SNOW COLD CASE

THE MYSTIC SNOW GLOBE MYSTERY SERIES:
BOOK 1

M.Z. ANDREWS

Snow Cold Case
The Mystic Snow Globe Mystery Series: Book 1

by
M.Z. Andrews

Copyright © 2017 by M.Z. Andrews

Print ISBN-13: 978-1979953344
Print ISBN-10: 1979953341
VS. 10052018.05

Editing by Clio Editing Services
Cover Art by Robert Brown

To my husband.
Thank you for your continued encouragement, your sage advice, and most of all for your love.

CONTENTS

"*E*wan's hands trembled as his fingers unfastened the small ivory buttons on Jacquelyn's blouse. Pushing the flimsy piece of silk to the floor, he caressed the smooth curves of her shoulders while goose bumps rippled across the swell of her heaving breasts. Ewan desperately craved the taste of her skin, his loins pulsing with desire." Johanna Hughes spoke the words aloud as she typed them into her dinosaur of a computer.

With pursed lips, she blinked behind her oversized black-rimmed glasses, staring at the small black letters on the glowing white screen. In front of her, a single strand of Christmas lights flickered, illuminating her frosty window. "His loins pulsing with desire," she repeated, tipping her head sideways and wrinkling her nose. "Is that real?"

Pulling off her glasses, she looked down at Rocky, the pony-sized English mastiff lying in the shadows at her feet. "Can loins really pulse with desire, Rocky?"

Hearing his name, he lifted his head and looked up at her curiously.

"Have your loins ever pulsed with desire?"

He grunted and laid his head back down on his front paws.

"Right," she agreed. "Mine either."

Johanna tossed the glasses down onto her overflowing desk. The slight motion sent a poof of air across the desk, and a wad of crumpled tissues blew to the floor. She ground the heels of her hands into her eyes and sat back in her chair. Her arms fell to her sides, her head lolled back on her neck, and her feet splayed out in front of her.

"Gah! Rocky! I can't do this! I'm a fraud! I'm a fake! I'm not qualified to be writing about loins pulsing and breasts heaving. My breasts haven't heaved in… in… ugh! I'm not sure that my breasts have ever heaved!" she cried, grabbing a half-handful of breast in each hand.

He looked up at her again and tilted his head sideways, as if to say, "What about that one time?"

She swatted at his meaty rump playfully with the palm of her hand. "Oh, that guy didn't count. I faked the heaving breasts, just like I faked the noises." Then she dropped her eyebrows. "And I thought we promised never to bring that up again. It was years ago, and I was in a bad place. Cut me some slack."

Rocky's retort was to stand up and trot into the kitchen, where he buried his head in an empty stainless steel bowl.

"It's not like you've never had a random hookup either," she hollered after him. "Neither one of us will forget that day in the park. That little dame with the bow in her hair. You know, it's lucky you didn't get that one knocked up. There's no way you could have afforded the child support on your salary."

She turned her attention back to her computer screen and put her glasses back on her face. "Blah, blah, blah, loins pulsing with desire." She stared at the screen as she debated what perfectly selected eloquent words should come next. "Umm..." she mused aloud. Her brain rolled through all the possible scenarios until finally, it was like a lightbulb turned on inside her head.

"Then Jacquelyn came to her senses. She decided to say screw sex, no pun intended. Screw love. Screw happy endings. Screw finding your soul mate," Johanna typed, smiling to herself all the while. "The end." She punctuated the finale with a perfunctory nod. She flipped the lid of her boxy laptop closed and then stood up and let out a deep sigh.

"I quit, Rocky. What made me think I could try my hand at romances? I have no business straying away from the day job." She ripped off her glasses once again and tossed them down onto a stack of books. The title of the top book read *Mrs. Plum in the Ballroom*, by Hanna Hughes.

Rocky pulled his heavy jowls from his bowl and looked up at Johanna. Wordlessly, he bore the brunt of his weight on his left leg, and with his right, he shoved the bowl halfway across the wooden floor, where it landed at Johanna's feet.

She gave him a lopsided grin. "Hint much?"

"Woof!" he agreed, his head jerking upwards.

Carrying his bowl, she walked towards him, taking in his sizable girth. "But you just ate!"

"Woof!"

"I realize that, but, buddy, you're looking heavier than usual." She tossed his bowl down next to the lit sugar cookie candle on her antique drop-leaf table and flipped on the kitchen light.

That was when she caught sight of herself in the mirror on the other side of her small Manhattan apartment. She groaned and turned to face it head-on. Who was she to talk about appearances? She hadn't changed out of her sweatpants in two days. Her partially bleached grey-and-red Seawolves crewneck was covered in bits of last night's boxed mac 'n' cheese, and only the upper two-thirds of her stringy brown hair was still tied back in a crooked ponytail. She wore no makeup, she couldn't remember the last time she'd brushed her teeth, and she was pretty sure she felt a zit coming in just above her lip.

While staring in the mirror, Johanna curled her lips around her front teeth and touched the little mound, pressing on it hard enough to feel the familiar sensation of an under-the-surface pimple. Yup. It was a pimple alright. She looked at her dog. "I really thought by thirty-five I'd be done with zits. If not, what are the perks of aging?"

He tilted his head to the side.

She closed her eyes, lifted her brows, and shrugged. "Yeah. I don't know either." She gave a glance towards the window and felt a sudden pang of guilt that she hadn't taken Rocky out since breakfast. Of course the dog walker had given him a nice midday stroll, but Johanna knew it was her turn. The drizzle of rain coming down from the mottled grey sky didn't look tantalizing. "You wanna go outside?" The inflection in her voice and the tilt of her head hinted that she hoped like mad he'd turn her down.

But the minute he heard the words, Rocky's butt was off the ground, and he was on the hunt for his leash. He returned to her seconds later with the nylon strap in his mouth.

"Oh, fine," she agreed. She was at a stopping point anyway. A stopping point in her new book and a stopping point in her romance writing career. She was going to stick to what she knew best. Mysteries.

Johanna sat down on the small padded antique bench that she'd ordered off eBay and pulled her midcalf neoprene Bogs on over her sweatpants. She wondered why she'd ever thought of writing a romance novel anyway.

Because you thought, if you can't have love, why not write about it? she answered herself matter-of-factly.

Annoyed at her own snottiness, she opened her small coat closet, pulled out her decades-old pink winter coat and tugged it on over her sweatshirt. One final look in the mirror made her brown eyes bulge.

"My God. I'm a hot mess!" she cried.

Rocky sat by her side, staring at his reflection in the mirror as she reconsidered her words.

"I know what you're thinking. Don't say it. You have to be hot to be a hot mess, I know. Fine. I'm just a mess," she sighed. She pulled the ponytail holder from her hair and tossed it on the entryway table. Combing her fingers through her thick tresses, she carefully smoothed the flyaways before pulling the pink puppy hat her grand-mother had crocheted for her on over her crazy hair. She tugged on the long earflaps that ended in little pink balls of pink yarn and tucked her hair in all around.

"Better?" she asked him.

Rocky groaned.

She frowned at him. "Like I care? It's not like I have to worry about any friends seeing me out and about. You're my only friend, and you like me just the way I am, right?"

He whined at her, causing her shoulders to stoop. "Oh, fine. I'll brush my teeth, and *then* we'll go. Okay?"

"Woof!" he agreed cheerfully.

She leaned over and gave him a thankful scratch around his ears, fastening his leash to his collar. "Thanks, Rock. I love you, too."

*W*ith her posture straight and her elbows bent at precise ninety-degree angles, Johanna and Rocky power-walked their usual path through the twinkling lights of Central Park. The brisk air both numbed and pinkened Johanna's cheeks and caused her breath to puff out in front of her like a little cloud against the darkened sky.

Johanna was thankful that the sleety-rain crap they'd gotten all day had slowed to a drizzle, though she wondered why it couldn't just get it over with and snow already. Christmas was only a little over a week away. The tree in Rockefeller Center was up. The shops on Fifth Avenue all had their windows properly dressed. The ever-charming Winter Village at Bryant Park was fully stocked, and every street corner in her neighborhood had the blended aromatic woody scents of fir trees mixed with the clean, fresh scents of pine. The seasonal magic of New York City at Christmastime could only be made more magical by adding snow.

Catching sight of a squirrel on a bench, Rocky halted his steady trot along the path. "Woof!" he barked, letting out a white puff of air. His upper torso lunged forward onto his front paws, his head lowered, and his rear end wagged in the air.

Johanna patted Rocky's back end. "Show-off."

"Woof woof!" Rocky's front end bounced excitedly, but the squirrel, used to the multitude of dogs in the park, didn't even contemplate moving and continued nibbling on the nut he held.

Johanna sighed but took the momentary break in their walk to squint up into the darkness. The lights of the park illuminated the drizzle in the black sky, giving the slow-falling rain a hyperspeed appearance. It reminded her of when she was a kid and used to lie on the grass in front of her house when it rained and look up into the sky. "All systems are a go," James would say before grabbing her hand. "Warp speed ahead!"

Johanna had to swallow down the lump in her throat that seemed to come out of nowhere. *James.* This time of year always made thoughts of him more frequent than usual. But she didn't have time to dwell on the thought as, without warning, Rocky launched himself after the squirrel and jerked her forward, pulling her straight into the bench.

Johanna howled, doubling over as the lip of the seat caught both of her legs just below the knees. Unwittingly, she let go of the leash, giving Rocky the opportunity to jump the low fence, following the squirrel across a strip of water-logged grass.

From the path, Johanna nursed her sore shin bones and watched as Rocky frolicked in the sloppy patch of mud just beyond the fence. "Rocky! Get back here! Look at you. Now you're all filthy!"

"Woof, woof!" His tail whipped the frigid air as he stared up into the tree where the squirrel now taunted him.

"He's not going to come down. Now get over here, or we're going home."

Rocky lowered his head. Her tone told him that she wasn't playing. She waved her hand at him, and Rocky looked up at the squirrel again. "Woof, woof!"

"Alright, then I'm going home, Rocky. I mean it!" Johanna threatened as she limped ahead on the path, her shin bones throbbing.

She knew the second she began to get too far away from him, he'd follow. Rocky was a good companion. Steady, loyal, protective, and he listened most of the time. She also knew that he was scared of losing sight of his caretaker and food provider, and she was right. She hadn't gotten more than fifteen feet away from him before she found Rocky trotting by her side again.

She looked down at him disdainfully. "You pulled me into a bench, Rocky."

Panting happily after his little excursion, he glanced up at her as they walked. Her scowl caused him to look away.

She tipped her head to the side. "Really? You don't have anything to say? That hurt, you know!"

"Ow-ow-wow!" he barked.

"Yeah, I know. You didn't mean it. You just wanted to make a new friend. I can understand that," she sighed. "I wouldn't mind making a new friend myself."

Rocky looked up at her again, his big brown eyes full of nothing but love, and barked.

She patted the top of his head. "I know you're my friend, buddy. I was thinking less fur friend and more *real* friend." She sighed. It had been so long since she'd actually spoken to someone besides Rocky or her family or the bagel-and-coffee guy that she didn't even know if she'd know *how* to have a human friend anymore. Johanna looked down at Rocky's now muddied body and sighed. "We're cutting this walk short, Rocky. You're filthy, and my shins are killing me."

He hung his head.

"Oh, darn it!" she cried, stopping on the path. "I just remembered. I have to stop and pick Mook up her Christmas present. Dad said her mixer went out."

At the first available spot, they veered off the path to head towards home. The same squirrel that had taunted Rocky earlier now darted ahead of them, catching Rocky's attention yet again. He barked excitedly.

"Oh no, you're staying with me," she warned, keeping a firm hold of his leash. But Rocky's behemoth size was no match for Johanna's small frame. He took off on a dead sprint, pulling Johanna along for the ride.

"Rocky! Stop!" she hollered at him, barely able to keep up with him due to the stinging pain just below her knees. The cold air burned her lungs as she inhaled. "Rocky!"

They'd gone quite a distance when finally, Rocky was able to pull his leash loose from Johanna's hands and he took off, dragging it down the pathway. Johanna chased after him, shouting his name. "Rocky!"

That was when she saw *him* coming towards them. The man she passed at least three nights a week on their nightly walks. He was medium-height. Average build. His hair looked like a soft patch of curly yellow silk. Johanna assumed he was a businessman of some sort as every day he wore a tailored suit and tie and carried a messenger bag slung over one shoulder. He always walked with his eyes glued to the cell phone out in front of him, affording Johanna plenty of time to drink in his handsomeness. He didn't have supermodel good looks or anything like that, but he had kind eyes that crinkled in the corners every time he noticed Rocky, and he had perfect posture, which Johanna thought gave him an air of confidence and made him that much more attractive.

But today, the scene that unfolded in front of her didn't give her the time to gawk at the handsome stranger. Today, Rocky's one-track mind set him on a collision course, headed straight for the well-dressed man.

"Rocky! No!" Johanna yelled from too far away to stop him. Her heart beat wildly in her chest. Whether it was from the physical exertion of her run or the anticipation of what was about to happen, she couldn't be sure.

Johanna's two-word scream made the man in the suit

glance up from his phone—just not in time to make a differ-ence. The pony-sized animal crashed headfirst into the man, catapulting him backwards onto the wet trail. Rocky's momentum carried him right over the top of the man, soaking his beautiful suit from stem to stern with a disgusting layer of doggy sludge.

*J*ohanna's jaw dropped as she caught up to Rocky and the man. Though it was dark in the park, she could clearly see the layer of grey sludge coating the man's expensive-looking suit.

"Rocky!" she breathed with her hand covering her gaping mouth. "Oh my goodness, sir…I—I'm *so, so sorry!*"

Rocky apologized too by covering the man's face with a thick film of doggy slobber. The man tried to cover his face with his arms, but he was no match for Rocky when he wanted to lick something.

"Get off, Rocky!" Johanna hollered.

Sure that the man was playing with him and enjoying the impromptu bath, Rocky continued to lick.

Johanna had to heave all of her weight against her dog to force him off the stranger, and as she did, she accidentally dropped a knee onto the man's stomach. He reflexively curled up and let out a "Doh!" sound.

"Oh my God," she breathed with wide eyes as she struggled to climb off of him. When she was finally on her feet, she leaned over him, her little pink balls of yarn dangling just a few feet above his face. His eyes were pinched shut, and his face screwed up into a grimace. He smelled like sandalwood and wet dog all at the same time.

"I—I—I am *so, so sorry!*" She moved her hands around his head awkwardly, not sure if she should make a pillow behind his head, or if she should drag him up to his feet. "Sir? Umm… are you alright? Are you hurt?"

With his eyes still closed, the man let out a wheeze and tried to sit up, but Johanna was still bent over him. Their foreheads collided. The man's head bounced backwards against the path. "Oh!" he screamed, as both muddied hands went to hold his head.

Johanna let out a similar scream, as she reeled backwards. She rubbed the tips of her fingers against her temples and stared down at the man. Horror filled her body. Not only had she and Rocky soaked his beautiful suit in mud and park sludge, but they'd both done more physical damage to him than if he'd been in a WWE match. While he nursed his sore head, Johanna spun around on her toes, unable to face him. What should she say?

When she heard him let out another groan, she turned back around to see him lifting his head trying to look down at his suit.

"Oh, sir," she gushed. "Are you alright? Can I help you up?"

He held two hands out in front of him to keep her from touching him. "No, no. I'm okay, I'm okay," he assured her.

Johanna's could barely feel the throbbing in her head and shins as her stomach turned. She'd always thought that someday she'd get to talk to the stranger in the park. She'd dreamt it would have been a beautiful day and she'd have actually done her hair and put on an attractive workout outfit. She'd have been walking Rocky, and he'd have been on his best behavior, of course. The man would have stopped her to comment on what a nice dog she had and somehow their conversation would turn to the weather, and then he'd mention he'd seen her several times a week for the last few years. She'd think of something witty or clever to say. He'd ask her name… she'd ask his… maybe together they'd walk with Rocky to get coffee…

With her heart in her throat, Johanna sighed. She'd never have imagined in a million years that their first official meeting would have been on a cold, rainy night in December when she hadn't showered in two days, and that it would result in his destroyed clothes, broken ribs, and a concussion.

"Please—I—I'm so, so sorry," she stuttered, the words coming out of her mouth like Heinz ketchup from a glass bottle.

As he regained his wits, the man struggled to sit up. "I'm okay. Looks like my suit didn't fare quite as well."

Johanna reached down and held a hand out to him. Grudgingly, he took it and allowed her to help pull him to his feet. "I see that. I will totally pay your cleaning bill. Or —or buy you a new suit!"

As he steadied himself, the man gave her a forced smile. "I appreciate that, but really there's no need. This suit was headed to the cleaners anyway. I think it will be fine."

"Oh, please, I feel terrible," begged Johanna, her heart throbbing in her chest. Her fingertips gathered on the little patch of skin just below her nose. She delicately fingered the painful little mound above her lip uncomfortably, and suddenly she became completely aware of how she looked. At least her breath didn't stink, and it was dark. That was something.

"Really, it's alright. No serious damage done. That's a pretty big dog you've got there," he remarked, examining his muddy hands.

Johanna watched Rocky running circles around a tree. She shifted uncomfortably in her rain boots. What was she supposed to say? She didn't generally communicate with other humans, at least not face-to-face, and where some women might know exactly how to flirt their way out of a situation such as this, Johanna did not. "Yeah. He's an English mastiff."

"I thought so," he said with a nod, finally deciding to wipe his hands on his already dirtied trousers. "What's his name?"

Johanna tugged on the little puff balls of yarn hanging just above her breasts and suddenly remembered the hat she was wearing. Her grandmother had crocheted it for her when she was in the seventh grade. It had a pink dog face on it and two little dog ears that poked out of either side of her head. She wanted to crawl into a hole. "Umm, his name is Rocky, er, Rockland Gable Hughes, Rocky for short," she rambled uncomfortably. "Your back is soaking wet. You've got to be freezing. Would you like to wear my coat?"

The man looked at her faded pink coat and lifted an eyebrow. "Uh, thank you, but, uh, I don't think I'd fit into it."

Johanna nodded and looked down at her hands awkwardly. *You're such an idiot! Of course he can't fit into your ridiculously ugly coat! Why did you wear the stupid thing anyway?!* "Oh, sure. What was I thinking?" She shook her head. "Well, I better not keep you, since you're probably freezing. Again, I'm really sorry about my dog, a-and the mud. And your stomach… and your head."

The man waved a hand as he really looked at her for the first time. His smile softened a bit. "Don't feel bad. Really, it was my fault. I wasn't looking where I was going, or I would have seen Rocky coming. Too engrossed in work as usual. I'll be good as new as soon as I get a warm shower. No worries, alright?"

Johanna bit the inside of her lip and nodded uncomfortably. She felt tears burning behind her eyes, but she forced them back. "Okay," she whispered, pursing her lips in a tight smile.

The man gave her a half-smile and a little wave. "Goodbye," he said before heading on his way.

When he'd turned his back to her, Johanna watched him go and felt her insides churning. "What an idiot you are, Johanna," she whispered to herself. "Five years of seeing that man on this very path and you can't wear a decent coat and a normal hat?" She threw her hands down on either side of her and turned around to chase after Rocky. "And you offer him your coat? Like you're what? *A man?!*" She pounded her forehead with the palm of her hand. "No wonder you don't have any friends!" She lifted her brows animatedly as she chastised herself. "No, really. You shouldn't be allowed out of the house. You're an embarrassment to the human race.

"We're leaving, Rocky, and if you're not over here in two shakes, I'm going without you," shouted Johanna, her tone firmer than it had been with Rocky in months.

From across the fence, Rocky stared at her, frozen. She waited a solid ten seconds and then took off. He barked but gave up on his squirrel chasing and met back up with her on the path.

"I'm so mad at you, Rocky! I can't even. You haven't behaved that badly in… in… well… in a long time."

He hung his head.

"Of all the people to maul, you have to pick *him?!*"

Rocky let out a guttural growl.

"Because it… it's… him! He's so… so…ugh," Johanna sighed and rolled her head back on her neck. He was so what? She didn't even know how to finish that statement. *Perfect* was what she wanted to say, but how in the world did she know if he was perfect? Just because he *looked* perfect. And *smelled* perfect. And was ridiculously kind to her when her horse-dog knocked him into the mud and she clumsily beat him to a pulp. Okay, so maybe he was perfect. But that didn't mean anything. He was also probably perfectly married. Or perfectly gay. Or perfectly allergic to awkward writers who rarely left the house.

Johanna swallowed hard, fighting back the tears. There was only one man in her life who had ever accepted her awkwardness, and he was gone. She was sure she'd never find another man like him. So sure that she'd never even tried looking.

James had been her childhood sweetheart. Living next door to her family growing up, he'd relished her pitiful clumsiness—calling her adorable rather than awkward—laughed at her stupid jokes, and loved her face even without makeup—so much so that she'd never learned to wear the stuff properly and was now a thirty-five-year-old who didn't know how to apply eyeliner. James didn't care that Johanna was a homebody who preferred books and dogs to people. And it didn't bother him a bit that she liked watching old reruns of *Murder, She Wrote* and *Columbo* in her pj's instead of going to the movie theater or out to a club on a Saturday night.

James and Johanna had seen each other through every major life event. High school *and* college graduations. The deaths of both Johanna's mother *and* her grandmother. James's first big job at the *Times*. Johanna's first hit novel. James's first big job loss. But through everything, they'd managed to come out on the other side together. They'd even promised to spend their lives together and sealed the deal with an engagement and the dream of a winter wedding.

But then the unthinkable had happened, and Johanna had been left alone for the single most important event in both of their lives. She'd been left alone when it was time to bury him.

3

"*J* can't believe they're sold out of mixers!" complained Johanna as she left the pet-friendly home goods store with Rocky by her side. "I should have just ordered it online the minute Dad mentioned it." Of course, Johanna had been too cheap to pay for postage and too busy writing her most recent book and mothering a two-hundred-pound mastiff to have paused to one-click it on Amazon and now she was up against a deadline. Her family's pre-Christmas get-together was now knocking on her door.

Standing on the sidewalk, she glanced around at all the busy shops, debating which other stores might carry a mixer *and* be pet-friendly. While she stood hugging her coat around her and wishing she'd thought to bring gloves on their walk, Rocky let out a series of barks.

"What?" Her teeth chattered as she squinted up into the dark sky, wondering if there would be snow on the ground by the time she woke up in the morning. "You ready to go home?"

"Woof!" He tugged on his leash, begging her to follow him.

Johanna followed his gaze to see the furriest grey cat she'd ever seen lying in the display window of an antique shop. She chuckled. "I see her. She's lovely, but you've already had your fun for the day, chasing after that squirrel. I think it's time to go home."

"Woof, woof!" he argued, tugging her towards the shop.

Johanna sighed as she noticed the pet-friendly sign in the window. She felt herself relenting. She rather enjoyed antique shops. All the fun little treasures one could find, each of them with a story to tell. "Oh, fine, we'll go in. But you'd better be on your best behavior, because if you're naughty, we're going straight home." She pulled him to her and patted his side.

Johanna pushed the door open, and immediately the scent of fresh red cedar and cinnamon sticks engulfed her, delighting her senses. A Christmas tree decorated with antique ornaments and strands of colorful lights was front and center in the shop, with an old Radio Flyer sled leaning against it. Festive garlands with big red silk balls hung from the raw-cut cedar rafters, and the song "Winter Wonderland" played on a crackly old radio.

An elderly man behind the counter gave Johanna a smile and a nod. "Good evening, are you looking for anything special?"

Rocky went right for the cat in the window, pulling Johanna along for the ride.

Johanna threw him a smile over her shoulder. "We saw your cat in the window. Rocky had to come check it out."

The balding man nodded. "She's a bit of a salty thing, that one. Not my cat, but the darn thing won't leave."

Johanna gave him a funny look. "Maybe you just need to put her outside."

The man sat back down on his stool and chuckled warmly. "Oh, I've tried. Dozens and dozens of times. I put her outside, and she always sneaks back in."

Johanna looked at the cat. The long, fluffed-up grey hair around her neck gave her the appearance of a lion with a mane. "You'd think someone would adopt her; she's a beautiful cat."

The man pointed at a sign in front of his counter. It read, *Free Cat.* "I've probably had a handful of people take her home with them. She always comes back."

Johanna tipped her head to the side. "Isn't that something? She must really like your shop."

He threw his hands up. "I guess. I don't know what else to think. I'd be okay with her staying if she was a little bit more lovable."

Johanna's brows lifted. "I've yet to meet an unlovable cat."

"Try and pet her," he urged, shooing his hand towards the cat. "She's a spirited one."

Rocky's head rested on the sill of the deep window display. The cat was feet away, curled up in a ball, watching traffic go by. Johanna kept a close hand on his leash, fearing that he might suddenly bolt ahead and jump into the window.

"She looks comfortable," said Johanna to the shop-keeper. "I think I'll just let her be. Come on, Rocky. We might as well browse while we're here."

"We're having a Christmas sale. Twenty percent off a purchase of thirty-five dollars or more."

Johanna nodded at him. "Thank you." She tugged on Rocky's leash. "Let's look around, buddy."

Grudgingly, Rocky left the window but kept his eyes firmly planted on the cat while Johanna browsed the holi-day-themed home decor items near the window. "You don't happen to carry stand mixers, do you?" Johanna shouted towards the counter.

"I just sold one this morning," he said. "It was my last."

Johanna's mouth swished to the side. *Darn it.* She'd be hard-pressed to get one delivered in time now.

Rocky let out an excited bark. Johanna turned to see the cat had jumped out of the display window. Rocky tugged on his leash, wanting to follow her as she took slow, deliberate steps towards the counter. "No, you'll get us in trouble," Johanna hissed at him, pulling him close to her side.

He stood frozen with pert ears watching intently as the cat sauntered off. She almost seemed to flirt with him, wagging her fluffy tail back and forth as she gazed back at Rocky, her brilliant green eyes glowing like emeralds against a furry grey blanket. "Woof!"

"Yes, she's very pretty," agreed Johanna, unable to take her eyes off of the cat. *How can a cat like that be unlovable?* she wondered as the cat took off deeper into the store until finally, she was completely out of sight.

Agitated now, Rocky wagged his tail furiously. He fidgeted about awkwardly like he suffered from restless leg syndrome or was trying to dance, but had four left feet.

Johanna gave him a sad smile. He was always such a good boy, his previous escapade excluded, cooped up in her apartment all day. So, when he got a chance to get out of the house, she liked to make him happy. "You really want to follow her, don't you?"

"Woof!"

"Alright, alright. We'll see what she's up to, and then we'll go. Okay?"

Rocky strode ahead. With his head to the ground, he sniffed out her trail. Together Johanna and Rocky wound their way through the antique shop. Johanna held his leash tightly, scared that he would bulldoze his way through the store and destroy a china display or some expensive crystal vase or something, but he only led them to a staircase, barking at the base of it.

Johanna craned her neck to see if there were more antiques up there or if it was just for employees.

"You can go up there," said the man at the counter. "There are lots of collectibles up there, so you'll want to hang on to him."

"Thank you," said Johanna, wrapping his leash around her hand in several tight loops. She turned to Rocky and whispered, "Careful."

Excited, he bounded up the stairs with her close behind. Upstairs, they discovered rows and rows of carefully displayed items. Rocky dragged Johanna along until finally, they both caught sight of the cat again. She sat on the floor at the base of a large shelf, watching them with her head tilted to the side and that big fluffy tail calmly swatting the floor. She looked both regal and suspicious, as only cats could, and it occurred to Johanna that if she didn't know better, she'd think the cat was egging them along.

As they approached, the cat sprang up onto the third shelf, where she reached up higher to put her paw on a snow globe. Drawing her attention to it, the cat meowed and waved her fluffy tail at Rocky.

"Woof!" Rocky barked excitedly.

Johanna couldn't help but smile at Rocky. She knew he wanted nothing more than to snuggle the cat and coat her in a pool of slobber until her fur was like wet cotton candy smashed against her body.

"No, Rocky, you leave her alone."

Now, Johanna's eyes were on the snow globe. She lifted it to look at it more closely. The weighted brass base was embossed with swirls and stars, and inside the glass ball was a bedroom scene. A beautiful young woman with long, wavy chocolate-brown hair sat at a sewing machine sewing a dress. Beside her stood a mannequin wearing the most beautiful wedding gown Johanna had ever seen. There was a wardrobe full of dresses behind her and a four-poster bed. A soft smile covered Johanna's face as she gave the globe a shake and the snow erupted, coating the dress and the girl's hair with a blanket of white.

Johanna blinked back tears as her hand went to her mouth to cover the giggle escaping her lips. Something about seeing the wedding dress in the snow globe at Christmas time made her oddly emotional and happy at the same time. Even though they hadn't picked a date, she and James had agreed on a winter wedding.

"It's beautiful," she whispered, not sure if she meant the globe or the dress. She shook it again, and as she watched the delicate, glittering flakes fall she felt a sudden mystic connection to the globe—as if it were calling to her. The feeling overwhelmed her, causing Johanna to hastily put the globe back on the shelf and withdraw her hands as if it had shocked her.

"Woof!" said Rocky.

"There's something mysterious about that globe." She looked down at him, her almond-shaped brown eyes darkening. "I think it's time for us to go, buddy."

The cat leapt off the shelf then, and as Rocky and Johanna watched, she seductively waltzed a figure eight between Rocky's legs to rub up against Johanna's boot. Johanna lifted an eyebrow, shocked that the cat was being so friendly after the clerk had said she was so *unfriendly*. She leaned down and petted the cat's beautiful grey fur.

"You are a lovely little thing," she cooed as the cat purred contentedly. "I can't believe that man called you salty! You hardly seem salty to me."

Rocky sniffed the cat in a friendly manner but refrained from the licking Johanna was sure he wanted to do.

The cat meowed again. This time what came out was more of a warbling sound, like the melody of a song.

A smile covered Johanna's face. "You can sing? Well, aren't you talented!"

The cat's melodic singing continued until finally, Johanna stood up in a trance and nodded. "Yes, I think I'll get the snow globe."

4

*J*ohanna shuffled the large cardboard box and Rocky's leash to her other arm while she dug out her apartment keys. Rocky barked in the direction of the stairwell from which they'd just come, causing Johanna to cast a backwards glance in that direction.

"Well, I'll be! She *is* still following us," said Johanna, sticking her key into the doorknob. "That's bizarre."

The furry grey cat from the antique store peered around the corner at them.

Rocky bounced around on his front paws. A friend had come home to play with him, and he couldn't be more excited about it.

Johanna threw the apartment door open but stood in the hallway for an extended moment, looking at the cat curiously. She hadn't let the furry creature into her building, but it was rush hour, and between those coming home from work and those headed out for supper, someone else could have easily let the cat slip in. *Should I take her back to the antique shop even though she wasn't his cat?* Johanna wondered, tilting her head sideways.

With Rocky bouncing around like a three-year-old that had to pee, Johanna knew exactly what he wanted. Rocky wanted Johanna to invite the cat in, but she didn't know. The antique store owner had said that the cat had taken up residence and then wouldn't leave. What if she decided to take up residence in Johanna's apartment? Johanna wasn't sure that she could handle a two-hundred-pound mastiff *and* a cat in her small apartment.

"Go on." She shooed the cat back towards the stairs as it crept towards them.

At Johanna's urging, the cat stopped walking and sat down primly. Training her green eyes intently on Rocky, she flipped her long fluffy tail back and forth. "Meow," she said sweetly.

Rocky let out a chuff.

"I think she's sweet on you, Rocky," said Johanna, shooting him a wink and a crooked smile. "I guess you've still got it."

He barked and then put his head on his paws, leaving his rump sticking up into the air.

"Oh, oh, right." She chuckled. "You never lost it. Come on, bud, time to go inside. I'm getting hungry. You want dinner?"

That got his attention. He stood up and, forgetting about the cat, trotted inside the apartment. Johanna smiled at the cat. "Time for you to go home, sweetie. Night-night."

Johanna followed Rocky inside the apartment, and just as she slammed the door behind her, she caught a glimpse of the cat trying to make it inside before the door closed, but she narrowly missed. *What a funny little cat.*

Johanna set the box with the snow globe down on her side table. "Talk about your impulse buy," she said to

Rocky, who sat next to his food bowl waiting patiently. Tossing her keys down onto her comfortably tattered sofa, she pulled off her hat and coat and strode into the kitchen. "What in the world do I need a snow globe for? At least it was on sale."

"Woof!"

"I know, I know. Walk equals dinner. It's coming." She lifted his food bowl and walked it over to the giant plastic container that held his food. Giving him a generous portion, she walked back to her front door, where she opened the box and pulled out the snow globe. "I mean, I don't even know where I'm going to put it! It's just one more thing for me to dust." Her eyes glanced around her unkempt apartment. "Or not dust, if we're being honest."

She shook the globe and watched the snowflakes fly. It was so pretty in there, but what she really loved was the dress on the form. If she ever got married, that would be the exact dress she would pick to get married in. She sighed.

"Who am I kidding, Rocky? You have to find a man to get married. You have to have a social life to find a man. And you have to be social to have a social life."

Johanna walked to her computer desk with the globe in hand. She slid all the empty coffee cups into her garbage can, followed by a heaping pile of wadded-up tissues and crumpled sticky notes, and then she moved a big stack of books to her bookshelf.

"There, now I've got room for you!" She put the snow globe down next to her laptop. "Perfect. Now I've got one more thing to distract me from my writing. Just what I needed."

Pulling the full garbage liner from her wastepaper basket and grabbing the empty cardboard box, she carried the trash out into the hallway. "Taking the garbage out,

Rock. I'll be right back," she hollered, though Rocky didn't bother looking up from his bowl.

After returning to her apartment, Johanna found the grey cat sitting in front of the closed door, staring at it. When she saw Johanna, the cat stood up, arched her back in a stretch, and then wrapped herself around Johanna's legs. "Meow."

Johanna squatted down and met the cat eye to eye. "You're still here?" She scratched the cat under the chin. "I'm sorry, but I don't have room for another pet in my apartment. Don't you have a home?" For a second, Johanna thought the peculiar feline had shaken her head, but reconsidering it, Johanna was sure she'd just imagined it. It had been a long day of writing, after all, and her eyes were likely fatigued. They were always playing little tricks on her like that.

"Well, I'm sorry. You're beautiful and all, but I just can't keep you," said Johanna, stroking her fur. She gave her one more scratch behind the ears and then scooted her body out of the way. "Bye-bye."

Johanna stood up, opened the door to her apartment, and walked inside. Once the door was shut behind her, she was shocked to discover that the cat had managed to dart in behind her.

"Hey!" she shouted. "You sure are fast!"

Done with his food, Rocky glanced up to see the cat standing in his living room. "Woof!"

Johanna dropped her eyebrows. "Yeah, I know you're excited, but we can't keep her."

The cat looked up at Johanna, her big green eyes pleading silently. *Please let me stay*, they begged.

Johanna felt her defenses crumbling. She bent over and picked the cat up. Holding her in her arms, she ran her hand down the cat's thick, soft, luxurious fur while Rocky circled Johanna anxiously.

"Oh, fine," she finally sighed. "You can have something to eat, but then you're going outside!"

"Meow," the cat seemingly agreed.

Johanna put the cat down next to Rocky. "Play nice while I look for something that she might want to eat."

Immediately, the cat darted towards Johanna's desk and hopped up on her chair and then onto the desk, where she promptly sat down next to the snow globe and peered inside.

"Oh, I see. I took something from your antique shop. Is that it?" Johanna lifted her off the desk and put her back on the ground. "You can't get on my desk, though. No, no," she added, wagging her finger at the cat. Then she looked at Rocky. "Rocky, entertain her while I go pour her some milk."

Rocky let out a happy-to-oblige "woof" and gave the cat a sloppy lick across the face, something Johanna was sure he'd been dying to do since they'd met her. One would have thought he'd slapped her across the face, the way she reacted. Her green eyes widened, and she let out the most god-awful "rawr" Johanna had ever heard. The next thing she knew, the cat had her claws extended and had reached out and swiped Rocky across the nose.

Whimpering and now nursing a scratched-up nose, Rocky backed away from her. He had been raised a bit of a sheltered dog and as such had never been treated like that before. Especially by a cat! He didn't know what to make of it.

Johanna's eyebrows lifted. "Oh! So the claws come out! The clerk was right. You *are* a salty girl." She patted Rocky's head. "He was only showing you affection." Johanna headed straight for the kitchen to pour the milk. "If that's how you're going to be, I think we'll just let you drink your milk in the hallway."

Suddenly, the cat's attitude appeared to change. She pranced over to Rocky and rubbed her body against his muscular leg and then rolled to the floor, where she looked up at him sweetly, almost begging him to cuddle with her.

By the time Johanna returned with the small saucer of milk, Rocky and the cat were playing nicely. She sighed. *Now what?* Kick the cat out and make Rocky be lonely again? The thought of breaking his heart broke *her* heart. She plopped down at her desk chair and watched them play. Johanna couldn't do that to him.

"Fine," she relented. "She can stay until morning, but on our morning walk, we're taking her back to the antique store!"

---

a sparse Charlie Brown–type Christmas tree stood in the corner of Johanna's living room next to the radiator. With its crooked stem, misshapen branches, and lack of needles, some might have thought it to be a pity purchase, but Johanna had found herself quite excited about her discovery. All the other Christmas trees were bigger, denser, more beautiful, and more coveted by the masses. This Christmas tree was the awkward, misunderstood one of the group, and Johanna felt a kinship towards the tree that made her excited to decorate it proudly with her grandmother's glass bulbs, single strands of tinsel, and a string of hand-strung popcorn.

Colored Christmas lights blinked on and off in random fashion in the living room window, and the television set glowed blue-green against her living room wall later that evening.

Curled up beneath a blanket next to Rocky and Natasha, the moniker she'd assigned to her furry overnight guest, Johanna fast-forwarded through the commercials on her Hallmark Channel Christmas movie and sighed. She'd just watched a romantic Christmas proposal, and now her heart was heavy. Most days she valued her independence and treasured her solitary lifestyle, but moments like this, sitting alone on a cold winter evening, made her wish for a companion.

Taking a sip of her wine, Johanna reached over and clicked on the lamp on her end table. She pulled her feet into her body pretzel-style and exchanged her wineglass for her new snow globe. Giving it a good shake, Johanna watched the glittery flakes cover the wedding gown, as she'd done dozens of times since she'd brought it home only a few hours ago. She couldn't put her finger on it, but something begged her to continue shaking it. Like a song stuck in her head that begged to be sung, Johanna just couldn't make herself stop.

"Ugh, no matter how many times I shake this globe, I'm never gonna get to wear this dress," Johanna finally sighed, her words only slightly slurred by her third glass of wine. "It's gonna be you and me forever, Rocky. You're the only man I need in my life." She patted his butt, causing Rocky to lift his heavy head and look at her with big sad eyes.

"Oh, don't look at me like that." Johanna scowled at him. "Because when your pet starts feeling sorry for you, you know your love life really has gone to hell in a handbasket."

She focused her attention on the girl in the globe. "She's a pretty girl. I wonder if she made that dress herself."

Natasha uncurled herself from Rocky's embrace and hopped over him to curl up next to Johanna. "Meow."

Johanna showed her the snow globe. "You like the girl in the globe?"

Natasha's green eyes stared at the glass ball. Johanna was sure she was staring right at the girl.

"I feel like you can understand me," said Johanna, scratching Natasha's chin. "Isn't that ridiculous?"

"Meow."

Johanna took another sip of her wine and, without looking at the globe, gave it a solid shake. When the glittery flakes had settled, she looked back down at it and was shocked to discover that the wedding gown was no longer on the dress form. It was on the girl! And the girl wasn't seated at her sewing machine anymore. She was now standing!

"Oh my God!" Johanna breathed. Bolting upright, she practically threw the snow globe onto her coffee table. "Did you see that?!" she asked Natasha.

Natasha leapt off the couch and onto the coffee table.

Feeling the sudden tension in the room, Rocky sat up too.

Johanna wondered if she'd just imagined the girl in a different position or if the wine was stronger than she'd thought. "I swear she was sitting at the sewing machine just a few minutes ago! Tell me you saw that!"

Natasha put a paw on the snow globe. "Meow," she said plainly.

And now it felt as if the cat was talking to her. Johanna rubbed the heels of her hands against her forehead and sucked in a deep breath. *Breathe, Johanna, breathe. There's no way the girl in the snow globe moved and the cat talked to you. You're seeing things! Your eyes are fatigued! You're drunk. You — you've read too many fantasy novels and watched too many magical Hallmark movies!*

And then the warbling began again. It started out deep

in Natasha's throat, but slowly it became a melody. It was the same song she'd sung to them in the antique store.

Johanna's eyes widened, and her pulse quickened. But suddenly she felt drawn to the globe once again. She lifted it with both hands and gave it another shake. And another. Again and again she shook it until she noticed a glowing glimmer of light emanating from inside the base of the globe.

Johanna peered down at it. The shimmering lights glowed through the snow, forming letters, and then words! She had to squint to read it. *"There's no star too far away,"* she whispered, before having to shake the snow globe again to keep the snow at bay. *"And no wish too grand. Shake the snow globe and make a wish, the magic's in your hands."*

Johanna's heart raced. *Make a wish?*

Rocky's head tilted sideways as he stared at the globe too.

"You can see it too, can't you?!" she asked excitedly.

Rocky jumped off the sofa and ran to her bedroom.

"Scaredy-cat!" she hollered after him.

Natasha still sat with her tail thwacking the coffee table. Cool as the proverbial cucumber.

Johanna eyed her suspiciously. "You're not scared. Why aren't you scared? Cats are the jumpiest animals alive, and you're over there chillaxing!"

Natasha didn't flinch.

Johanna sighed and turned her attention back to the globe. "I'm supposed to make a wish? So it's a mystical snow globe?" she wondered aloud. What should she wish for? She cast her eyes towards her apartment window. Snow. She should wish for snow. "Fine, I'll play along. What's the harm?" She shrugged.

"I wish for…" She stopped. She had been just about to say the words, *I wish for snow*, when the girl in the wedding dress caught her eye again. What she *really* wanted was to meet a nice man and get married. Should she wish for a husband? Was that what she really wanted? Johanna slumped backwards against the sofa as tears burned at her eyes. No. The truth of the matter was, she missed James. She missed her best friend. *Yes.* She wanted to find the love of her life and get married so that she wouldn't be alone anymore, but in reality, she wanted to find and marry her best friend. *Is it creepy to wish for a dead man to come back into my life?* she wondered.

Goose bumps rippled down Johanna's legs as the words she felt in her heart finally came to her. Her spine straightened. She shook the snow globe one more time as tears of loneliness coursed down her cheeks and dripped onto the glass.

Sniffling, she whispered, "I don't want to be alone anymore. My wish is to find my best friend again."

Johanna didn't even have time to wipe the tears from her face before it began to snow in her apartment.

ohanna's eyes widened and her breath caught in her throat. *Snow?! Okay, I'm dreaming right now,* she told herself, pinching her eyes shut. *But I can feel the flakes on my face.* She forced one eye open and then held her arms out on either side, allowing the cold flakes to hit her arms.

"But I didn't wish for snow," she whispered before letting out a little giggle.

As the snow in her apartment began to come down harder, the snow globe in her lap began to shake, whipping up a snowstorm inside the watery world. Johanna's pulse quickened.

"What in the world?" she said, putting the glass ball on the coffee table next to Natasha. Wind whipped around her as the flurry of flakes in her apartment continued. Suddenly, the snow globe emitted a brilliant burst of light, followed by a deafening sound like thunder cracking overhead. Thinking it was some kind of bomb about to explode, Johanna curled into a ball and covered her head with her arms, her heart beating erratically in her chest. But instead of an explosion, seconds later, the whole apartment fell eerily silent.

Johanna waited for almost an entire sixty seconds before she slowly uncovered her head, afraid of what she was going to see and wishing to God that Rocky hadn't high-tailed it to the bedroom. Where was her protector when she needed him? As she slowly forced one eye open, Johanna was happy to see that it had stopped snowing in her apart-ment and Natasha still sat calmly on the coffee table staring at her with Rocky nowhere in sight!

Surely that hadn't just been a figment of her wine diluted imagination! Because if it was, she needed to get to a hospital stat and have a CT scan done on her brain!

"Natasha, please tell me you saw that too and that it wasn't a brain tumor," she begged, suddenly wondering which scenario was worse—a brain tumor or having the cat tell her she'd seen it too.

"Well, first of all, my name isn't Natasha, it's Esmerel-da," said the cat quite plainly. "And second of all, it's not a brain tumor, I saw it too."

Johanna's eyes nearly bugged out of her head as she scrambled up onto her feet as she climbed up the sofa.

"Ahhhh!" she screamed, her heart throbbing wildly in her chest. "Rocky!"

The cat rolled her eyes and jumped off of the coffee table. "Oh, what's that big buffoon going to do to save you? *Lick me to death?*"

"Essy!" hissed another voice in the room. "Be nice."

Johanna didn't think she could take any more, but slowly her head swiveled to her left to see a young woman in a wedding dress standing in her living room.

"Ahhh!" Johanna screamed again, holding her blanket to her chest while standing on the sofa. "Ahhh!"

The young woman held out a steadying hand. Her long

brown hair fell over her shoulders in smooth waves, and Johanna had the uncanny feeling that she'd seen her before. "Oh, I'm so sorry we scared you. Please! We aren't going to hurt you!"

Johanna's eyes darted around the room as she wondered where she'd put her cell phone. "Siri, call 911!" she shouted, praying that her phone wasn't buried beneath a pillow somewhere.

When the familiar Englishman's voice didn't answer her, she glanced back at the young woman. "W-where did you come from?" she demanded.

The woman pointed to the snow globe on the coffee table with the narrow end of a short, ornately decorated wand. "Don't you recognize me? I came from in there."

Johanna's body trembled as she glanced down at the snow globe and was shocked to suddenly realize that the girl that had been inside the globe, the one wearing the wedding dress only seconds ago, was gone!

"No, no, no... i-it can't be... You can't be her! That's not possible."

The woman sighed. "I'm really sorry we scared you, but yes, I *am* her."

Johanna's head shook. "Wh-who are you?!"

The young woman's emerald green eyes lit up. "Oh, right! How silly of me. I didn't introduce myself. I'm Whitley Snow. You've already met my sister, Esmerelda."

Johanna's eyes flickered towards the cat. "Th-the cat is your sister?" Even the words coming out of her mouth sounded ludicrous.

Whitley smiled. "Twin sister, to be precise."

"I'm the good-looking sister," said Esmerelda, rolling her eyes. "Not that you can tell in my present condition."

"And you are?" asked Whitley, extending a hand to Johanna.

Johanna stared at the young woman's slim hand uncomfortably. Was she supposed to shake the hand of her brain's delusional, fantastical concoction? Something about that seemed off.

"I'm Johanna Hughes," she finally said, not taking the hand offered. Her forehead creased as she frowned. "I'm so confused. How is it possible that you are here, and she is a cat, a-and *you're sisters*?!"

Whitley smiled at her patiently. "It's actually a very long story, and I don't want to bore you with the details. But I hear you like my dress," she said, changing the subject.

"Your dress?"

Whitley motioned to the dress she was wearing. "My wedding dress."

Johanna lifted a brow. "Who told you that?"

"I heard you say it was beautiful," Whitley explained, swaying her hips to give the dress a little motion before spinning around in it. "I feel like that's why we were brought together. In fact, I'm sure of it!"

"My sister thinks she's a seamstress," said Esmerelda, jumping off the table. "Do you have any more milk? I'm so thirsty. That antique store owner kept trying to feed me generic brand dry cat food. Do you know how *disgusting* that stuff is?"

Whitley lifted a brow. "I *am* a seamstress. Of course, I didn't actually *make* this dress. I only tweaked it."

"Tweaked it?" Johanna asked, not sure what to make of everything that was happening.

Whitley smiled. "I added this sash! And the lace over the bodice and the little cap sleeves. Do you like it? I think it adds a little something extra myself."

"It's very beautiful," Johanna agreed. "I don't understand. How is it possible that you were in there and now you're out here?"

Whitley giggled. "Let's not get hung up on those details, shall we? I don't really know how it all works. Let's just say it's a magical snow globe, and I'm here to grant a wish."

Slowly Johanna crawled down off the sofa. "Like a genie?"

Johanna heard Esmerelda choke on a laugh from the kitchen. "No, not like a genie. What an idiot. Like a witch."

"Essy, don't be rude!"

"Well, she asked a dumb question. Dumb questions are asked by dumb people," she snapped back to her sister.

"That wasn't a dumb question. She shook the globe to make a wish. I can see how she'd think it was like a genie. Rub the lamp, get a wish. Shake the snow globe, get a wish."

"Whatever. I'm waiting for my milk," she snapped impatiently.

Johanna glanced at Whitley, her eyes round, not sure what she should do. "So…am I supposed to feed the insulting cat?"

Whitley shrugged. "It's up to you. I'd make her promise to be nice if you're going to feed her."

Johanna sighed, put her blanket down on the sofa, and went into the kitchen. Pulling the half gallon of milk from her fridge, she looked down at the puffy grey cat. "If I feed you again, do you promise to be nicer?"

"To who?" asked Esmerelda, lifting the whiskers over one eye suspiciously.

A chortle escaped Johanna's lips. "To all of us! To me. To your sister. And especially to Rocky."

Esmerelda groaned. "I have to be nice to that overgrown meathead? He's so gross."

Johanna's jaw dropped. "Uh! Rocky's not gross! He's sweet and lovable and kind!"

"He's a walking bowl of slobber. Do you know how many times I've had to bathe myself since I met the dufus?"

Johanna put the carton of milk back on the counter. "Okay. Let's get a few things straight. You can't call Rocky a dufus and expect me to feed you."

The cat stood up and stretched before finally sitting back down and curling her tail around her. "Oh, fine. I won't call your fleabag a dufus anymore."

"You can't call him a fleabag either," said Johanna.

"Ugh. Fine." She pawed her forehead. "Milk?"

Johanna lifted the empty saucer from the floor and filled it with milk. "Boy, that clerk was right. You *are* a salty little thing!"

"Ugh! That guy was the worst. He kept kicking me out. It's like, what? Twenty degrees outside, and I have *no shoes on*, and he wants me to go find a new place to live? Are you kidding me? It's Christmas! Where's his Yuletide spirit?"

"You were intimidating his customers!" argued Whitley. "I don't blame him one bit."

Johanna walked back into her living room. "So you two *lived* at the antique store together?"

"We've been there for a few months," said Whitley. "We've been bounced around quite a bit over the last year. It's been exhausting, so we're both more than thrilled that you brought us home."

Johanna didn't know what to say. She'd brought the *snow globe* home, not a snarky cat and her weird genie sister. "Yeah, about that…"

Whitley held out a hand to stop her from saying anything more. "We came to deliver your wish."

"My wish," sighed Johanna. "I wished for a best friend."

Whitley's head bobbed excitedly as she pointed to herself. "Best friend!"

Johanna's eyes widened. "Oh, don't tell me *you're* the best friend?"

Whitley squealed as her green eyes flashed with youthful exuberance. "I think I am!"

Johanna's lip curled. "Umm, don't take this the wrong way, but I was actually wishing for a *man*."

Esmerelda nearly choked on her milk from the kitchen. "Oh, sister, aren't we all!"

Whitley's nose scrunched up as she looked at the wand she held in one hand. "Yeah, I'll be honest. I have *some* magic, but I can't make *men* appear out of nowhere. But I can move the furniture so you can vacuum underneath your sofa."

She flicked her wand towards the sofa to prove it, and a little fizzle of electricity sputtered out with a staticky *pfft* sound.

Whitley frowned and looked at the end of her stick. "Are you kidding me?" She flicked her wand again, and this time nothing at all came out. She looked up into the sky. "We have to do this with no *magic*?!" She slammed the wand down by her side. "Well, this is just great."

Johanna cocked one eyebrow up. "So you're telling me you *can't* make a man magically appear out of nowhere?"

"If she could, my life would be a heckuva lot better than it is right now," said Esmerelda.

Whitley put a hand beside her face. "Don't mind her, she's a bit of a man-aholic," she whispered to Johanna.

"And going through withdrawals!" shouted Esmerelda from the other room. "Don't forget, cats have amazing hearing, dear sister."

Whitley rolled her eyes and then looked around the room. "This is just too much. I think I need a minute. Do you mind if I sit down?"

Johanna pointed to the gown. "In that dress?"

Whitley's eyes dropped to look at the long layers of white satin. "Oh, right. You know, you really should try this on. I honestly think it's meant for you. I mean, that's *got* to be the reason that we're here."

"To give me a wedding dress?" scoffed Johanna. She looked at the dress. It *was* beautiful. "I mean, I wish I had a reason to need it. It's a gorgeous gown, but I'm not getting married anytime soon."

Whitley shrugged and wrestled with the zipper behind her. "Neither am I, but I put it on. Aren't you curious what it would look like on you?"

Johanna sighed. If she was being honest, she had to admit that she had envisioned herself wearing the dress, but that was *before* the dress had actually shown up in her living room! "This whole thing just feels surreal."

"Surreal?" asked Whitley, still working on trying to reach the zipper. "How so?"

"Do you need help with that?" asked Johanna.

Whitley sighed with relief. "Yes! That would be fabulous!"

Johanna went around behind her and unfastened the three little satin buttons at the top of the dress, then undid the hidden zipper the rest of the way. "There you go."

"Oh!" breathed Whitley. "Thank you!" She immediately let the dress fall to the ground.

Johanna quickly discovered that Whitley had been completely naked under the dress. Johanna put a hand beside her eyes to shield the naked woman from her view.

"You didn't come prepared, did you?"

"To be honest, this is our very first rodeo. I had no idea I was going to be spat out of the globe like that! All of my clothes are in my bedroom, and my bedroom is… well… it's in there!" She pointed to the snow globe with her wand.

"You don't happen to have something I could wear, do you?"

Still keeping her eyes off of the naked woman in her apartment, Johanna padded towards her own bedroom. "Right. I'll just see what I have."

Seconds later she returned with a pair of sweatpants, some underwear, a t-shirt, socks, and Rocky. "Will this do?"

"Yes, perfect. Thank you." Rocky barked at Whitley as she took the top and pulled it on over her head.

"Oh. This is Rocky. Rocky, this is Whitley," said Johanna patiently. Then she added with a whisper, "She's a figment of my imagination."

Whitley smiled at Rocky. "It's nice to meet you, Rocky," she said with a cinnamon-roll-sweet voice. She patted his head, changing his opinion of her almost instantaneously. "I'm not a figment of your mommy's imagination. I'm real. See, you can feel me petting you, can't you?"

"Woof!" agreed Rocky.

"I thought so." She pulled on the underwear and pants Johanna had given her.

"And that's Esmerelda," Johanna said to Rocky, pointing at the cat in the kitchen.

A groan escaped Esmerelda's throat. "Oh, we've met. Honestly, *not impressed*." She strolled into the living room and looked up at the big dog as he high-stepped around her, unsure of what to make of hearing his little furry play-mate suddenly speaking in a human voice. A low rumble formed in his throat.

"It's okay, Rock, relax," said Johanna, calmly scratching his head.

Esmerelda held a paw up to her nose. "Ugh, the kid stinks. He smells like the love child of a skunk and a pig. What do you feed him anyway?"

Johanna groaned. She'd just bathed him a few hours

ago, thanks to his little evening romp in the mud at the park. Despite that, the cat had a point. Rocky *didn't* smell very good. He had a bit of a gas problem. She was working on it, but when he got scared, it seemed to mess with his stomach.

"It's because you two freaked him out," she muttered, wanting to add that they'd freaked her out as well. "He's got a nervous stomach, and talking cats don't help."

Esmerelda rolled her eyes and bobbed her head towards the gown her sister had just shed. "Whatever. You should try that dress on."

Johanna looked down at the cat and lifted a suspicious brow. "Why do you two want me to try the dress on so badly?"

Whitley smiled and pointed her wand at the dress. When it didn't do anything, her head lolled back on her shoulders.

"Ugh, are you kidding? I have to pick up my own *clothes* from now on? This is *not* going to be fun." She walked over to the dress and picked it up, giving it a little shake to loosen the wrinkles. Then she held the dress up to Johanna's body and smiled. "We just think it would look pretty on you. I'll tell you what. I'll make you a deal. If you try on the dress and it fits, I'll let you keep it."

Johanna shook her head as if she were confused. "You're going to *give me* a wedding dress? Why in the world would I want a wedding dress? I'm not getting married!"

"Well, you might get married someday, silly," said Whitley with a perky little smile.

Esmerelda jumped up to sit on the arm of the sofa. "Yeah, miracles do happen, I'm told," she said dryly.

"Es!" snapped Whitley, sitting down on the little wooden chair next to Johanna's floor-to-ceiling bookcase and pulling on her socks.

"Listen, girls. This whole good cop bad cop thing you've got going on is entertaining and all, but I'm afraid you've got me completely befuddled. The two of you show up in my life, claiming you aren't a tumor in my head, and you want to be my new best friends, you've got a broken magic wand, you somehow made it snow in my apartment, and now you want to give me a wedding dress. I've got to be missing something!" said Johanna, feeling like she was going nuts.

Whitley sighed and slumped back in her seat. "Oh, Hanna—can I call you Hanna?" She didn't wait for an answer before continuing. "I honestly don't know what's going on. Esmerelda and I are new to this whole fairy godmother thing. All I know is that I have these dresses in my snow globe and they need homes. You were drawn to my snow globe for a reason, and unfortunately, that's all I know."

"Fairy godmother thing?" chuckled Johanna. "You don't even have any magic! And *that's* what you're calling yourselves? My fairy godmothers? Who am I, then? Cinderella?"

"Well, what else would you call us?" pouted Whitley. "Back home they called us witches, but I really find that term offensive. The word *witch* makes me think of black hats, pumpkins, and evil laughs." She shuddered. "I like a good hat just as much as the next girl, but pointy hats? Not my style."

"Riiight…"

"Listen, would you *please* just try on the dress? I have a closet full of dresses that need homes before my sister and I can be set free, and I literally think it's the reason why we were sent to you."

Johanna lifted the snow globe from the coffee table and held it to her face. Squinting, she peered in at the wooden wardrobe stuffed with an assortment of colored dresses. "You have to find homes for *all* of those dresses?"

With a pout on her face, Whitley nodded.

"Or what?"

Whitley stared at Johanna blankly. "Or else I'm stuck in that globe forever."

6

*J*ohanna spun around slowly, staring at her reflection in the full-length mirror. The dress fit like it had been made for her. The sash accentuated her small waist, and the little lace cap sleeves covered enough skin that she didn't feel naked, but still made her feel feminine and beautiful. The length was perfect, not so long that she would have to lift it to drag it around behind her, but long enough that she felt like a princess.

"It's beautiful," she breathed, unable to take her eyes off of the dress.

Whitley's hands clasped in front of her and she fought back a squeal. "Oh, Hanna! You look *gorgeous!*"

"When's the last time you washed your hair?" asked Esmerelda from the floor.

"Es!"

"What?! It looks like she poured a quart of motor oil on it and then let it dry naturally."

Johanna winced as a hand went to her head self-consciously. "I read it was bad to wash your hair every day."

"Yeah, you don't have to wash it *every day*, but you should certainly wash it more than once a year!"

Johanna lowered her brows and scowled at the cat. "I thought you were going to start being nicer."

"Were those my exact words? No. And I certainly didn't promise to lie."

"Never mind my sister," said Whitley, her green eyes shining. "The point is, the dress is beautiful. It fits you like a glove! So, it's all yours if you want it!"

Johanna lifted a shoulder. She *loved* the dress, but she also didn't want these girls to think that they were doing her any kind of favor. She didn't *need* the dress. "It's alright."

Whitley's face dropped. "You don't love it?"

Johanna mustered up a half-smile. "No, I do. I just don't need it or anything. I'm probably never going to get married."

Esmerelda looked up at her then. "How old are you anyway? You've gotta be knockin' on thirty."

"I'm actually thirty-five, why?"

Esmerelda's eyes widened and her little mouth gaped. "You're *thirty-five years old*?" she spat.

Johanna put a hand on her hip. "Yes, I'm thirty-five years old. What's wrong with that?"

A little snicker escaped the cat's mouth. "You're thirty-five and not married?"

"Yeah, so?"

"Where did your life go wrong?"

"Essy!" chastised Whitley.

"Well, that's rude!" said Johanna, giving the cat a fiery-glare. "I'll have you know I've got a great life!"

"Sure ya do…"

Johanna's dander was up now. "I do! I have a great

apartment. I live in a great city. I love my career. I have an amazing dog. I—I love my family…"

"And yet you spent your Thursday night on the couch, watching a sappy Christmas movie with a glass of wine from a box and shaking a snow globe, wishing for a man?" Esmerelda's green eyes swiveled up towards the ceiling. "Yeah, real great life."

Johanna's eyes burned with the same tears that had gone unshed earlier. She knew she had a great life. She did! And she didn't have to prove that to anyone! How *dare* this —this—*talking cat* criticize her life! Swallowing back the lump in her throat, Johanna looked at Whitley expectantly.

"So now what? You gave me the dress. Now you can go back to your snow globe? Rocky and I would be happy to walk the two of you back to the antique store so you can freak out another unsuspecting shopper."

Whitley grimaced. "Well, it doesn't exactly work like that."

Johanna shook her head in dismay. She suddenly had a desperate need to have the two figments of her imagination out of her head and out of her apartment, immediately. She strutted over to her apartment door and opened it, swooping the air with a hand. "You said you had to give me the dress. I accept. Thank you. Now you can go."

Whitley pursed her lips. "Umm. So that's *part of it*."

"Part of it? You didn't tell me there was more."

Whitley flicked her magic wand towards the apartment door, forgetting that it didn't work. She sighed and shook her head, walking over to it and shutting it manually. "I know. I don't exactly know *all of it*, but I do know a little bit more," she admitted, pinching one eye shut.

Johanna's face dropped. "Ohh-kay?" she drawled.

"That dress was pre-owned."

Johanna held the flared skirt out on either side of herself and looked down at it. "It's in really good shape for being pre-owned. It doesn't even look worn. Regardless. I'm totally okay with that. I still accept the dress. Now you can go."

Whitley scratched her head before continuing. "I really don't know *who* wore it before. Or for how long or anything. All I know is that it was pre-owned and there's a mystery surrounding it."

"A mystery?" The word hung in the air. Johanna was a mystery writer after all. "What do you mean there's a mystery surrounding it?"

Whitley's head bobbed up and down slowly. "Yes. I wish I knew what I meant. I was told that there's a mystery surrounding all of the dresses in my wardrobe. I don't know what that means. I just know that we have to figure out what it is and then solve it."

"We?" Johanna practically sneezed out the word.

"Yes, *we*," chimed in Esmerelda from the floor. "And if you don't help us, *you* get to take Whitley's place in the globe, and your horse over there gets to play the role of your trusty sidekick, got it?"

"What?!" demanded Johanna, her jaw dropping.

"Yup!" she added. "If you don't help us solve the mystery, then you and Slobber Boy get to take our places."

"I didn't agree to that!" gasped Johanna.

Esmerelda leapt up into Johanna's arms. She poked a paw into the woman's chest and looked directly into her eyes. "You put on the dress. You help us with the mystery."

Johanna's big brown eyes were wide as she sputtered, "B-but I didn't *ask* to put on the dress. You two forced me!"

Whitley clambered to her feet and plucked Esmerelda from Johanna's arms. "Essy, tell the—"

"Bup, bup, bup." Esmerelda put a paw to her sister's mouth. The twins made eye contact for the briefest of moments. "She helps us or she's the new genie in the lamp, *right, sis?*"

Whitley looked down at the snow globe sorrowfully.

Whitley let out the breath she'd been holding and made a face at her sister. Then she looked at Johanna. "Es is right, Hanna. Either help us solve the mystery or you're the new genie in the lamp."

Johanna's mouth opened wide. "But I don't wanna be the new genie in the lamp!"

"Then help us solve the mystery of the dress," countered Esmerelda, leaping back down onto the floor.

Johanna lifted the hem of her skirt and rushed over to the cat. "What mystery? What's to solve?"

Esmerelda shook her head. "Part of the mystery is figuring out what the mystery is."

"But how are we supposed to do that?!"

"There's a dry cleaning tag," whispered Whitley. Her head hung low and her tiny voice was barely audible.

"What?" snapped Esmerelda.

"There's a dry cleaning tag," she whispered a little louder.

Esmerelda gave an exasperated sigh. "A dry cleaning tag? What's that supposed to mean?"

"Hanna, did you happen to notice the dry cleaning tag when you put the dress on?"

Johanna shook her head. "I didn't notice anything."

"It's inside the dress," whispered Whitley. "Attached to the manufacturer's label."

Johanna's eyes brightened as she nodded. "Oh!"

Esmerelda's gaze ping-ponged back and forth between the two women. "I don't get it. So the dress got cleaned before it got given away to the secondhand store. What's that supposed to mean?"

"It's a clue," explained Whitley.

"How is it a clue?" Esmerelda rubbed her paw against her temples.

"If we can find the dry cleaners that the tag came from, maybe we can find another clue to help us figure out what the mystery is." Whitley shrugged. "It's all we've got right now."

"Wait. That's the *only* clue?" Johanna's voice rose an octave. "So, let me get this straight. We have to solve a mystery. No idea what kind of mystery, just a mystery. The dress could have been stolen. The owner could have been abducted. There could have been a fire. We don't know. And the *only* piece of evidence we have to go on is a *dry cleaning tag*?"

Whitley's head bobbed. "Yup."

Johanna sprawled her hands out wide as she shook her head. "Impossible. There's not enough evidence."

Whitley's bottom lip pouted out. "It's not impossible. It's going to be *hard*, especially since I don't have my magic, but it won't be impossible. I have faith. I've read a lot of mystery novels. I think we can do this."

"Yeah, well I've *written* a lot of mystery novels and I don't think we can do it," said Johanna with a furrowed brow.

Whitley sucked in her breath. "You're a mystery writer?"

Johanna nodded. "I like to think so."

"What have you written?"

Johanna plodded over to the bookshelf in her new wedding gown and pointed at the row of titles she'd penned. "These are mine."

Whitley's eyes widened. "*You're Hanna Hughes?!*"

A soft smile covered Johanna's face. "You've heard of me?"

Whitley shook her head. "No, but wow! Look at all the books you've written!"

Esmerelda laughed from the floor.

Still in awe, Whitley blinked rapidly. "So you've *written* mysteries, and I've *read* mysteries. We're gonna *kill* this case. Pun intended!" Whitley laughed.

"Oh geez. Now she thinks she's a sleuth *and* a comedian," groaned Esmerelda.

"When can we start?" Whitley asked excitedly.

It was well past midnight when Johanna looked down at her dress and then at the dark sky outside her window. "I can't believe this," she sighed. "I have so much work to do tomorrow, but I'd like to get you two out of my life. I guess we'll start in the morning."

Whitley squealed, clapping her hands.

Esmerelda made a beeline for the bedroom and hopped up on the bed. Kneading the soft comforter with both paws, she curled up in a ball. "So where are you two sleeping?"

7

"*I*'m sorry, those tags have been discontinued," said the burly red-faced man behind the counter. His sweaty brown hair curled up around the base of his neck, and his maroon t-shirt boasted big round armpit stains.

"Yeah, but what does that *mean*?" Johanna asked, tipping her head sideways and trying to understand what he was telling her.

"It means we don't use those kinds of tags anymore. What else do you want me to say?" asked the man in a thick New York accent.

Johanna sighed. She was getting nowhere fast with the growly dry cleaning clerk, and the overpowering stench of the dry cleaning chemicals nauseated her. "How long ago was it discontinued?"

The man threw up his hands. "How am I supposed to remember that? It's been years!"

"But this was definitely *your* tag at one time?"

He closed his eyes and lifted his brows while bobbing

his head. "Yeah. I mean, it says Duncan Dry Cleaners on it, doesn't it?"

"Is there any way you can look the number up in your computer system?"

"For what?"

"I need to know whose dress it was."

"You're the one carrying the thing. It ain't your dress?" he asked, wiping beads of sweat off his brow with the back of his hand.

"No, it's not my dress. I got it from a secondhand store. I need to know who the original owner was."

"Why do ya need to know that?"

Johanna turned her head towards Whitley, wondering if she had an answer to that question. "Why do we need to know?"

Whitley shrugged. "Because the original owner might want it back," she said weakly.

"You're askin' me?" He made a face as he peered over Johanna's shoulder.

Johanna's eyes narrowed as she glanced at Whitley again. She threw a thumb over her shoulder. "No, I was asking her."

The man behind the counter threw both hands on his hips. "Is this some kind of joke? 'Cause I got a lotta work to do in the back and I don't have time for this."

"Umm, Johanna, I don't think he can see me," Whitley whispered.

Johanna cringed internally. *Of course he can't, I'm the one with the brain tumor.*

Much to Johanna's surprise, Whitley had still been sleeping on her sofa when she'd awoken that morning, and Esmerelda had still been a talking cat. Johanna had thought for sure she'd wake up in the morning and discover that the night before had all been a dream, so when it wasn't, she was more than a little disappointed.

Johanna glanced out the window. Esmerelda sat calmly on the sidewalk with her tail fluffed up around her legs while Rocky bounced around her, trying to entice her to play with him. Johanna scratched the base of her skull with a finger and pursed her lips.

"Right, no, sorry. I was talking to myself. I do that sometimes. What I meant to say was, I just need to know. Isn't there some way you can just punch this number in your computer and have it spit out a name?"

The man let out an exasperated sigh like Johanna was really getting on his nerves. "No, I can't do that for two reasons. A, we don't disclose our customers' personal information, and two, that number don't mean anything anymore. It's too old. We purge our records once a year, and that tag has to be *at least* five years old."

"Ask him if he remembers the dress," suggested Whitley, hope widening her eyes.

"Well, at least tell me if you *remember* the dress," said Johanna, holding up the dress by the hanger and lifting the plastic sheathing.

The clerk glanced at it for a split second with lifted brows. "Lady, I started workin' here in '03. Do you know how many wedding dresses I've cleaned since '03? Probably a couple thousand. At the least. Ya know what I'm sayin'?"

Johanna sighed. "There's *nothing else* you can tell me about this dress?"

He rubbed his forehead again and then took the hanger from her. He spun the dress around and looked down inside it at the dry cleaning tag that was attached to the manufacturer's label. His head shook and one side of his mouth bunched up. Finally, he sighed and handed the dress back to Johanna.

"This is an A tag." He said it like it should mean something to her.

"An A tag," she repeated.

"Yeah, ya know. Like an alteration tag. This was here getting altered, not cleaned."

Whitley's brows sprang up. "Ask him if we can talk to the seamstress!"

Johanna waved a hand at Whitley. She already knew that. "Sir, is there any way that we can speak to your seamstress?"

"You wanna talk to Virginia?"

"Is she your only seamstress?"

He nodded. "Yeah, she's been here going on twenty-five years."

"She would have been here when this dress was altered?"

"Well, yeah. I'm sure she did the alterations herself. There's no one else here that could have done it," he said.

Finally, maybe we've got a break in the case! "Can we talk to her?"

"I mean, I guess, but she's like a hundred years old. She ain't gonna remember that dress any more than I am."

"Please, sir. It's really important that I get this dress back to its rightful owner," begged Johanna. It was even more important that she get this mystery solved so she could get rid of the two nutjobs taking up residence in her apartment.

He sighed and cast a backwards glance over his shoulder. "I guess I can see if she's got a minute. Just a second."

"Thank you," said Johanna as the man disappeared through a door behind the counter.

"This is so exciting! I'm solving mysteries with a real live *mystery writer*!" squealed Whitley.

Johanna puffed air out her nose. Just because she *wrote* mysteries didn't mean she had ever actually solved a *real* mystery. This was all new to her. "Well, calm down. Chances are Virginia won't remember this dress either."

"She *has to*," said Whitley. "We have nothing else to go on!"

"Ma'am," said the gruff voice from the doorway. "Virginia said you can bring the dress back and she'll take a look at it." He gestured for Johanna to follow him.

"Thank you." She folded the dress over her arm and followed the man through a short hallway until they got to a sewing room.

The man ushered Johanna in but stood in the doorway. "This is Virginia. She'll show you out when you're done. Virg, I'm headed back to work."

An old woman with white hair bundled on top of her head in a butterfly clip looked over her glasses at Johanna. "Sure thing, Herb," she said to him before he disappeared.

Johanna glanced around the cramped room. Spools of colored threads on wooden racks lined the upper half of one entire wall, and rows of different-colored zippers hung below it. There were several different sewing machines on small tables, and a dress form held an elegant little black dress pinned around the hem.

The woman turned to Johanna. "Now, what can I help you with? Herb said you had questions about a dress I altered?"

"Yes," said Johanna, holding the dress up. She hung it on a wooden coatrack near a sewing machine. "I got this dress from a secondhand store, but I was hoping to find its original owner. The only clue I have to go on is the dry cleaning tag inside the dress. Herb said it was an alteration tag from at least five years ago. I wondered if maybe you remembered the dress?"

"Ah." Virginia scooted herself over to the dress on her rolling chair. She lifted the plastic bag. "I alter a lot of wedding dresses."

"I know, but maybe you could just take a look?"

Virginia was already looking the dress over, pulling on the fabric, and then smoothing it with her time-worn hands. Finally, Virginia's white brows dropped. "These aren't my alterations." She touched the lace and the sash.

"Yes, those were added later," said Johanna.

The woman nodded and turned the dress around. She'd studied it for only a few seconds when something about it made her breath catch in her throat. "I put in this zipper!" she said with a soft reminiscent smile.

"You remember the dress?" asked Johanna, her brown eyes brightening. *What luck!*

Virginia frowned. "Unfortunately, I do."

"What do you mean, *unfortunately*?" Johanna glanced up at Whitley, whose smile was slowly fading.

"Well, I remember this gal clearly. She came in on the morning of her wedding rehearsal to pick up her dress. I had her try it on one last time, just to be sure everything fit properly, and wouldn't you know, the zipper broke!"

Listening to the woman's story carefully, Johanna nodded at her encouragingly.

"She was *so* disappointed, because she had a list of things to do before her rehearsal dinner, but I promised her it wouldn't take me long to replace the zipper. She was going to wait here for it, but then she got a message on her phone."

Johanna's eyes narrowed. "A message from her fiancé?"

Virginia shook her head. "No, it wasn't her fiancé. It was someone wanting to look at a house."

"Look at a house? What do you mean?"

Virginia's hand shook as she pointed to the dress. "The

woman was a realtor. I guess she was quite the go-getter. Every time she stopped in for a fitting, she was in a rush. Buzzing here, buzzing there." Virginia swatted the air with her hand.

"So she was a realtor and someone asked her to show a house on the day of her wedding rehearsal?" asked Johanna, her eyebrows lifting in surprise.

"Boy, she must have really been dedicated to her job," said Whitley from the corner. "I don't think I would have gone to work the day before my wedding!"

Unable to see or hear Whitley, Virginia gave a small nod. "Yes. I was surprised too. She told me that if it were just any house, she'd have suggested they choose a different realtor, but she said that this particular man asked for her by name, and he wanted to see a twenty-five-million-dollar listing! She said the commission on that one piece of real estate alone would pay for her *entire* wedding *and* honeymoon!"

"Wow!"

Virginia nodded. "Wow is right! I remember shooing her off!" she chuckled. "I remember saying, 'Go, go. I'll get the zipper fixed while you're gone!'"

"So then what happened?" asked Johanna, hanging on Virginia's every word.

The old woman's eyes widened, lifting the heavy wrinkles in her forehead. "She never came back."

Johanna shook her head in confusion. "What do you mean she never came back?"

Virginia threw up both arms. "I mean, I fixed the zipper. I bagged it up for her, and then she never showed up to pick it up."

"Did you try calling her?"

"Yes, of course I did. I left her several voicemail messages. She never returned any of the calls. And then eventually, the dress went into our overdue pile."

"What happens to the dresses in the overdue pile?"

"Oh, every so often the company either sells the garments or donates them."

"So that would have been how it got to a secondhand store?" asked Johanna.

Virginia nodded. "Very likely."

"Didn't you find it bizarre that she never came back for her wedding dress?"

"Oh, of course I did. But I thought, you just don't know what happens sometimes. Maybe she and her fiancé got in a fight and split up. It's really none of my business. Of course I was always *curious* as to what happened." Virginia looked at Johanna with interest. "Why are *you* looking for the owner?"

Johanna sighed and glanced at the dress. "Honestly? I really don't know. Something just begged me to return this dress to its original owner. Like there's a mystery to be solved."

Virginia smiled at Johanna softly. "How sweet of you, dear. But it's possible the woman who owned this dress didn't *want* her dress back. Perhaps it would be just too painful for her to see it again."

Johanna frowned then. She hadn't thought of that. "It's possible," she agreed. "But I have to try. Do you remember the woman's name?"

Virginia shook her head softly. "She signed the dry cleaning ticket as F. Marshall. I always called her Miss Marshall."

"Do you still have the ticket?" Johanna asked, sitting up straighter.

Virginia stood up and went to the small desk in her workspace. She pulled open a drawer and rifled through some papers. "Aha!" she said with a smile, pulling a paper from the drawer. "Here it is." She handed it to Johanna.

"It's even got her phone number on in it. Now you can track her down!"

Johanna's heart leapt for joy. She felt one giant step closer to returning the dress to its rightful owner and solving the mystery. "Oh, Virginia, this is great. Thank you!"

"Just don't tell Herb I gave it to you," she whispered. "The boss wouldn't take too kindly to me giving out customer information, and at my age, I can't exactly go looking for a new job."

Johanna beamed. "Oh, Virginia, my lips are sealed!"

8

*R*ocky snorted happily and bounded forward when Johanna and Whitley emerged from the dry cleaner's minutes later.

"Oh, it's *about time*," Esmerelda drawled, rolling her eyes. "This kid whines more than a four-year-old with a tummyache."

"Well, then, you two should have gotten along well together," said Whitley with a half-smile.

"Ha-ha, very funny," snapped her sister, swishing her tail back and forth. "Just so we're clear, you two aren't leaving me alone with this buffalo anymore. I'm a cat, not a dog sitter."

Johanna hugged Rocky's head to her stomach. "Oh, did you miss Mommy?"

Rocky's tail stirred the frosty air excitedly as she gave his ears and jowls a good jostle. He pulled himself loose from Johanna and walked over to Whitley next, looking up at her with his big brown eyes.

"I think he wants *you* to give him a little love," said Johanna with a smile.

Whitley grinned from ear to ear. "My pleasure!" she chirped, giving him a hug.

"What did you find out?" asked Esmerelda.

"The first thing we found out is that the clerk couldn't see your sister," said Johanna. "He thought I was crazy."

"You probably are. But that wasn't what I meant. Do we have a name?"

"We have a last name and a first initial. F. Marshall. The woman dropped off the dress to be altered and then never came back for it," said Johanna, untying Rocky's leash from the pole outside the cleaners. "We did get a phone number."

"Oh, man, that's going to make solving this mystery so much easier," sighed Whitley. "Can we call it now?"

Wrapping Rocky's leash around her hand, Johanna pulled her phone out of her pocket. "We can sure try." She punched the number in and put it on speakerphone.

It rang and rang and then went to voicemail. "Hey, you got my answering service. You know what to do," said a young woman's cheerful voice.

"Leave her a message," hissed Whitley in a whisper.

Johanna nodded, silencing Whitley. "Hi, my name is Johanna Hughes. I was hoping to speak with you. If you could give me a call back, I'd really appreciate it," she said before adding her phone number.

"Well, fingers crossed she calls us back!" said Whitley.

Johanna groaned. "She never called Virginia back. Chances are she's not going to call us back."

"Who's Virginia?" asked Esmerelda, jogging to keep up with the rest of them as they walked down the street.

"She was the seamstress who did the alterations on the dress. She remembered the woman who owned the dress. She said she was a realtor, and someone texted her out of the blue to show him a really expensive listing on the day of her wedding rehearsal."

"Did she go?"

"Yeah, she told Virginia that the commission on the sale of that single property would pay for her entire wedding *and* her honeymoon," said Whitley. "She *had* to go."

"But then she never came back," added Johanna.

"Ugh, this woman went to *work* on the day of her wedding rehearsal and never came back for her dress? Lame," groaned Esmerelda. "See, this is why women shouldn't work. They should just meet a man and get married, and that's it."

Johanna's jaw dropped. "You don't think women should work? What decade are you girls coming from, anyway?"

"We're coming from the same decade as you," said Whitley with a laugh. "My sister just never had a job. I, on the other hand, was a budding fashion designer. I had big plans to move to the city before I was *incarcerated*."

"How did that happen anyway?" asked Johanna. She'd been wondering what the story behind the twins was since she'd met them less than twenty-four hours ago.

Esmerelda groaned. "It's Whitley's fault, ask her. She's the reason we're in this predicament."

Whitley stopped walking and stared down at the cat. "*My fault?!*"

Esmerelda didn't stop, but instead hollered over her furry shoulder, "Admission is the first step, you're making progress."

Whitley thundered ahead. "This is not *my fault*, Esmerelda Snow. This is *your fault*. You're the one who refused to solve the mysteries with me like we promised Dad."

"I didn't promise Dad anything. That was you. I also didn't ask you to alter those dresses. That was your doing!"

Whitley slammed her arms down to her sides. "I did it *for you!*" she hollered.

"Sure ya did. Keep telling yourself that, sis. You did it for yourself."

"No, I didn't!"

Johanna's head bounced back and forth between the sisters. She rubbed her temples. "Can you two knock it off? You're giving me a headache."

Whitley let out a frustrated "Ugh!" and then strutted past Johanna and Rocky.

Just as she did, Johanna's phone rang.

"It's her, it's her!" shouted Johanna excitedly, touching the little green phone symbol.

Whitley turned around and rushed back to Johanna's side. "Put her on speaker!"

Johanna nodded. "Hello?"

"Hi, this is Penny returning your call."

"Penny?" asked Johanna with a frown, wondering if perhaps that F on the dry cleaning ticket had actually been a P. "Penny Marshall?"

"No, Penny Greenway."

"Oh," sighed Johanna, feeling defeated. "I was trying to get in touch with an old friend. I'm sorry. I must have the wrong number."

The woman on the other end of the phone paused before answering. "You're looking for a Marshall?" she asked.

"Yes. Is she at this number?" Johanna's hopes lifted for a moment.

"No, but I'm pretty sure I was assigned her old number. I've had it for several years now. The woman who owned the number before me must have been a realtor, because for a while I got a lot of calls about realty listings. I almost switched numbers because I got so many calls for her."

"Yes, the woman I'm looking for was a realtor. I don't suppose you have a forwarding number?"

"I'm sorry. I don't."

"Oh, that's too bad. Well, I'm sorry to have bothered you," said Johanna, preparing to hang up.

"I do know what realty company she worked for, though," said Penny.

Whitley's eyes widened excitedly and she clapped her hands together quietly.

"You do? Oh, that would be very helpful! Which company?"

"It was Four Seasons Realty," said Penny.

Johanna wanted to cheer, too, but she reined herself in. "Oh, Penny. Thank you so much!"

"No problem, I hope you find the woman you're looking for!"

Johanna smiled. "So do I!"

"*A*re we just going to go in there and ask for an F. Marshall?" asked Whitley, looking around nervously.

Johanna peered through the glass doors. It was well past lunchtime. Against Esmerelda's wishes, they'd taken her and Rocky back to the apartment again because it was too cold to leave a dog and a cat out on the city street for any length of time, and the realty office they now stood in front of had a sign that clearly read *No Animals*. A woman with a pen stuck in a messy bun on top of her head sat at a desk answering the phone.

"What else would we do?"

Whitley giggled. "I don't know, we could be sneaky and pretend to be buying a house and ask for Miss Marshall?"

Johanna knew that Whitley was having a good time with the mystery, but she wasn't. She had a million things she needed to be doing, including a book she needed to finish writing, and investigating a mystery with no crime, no suspects, and no clues was not one of those things.

"Or we could just tell them we're looking for Miss Marshall and then talk to her like normal adults."

The smile on Whitley's face faded. "Or we could do that," she agreed in a small voice.

Johanna nodded. There was no reason for them to beat around the bush. They weren't going to get anywhere in solving the mystery if they did that. "That's what we'll do. Come on."

"Don't forget, they can't see me," whispered Whitley as Johanna opened one of the glass doors.

"Then why are you whispering?" Johanna whispered back out of the side of her mouth.

Whitley giggled. "Good question."

"May I help you?" asked the woman at the desk, hanging up the phone.

"We're here to see Miss Marshall," said Johanna.

The woman behind the desk lowered her eyebrows. "Hmm. Miss Marshall? I don't believe we have any agents here by that name."

Whitley stomped her foot down on the floor. "Oh, darn it! She doesn't work here anymore!"

"I see," said Johanna, not prepared to give up just yet. She'd half-expected the secretary to say that since her phone number had changed. "She used to be a realtor here, maybe five or six years ago. Maybe even more. But I think Marshall was her maiden name. It's possible she's married since then."

The woman smiled. "Ah. I'm new. I wouldn't know

those things. Can you hang on? I'll let you talk to Mr. Shaw. He's the boss, he'll know."

"Thank you."

Johanna and Whitley turned their backs to the receptionist and examined the pictures on the wall while the woman called her boss. Several framed pictures of happy home-owners with keys to their new homes, shaking realtors' hands, covered most of one wall. Another picture was of a stocky man shaking hands with a tall, thin man, captioned *Tim Shaw, Managing Broker* with a little placard beneath it, *October 2011*.

Suddenly a voice boomed behind them. "Hello, I'm Tim Shaw, may I help you?"

Johanna turned to see the stocky man in the picture standing in front of them. He had straw-like blond hair with a bit of a cowlick in the back and a chubby red smiling face, and he wore khaki trousers and a short-sleeved white button-down shirt. Johanna reached her hand out to him.

"Hi, Mr. Shaw. My name is Johanna Hughes. Several years ago, maybe five or more years, I worked with a realtor by the name of Miss Marshall. I'm having a hard time remembering her first name. I was hoping to possibly work with her again?"

Whitley elbowed Johanna in the ribs. "You're welcome," she hissed.

Tim's bright smile faded. "Oh, I'm so sorry to have to tell you, but Felicia Marshall passed away six years ago."

Whitley sucked in her breath and covered her mouth with her hand. "Oh my goodness!"

Johanna felt her stomach sink. When Virginia had said she had never come back for her dress, the thought had crossed her mind, but she hadn't wanted to say it out loud. She put a hand to her stomach as her jaw dropped.

"Oh, no! I'm so sorry! How did she die?"

Tim frowned. "She was found dead in a park. An apparent mugging gone wrong."

"Oh my God," breathed Johanna. "That's terrible!"

Stunned, Whitley took a seat in one of the lobby chairs. "This is *horrible*! I thought we were only going to be returning the dress to the woman. I never thought for a second we'd find out she was dead!"

The mystery writer inside of Johanna had gotten her interest piqued now. How curious was it that Felicia Marshall had received a suspicious request to show a house on the morning of her wedding rehearsal and then had been found dead later that day? Was that simply a coincidence, or was there more to the story?

Tim nodded. "It certainly was horrible. She was a great coworker and an amazingly hardworking realtor. We all loved Felicia."

"Wow, I'm in shock," said Johanna, unsure of what to do next. That mystery without a crime or a victim they'd been trying to solve had just become a mystery *with* a crime *and* a victim.

"I completely understand," said Tim, nodding sadly. They all seemed to observe a moment of silence in Felicia's memory, and then he looked up at Johanna curiously. "Is there a listing you were interested in looking at? I can certainly get you to another realtor. Janet Sandborn took over most of Felicia's clients."

Johanna's mouth opened, but nothing came out.

"Tell him yes," said Whitley, shooting up out of her chair. Having recovered from the shock of finding out that the dress's owner was dead, she now stood next to Johanna with a determined look on her face. "Tell him we want to see some apartments."

Johanna swallowed hard and nodded. "We'd like to look at some apartments."

"We? Do you have someone coming to look with you?"

Johanna cleared her throat and blanched. "I'm sorry. I meant, *I'd* like to look at some apartments."

Tim smiled kindly. "I'll let you talk to Janet. She knew Felicia too, and she's one of my best agents. She'd be glad to help you."

Johanna gave him a tight smile, the kind where her smile didn't make it all the way to her eyes. "Thank you."

Minutes later, Johanna and Whitley sat side by side in matching chairs in front of Janet Sandborn's desk. The spiky-haired blonde stared at them from beneath a set of extremely long, obviously fake eyelashes.

"Tim says you're looking for an apartment?" she asked as her long red fingernails clicked her computer's keyboard.

Johanna held her breath, puffing out her cheeks. She released it uncomfortably. "Actually," she began, dragging out the word, "can I just be honest with you?"

Janet's fingers stopped clicking on the keys. She looked up at Johanna curiously. "Of course."

Johanna swallowed hard. "This is probably going to sound really weird."

"Okay?" Janet's over-drawn eyebrows knitted together curiously.

"I recently acquired a wedding dress from a secondhand shop. It had a dry cleaner's tag inside it that led me to discover that the dress was owned by Felicia Marshall."

Janet's mouth gaped open. "Felicia Marshall! Wow, I haven't heard *that* name in a while."

Johanna nodded. "Mr. Shaw just broke the news to me that Felicia passed away six years ago."

Janet sucked in a deep breath and pursed her lips. "Yes, six years ago. That sounds about right," she agreed stiffly.

Sensing that Janet's body had tightened up slightly,

Johanna leaned in and cocked her head to the side. "Did you know Felicia well?"

Janet leaned back in her black desk chair and, putting her elbows on the armrests, steepled her fingers. "I mean, we were coworkers."

Johanna leaned forward. "I'm sensing something. Did the two of you not get along?"

Janet shrugged. "We got along alright. It's just that Felicia was... I don't know how to say it exactly." She shifted in her seat. "Let's just say that Felicia was a shark."

"A shark? How so?"

The rouged apples of Janet's cheeks squished up into her eyes as she faked a smile. "She had a tendency to steal other people's clients."

"Oh, I see. Did she ever steal any of your clients?"

Janet lifted a shoulder and gave a smarmy grin. "I always got them back."

"Was anyone suspicious about the way that Felicia was killed?"

"Not that I know of. I mean, I really didn't ask a lot of questions or anything, so they might have been. You'd have to talk to her family or her fiancé."

Johanna nodded, she planned to! "Did you know her family or her fiancé?"

"I never met any of her family. I only met the fiancé once. He stopped in here to take Felicia to lunch one afternoon. I think he and Felicia both had similar personalities."

"In what way?" asked Johanna.

Janet made a face. "I don't know. It was just a sense I got. He seemed just as work-oriented as she did."

"Do you know his name?"

Janet thought about it for a second. "Mmm, pretty sure it was Mitchell."

"Is that a first name or a last name?"

"First."

"Mitchell what?"

Janet shook her head. "I honestly have no idea. Felicia just used to ramble on about Mitchell this and Mitchell that. That's all I remember." She thought about it for a second and then held up a finger. "I do remember that he worked for an architectural company or an engineering company nearby, but I couldn't tell you which company."

Johanna smiled at her. "Okay, that might be helpful."

Janet furrowed her brows. "So what's this all about? You found her wedding dress and what? You're trying to put together the pieces of her life?"

"I wish I knew what this was about." Johanna sighed inwardly, wishing she had a better reason to tell Janet, but she didn't. She wasn't completely sure what she was doing. "There's just something telling me I have to find out the truth about Felicia Marshall's death."

9

*T*he sun hung low in the western skyline by the time Whitley and Johanna returned home later that evening. It was hardly visible behind the grey, moisture-laden clouds enveloping the city. During the train ride home, the temperature had dropped another ten degrees, making it officially cold enough to snow, but a single snowflake had yet to fall.

Esmerelda was sitting in front of the apartment door with a scowl on her face when the two women entered. "What part of not leaving me alone with the slobber king did you two not understand?" she demanded, her green eyes flashing. She stood up and spun around so the two women could see all sides of her matted fur. "Look at me! I'm wilted!"

Whitley couldn't help but giggle when she saw her sister dripping with doggy saliva.

Johanna glanced over at Rocky, who sat quietly in a corner with his head drooped low between his shoulder blades. "Oh, Rocky, did the kitty get mad at you?" she asked him tenderly.

He lifted his eyes slightly without moving his head and let out a little whine, but refused to make eye contact with Johanna.

She pulled off her winter coat and rushed to his side to cuddle his head. "I've never seen Rocky so upset," said Johanna, stroking his head sweetly. "Were you mean to him?"

Esmerelda hopped up on the kitchen table. "Define mean?"

"Did you yell at him?" Johanna's heart twisted in her chest. The thought of someone being mean to her dog lit a fire inside her belly.

Esmerelda tipped her head sideways. "Mmm. Define yell?"

"Esmerelda! You cannot be mean to Rocky. Do you not remember our agreement? You promised not to be mean to him."

Esmerelda waved a paw in the air. "No, no. Rewind the tape. I promised not to call him a flea bag or a dufus. I didn't say I wouldn't be mean."

"Well, obviously that's what I meant!" hollered Johanna. "Rocky is very tenderhearted. He doesn't respond well to yelling."

Esmerelda sat back on her two hind legs and threw her front paws up in the air in a shrug as she cast a sideways glance over to Rocky, who still sat quietly. "I don't know. Looks to me like he responded just fine to yelling. He hasn't tried to lick me once since I yelled."

Johanna gave Whitley a sideways glance. "Can you talk to her?"

Whitley sighed. "If you want Hanna to help us, no more yelling, Es."

Esmerelda rolled her eyes and put her front paws back

down on the table. "Oh, fine. No more yelling. Can I have dinner now? I'm *starving*. You really do need to get some tuna fish or something. This all liquid diet is a killer."

Johanna groaned as she poured Esmerelda another saucer of milk and scooped Rocky out a bowlful of food. "Come here, Rocky. The mean kitty is going to leave you alone," she promised.

Rocky whined as he watched the cat lapping the milk in the kitchen. His bowl sat only a few feet away from her, but it was obvious he wasn't coming anywhere near her. With her feet, Johanna scooted the bowl over to the front door. Rocky gave her a thankful "Woof!" before burying his head in his bowl.

Johanna spun on her heel and padded over to her computer desk, where she slid into her comfy padded seat and put on her glasses. She opened her laptop, gave her touchpad a little click and waited for it to boot up.

"Now, we need to see what we can find out on the internet about Felicia Marshall's murder."

"You figured out her first name?" asked Esmerelda, lifting her head from her saucer of milk.

"Yes," said Whitley sadly. "We also found out she died six years ago."

Esmerelda sucked in her breath. "The dress belongs to a dead girl? How creepy is that?"

"Essy, that's mean!"

"I wouldn't call it creepy," said Johanna, navigating her computer to the internet. "It's worrisome. I feel like this mystery we're supposed to solve is about figuring out who murdered her."

Esmerelda abandoned her bowl and raced into the living room. "Wait, she was murdered?"

"We were told by some of the people at the realty office

that it was a mugging gone wrong, so it's my guess you two were sent here to figure out who killed her." Johanna typed "Felicia Marshall mugging" into the search engine. She clicked on the first article that popped up and read the headline. "Missing Realtor, Felicia Marshall, Found Dead in Hudson River Park."

"Ugh, this just makes me so sad," said Whitley as she fell onto the sofa.

"It says Felicia Marshall was discovered by a homeless man in the Hudson River Park," said Johanna, skimming the article. "Her jewelry and her purse, including her wallet, phone, and car keys, were all missing. Her car was discovered abandoned a few blocks away. She was shot twice, once in the stomach and once in the chest. The police ruled it a mugging gone bad, but no suspects were ever arrested."

"So she was shot during a mugging and we're supposed to track down the mugger?" asked Esmerelda. "How in the world are we supposed to do that?"

Johanna shook her head. She had no idea how they'd piece it together either. She straightened her glasses and clicked on another link.

"I found her obituary. There's a picture of her." She pointed at the professional head shot of a beautiful, put-together woman with smooth shoulder-length blond hair, blue eyes, and narrow glasses in a grey suit. No doubt it was one that had graced a realty billboard or the side of a bus stop bench in her time.

"She was beautiful," whispered Whitley.

"Yeah." Johanna had to swallow hard to keep from crying. Having a face put to the name suddenly made it all real for her. This wasn't just some puzzle that they were trying to solve now. This was an actual *person* who had been killed. The realization that *that* was the woman who had owned the dress and that *that* was the woman who hadn't made it to her wedding tugged at her heart. Her own fiancé hadn't made it to their wedding day either, and it had crushed her. So much so that she'd closed up her world and buried herself in her career for the past decade.

"Ohh," Whitley cried, bursting into tears. "This is so sad!"

"You didn't even know her," snapped Esmerelda, but Johanna could hear a little less sting in her words.

"I didn't have to know her!" Whitley bawled. "I have a heart!"

Johanna shoved down her own pain. They didn't need two blathering women in the apartment. She had to stiffen her resolve in order to focus on the facts of the case.

"Girls, her parents were Gene and Dawn Marshall, and her fiancé was Mitchell Connelly."

Johanna typed both into the computer. After a little bit of clicking and scanning, she announced, "I found an address for a Gene and Dawn Marshall in Brooklyn. I'm pretty sure it's her parents. But there are lots of Mitchell Connellys in this city. I have no idea which one would be him."

Whitley wiped her eyes on the sleeve of the long-sleeved UCHS t-shirt that she'd borrowed from Johanna and sat up. "Look up 'Mitchell Connelly engineer' or 'Mitchell Connelly architect'! Janet said he worked for a company like that."

Johanna nodded at the good idea. She typed "Mitchell Connelly engineer" into the computer. A smile spread across her face. "I got a hit! There is a Mitchell Connelly, structural engineer for a company in Midtown. It has to be him!"

"We've got to pay her parents and her fiancé a visit," said Whitley.

Johanna paused. The thought of having to face the people who had lost their daughter brought her right back to the nights she'd spent comforting James's family after he'd been killed in the accident. It had been so painful that she wasn't sure if she could relive that. She already felt awkward around people, never knowing what to say or how to act, but the fact that this particular one hit so close to home terrified her even more. "I—I don't think I can…"

"You don't think you can what?" asked Esmerelda, giving her a look.

"I don't think I can meet her parents and her fiancé. I wouldn't know what to say."

"You don't have a choice," said Esmerelda. "Unless you want to be stuck in that glass ball for the rest of your life."

Johanna's stomach turned. She'd about had it with the snarky cat. She didn't need the added pressure of a threat. "Just can it, Esmerelda. I'm tired of your attitude. Whitley and I really don't need you to solve this mystery, you know. You're just dead weight. I can easily return you to the antique store and you can just find someone else to feed you."

Esmerelda sucked in her breath indignantly. "Dead weight?! I'm not dead weight!"

"You are dead weight. You're mean to my dog. You're rude to me and your sister. You haven't contributed anything valuable to solving this mystery. Why do we even keep you around?"

"Uh! Whitley, are you just going to stand around and let her talk to me like that?!" demanded Esmerelda.

Whitley wrinkled her nose. "I hate to say it, but she has a point, Es. I've told you for years that you catch more flies with honey than you do with vinegar."

"That's, like, the dumbest saying *ever*. How am I supposed to know what that means?" she pouted. "I don't even like honey or vinegar."

When Whitley and Johanna didn't respond, Esmerelda leapt off the arm of the sofa and strutted off towards Johanna's bedroom. "Whatever. I'll just go to bed, then."

"You're not sleeping on my bed," Johanna hollered after her.

Esmerelda just wagged her fluffy tail in the air. "Goodnight."

When she was gone, Whitley turned to look at Johanna. "Hanna, as much as I know you don't want to go meet Felicia's parents and her fiancé, I think we have to pay them a visit. We need to find out more about what happened the day of her wedding rehearsal." Whitley glanced out at the darkened windows. "It's already getting late, but I think we should go first thing in the morning."

Johanna sighed and glanced across the room at Rocky, who had curled up on his big square doggy bed in the corner. Even if she wanted to go, she couldn't do it tomorrow. "I can't tomorrow. I have plans."

"What plans?" hollered Esmerelda from the bedroom.

"I thought you were going to bed," Johanna hollered back.

"What plans?" Esmerelda repeated.

"Family plans. None of your business!" Johanna groaned. She still hadn't gotten her sister's mixer, and there was no way she was going to find one before the party.

"Wait, you're leaving?" asked Whitley, her thin voice raising an octave. "But we have so many things to figure out! We were finally getting somewhere!"

Johanna shrugged. Her heart was heavy, and she suddenly wished she could just crawl up in a ball next to

Rocky. "I'm sorry, but we're having a Christmas party at my Dad's house. I have to go."

"Oooh, I wanna go to a Christmas party!" said Whitley with bright eyes.

In a flash, Esmerelda was back in the living room. She sprang up on top of Johanna's desk and pointed a paw at the two women. "Listen. I was left alone with that nuisance to society all afternoon. I am *not* going to be left alone with him all day tomorrow too while you go and have fun at a Christmas party."

Johanna shrugged. "Then I'll let you out and you can go find somewhere else to keep warm."

Esmerelda pawed her forehead.

Whitley smiled excitedly. "I have a better idea! How about you take us all with you?"

Johanna shook her head. "Oh no, I'm not taking Mean Cat and Invisible Girl to my dad's. My sister will think I've gone mad. She already thinks I'm a little crazy."

"And she wouldn't be wrong," said Esmerelda under her breath.

Johanna stared at the grumpy cat. "Isn't there a meme somewhere that you need to go put your face on?"

"I don't know what that means, but I'm sure I take offense. Listen, unless you want to be stuck in a snow globe for the rest of your life, I suggest you keep us happy. My sister and I want to go to a Christmas party, so we're *going* to a Christmas party."

Johanna grimaced. "Fine," she sulked. "Come to my family's Christmas party. But I'm telling you, it's not going to be a fun time."

"Why not?" asked Whitley.

Johanna rubbed her forehead. "Let's just say my family has… issues."

"What kind of issues?"

"You know, just the regular, annoyingly intrusive family stuff. Don't say I didn't warn you."

Esmerelda strutted past Whitley and Johanna towards Johanna's bedroom, her tail batting the air. "Consider me warned. I'll see you both in the morning. I need my beauty sleep now. I've got a party to attend tomorrow!"

10

*R*ocky fidgeted on the doorstep next to Johanna and yawned. His breath puffed out in front of him in a cloudy vapor mist. Around them, the small patches of grass were still a crispy white from the night's frost.

"Why'd we have to get here so early?" Esmerelda complained, laying her chin on Johanna's shoulder. She'd whined so much about the freezing sidewalk on the way there that Johanna had been forced to pick her up and carry her for the rest of the trip.

"You didn't have to come," Johanna whispered in her ear. Her cheeks still burned red from the train ride and the subsequent walk to her father's house. And not just from the subfreezing temperatures, but also because she'd felt like an idiot the entire way with both Rocky *and* Esmerelda in tow.

"Oh, but you positively *begged* us to come," sighed Esmerelda. "And we couldn't let you down."

"Very funny, Es. You're lucky she even brought us at all," her sister hissed from the step behind Johanna.

"What she said," agreed Johanna. Already stressing about the day ahead of her, she stared at the pine wreath in front of her and exhaled.

The door in front of them burst open and a younger, taller blond version of Johanna popped out, wearing an apple-green apron with holly-red rickrack trim and an elf's hat. "JoJo!" shouted the woman, throwing her arms around Johanna's shoulders. "Dad! JoJo's here!"

"Hey, Mook," said Johanna with a slow-moving smile. Her sister's real name was Melissa, but Johanna had been only eighteen months old when her sister was born, and the name Melissa had been too difficult for her to say when she was a toddler. *Mook* was what had come out, and it had stuck. Both her mother and father had started calling her that, and she'd never shaken the childish moniker since. "I missed you."

"Oh Gawd, I missed you too," she responded in her thick Jersey accent. She looked down at Rocky and threw her arms out wide. "Rockland Gable, give your Auntie Mook a hug!" she bellowed as he leapt up to put his enormous paws on either side of her shoulders. She wrapped her arms around her "nephew" while he lapped at her face excitedly.

"Where's my good boy?" called a male voice from inside the house, sending Rocky into a tizzy as he shot inside.

With Rocky gone, Melissa finally cast her brown eyes to her sister. "Where have you been? Why haven't you two been home lately?"

Johanna smiled. She loved her family a lot, but sometimes, it was hard for her to come home. There were a lot of painful memories and a lot of loss associated with the Union City, New Jersey, row house she now stood in front of.

"I've been busy. Books don't write themselves, you know."

Melissa suddenly noticed the furry grey scarf draped over her sister's shoulder. "Is that a cat?!" she demanded.

"Oh," said Johanna with a nervous smile. "Yeah, this is Esmerelda."

"You got a cat and didn't tell me?" Her brazen voice carried into the house as her eyes narrowed on Johanna. "What's going on with you?"

"JoJo got a cat?" asked Denny Hughes now standing in the doorway. "Hey, pumpkin. Merry Christmas."

"Merry Christmas, Dad." Johanna smiled as her dad enveloped her in a bear-sized embrace.

"So you did get a cat," he said, giving Esmerelda's fur a little tousle.

"She named it Esmerelda," Melissa chided.

"What kind of name is Esmerelda?" asked Denny.

"I didn't get a cat," said Johanna. "I'm just cat sitting her for a little while, and I didn't name her. She came with the name."

"Ah. What's old Rocky think of the two of you cat sitting?" asked Denny, thumbing the air.

"He likes her. She's like a new toy to him."

"Well, we all know what he does with his toys," said Melissa. "She's such a pretty cat. You're going to have to keep the two of them separated so he doesn't chew off all of her fur."

Johanna grimaced. "Esmerelda's pretty good about keeping Rocky in line. They've had a few scuffles, but I think they have an understanding now. He understands that she has a strict no-licking policy."

Denny smiled and then took a step back into the house. "Well, what are we doing standing out here? I'm not paying to heat all of Jersey. Come in, come in."

Her childhood home smelled like pine needles and turkey, and Johanna's heart warmed to see her mother's Christmas decorations scattered about. The tree in the living room to her left caught her attention. "You sprang for a real tree this year, Dad?"

Denny rubbed a hand against his thinning hair and shifted on his feet. "Oh. Yeah, I, uh, I thought it might be nice. Whaddaya think?"

From behind Johanna, Whitley sucked in her breath. "Oh, Hanna! This is where you grew up? It's so warm and cozy! And the tree is beautiful! Is it okay if Essy and I go exploring?"

Johanna nodded as she unwound the cat from her neck and sat her down on the well-worn carpet. Trying not to call attention to the nod she'd given the two of them, she turned her back to them and they took off towards the living room.

"Yeah, Dad. The tree's beautiful." While she was being honest, the tree *was* beautiful, but it was a bit of a shocker to her that her father, who was a bit of a cheapskate, had splurged on a live Christmas tree. Johanna couldn't remember a single live tree she'd ever had growing up. "You rearranged the decorations this year, too. Usually we put the good garland in the doorway, not on the balusters. Did you do the decorating this year, Mook?"

Melissa held up two hands and then took the gift bags from Johanna's arms. "Don't look at me."

"Huh. I guess it's okay," said Johanna slowly, her eyes taking everything in. It wasn't how her mom used to decorate, but she would just have to get over it. Johanna craned her neck to look past the entryway where they stood and towards the kitchen. "Where are Kevin and the kids?"

"Henry and Lex are upstairs watching cartoons in my

old room, and I sent Kev to the market. Dad didn't get everything on the list I sent him."

"I did too get everything on the list," said Denny gruffly. "Your sister wasn't specific with some of the things she wanted, and now she's blaming *me*."

Melissa rolled her eyes. "Seriously, Dad. How am I supposed to make Mom's famous cinnamon roll apple pie with red delicious apples? Those are like the worst baking apples there are."

Denny looked at his oldest daughter and lifted his brows, sending a sharp crease running across his forehead. "She said apples. I bought apples. If she wanted a certain kind of apples, don'tcha think she shoulda told me?"

Johanna couldn't help but smile as she shed the good hat and coat she'd worn. Her family's big, boisterous personalities warmed her heart. Even though the noise and the chaos would get old before the sun went down, and she knew she'd crave the silence of her Manhattan apartment, for now, this was exactly what she needed.

"Oh, you're wearing the shirt I gave you last year for Christmas," said Melissa with a broad smile. "See, what did I tell ya? Green's your color."

"Thanks, sis." Johanna turned around to hang her coat and hat on the wooden coatrack in the entryway.

When she did, her sister grabbed the back of her blouse. "What is this?"

Johanna froze and glanced over her shoulder. "What?"

"The tag's still on it!"

Johanna felt her face flush. *Shit.* "Is it?"

"Is this seriously the first time you're wearing it?"

"Umm, nah. It can't be. I'm sure I've worn it before." Johanna crossed her fingers inside her pants pockets and prayed her sister would just drop it.

"I got you this blouse so you'd have something nice to

wear out on a date, since all you seem to own are sweat-pants, old t-shirts, and crewneck sweatshirts."

"Well, yeah," agreed Johanna, making her *duh* face. "It's a *great* date shirt."

"And yet you haven't worn it on a date."

"I'm pretty sure I have."

"It still has the tag on it."

"I just probably wore a jacket over it."

"You didn't wash it?"

"Well, if I only wore it for an hour or two or whatever, then I probably just hung it up after."

Melissa stared at her, her brown eyes like lasers on Johanna's face. "Liar."

"Quit!"

"Dad, JoJo's lying," shouted Melissa, even though her dad was standing only a few feet away.

"Dad, make Mook stop harassing me."

Denny ran a hand over his head. "You two aren't seriously going to do this all day, are you? It's our Christmas party."

"Maybe," said Melissa with a frown and a one-shoulder shrug. "If JoJo keeps lyin' to me."

"I'm not lying!"

"When's the last time you went on a date, then?"

Johanna groaned internally. She couldn't believe the interrogation was starting already. She thought she'd have at least a few hours before anyone would ask her about her social life. This was way too early in the day. She wanted to turn around and leave. "I don't know. Thursday?"

"Of what year?"

"Mook! Can we not do this? I literally just walked in the door."

"I can't help it. I worry about you. It's not healthy to be alone so much."

"I'm not alone. I have Rocky."

Melissa's hands gestured wildly in the air. She'd always been a hand talker. "Rocky is great and all, but he doesn't count."

"Dad, tell Mook that Rocky totally counts."

Denny glanced back at Rocky, who was quietly gnawing on the dog bone he'd laid out for him. "Rocky doesn't count, JoJo. I'm sorry. He's a great dog and companion and all, but your sister's right. You need human interaction in your life."

"I get human interaction! You guys are overreacting!"

Melissa narrowed her eyes and put her hands on her hips. "Really? When's the last time you talked to a real live man? Like not someone on the internet."

"This morning!"

"A man *besides* the bagel guy, JoJo."

Johanna's mind flipped backwards to the man Rocky had ran over in the park. "Thursday night, I told you."

"Really?" Melissa said the word like she didn't believe her.

"Really."

"You had a date on Thursday night?"

Johanna swallowed hard before spitting out an anxious "Yeah."

"With a man."

"Yes, with a man!"

Melissa glanced over at Johanna's dog. "What'd you do with Rocky?"

"Took him with."

"How long have you been seeing this guy?"

"What is this? An interrogation? Daaaad. Make her stop!" Johanna whined.

"Mook. Ease up," their father said quietly.

"I will ease up when she tells me what I want to know!"

Melissa turned to Johanna. "How long have you been seein' him?"

Johanna shrugged. "I've been seeing him on and off for the last five years." It wasn't a lie. It was the truth. A bit of an intentional misdirection, but the truth.

"You've been seeing a guy on and off for the last five years and you've never told us?!" Now Melissa was interested. Even her father looked at her with shock in his eyes. "What's his name?"

Shit. "Um," she swallowed hard. "Mitchell." The name of Felicia Marshall's fiancé was the first name that popped into her head.

"What does he do for a living?"

"He's an engineer."

"JoJo, you've been dating an engineer for five years and you haven't told us. I'm shocked," said Denny.

Johanna's arms suddenly felt chilled as all the heat in her body went to her face. "Dad, it's not serious. We literally lead our own lives and just bump into each other on occasion." *Still not a lie.*

Melissa's hands exploded in the air next to her temples. "My mind is literally blown right now. Like *literally*."

Johanna felt a sudden pang of guilt. How had she gone from being single to having an on-and-off boyfriend in a matter of seconds after arriving at her Dad's house? She swallowed hard.

"Can we start cooking now?" She walked towards the kitchen.

"I guess...," said Melissa slowly, still in a state of shock. Following Johanna into the kitchen, she quickly recovered. "But I want to hear everything about this guy!"

11

"*A*untie JoJo!" shouted Lexi Hughes-Donovan as she flew down the wooden stairs at breakneck speed and launched herself into Johanna's waiting arms.

"Lex Luthor! I've missed you so much!" Johanna wrapped her arms around the ten-year-old and stroked her blond hair. Hearing the wood floor creak, she glanced up towards the top of the stairs to see a dawdling eight-year-old carrying a small electronic device. "Henry the Eighth, where's Auntie JoJo's hug?" she hollered up at him.

He pulled his big brown eyes off his game and a slow smile spread across his face. "Hi, Auntie," he said shyly, continuing down the stairs. Henry had always been the most like his aunt Johanna. The two of them were by far the most introverted of the Hughes clan. When he landed on the last step, he hugged her around the waist.

Johanna's heart melted to have her two favorite munchkins hugging her at the same time. She wished she could screenshot the moment in time and hold on to it forever. "I brought you guys presents," she managed to choke out over the lump in her throat.

Immediately they both let go of her and raced each other to the living room. "Presents?" they cheered in unison.

"Can we open them now?" begged Lexi.

"No, you can't open them now. You have to wait until after dinner, when we all open presents together," shouted Melissa from the kitchen.

"Oh, but Mom!" whined Lexi.

"Yeah, but Mom!" agreed Johanna. She'd been so excited to see their faces that she was just as disappointed as they were.

"No *but Mom*s. Why don't the two of you help me finish setting the table?"

When their little faces crumpled, Johanna chucked them both under the chin. "The faster you set the table, the sooner we eat. The sooner we eat, the sooner we get to open presents!"

"I'm doing the silverware," shouted Lexi, taking off towards the dining room. "You're pouring the water."

"You're *both* pouring the water," Melissa answered.

"Hey, don't forget to go say hi to Rocky!" said Johanna, pointing back towards the kitchen.

Henry's brown eyes lit up like fireworks on the Fourth of July. "You brought Rocky? Yay!"

Johanna nodded. "I brought a new friend, too. Her name is Esmerelda. I think you're going to like her a lot. They're both in the kitchen."

"Yay!" they cheered as they raced off towards the kitchen.

Johanna giggled as she continued on her path towards the living room, where she snuggled up on the sofa next to her dad.

He put his arm around her. "How's dinner coming?"

"Almost ready. We're just waiting for the gravy to thicken," she said, laying her head on his shoulder. "Are you two hungry yet?"

Melissa's husband, Kevin, tossed his head backwards. "Starving. We've been up since five. All I've had to eat are the scraps you two have been throwing my way."

"And the chips and that homemade dip Mook pulled out around one o'clock," Johanna reminded him.

"Oh yeah, I had a few chips. I forgot about that."

"And the Christmas cookies you've sent the kids in to sneak out for you."

He smiled. "Oh yeah. And those."

"And the beers," she added, pointing at the drink he held. She was pretty sure it was his third.

"Right. And the beers." He grinned at her. "You don't let anything slip past you, do you?"

"Nope!" she agreed proudly.

He groaned. "You'll make some man an excellent game warden someday, JoJo."

Denny chuckled.

"Thank you!" Johanna answered brightly.

"So tell me, how's the book business going these days," asked Kevin, crossing one gangly leg over the other.

"Great! My new book is due out in two months. I'm so close to completing it that I can taste the finish line."

"Oh yeah? What's that taste like? Chocolate?"

Johanna grinned as she leaned forward and swatted at his legs playfully. "Something like that." She looked up at her father, whose belly shook as he laughed too. "So, what's new in the IT business?"

Kevin leaned forward. "Everything! Everything's always new in IT. Gotta keep up with the times."

"Like whatcha working on now?" she asked.

"Cybersecurity mostly. Cybersecurity is hot right now with all the data breaches on the news lately. Everyone wants to make sure their data is secure, so we've been doing a lot of work for companies, helping them beef up their firewalls."

"Sounds like something that's over my head," said Johanna with a giggle. "I'm still using the same laptop I got in college. I'm pretty sure I haven't updated my virus protection since the Bush administration."

"Didn't you graduate in '04?"

Johanna nodded. "Remember the 'Dude, you're getting a Dell' commercials?' Dad got me a state-of-the-art Dell my freshman year!"

"Cost me a bundle!" Denny agreed.

His brow lifted. "You're using a seventeen-year-old Dell? And it's still functional?! So you're running what? Windows 2000?" he asked incredulously.

She shrugged. "I would assume? Like I know. I do know it was one of the first laptops with Wi-Fi at the time. Besides using it to Google things once in a while, I only use it to run Word. That's all I need. I've got my phone for everything else."

"Wow. Now I know what I'm getting you for your birthday," he said with a chuckle.

The doorbell rang and Johanna could hear Rocky's feet on the linoleum in the kitchen as he made a mad dash for the entryway. She glanced up at her father. "You expecting someone, Dad?"

"I'll get it!" Melissa hollered from the other side of the house.

With an arm slung over the back of the sofa, Denny scratched his thumb against his eyebrows as Johanna sat forward on the edge of the couch.

"Oh, uh, yeah, I, uh, was gonna tell you."

Johanna's brows crumpled together. *Who else could he possibly be expecting?* she wondered. "Tell me what?"

As Johanna's eyes swung over to look at Kevin curiously, he lifted his beer to his lips and took a big gulp.

"Dad? Did you invite someone else to Christmas dinner?" Something about the two men's reactions set Johanna's heart pounding in her chest.

"Dad!" called Melissa from the entryway. "Maureen's here!"

With her brows still bunched up, Johanna turned to her father. "Maureen? Who's Maureen, Dad?"

"Oh, I, uh, I work with her."

"You invited work people to Christmas dinner?" Johanna was confused.

"I'm going to go help Mel in the kitchen," said Kevin, taking off like a shot before Johanna could turn her questions towards him.

"Well, umm, not exactly, pumpkin," said Denny.

Johanna noticed the sweat beads glistening on her father's forehead, but before she could say anything, there was a busty big-haired brunette standing in the wide doorway between the entryway and the living room, and Rocky was barking like mad.

"Merry Christmas, Denny. Oh, you must be JoJo," she cried, throwing her arms out wide and rushing towards Johanna. "Your father has told me *all* about you! I'm so happy to *finally* get to meet you!"

Finally get to meet me? Johanna wondered as the woman threw her arms around her shoulders. *Finally?!* "I'm sorry, I guess I'm out of the loop here. Who are you?"

The woman promptly let go of Johanna and took a step back, gasping. "Denny Hughes! Have you still not told JoJo about us?"

Johanna sucked in a breath. "Us?!" Her head pivoted to stare at her father, who was struggling to get up off the sofa.

"Dinner!" hollered Melissa from the other room.

Rocky leapt around Johanna and barked excitedly. He wanted to play with the new guest.

Johanna suddenly felt sticky under her armpits. She waved a hand in front of her face. "Is it hot in here?"

"Denny!" shouted the woman, her amber eyes blazing.

"Now, Mo, don't get mad. I hadn't found the right moment," he began uncomfortably.

"The right moment?" she asked, lifting her bushy brown eyebrows. "We've been together for nearly a year. You haven't found one single moment that you could tell her about us during that year?"

Johanna's ears were ringing now. "Year?" she gulped.

Melissa poked her head into the living room. "Kev and the kids are all at the table. I don't want the turkey to get cold. We should eat."

"You knew about this?" Johanna asked, pointing at her sister.

Melissa grimaced. "I haven't known *the whole time*."

"But how long?"

"I mean, I've known awhile," she admitted, playing with the bracelets on her wrists.

"How long is awhile, Mook?"

She shook her blond hair and the little Christmas bells attached to her earlobes jingled. "A few months?"

"A few months!"

"Grandma Mo, Grandma Mo!" cheered Lexi as she came running into the living room and threw her arms around Maureen.

Johanna's heart stopped as she reeled around to stare at her father. "Grandma Mo?!"

"Your sister's right. I think we should eat," he said with a nod.

"So she's your dad's girlfriend?" asked Whitley, teetering on the edge of the mustard yellow bathtub in the Hughes family's upstairs bathroom.

Johanna, who had excused herself in an attempt to gather her bearings before returning to the family dinner, was palms down on the bathroom counter with her head slung low between her shoulder blades. Dejectedly, she lifted her head and stared at her reflection in the bathroom mirror. "That's what I'm gathering."

"But he never told you about her?"

"Nope."

"Isn't it kind of awkward that you had to find out now of all days?" Whitley crinkled her nose.

"Yup," she agreed, even though awkward didn't begin to describe what she was feeling.

"Whoa. Sucks to be you right now."

"Yup." The two women were silent for a moment as Johanna tried to gather her thoughts.

Finally, Whitley piped up again. "So, you don't like her?"

Johanna watched her reflection frown. "Like her? I don't even know her. I had no idea she even *existed*! How am I supposed to know if I like her or not?"

"Why wouldn't your dad tell you about her?"

Johanna threw up both arms. "I have no idea."

Whitley still looked confused. "So, is she different from his other girlfriends or something?"

Johanna made a face. "Yeah, she's different. *She exists!*"

"She exists? What's that mean?"

"As far as I'm aware, my dad has never had a girlfriend since Mom died."

"Aww, your mom died? That's so sad," said Whitley

with big, puppy dog eyes. "I lost my mom too. I was just a little girl. How long ago did yours die?"

"When I was in college," whispered Johanna. Just speaking about her mother made tears burn in her eyes.

"You're thirty-five, right? So that was kind of a long time ago?"

"Yeah."

"So why is it weird for your dad to be dating again?"

Johanna sighed. She didn't really know how to explain it. "It's not *weird* that he's dating, I guess. I mean, I always assumed he would *eventually*."

"So, it's not eventually yet...?"

"I suppose it is," she said, crossing her arms across her chest and turning to lean her butt against the edge of the bathroom counter. "It's just that for the first few years after Mom died, Dad never mentioned dating. I was thankful, because back then, I wasn't ready for him to get over losing Mom, and I certainly wasn't ready for a stepmom. And then, I got engaged and the world was this happy place and I wanted Dad to be in that happy place with me."

"Wait. You were engaged?!" asked Whitley, her mouth agape.

"Yeah. It was a long time ago," Johanna whispered.

"What happened?"

"Can we not talk about that? I don't want to get into the details."

Whitley shrugged but let it go.

"So when I was engaged, I was ready for Dad to start dating. Mook and I suggested women to him all the time. We both wanted him to try dating websites, which he refused, of course. But he was never interested. He said he had us, and then Lex and Henry came along and he loved to babysit and be the doting grandfather, and dating was never on his priority list."

Whitley shook her head. "What changed for you?"

With wet eyes, Johanna looked down at her hands. She wasn't sure if she could say the words. Her voice was weak as she continued, "Umm. My fiancé—his name was James —he, uh, he passed away."

"Oh, Hanna!" breathed Whitley. She stood up and threw her arms around Johanna's shoulders. "I'm so sorry!"

"Thanks." She gave Whitley a tight smile and dotted at her eyes with a tissue. "I'm okay, it was a while ago. Just being home and, I don't know, this time of year always does this to me, I guess."

"After James passed away, you weren't ready for your dad to date anymore?" mused Whitley with a knowing nod.

"Yeah, I guess. I leaned on Dad a lot. He'd loved James too, you know. At that time, James's family lived next door, so Dad had watched us grow up together, and losing him was really hard on both of us." Johanna smiled through the fresh tears. "We bonded over our loss, Dad and I. And it was almost like he'd lost Mom all over again because he felt my pain so deeply. He just knew what I was going through."

"Wow," Whitley said, stunned to hear Johanna's story. "That's so sad."

"So, I guess I felt like Dad and I both had this unspoken pact. Neither of us would date until the other was ready."

"But surely you didn't think that would last forever?"

Johanna smiled and brushed her hair back from her face. "I know," she whispered. "I knew it wouldn't. I just would have appreciated a little warning, I guess. Mook's known about this for months."

"Yeah, I would have been furious if Essy know something important about our dad for months and didn't tell me."

"Right?" asked Johanna. "And not even that. They've been dating for almost a year! That's *twelve months* that Dad didn't tell me himself!"

Suddenly there was a knock at the door. Johanna glared at it. "What?!"

"Who ya talkin' to in there?" boomed Melissa's voice.

12

"*I*'m talking to myself!" Johanna hollered back, having forgotten for a moment that no one there could see or hear Whitley.

"Can I come in?" asked Melissa from the other side of the door.

"No."

"Oh, come on, JoJo. Lemme in."

"Go away, Mook. I need a minute."

"Don't make me bust down this door!"

"Dad would kill you if you busted the door."

"Open this door right now, JoJo!" It was her father's voice outside the door now.

Johanna sighed and glanced at Whitley.

"Let him in," she begged. "Give him a chance to explain."

"But I don't want to," Johanna whined.

"Who's she talking to in there?" she heard her dad asking her sister.

"Herself," said Melissa.

Johanna heard Maureen's voice next. "Maybe I should talk to her. You know, woman to woman."

Oh God, please no.

"I don't think she'd like that very much," said Kevin.

"What's the matter with Auntie JoJo?" asked Lexi.

"Woof!" barked Rocky from outside the door. Johanna could hear his tail thwacking against the sheetrock in the hallway.

"Are you *all* out there?!" asked Johanna as she peered in the mirror to make sure she had dried all the tears.

"No. Henry's downstairs on his tablet," hollered Lexi. "Want me to go get him?"

Johanna opened the door to see the whole family, with the exception of Henry, staring back at her. They smiled in unison.

"Listen, JoJo, I'm sorry I didn't tell you about Mo," said Denny. "Can I come in and we can talk about it?"

"No," Johanna sniffled.

"For what it's worth, JoJo, I told your father to tell you about me *months ago*," said Maureen. "I remember it was, what, Easter when we told Melissa, and even she said we should tell you."

"*Easter*?!" Johanna stared at her sister. "You've known *since Easter*?!"

"Sweetheart, that's not helping," said Denny, patting his girlfriend's hand. "Can you all please go back downstairs? I need to speak to my daughter alone."

Melissa nodded as she herded the family back down the wooden staircase. "That's right. Show's over. Keep it movin'," she prodded. When they'd all gone, Melissa turned around. "Alright, now we can sort this out."

Denny stared at Melissa. "Mook, I want to speak to JoJo *alone*."

"We *are* alone."

"Just me and her."

Melissa curled her lip. "Like, without me?"

"Yeah, without you."

"But, Dad!" she whined.

He pointed at the stairs. "We'll be down in a minute."

Melissa wrinkled her nose and grunted but turned and headed back downstairs.

Denny closed the door and looked at his daughter. "I'm really sorry, JoJo. I should have told you about Mo."

"Yeah, you should have!"

"Ya gotta understand! At first, I didn't know what was gonna happen between me and her. I didn't wanna go around sending out announcements it if it turned out to be nothin'. Ya know. I wanted it to be *something* first."

Johanna's heart thumped against the wall of her chest. Even though she knew the answer, she had to ask, "So it's *something*?!" She sniffled into her wadded-up tissue.

"Well, yeah, of course it's something. Mo's a great woman. The kids love her. She takes really good care of me. I think you'll like her."

"That's not the point," said Johanna stubbornly.

He hung his head, the light bouncing a glare off his thinning scalp. "Yeah, I know it's not the point. I'm sorry I didn't tell you. I just wasn't sure that you were ready to hear about me dating."

Johanna played with the skin webbed between her fingers. She still wasn't ready to hear about him dating, but she didn't feel like she could say that. Not now anyway. It was too late.

"But now that I know that you've been seeing someone on and off for the last *five years* and didn't tell me, I guess I don't feel so bad."

Johanna closed her eyes. Of course *that* would come back to bite her in the ass. "Yeah," she whispered.

"So when are we gonna get to meet this Mitch guy?"

"His name is Mitchell, Dad."

"He doesn't like to be called Mitch?"

Johanna shrugged. She didn't know if he liked to be called Mitch or not.

Denny leaned his bottom against the tile counter. "So if we're both ready to start dating again, maybe we need to be okay with each other dating again. Right?"

Wrong. "Right," she whispered.

"Alright, then! Come meet Mo. You're gonna like her."

"Was she the one who decorated the house?"

Denny sighed. "Yes. And I think she did a great job. Don't you?"

Johanna sniffled and then lifted her lip. "She put a star on the top of the tree. Mom always put our angel up there."

"That angel was so old it was falling apart, JoJo. I didn't want it to get destroyed. I wanted you girls to have it someday."

"But you never got a live tree when Mom was alive." The fact that he'd splurged for this new woman and not her mother really hurt something deep inside Johanna. Maybe that was silly, but it hurt nonetheless.

"Your mother never wanted a live tree."

"How could she not have wanted a live tree?"

"She was just as frugal as I was. She thought it was a waste of money to buy a live tree year after year, just to throw it away in the new year."

"She thought that?"

"Yeah, she thought that! She wanted to spend the money on you and your sister instead of on a tree that dried the house out."

Johanna felt a little bubble of laughter rise to the inside of her throat. "That sounds like something Mom would say."

"Because it is!" he said with a broad smile. "JoJo, I get that this is all new to you, but I just want you to be happy for me. Mo makes me happy."

Johanna's shoulders slumped. She wanted her dad to be happy too. "Well, she better, or she'll have to answer to me and Mook."

"You think I don't know that?!"

Johanna smiled as her dad threw an arm over her shoulder.

"Come on, pumpkin. Let's go downstairs and eat. I'm starving."

"Me too."

"*I*t's a smartwatch," explained Johanna, leaning across the sofa's arm and Denny's lap to point at the screen. "It's got Bluetooth. It can do anything from tracking your heart rate and counting your steps to checking email or making a phone call. Now there's no reason I shouldn't be able to reach you."

"Again, JoJo, you've got that game warden thing on lockdown," said Kevin, winking at her from across the room. "That's exactly what men love is to be able to be reached by the women in their lives twenty-four seven."

Johanna giggled. "Or, it's just an attractive watch, Dad. Whatever."

Denny leaned over and kissed his daughter on the cheek. "It's beautiful, pumpkin. I love it. Thank you!"

Suddenly they heard Esmerelda let out a "Rawr!" on the other side of the room. All heads turned to see Rocky bouncing around the cat. Esmerelda's grey fur was fluffed up around her and her claws were bared.

"Rocky!" Johanna shouted. "Are you antagonizing Essy?"

"Woof!" He was being playful and she knew Esmerelda could handle herself, but still, Johanna worried about the two of them getting too carried away.

"You leave her alone. Go lay down," said Johanna, pointing at the other room.

Rocky let out a whine but kept his eyes trained on Esmerelda.

Johanna turned to face her sister next. "You're next, Mook." She pulled a card out of the backpack she'd brought along and handed it to her sister.

"Ooh, a card. Is it filled with cash?" laughed Melissa, shaking the envelope next to her ear.

Johanna shrugged with a mischievous smile. "Open it!"

"I am, I am!"

Melissa tore into the envelope and fake-read the sentiment on the outside of the card before opening it. A folded piece of paper fell out. She unfolded it to discover a picture of a stand mixer.

"Tada!" shouted Johanna with a little giggle.

"You got me a picture of a stand mixer?"

"No, I got you a stand mixer. It'll be delivered sometime next week. I'll email you the tracking number if you want."

"Oh, nice. Didn't want to lug the thing from Manhattan to Jersey?" asked Kevin.

Johanna smiled broadly. *Well, that makes sense, doesn't it?* "Yes, absolutely." She pointed at the paper. "I got you the deluxe one with all the extra attachments. I think you can make sausage and pasta with it."

"Oh, JoJo, this is so sweet! Dad must have told you mine died last week?"

"Yeah, he mentioned it."

Melissa stood up and gave Johanna a hug. "Thanks, sis.

I'll make you some cookies when I get it. I'll bring them to the big family get-together next weekend."

That piqued Whitley's attention. Sitting cross-legged on the floor next to Henry, who was quietly playing with the new electronic game Johanna had gotten him, she lifted her head. "What big family get-together?"

Johanna shook her head at Whitley to silence her. "Oh, I almost forgot about that. What time does it start?"

"Well, it's Christmas Day, so I'd say we could go over there anytime," said Melissa.

Denny shook his head. "Jack said we can all start coming anytime after ten."

"It's at Uncle Jack's this year?"

"Yeah," said Melissa. "Kev and I can pick you up if you want. We're picking Dad up."

"Sounds good," said Johanna. "Are we supposed to bring anything?"

"No, Aunt Lucy said they were taking care of the meal, so we're good. Are you coming, Mo?"

All heads turned to Maureen, who sat with her hand resting on Denny's knee. "And get to meet the rest of the Hughes family? I wouldn't miss it!"

"Hey, I got a great idea," said Denny, pointing a finger at Johanna. "Why don't you bring your new guy?"

"What new guy?" asked Whitley, bright-eyed from the floor.

Johanna shook her head wildly, her eyes open wide like a deer caught in the headlights. "Oh, gosh. Thank you for thinking of him, but no. He's got his own... umm, family thing. We're spending Christmas apart."

"Oh, JoJo, that's so sad!" said Melissa. "You finally get a boyfriend and now you two aren't going to spend it together?"

Whitley's brows dropped. "Wait. You have a boyfriend? You never told Es and me!"

"He's not my boyfriend, Mook. I told you, he's just this guy I bump into now and again."

"Do you hear how coy she's being?" asked Melissa, swatting at her husband's arm. "My sister, the tight-lipped one! She never tells us anything. We didn't even know she'd gotten engaged to James until he told his folks and they casually mentioned it to Dad while he was taking out the garbage one morning."

Johanna's head shook wildly. Things were getting out of control. Maybe it was time to just tell them the truth.

"Rawr, rawr!" hissed Esmerelda from the other side of the room.

"Woof, woof!"

Johanna buried her head in her hands. Her cheeks were warm to the touch. Had someone turned up the heat?

Denny reached out and put a hand on his daughter's arm. "I don't care how serious you two are, JoJo. I want to meet him. It would mean a lot to me. *I'd* feel so much better about dating again if I knew that *you* were happy and dating again."

"But, Dad...," she began uncomfortably. She wasn't sure what the right words were to explain that she'd sort of embellished the truth.

"Rocky, no," hissed Whitley.

Johanna's eyes followed Whitley's gaze to see Rocky had caught hold of Esmerelda between his massive paws. She batted at his nose with her claws, but by now, he was used to it. "Oh, Rocky! Let her go!" shouted Johanna.

He snorted. Refusing to let go of Esmerelda, he licked her underside with big broad strokes. Johanna stood up and padded over to the pair. "Rocky, I mean it. Let her go!"

Johanna had to use all of her might to lift Rocky's front

paws, and the minute she did, Esmerelda escaped his clutches and ran directly for the Christmas tree, scampering up its branches.

"Essy, no!" Johanna and Whitley screamed in unison, though no one could hear Whitley's voice but Johanna.

Rocky leapt over Henry and Lex's heads and onto the coffee table, and then in one more leap he was flying towards the Christmas tree.

"No, Rocky!" Johanna felt the words come out of her mouth in slow motion as she tried to stop him from hitting the tree with his clumsy paws, but it was too late.

As he lunged, his paws caught hold of the branches and tugged them down, and in one fell swoop, the tree was on its side with a blistering thud.

*J*ohanna hugged her sister tightly. "Tell everyone again how sorry I am," she begged.

"They know it's not your fault, JoJo. I don't understand why you're running off," said Melissa.

Johanna couldn't tell her sister the truth. That as naughty as he'd been, Johanna was thankful that Rocky had created the diversion that he had. It had given her the perfect reason to make a hasty exit. "I'm just so embarrassed," she said. It wasn't a lie. She was embarrassed about Rocky's behavior, but she was also glad to be leaving. She was tired of answering questions about her social life. "I'll see you all on Christmas."

"I'm picking you up, right?"

"I don't know, Mook. If Maureen's going to be riding with you, there might not be room for Rocky and me in your van."

"We can make room!" said Melissa. "I'll strap a kid to the roof." She smiled as she leaned against the door frame.

"As much as that sounds like fun for Lex and Henry, I think I'll have to insist that they stay in the car," said Johanna with a forced chuckle. "I think I'll just get there on my own. I'll take a cab or something."

"That's gonna cost you a bundle," argued Melissa. "Just ride with us."

"We can talk about it later," said Johanna. She leaned over to scoop Esmerelda up from the front step and hoisted her back up on her shoulder. "Listen, Mook, I gotta get the kids home. I think their bad behavior is an indication of just how tired they are. You've got kids, you understand how that goes."

Melissa lifted her brows and sighed. "Yeah, I get it."

Johanna stepped down the concrete front steps towards the curb, where a cab was waiting for her.

"You should have just let me have Kevin drive you home."

Johanna waved a hand at her. "Nah, a cab's fine."

"Hey," shouted Melissa, pulling the door shut behind her. "I know that Dad dating again is kind of a big shock to you. I'm sorry I didn't tell you sooner. I probably should have, but I felt like it wasn't my place."

Johanna swallowed hard. "It would have been nice to know sooner," was all she could manage to spit out.

"I know."

Johanna began to walk away.

"He was really depressed, you know," Melissa called out.

Johanna turned around. "What?"

"Dad. He was really depressed before he met Mo."

"He didn't seem depressed to me."

"You don't visit as often as I do. You didn't see it," said

Melissa. "He wasn't dating because he knew you weren't ready."

Johanna put a hand to her chest. "Because of me?"

Melissa nodded. "It would be good for him to see you happy."

"I am happy," whispered Johanna. It was a mostly true statement.

"Then bring Mitchell to Uncle Jack's."

"Mook, I—"

"He won't commit to her until he knows you're in a good place. He's sixty-three, JoJo. He runs around this big old house alone. Don't you want him to get remarried and be happy again?"

"Well, yeah, I mean, someday…"

"Mo's a great gal. You'd like her if you gave her a chance. Dad would be lucky to get to spend the rest of his life with her, and we'd be lucky to have her for a stepmom."

"I'm sure she's lovely…"

"Don't mess this up for him, okay?"

"Mess it up?"

"All I'm saying is, it would help everyone a lot if you brought the guy."

"But…"

Melissa rushed down off the stoop and threw her arms around her sister. "I love you, JoJo."

Johanna squeezed her eyes shut as she hugged Melissa tightly. "I love you too, Mook."

13

$\mathcal{E}$smerelda lay on her side on the hardwood floor of Johanna's apartment. A solid stream of sunlight poured in from the window, warming her as she bathed herself while everyone else slept.

Things had changed for Esmerelda when she'd become a cat. She was no longer able to wear makeup, and she didn't get to curl her hair or wear pretty clothes anymore. All she got was a body full of thick grey hair that knotted and clumped if it wasn't taken care of properly. She'd quickly learned that fact after her first few days on a dirt road in her new body. But after observing some wrong-side-of-the-track street cats, she'd learned how to groom herself in the way that felines did.

Bathing wasn't a task Esmerelda enjoyed. In fact, she found it downright humiliating and disgusting that she had to *lick* her own body in order to clean it, but she had no choice. Up until recently, there had been no one else willing to do it. And now that she lived in close quarters with someone who *was* willing to lick her—*frequently*, in fact— she discovered that that wasn't any better. The live-in slobber guru had the worst breath she'd ever smelled. It was a combination of rotten garbage and bacon bits and made her fur smell like that of a long-deceased dead animal. It nauseated her to have to clean herself up after Rocky had had his way with her, but she couldn't very well be known as the "stinky cat." Whitley would never let her live that down.

The oversized bucket of slime himself slept soundly in his king-sized doggy bed less than twelve feet away from Esmerelda. Well, as soundly as he could. Rocky had a snoring problem that, while utterly annoying and sleep-disruptive, was like Esmerelda's alarm system. When the snoring stopped, she was on high alert. And since the snoring had ceased almost a half hour ago, she kept a watchful eye on him as she worked to clean herself, knowing full well that the minute he awoke, she'd have to go into hiding again to escape his unwelcome morning greeting.

"Good morning, Essy," said Whitley from the sofa. "What time is it?"

"Like I know?" hissed Esmerelda from the floor, shooting a glance towards Rocky. "Be quiet. You'll wake the beast."

"Has Hanna come out of her room yet?"

"No." Esmerelda stopped licking and sat upright. She preferred to do her bathing in private. It was rather uncomfortable and embarrassing to be caught licking her nether regions when her sister, or anyone else for that matter, was watching. "She came out and made a bowl of ramen noodles after you fell asleep last night, but she walked it right back into her room and shut the door. She didn't even talk to what's-his-name over there."

Whitley sat up and rested her chin in the palm of her hand. "I'm worried about her, Es. It's been over twenty-four hours. I don't think it's healthy for her to lock herself away like that, is it?"

Esmerelda rolled her eyes. "I don't know, and honestly, I don't care. All I know is that we need to get this mystery solved so we can move on to the next dress and get me out of this fur blanket."

"Essy, it's our job to help Hanna. We can't just abandon her. She's giving us a place to stay. You should be more grateful."

"I'd be more grateful if she bought me something good to eat and kept her mutt away from me."

"Maybe she'd do that if you were a little bit *nicer*."

"Good morning, girls," sang Johanna as she threw open her bedroom door. She peered out the window at the sun, which had already defrosted the cityscape below. "Looks like it's going to be a nice day!"

"Hanna!" exclaimed Whitley, "You're up! Are you alright?"

Johanna smiled at her. "Of course I'm alright. Why wouldn't I be?"

Whitley cast a glance over at Esmerelda. She wrinkled her nose. "I don't know. Because you stayed in your room all day yesterday? And because you lied and told your dad you had a boyfriend, and now he wants you to bring your nonexistent boyfriend over on Christmas Day to meet your whole family? And because you had a fiancé and he died? And because Essy and Rocky knocked over your family's Christmas tree? And because your dad's dating again, and he and your sister didn't tell you?"

Johanna stared at Whitley.

"Smooth, Whit. Smooth," snarked Esmerelda from the floor.

Whitley put a hand to her mouth. "Oops."

Johanna padded towards the kitchen to pull a coffee

mug from the cupboard. "It's okay, Whit. I've had time to think about everything, and I'm alright."

"You are?"

Johanna nodded her head as she put her cup underneath her one-cup coffeemaker, inserted a flavor pod, and punched a button on the machine. "Yes. I am. I came to a realization this morning."

"A realization? What realization?" asked Whitley.

"I decided that things in my life took a turn for the worse when I met you two."

"Thanks?" said Whitley uncomfortably.

Esmerelda let out a little chuckle.

"I don't know that I mean that in a *bad* way, per se. I mean, Whit, you're a sweet girl. Es, you're a salty girl. Together you're fine. Whatever, right? But the point is, from that point in time forward, my life sort of went into a tailspin. So, what I've decided is, we need to get this mystery solved so I can get the two of you out of my life and move on. I have a book that needs to be written by the end of the month or I won't make my deadline. I'm setting a goal. I want this mystery solved by Christmas."

"But that's in a week!" breathed Whitley.

Johanna gave a perfunctory nod. "Yup! We're going to have this mystery solved by Christmas. I've been pretty laid-back about it up until now, but from this point forward, we're going balls to the wall."

Whitley's eyes widened. "Balls to the wall?"

"Yup. Starting today!" She scratched her head. "First, I'm going to go shower, then I'll take Rocky out for his morning walk."

"Wait, you're going to *shower* today?" asked Whitley. "But you just showered yesterday."

"I can't shower every day?"

"Well, it's just that we were under the impression

that..." Whitley's words trailed off.

Esmerelda looked at her with a snicker bubbling up inside her chest. "It's just that we thought you were a gross human being who only showered in odd months."

"Essy!"

"What?! It's essentially what you were thinking!"

Whitley grimaced, but bit her lip.

"Oh, I'm not *that* bad. Yes, I'm a bit lax with my desire to shower, but that's only because I never go anywhere or do anything. I used to shower every day when I actually left my apartment on a regular basis."

"When was that?" asked Whitley.

"Oh, you know. There was a time. When James and I were dating, I took showers every day. And when I was in college. So anyway, I was thinking today, after my walk with Rocky, we should start interviewing some of Felicia's family. You know, get a little intel, see what we can find out."

Esmerelda glanced over at Rocky, who had heard his name. His ears perked up and he yawned. She prepared herself to move to higher ground.

"I think we should start with her fiancé. When people are killed, it's always the spouse or the fiancé that did it, right?" said Whitley.

Johanna smiled at her. "My thought exactly!" She pulled her cup of coffee from the machine and gave it a stir.

"How about you and your newfound attitude hit me with a little milk before you go shower?" asked Esmerelda, who had leapt up on top of the kitchen table.

Johanna pulled open the fridge and extracted the carton. She poured Esmerelda a small saucer of milk and put it on the table. She glanced at the time on the clock above her table. "Oh gosh, I slept in longer than I realized. I better get moving. Nature's gonna be calling Rocky soon."

"We're all going with you to the fiancé's, right?" asked Esmerelda, lifting her head from the saucer to look at Johanna.

Johanna tipped her head sideways. "I'm sorry, Es, but no. Whit and I will go. Felicia's fiancé is an engineer. They aren't going to allow pets in an engineering office."

Esmerelda knitted the whiskers over her eyes together. "You can't be serious. You know how he treats me! I don't want to be left alone with him!"

"I'll put you in the bedroom while we're gone, then."

"I don't want to be stuck in there all day, that's not fair! Put *him* in the bedroom!"

Johanna looked at Rocky, who had just gotten out of bed to stand by her side. She scratched his ears. "He can't be trapped in my bedroom all day either. He'll freak out and eat all my stuff."

"So *I* have to get locked in there? What am I supposed to do all day?"

Johanna shrugged. "Fine, I'll put you in the hall, and you can find somewhere else to hang out all day."

"But there's no food in the hall!" Esmerelda protested. It was also cold in the hall. And scary, with weird people everywhere and random dogs and bad smells. Esmerelda screwed her face into a pout. "Fine. I'll stay in your room."

Johanna nodded with a smile. "Great! I'll go get ready, then!"

---

*D*espite Whitley's incessant chatter, Johanna was in her head as the duo walked from her apartment in Kip's Bay to Mitchell Connelly's engineering office in Midtown. Thinking ahead, Johanna had called Mr. Connelly's office and verified with his assistant that he was in.

Once she'd scheduled the appointment to see him, she'd felt her stomach do an immediate flip. She was going to have to talk to the almost-widower and figure out a way to explain to him that she was trying to solve Felicia Marshall's murder. The thought was nauseating at best, and her first instinct had been to retreat, run, find someone else for the job. But as she'd told Whitley and Esmerelda that morning, the mystery needed to be solved in order for her to get her life back together. She and Rocky needed the solitude of an empty apartment again and for things to get back to normal so she could go back to hiding herself away from the world in peace and quiet.

"So, what are you going to say?" Whitley asked Johanna as she pulled open the tall building's heavy glass doors.

Johanna didn't know. She'd been running possibilities through her mind the entire way, but she had yet to settle on anything. "I don't know. I guess honesty is the best policy. I'll just tell him I'm researching his late fiancée's murder, and I have a few questions for him."

Whitley's face grew serious as she stepped onto the elevator between Johanna and a broad-shouldered white-haired man in a dark suit. "You have to be careful. You don't know anything about this guy."

"I know, I'll be careful. Don't worry."

The man turned to look at Johanna curiously. "Excuse me?"

Johanna felt her cheeks heat up. "Oh, I was just talking to myself."

The man turned his back to her without saying another word.

"And don't talk to me in front of him. He'll think you're crazy," whispered Whitley.

Johanna inhaled a deep breath as she stared at her distorted reflection in the elevator doors. Her heart felt like it was going to pound a hole through her chest. Talking to strangers already gave her anxiety, but this was different. This was more than just social anxiety. Without setting eyes on him, she could already feel this man's pain, and she was scared she'd lose it. *Deep breath, JoJo. You can do this. You're a professional. You've got this.* Her little internal pep talk did little to quell the queasiness in her stomach.

The elevator doors slid open with a ding. Johanna felt lightheaded as she stepped onto the eleventh floor with Whitley by her side. As they turned, the doors behind them closed, and when they did, Johanna paused briefly to collect herself. She inhaled a deep lungful of air and then exhaled it in little rapid bursts, like a pregnant woman in labor.

"Are you going to be alright? You don't look so good."

"I'll be okay," puffed Johanna, her hands shaking by her sides.

The glass doors to the engineering office loomed ahead at the end of a long hallway lined by waist-high wainscoting and a patterned designer rug. Johanna's mouth went dry. They were really here. She turned around to retreat back into the elevator.

"Whoa, whoa, whoa. Where are you going?"

"Home. I can't do this. This is crazy. This poor man. He lost the woman he loved. He doesn't want us dredging up old memories." Johanna wrung out her hands.

"You don't think he would want to know the truth behind Felicia's murder?"

"What truth? We don't know anything other than the truth he already knows."

Johanna glanced over her shoulder at the engineering offices. Through the glass door, she could see a heavyset young man with a man bun flipping through a magazine at the desk. Their eyes met momentarily. Johanna turned her back to him. "I can't do this."

"You *can* do this. There is a mystical force at work here, Hanna. It wants us to figure out what really happened to Felicia Marshall. It's *drawing* us to this man. You can't quit now."

"What am I supposed to say to him?"

Whitley took Johanna's hands in hers. "Honesty is the best policy, remember?"

Johanna let out a breath and nodded. "Right."

Together they turned and walked to the end of the hall-way. Johanna pulled the door open and let Whitley go in first. The man at the counter looked up from his magazine. "Hello. Do you have an appointment?"

Johanna felt herself nod. "Yes. Johanna Hughes to see Mr. Connelly at one thirty."

The man tapped the eraser of his pencil against a computer screen. "Hughes? Yes, I've got you on Mr. Connelly's schedule. You can have a seat and his assistant will be out to get you shortly."

Less than five minutes later, a thirty-something-year-old blonde woman in a pinstriped grey pantsuit stood in front of Johanna and Whitley. She extended a hand to Johanna. "Hi, I'm Darcy Carr. I'm Mr. Connelly's assistant. Right this way."

With a clipboard tucked under her arm, Darcy led them through a maze of offices and cubicles.

"Wow, fancy schmancy," whispered Whitley, trailing Johanna by a few steps.

"Shh," Johanna hissed at her.

Darcy looked over her shoulder, giving Johanna a curious glance. Johanna grinned innocently, but when Darcy turned back around, she scowled at Whitley, her expression clearly reading, "Quit talking to me!"

It wasn't like the fancy office had gone unnoticed by Johanna. In fact, the fancier the office got, the more Johanna felt the sudden urge to use the ladies' room. *This man is going to think I'm crazy! What am I doing?* she wondered.

Darcy stopped in front of a glass-enclosed office towards the back of the building and swung the door wide, letting Johanna and Whitley go inside first. Inside, the sparsely decorated office had a wraparound desk with a high-backed leather chair behind it, facing the office's oversized windows, which overlooked Manhattan. There was a conference table and chairs off to the right, and to the left, a little minibar with decanters of alcohol and glass tumblers on it and a mini fridge below it.

"Mr. Connelly, Johanna Hughes is here to see you."

"Thank you, Darcy," said a man's voice from the chair.

Darcy gave a curt nod and exited the room, pulling the glass door shut behind her. Slowly, the chair turned. "Good afternoon, Ms. Hughes."

"Thank you for seeing me today, Mr. Connelly," she whispered, unable to look up at him. She squeezed her hands together and focused on the pain she felt in her fingers instead of the desire to throw up.

"How may I be of assistance?" Johanna's eyes slowly lifted towards him, and as soon as she saw the soft blond curls on top of his head, her mouth gaped. *It was him!* Mitchell Connelly was none other than *him*!

The man sitting at the desk in front of her was none other than the man she'd passed by in the park for the last five years. It was the very same man that Rocky had bowled over the week before and the man Johanna had dropped a knee on and nearly given a concussion to!

As she stared at him in stunned silence, the blood drained from her face and her mind went blank.

14

"*H*anna," hissed Whitley. "Say something."

But Johanna couldn't speak. The beautiful man she'd made up stories about in her head for the last five years was now sitting in front of her. *Staring at her*. She knew his name now. She knew where he worked. *And now she knew that he was the one who had lost his fiancée!* The thought came to her fast and hard, knocking the air out of her lungs as if she'd just been plowed into by a Mack truck. Johanna struggled to suck air into her lungs. Her throat made a wheezing noise.

"Ms. Hughes? Are you alright?" the man asked, rising to his feet and rushing around the desk.

"Hanna! What's wrong?" asked Whitley, bending over with Johanna to look into her face.

But what could Johanna say? She couldn't very well *say* out loud what was going on! Not in front of *him*! She had to get it together fast.

"Mr. Connelly," she gasped, grabbing hold of his forearm.

"Yes! Ms. Hughes, are you alright? Do you need me to call 911?"

Johanna shook her head wildly. "Asthma attack." The lie squeaked out almost inaudibly. "Took the stairs."

Whitley looked at Johanna as if she were bonkers.

Mitch nodded and rushed to the bar. He leaned over to grab a bottle of sparkling water from the fridge, opened it, and handed it to Johanna. "Here, take a drink."

Johanna nodded and took a swig, fighting like mad to get her heart rate to slow so she could breathe normally. She had had anxiety attacks before, but none this embarrassing. When she'd drained half of the bottle, she looked up at him, her eyes were watery and her face ashen.

Concern colored his blue-grey eyes. But she could clearly see that he had absolutely no recollection of who she was. It was as if that night in the park hadn't actually happened. Maybe it had all been a figment of Johanna's imagination.

"Are you alright now?"

Johanna's breathing began to regulate itself. Even though her insides still felt like a mess of jiggly Jell-O, outwardly, she looked better. "I'm okay." She nodded, trying to convince herself.

"How about you sit down?" He pulled out a chair in front of his desk for her.

She gave him a tight smile and sat down. "Thank you."

Whitley sat down in the chair next to her, though Mitch couldn't see her. "What is wrong with you?" she demanded.

Johanna ignored her as Mitch walked around the desk and sat across from her. "So, Ms. Hughes, my assistant didn't tell me what you wanted to see me about. What exactly can I help you with?"

Johanna's mouth went dry. She took another drink from

her water bottle, draining it completely. It made a loud crinkling noise as she sucked the air from it. "Umm, do you have a trash can?" she asked uncomfortably.

He smiled at her with a look that clearly read he was doing his best to remain patient with her and held out his hand, taking the bottle from her. He tossed it into the garbage can without a word.

"You're going to have to speak, Hanna," prodded Whitley. "Tell him you're here to talk about his late fiancée."

Johanna opened her mouth. In all fairness, Whitley's words were what she'd planned to have come out of her mouth, but in the end, it didn't happen. "I was wondering if those stains came out of your suit," she said instead.

"My suit?" His light-colored eyes narrowed as he processed her statement.

Whitley's head waggled around on her neck. "What in the world are you talking about, Hanna? You sound like a crazy person."

Johanna gestured towards her own body. "You know. Your suit," she said again.

He shook his head, still not recognizing her.

"Umm, the mud. My dog?" she asked, squinching her eyes. "I—I had the hat. With the ears..." She pointed at her head and wondered why she couldn't just wear trendy hats to walk her dog like other nice women did.

"Your d—" Suddenly his eyes widened as he stared at her. "Oh! Your dog! Are you the lady from the park?" he asked incredulously.

Johanna's mouth gaped open. *The lady from the park? Is that how he thinks of me? I'm the park lady. That makes me sound like the homeless woman from* Home Alone. *The one who has all the birds covering her and scares the bejeezus out of Kevin.* "Umm, yeah, that's me," said Johanna, lifting her brows and nodding her head uncomfortably.

His gaze narrowed. "How'd you find me?"

Awkward, now he thinks you're like a park lady stalker or something. Her eyes swung downward, taking in the little etched glass desk plate with his name on it and the little glass business card holder next to it. "Oh, you dropped a business card," she fibbed, crossing her fingers under the desk.

"I did? Huh, I didn't even realize I had any business cards on me."

"Well, you must have. Because I found it. *Your* business card alright. Led me right to you!" she rambled. Not sure what to do with her hands, she finally crossed her arms and tucked them beneath her armpits.

"You are acting so weird," whispered Whitley, palming her forehead. "This guy's going to think you're a lunatic. You need to get it together, Hanna."

Johanna scratched the base of her scalp with one hand. "Right, so, umm, yeah. I just came by to see if the stains came out. Because otherwise, you know, I should probably buy you a new suit."

His blond brows pinched together. "Oh, like I said in the park, there's no need. I already had the suit dropped off at the cleaners, but I haven't gotten it back yet. I'm sure it's just fine."

"And your head? It's alright?" She touched the back of her own head.

"Oh, yes. Head, stomach. Both just fine."

Johanna nodded. "Right."

They stared at each other for several long seconds. Johanna didn't know what else to say or do.

Whitley's head bounced back and forth between Johanna and Mitch. "I have no idea what is going on, but this is so incredibly awkward. We're lucky Essy isn't here to see this right now."

Finally, Mitch put his palms on his desk and leaned forward as if he were preparing to stand up and see her out. "Was there something else, Ms. Hughes?"

Johanna let out a puff of air. "Oh, Mr. Connelly, it's Johanna. You don't have to call me Ms. Hughes," she said, extending a hand out across the desk.

"Right," he said, reaching his hand out to shake hers. "Well, then, Mitch is sufficient."

She gave his hand a little shake but held on a second too long. She liked the feeling of his firm handshake. He had muscular hands, not the hands of a businessman, what one would think those felt like anyway. She held on to him long enough that he had to tug his hand away from hers. In the process of her hand pulling back, the fitness band on her wrist bumped against a picture frame on his desk, which in turn toppled the cup of coffee next to it, sending a run of hot liquid across his desk planner.

"Hanna!" shouted Whitley, standing up to try and stop the cup.

"Oh no," breathed Johanna.

Mitch shouted, "Oh!" as he hastily stood up to keep the liquid from rolling off the desk and onto his pants, but it was too late. What wasn't absorbed by the desk planner wound up on his black trousers, and the other half ended up on his white button-down shirt.

Johanna's hand went to cover her gaping mouth. "Oh my God," she whispered as he reached onto the desk to grab his important papers from getting soaked.

"Paper towels, Hanna, paper towels!" Whitley pointed at the little table with the decanters. A stack of neatly folded paper towels was in a little basket.

"Right," shouted Johanna, rushing towards the towels. She grabbed a stack of the thick white cloths and rushed around the desk, where she began to blot at Mitch's shirt and trousers.

As she leaned over him, blotting his pants intently, Mitch stared down at her. "Umm, Johanna, I think I got this," he said with a wry grin and raised eyebrows. "Thanks, though."

Her eyes widened as she realized that she'd been rubbing in close proximity to his crotch. She handed him the paper towels, pulled her hands back, and stood up. "Oh, yeah, right." She wanted to crawl into a hole and die at that precise moment.

"You're really bad at this, aren't you," whispered Whitley. "It's like a car crash, I can't pull my eyes away from."

"I'm sooo sorry," gushed Johanna. "I can't believe I did it again!"

Mitch chuckled. "You definitely seem to have the clumsy thing down, don't you?"

"Yeees," she drawled, grabbing another stack of towels so she could blot at his desk planner.

"Oh, don't worry about that. It's shot. We'll just toss it," he said, lifting the mat off his desk. "Looks like it's done its job and soaked up most of the mess already."

Only a small bit of coffee remained around the outside edges of where the mat had been and on the silver picture frame. Johanna set up the now empty coffee cup and did her best to mop up the rest of the desk. "This isn't going very well," she admitted. "I'd wanted to make things right from the other day."

He nodded as he rolled up the desk mat and stuck it in the garbage can under his desk. "I can see that. I think maybe we should just call this all a wash. Is that alright with you?"

Johanna covered her forehead with her hand. Just by the feel of that small patch of skin, she knew her face was burning bright red. "Yeah," she whispered. She finished drying the picture frame, and as she went to set it down, she realized she recognized the woman in the picture. It was Felicia Marshall! Mitch's late fiancée.

"She's beautiful," whispered Johanna, straightening the frame.

"Yes," he agreed, his tone light. "Very."

"Your wife?" Johanna's heart hurt for even asking the question, but she knew she had to. She had to start somewhere.

"She was my fiancée."

"Was? You broke up?"

Mitch swallowed hard as he continued to wipe at his shirt. "She passed away about six years ago."

"Oh, I'm so sorry," Johanna whispered. "I know the pain of losing a fiancé. I lost mine several years ago too."

He stopped wiping his shirt and looked up at her with interest. His head cocked sideways. "Really?"

She nodded. "Yes. In a car accident." She swished her lips to the side and fought back tears.

"I'm so sorry."

"Thank you." She gave him a tight smile. "How did your fiancée die? If you don't mind me asking."

He exhaled slowly and then sat down on his desk chair. "The police say it was a mugging."

"You say that like you don't believe it."

He shrugged. "I mean, I have to believe it if I want to get any sleep at night, you know?"

"Yeah," Johanna whispered. She pointed at the picture as if a thought had suddenly come to her. "I feel like I've seen this picture before. What did she do for a living?"

"She was a realtor. I'm sure you probably saw her picture on a billboard or something. They were everywhere then," he said. Johanna could hear the proudness in his voice.

"Was she showing a house the day that she was mugged?"

Mitch's eyes darkened. "No. She was on her way to our wedding rehearsal. We're not really sure why she was on that side of town, but I'm sure she was doing something wedding-related that I just wasn't aware of."

"She was killed the day of your wedding rehearsal?" Johanna feigned shock, though it wasn't a far cry from how she actually felt. "That's terrible!"

He nodded. "It was pretty horrible."

"It's taken me a really long time to get over my James," Johanna admitted weakly. "I'm sure you've had the same problem."

He nodded. "I'm thankful for my career. It keeps me moving."

Johanna smiled a genuine smile then. Didn't she know it! "Me too. I'm a writer. A mystery writer, actually. My life is my career and, well, Rocky. You met him."

For the first time, the smile Mitch gave her actually seemed to reach his eyes. "I did meet Rocky. Friendly fellow."

"Yeah." Her grin widened. "Very friendly."

"I've seen him before, you know. On the trail through the park."

Johanna rubbed a hand across the back of her neck. "Oh, have you? I don't know that I'd ever seen you before." *You're going straight to hell with all these lies*, she told herself.

"I walk that way every night."

"Huh. Isn't that funny. I walk that way every night too."

Mitch lifted one brow. "He's a hard chap to miss."

Johanna giggled. "It's a good thing my building allows

pets. I'd definitely have a hard time hiding him from the landlord."

"Right," said Mitch with a soft smile.

"Right," agreed Johanna.

"Right," said Whitley. "So, are you going to ask him about Felicia's death or was this all just one big waste of time?"

Johanna turned her head and stared blankly at Whitley. What was she supposed to say to turn the conversation back around to Felicia that wouldn't be awkward? With her mouth hanging open, she looked at Mitch again. He had kind eyes. Their outside edges were webbed with smile lines, and he had a two-inch scar lining his left cheekbone. He looked rugged and manly and insanely sexy. The minute she noticed his handsomeness again, she once again became uncomfortable in her own skin and felt the urge to get out of there before she punched him in the nose or accidentally threw one of those decanters at him and took out his eye or something. "Right. Well, I should probably go." She stood up.

"Go!" cried Whitley, springing up too. "You haven't even asked him anything important about the case!"

"Yes, I'm sure I should get back to work." He said it without taking his eyes off Johanna, and without conviction.

Johanna walked towards his door as Whitley stared at her, mouth agape. Mitch rushed to get up and walk her out. As she thought of one more thing she wanted to say, she abruptly stopped and began to turn, but as she did, he crashed into her side.

"*Oof*," he breathed.

"Oh God. I did it again," she said sorrowfully, raising a hand to her temple. "I'm so sorry."

He grinned. "That one was my fault. I didn't leave a wide enough space cushion."

"I really shouldn't be let out in public," she admitted quietly. "I'm a hazard to society."

"I don't know. I think society might miss seeing that nice smile of yours."

Nice smile of mine? Her heart melted a bit then. "Oh. Thank you," she smiled awkwardly. "Okay, well, I appreciate you speaking to me today, Mr. Connelly."

"Mitch," he reminded her, holding out his hand to shake hers one last time.

"Mitch," she agreed, taking his hand.

"It was a pleasure to meet you, Johanna. It was very kind of you to check up on me."

"Maybe we'll bump into each at the park again someday."

He leaned on the door as he let her and Whitley out. "I'll make sure to keep my feet firmly planted when we do."

15

"*W*ell, that wasn't completely awkward or anything, was it?" asked Whitley, out of breath as she tried to keep up with Johanna's power walk down the busy street.

Johanna felt like she couldn't get back to the safety of her apartment fast enough. Her elbows resumed their familiar ninety-degree angle. "I told you I didn't know what to say."

"I didn't realize you'd be so awkward with what you *did* say, though. I take it you knew that guy?"

"We bumped into each other once. In the park. And let's just say, if you thought this encounter was awkward, then you'd agree that encounter was downright painful."

"Why didn't you ask him anything else about Felicia's murder?"

"You heard our convo in there! What was I supposed to do? Tell him I'd been sent by a mystic snow globe to investigate her murder? He'd think I was a complete loon! If he doesn't already think that!"

"Well, you could have started with the conversation

about her. Then it wouldn't have gotten so personal. He didn't even seem to know who you were."

Johanna's eyes swung towards the pavement. *Right. Not a clue indeed.* "I knew."

"Obviously. So now what do we do?"

"We'll have to see her parents and find out what we need to know from them."

"It won't be any easier," Whitley warned.

"I know. But I'm sure Rocky won't have knocked them into a pile of mud. It can't be any worse than that."

*G*ene and Dawn Marshall lived in a quintessential New York City brownstone on the northern tip of Brooklyn's Park Slope neighborhood. The sun shone brightly later that day, warming Johanna's face and reminding her that Christmas was only a week away, and it still had yet to snow a single flake yet. Standing on their front stoop, Johanna stared at her reflection in the glass and found herself hyperventilating once again.

"I really can't do this, Whit," she complained, shaking out her hands by her sides.

Whitley rubbed her back. "You can. I have faith in you. And it's the only way you're going to get rid of Essy and me."

Johanna's head bobbed. "Right." She blew out a breath. "Okay. Here I go." With her heart throbbing in her chest, she knocked on the front door, and she and Whitley watched through the glass as a woman in her fifties or sixties wearing a red cardigan, navy slacks, and narrow-framed glasses came to the door.

"Hello," she said, opening the front door a crack.

Johanna smiled hard. It was time to do this right. She

sucked up every bit of gumption she had in her body. "Hi. Mrs. Marshall?"

The woman's forehead crinkled slightly and the door opened a bit wider. "Yes?"

Johanna held out her hand even though she was quite sure it was clammy. "Hi. I'm Johanna Hughes. I'm a mystery novelist. I write under the pseudonym Hanna Hughes."

The woman's eyes bulged as the door opened even wider. "Yes, of course! I recognize you. I've been to one of your book signings!"

Johanna grimaced. What Mrs. Marshall probably didn't realize was that that book signing had been Johanna's very first and most definitely her last promotional event. Her agent had practically twisted her arm off to go, and in the end, she'd had such a bad anxiety attack that she'd nearly passed out before the event had even begun. It had taken a large dose of Xanax and an assurance that she'd never have to do it again to get Johanna to follow through on her obligation.

"The one at Barnes and Noble?" asked Johanna, trying to sound calm.

"Yes! It was for *DOA: The Deliveryman's Corpse*." Mrs. Marshall was excited now.

Johanna nodded, that had been one of her favorite books to write because she'd modeled the main character after her very own beloved UPS carrier, her father. "I remember that day vividly," she said with a tight smile.

Mrs. Marshall opened the door wider. "I feel like I have a celebrity at my door now! Do come in!"

"Thank you," said Johanna politely, holding the door open a second longer so that Whitley could trail in behind her.

"Shall we have a seat in the sitting room?"

"Yes, that would be lovely."

Mrs. Marshall's shoes made no sound as she led them across the tile floor and through a wide, arched doorway into a room with a soaring ceiling and the thickest door casings Johanna had ever seen. She gestured towards a formal pair of sofas that Johanna was sure pets were never allowed upon and just as sure that no one ever actually used. "Please, have a seat. Would you like something to drink? A cup of coffee or tea?"

The memory of the earlier event that day when she'd nearly choked herself to death during her anxiety attack replayed vividly in her mind. "I'd take some water if you have it?"

"Certainly! I'll just be a moment." Mrs. Marshall rushed out of the room, leaving Johanna and Whitley to look around the room.

"I can't believe she just let us in!" squealed Whitley. "You did *great*!"

"Thanks," muttered Johanna. She couldn't believe it had been so easy, either.

She surveyed the room, taking in the elegant decor. It was a family home, with beautifully taken portraits of people on the walls and a gorgeous Christmas tree in the corner with heirloom bulbs, sparkling tinsel, and red velvet bows. Johanna wondered if she'd ever have her own family home. Mook, of course, had outgrown the single-bedroom apartment in the city phase and grown into the married with kids, family home in New Jersey stage. Would that ever be something she would have for herself?

"Look," whispered Whitley. "It's Felicia!" She pointed to an oil portrait of the young woman.

"It looks like her senior picture," suggested Johanna.

"Here we are," sang Mrs. Marshall, carrying in a glass of water for Johanna.

"Thank you," said Johanna, taking a seat straight away.

"Now, tell me, to what do I owe this honor?" asked Mrs. Marshall as she took the seat across from Johanna and crossed her legs primly.

"I'm doing some research for an upcoming book, and I was hoping that perhaps you could help me," began Johanna tentatively. She'd have to do it right not to come off as a creeper.

Mrs. Marshall looked surprised. "I'd be happy to help, if I can."

Johanna set her water down on the coffee table. "I'm writing a mystery about a young woman who is killed during a mugging in Hudson River Park." Just the words caused a chill to ripple down Johanna's arms and legs and deflated the face of the woman sitting across from her.

"Yes," whispered Mrs. Marshall.

"I did some research and I discovered that you lost your daughter to a mugging in the Hudson River Park," said Johanna sadly. "I'm very sorry for your loss."

"Thank you." Mrs. Marshall's lips tightened as she nodded her head.

"I know it might be hard, but I was wondering if perhaps you and your husband might be willing to share your family's experience with me. It might help me to get a better understanding of the situation and the feelings of everyone involved so that I can relay that onto the page more authentically."

Mrs. Marshall swallowed hard and blinked her watery eyes. She was quiet for several long seconds, and Johanna wondered if the poor woman's wounds were too raw to discuss the event. "My husband's at work," she whispered.

Johanna's own tone softened. "I understand. Maybe I could just talk to you? But if it's too painful, I understand."

Mrs. Marshall's eyes took on a faraway look as her brows lifted. "We never understood it, you know."

Johanna remained quiet, allowing her to talk.

"She wasn't supposed to be in that part of town. It's boggled our minds for all these years."

"She was a realtor, right?" asked Johanna. "Perhaps she was showing a house in that neighborhood?"

Mrs. Marshall shook her head. "It was the day of my daughter's wedding rehearsal. I'm sure she wasn't showing houses that day. She and I spoke that morning and she was so stressed about all the little errands she still had left to do. She had an early appointment to get her nails done. She wanted to pick out new luggage for the honeymoon. She had to pick up her dress and the little gifts for her wedding party. I offered to do a few of her tasks for her, but she insisted she wanted to do them all."

Johanna gave Mrs. Marshall a tight smile. "So what happened?"

Mrs. Marshall threw her hands up on either side of herself lightly. "I don't know, to be honest. The rehearsal was at five thirty. I'd spoken to Felicia at eight thirty that morning, and then Gene and I were at the church by four forty-five. I had assumed Felicia would be early; she had a tendency to be places early. She was quite the go-getter, my Felicia," explained Mrs. Marshall.

"So, five thirty just came and went and no Felicia?" asked Johanna. The idea was heartbreaking.

"Yes," whispered Mrs. Marshall. "Oh, and poor Mitchell. He called and called her, but she never answered."

"Mitchell was her fiancé?"

"Yes. What a sweetheart he was. Those two were so suited for one another."

Johanna's heart burned in her chest. "How so?"

Mrs. Marshall leaned back. "Like I mentioned, my

Felicia was a go-getter. Just work, work, work. All day. Everyday. When she was in high school and other girls her age were out partying and going to dances and football games, my Felicia was home studying. She was very serious about her career and put that as her main priority for so long. She was almost thirty by the time she met Mitchell. Of course, I was shocked when she brought him home one Sunday night for supper, and even more shocked when they announced that they were engaged!"

Johanna tipped her head to the side. "You hadn't even met her fiancé before they announced their engagement?"

"No, neither Gene nor I had met him! But that was just like my Felicia. She treated her personal life just like her professional life. Everything that was done was done for a purpose and had an end goal in mind. She'd dated around here and there, but she always knew by the end of each date that it wouldn't work out. But when a friend introduced her to Mitchell, she said she knew almost immediately that things were different with him. He was just as career-oriented and focused as she was. It didn't bother him that she was so consumed with work, because he was just as consumed. Of course, I always thought that was no way to start a relationship, but it seemed to work for them."

"So how long had they dated before they announced their engagement?" Johanna hoped that Mrs. Marshall wouldn't notice her face flushing red for asking such a personal question.

"Oh, their relationship was very short. He was several years older than she was and a very serious man. They'd only been dating for three months when he'd proposed."

Whitley's jaw dropped. "Only three months! She hardly knew him!"

"That's not very much time to get to know someone," said Johanna quietly.

Mrs. Marshall nodded. "Felicia's father and I thought the same thing, and of course we were worried."

Whitley's green eyes were wide as she turned to Johanna. "You have to ask her if she thinks Mitch could have had anything to do with Felicia's death. You have to!"

Johanna looked down at her hands and rubbed her thumb against the smoothness of her nails. She cleared her throat and then looked up at the woman. "Mrs. Marshall, I hate to ask this, but I'm curious. Did anyone ever consider that perhaps Felicia wasn't mugged?"

"Oh, of course that thought crossed our minds! I suppose you're wondering if Mitchell was involved since they hadn't known each other for very long. I mean, how well could she have known him?"

Johanna nodded. She was thankful that she didn't have to spell that out.

"Well, the police checked all of that out. Mitchell was at work, and several of his colleagues were happy to verify that. He got there at seven that morning and didn't leave until five. He had had an important conference that day and was literally in a meeting with a half dozen other business associates from two until five. When he showed up at the church for the rehearsal it was almost a quarter to six. He was just sure that Felicia was going to be upset with him for being late. He had no idea that she wasn't even there yet as they hadn't spoken to one another all day."

Johanna blew out a breath of relief, thankful that he wasn't the killer. "So, the police figured out it wasn't her fiancé. Did they look at anyone else in her life?"

Mrs. Marshall lifted a shoulder. "They probably didn't do a good enough job. And I'll be honest; I didn't push it very hard. I was so devastated that I just wanted to put my daughter to rest. It was too painful to think about someone intentionally hurting my baby."

"I can understand that," whispered Johanna.

"But now, as the years have passed, and I've had more time to think about the circumstances surrounding her death, I admit that I have wondered if it was truly a mugging. Just because it made no sense to me that she was clear over in the Meatpacking District. I mean what in the world would she have been doing over there? She and Mitch worked in Midtown, and their apartment was in Lenox Hill. She always got her nails done at the same place and that was just a few blocks away from her office."

"What about the dress rehearsal? Where was that supposed to be—maybe she got sidetracked with car problems on the way to the church or something."

Mrs. Marshall shook her head resolutely. "No. She wanted to get married at our church, Saint Augustine's. So the rehearsal was just a few blocks from here."

"Did anyone ever ask the realty company if she had a property showing that day?" asked Johanna.

"The police did. They insisted they hadn't see hide nor hair of her all day, and if she'd had an appointment with a client, she hadn't let anyone there know about it."

Johanna wondered if maybe she should tell Mrs. Marshall about the wedding dress and the seamstress and her story about Felicia. *But then you'll have to explain how you wound up with her daughter's wedding dress and your whole cover about researching this for a story will be blown.* "Did Felicia have anyone that might want to hurt her?"

Mrs. Marshall's head shook so hard it made her carefully styled auburn hair shake. "If I thought someone had wanted to hurt her, I would have most certainly told the police, but there wasn't anyone. Felicia was very professional with everyone she came into contact with. I can't imagine anyone wanting to hurt her. I mean, what reason would they have? She didn't have much of a social circle because she worked so much. What she did have was a lot of money on her because she'd gone to the ATM that morning to get cash for the honeymoon. She was also dressed very nicely. Her nails were freshly done and she wore expensive jewelry, including a huge diamond ring. She was an easy target for someone wanting a couple bucks. I just don't understand why they had to kill her for it. She had to have tried fighting back." Mrs. Marshall was crying now.

Johanna moved herself to the other sofa and put a hand on Mrs. Marshall's hand as she felt her own heart squeezing. "I'm so sorry, Mrs. Marshall. How horrible of a feeling not to be able to have saved her from that."

Mrs. Marshall nodded and took the tissue that Johanna pulled from her purse. "It is. I'll never get to see my little girl again. She was our only child. Gene and I had been thrilled just to have her. So to have her taken from us…"

"I'm so sorry."

Mrs. Marshall sniffed and patted Johanna's hand. "But you're going to write a book about it? About my Felicia's case?"

The thought had occurred to Johanna. That she could actually write Felicia's story. She wondered if being so close to it now would make it more difficult to write or if perhaps it would make it easier and have more heart. "Maybe."

"If you do, tell the world what a wonderful girl my Felicia was. Alright?"

Johanna nodded. "I'll make her shine, Mrs. Marshall. Don't worry. I'll make Felicia shine."

16

That evening on her power walk through Central Park, with Rocky panting by her side, Johanna reveled in the silence surrounding her. The last few days had been nothing short of chaotic, stressful, and exhausting, and now the brisk air that filled her lungs felt cathartic and reinvigorating, and for the first time since Thursday, she felt her shoulders relaxing.

"Oh, Rock, I needed this," breathed Johanna. Her fists punched the winter air in the same precise rhythmic motion as her shoes beat the pavement.

"Woof!" agreed Rocky as he trotted by her side.

"Oh, don't I know it? You've had a rough week too, what with that darn cat staying with us and you two getting in trouble for knocking over Grandpa's Christmas tree. I bet you can't wait until things get back to normal too."

"Woof woof!"

"What would I do without you, buddy?" Johanna broke her stride for a single second to reach down and pat Rocky's head. "But don't you worry. I'm doing my best to get this cold case solved so we can send the Snow twins back to wherever they came from."

"Woof!"

"I mean, yeah, I agree, Whit's not so bad. She's actually kind of growing on me. But her sister, hoo!" squeaked Johanna. "She's nothing but vinegar, that one. It'll be so nice getting the apartment back to just us."

Rocky's head swiveled as a squirrel darted across the path in front of them. He ground his paws into the rough surface and came to an immediate halt. A low growl emanated from his throat.

"Oh no. Not today, buddy. I don't know what got into you that day, but that is definitely *not* happening today." She grasped his leash tighter with one hand and kept striding forward.

"Woof!" he barked, catching up to her.

As if she were watching the highlight reel, days after a big game, Johanna could clearly see the events of last Thursday playing through her mind. The squirrel eating a nut on the bench. Rocky tugging her forward, her shins being driven into the edge of the bench. She winced in memory. The mad dash down the trail after Rocky. The man coming up the path, staring at his cell phone. The collision. Her subsequent knee drop. Their banged heads. The offer to give him her coat. She closed her eyes for a split second, thoroughly embarrassed.

Now she knew exactly who that man was. Mitch Connelly, structural engineer and workaholic. His late fiancée was Felicia Marshall, and they'd only dated for *three months* before getting engaged. It had taken James precisely twenty-six years to propose to her. Of course, several of those years were spent in diapers and training pants and thus weren't to be included in the official count.

She shook her head as her feet heel-toed the asphalt next

to Rocky. How in the world had Mitch Connelly not kicked her out of his office? She'd come off as a fool, that much was certain. He probably thought she was one of those people that had escaped from a mental hospital and had thus been off their meds for too long. Of course, he had said something about her having a nice smile. Or maybe she had just invented that little compliment in her warped, delusional mind.

Johanna shook her head backwards into the fresh air. Her shoulder-length brown hair rode the waves of the breeze behind her. With no hat on her head, the tips of her ears burned from the cold, but it was a good pain. It made her feel alive and definitely not delusional. Maybe she hadn't imagined that little compliment after all.

"Woof woof!" barked Rocky, separating her from her thoughts. His front paws were off the ground as he bounced up and down.

Johanna glanced over at him and felt bad that she'd left him with Esmerelda earlier. The grouchy cat had probably yelled at him and made him sit in the corner all day and that was why he now had so much energy to burn. "Oh, you poor boy," clucked Johanna, giving him a face that said she felt sorry for him.

But Rocky kept bouncing, with his eyes trained on something up ahead. Johanna followed his line of sight as he stared. The sun had gone down hours ago, but the trail was somewhat illuminated. She could see a figure in a trench coat coming her way, but it was still too dark to make out who it was.

"Woof woof!"

It can't be. She squinted, trying to force the shadowy figure in front of her to be clearer. "Mitch?" His name came out of her mouth as little more than a breathy fog of condensation.

He was looking down at his phone again, but as he rounded the corner and heard Rocky's barking, his gaze shot up. He *searched* the path in front of him, Johanna was almost sure of it. Scared of her elephant of a dog, no doubt. But when he saw Rocky, he didn't look the least bit frightened, and then his eyes turned to Johanna next and darn it if it didn't look like he smiled at her.

Suddenly Johanna was thankful for the shower she'd taken that morning and the conscious decision she'd made *not* to wear her grandmother's crocheted hat and her pink coat on her walk. Since the weather had warmed slightly, she'd worn her plum-colored Under Armour windbreaker over her black leggings.

"Johanna? Is that you?" asked Mitch as he neared them.

Rocky couldn't be more excited to see his old pal, showing his excitement by rushing up ahead to Mitch and trying to leap into his arms as if he were nothing more than a six-pound Chihuahua.

"Rocky," chastised Johanna as she felt her face heating up almost instantaneously. She tugged on his leash. "Leave the poor man alone."

"Hey, Rocky, I thought that was you," said Mitch with a deep laugh. He took hold of Rocky's ears and gave them a solid jostle and a pat on the head.

As Johanna caught up to the two, she felt a nauseating flutter in the pit of her stomach, as if a bushelful of butterflies had suddenly been released. "Hello, Mitch." The simple pair of words came out of her mouth with a strange sense of confidence that felt foreign to Johanna.

"Twice in one day," he said with a light smile. "I guess it's my lucky day."

Pretty sure it's my *lucky day*, Johanna thought. "Or maybe your unlucky day where Rocky and I are concerned."

He shook his head. "Nope. I'd say my lucky day. It was nice visiting with you this afternoon."

His words delighted her. "It was nice visiting with you too."

With a hand still on Rocky's head, he continued, "It's not often I get a chance to meet someone who's been through what I've been through and understands how difficult it is to lose someone in your life like that."

Johanna's heart raced in her chest. Had he really enjoyed chatting with her earlier? Or had he just been able to sympathize with her and nothing more? "Yeah, no, I, uh, totally agree," she mumbled.

Rocky looked up at her. His heavy drooping eyes told her everything she needed to know. She sounded like an idiot.

"Would you maybe be in interested in having coffee with me sometime and we can commiserate together?" he asked. The park's lights reflected off his blue eyes, making them twinkle.

Johanna swallowed hard and then promptly choked on her own saliva as she tried to speak. She held a hand out as she coughed, her eyes watering.

"Are you alright?"

"Yeah," she gasped, trying like hell to regain a shred of composure. *It takes skill to choke on one's own saliva*, she told herself.

"I'm sorry I don't have any water to offer you. Is it your asthma again?" he said, his eyes narrowed with concern. "Do you have an inhaler on you?"

Oh God. I told him I had asthma. She wanted to slap herself upside the forehead. "It comes and goes," she assured him as the coughing fit finally settled. "Ooh, sorry about that." She put a hand at the base of her throat.

"No problem."

"Umm, yeah, I'd definitely like to go have coffee sometime."

"Then you can tell me all about being a mystery writer and what a fun career that must be."

Had she told him she was a mystery writer? Johanna lifted a brow. She'd been so embarrassed about spilling coffee on him that she'd wanted to block the entire conversation out. "Oh, ha-ha," she giggled. "Yeah. And you can tell me all about what's like to be a structural engineer." Her head waggled and she made a funny voice as she said "structural engineer." *Could I be any more awkward?* she wondered.

He laughed. "Unfortunately, I don't think being a structural engineer makes for any good stories, but maybe I can think of something interesting to share. There's this coffee shop just a few blocks from my office. Beans and Bagels. I've seen dogs in there before, so I'm pretty sure they're pet-friendly. Would you and Rocky be interested in maybe having a cup of coffee and a muffin or something with me tomorrow?"

"Oh, tomorrow?" asked Johanna with shock.

"You're busy tomorrow?"

No. She wasn't busy. She was just stunned he'd been serious. She just assumed he'd said, "Let's go have coffee," but what he'd really meant was, "I hope I never have to see your stupid, clumsy face anymore."

"Oh, no. I'm not busy. I usually walk Rocky in the mornings and get a bagel and a coffee on my way home, so he and I could definitely swing by your coffee shop."

A broad smile covered his face, brightening his eyes and making the cute little crinkles in the corners mesh up. "Well, great! What time works for you?"

Johanna patted Rocky's side. "Rocky's an early riser. We're usually out and about by seven."

"That's perfect. I'll just meet you at the coffee shop by... seven thirty?"

Johanna nodded. "Yeah, seven thirty works for us."

"You know where it is?"

With her lips firmly wedged between her teeth, she nodded again.

"Great." The smile never left his face as he walked back-wards down the path, giving her a little salute. "Well, I better get going. I'll see you both in the morning!"

Johanna gave him a little fluttery wave goodbye. She didn't trust herself to speak anymore. She was sure the words that would come out would be the incomprehensible ramblings of an undateable woman, and she didn't need any more help making a fool out of herself.

When he was completely out of sight and earshot, she looked down at Rocky. "Did that really just happen?"

"Woof!"

"It was probably just a sympathy invite." Esmerelda yawned and then slowly lowered herself into a prone position on the floor with her tail wrapped neatly around herself.

"Thanks." Johanna's jaw clenched as she scooped Rocky's food out of his container and set it down on the floor. She wished she hadn't told the girls about running into Mitch or that he'd invited her out to coffee the next morning. She was already nervous enough; she didn't need Esmerelda's attitude making things worse.

"Be nice, Essy. I think they bonded this morning. I think it's cute," sang Whitley.

Johanna shot her a wide-eyed grin. "You think we bonded?"

"Well, I mean, you both lost your fiancés. That's not something everyone else has gone through. Of course he'd want to talk to someone else who's been through it."

Johanna lowered her head as the grin dissipated. "Oh. You think that's all it was?"

"There's nothing wrong with that, is there?"

"No. I suppose not." She'd only hoped that maybe it would have been something more than just them commiserating together. But what was she thinking? Of course it wasn't more.

"You like him, don't you?" asked Esmerelda, opening one eye to make Johanna shift uncomfortably. How was it possible that a *cat* could make a grown woman feel uncomfortable?

"I mean… I just… you know. He seems like a nice— man. And, I think he's intelligent. And friendly."

"And hot?" asked Esmerelda.

Whitley giggled.

"Hot?" Johanna made her best I-have-no-idea-what-you're-talking-about face.

Esmerelda opened both eyes then. "Yeah. You know. Smoking hot. Sexy. Babelicious. Bangable."

"Bangable?!" Johanna's mouth went dry. "I certainly haven't… I mean, that never crossed my…"

"You haven't thought about what he'd look like naked?"

"Naked?! Of course not!"

Whitley sighed. "Essy, cut her a break, please."

"You two are so lame. Both of you. Goody two-shoes. Just once I'd like to meet someone else like me. Someone who says what they're really thinking. Don't talk to me anymore, I need my beauty rest. And please keep Mr. Wonder Drool away from me."

"You know, this could really work to our benefit, you

and Mitch going out for coffee," said Whitley, her green eyes sparkling.

"Are you serious? I get asked out to coffee by a man for the first time in my life, and I have to spend it digging for clues about how his late wife died?"

"What? You don't like that idea?"

"No, I don't like that idea!"

"Well, how else are we supposed to solve this murder? I mean, we're seriously out of clues here. Felicia's mom didn't give you anything to go on. Mitch didn't give us anything to go on. Her employers didn't give us anything. We're stuck."

Johanna lifted a finger and then slid down onto her desk chair and popped her laptop open. "I think you're wrong. I think we do have something. Her parents, her fiancé, and her employer didn't know about the house showing she got contacted about at the very last second. That means the police didn't know about it either. I think that's the key to all of this." Johanna slid on her reading glasses.

"Oh-kay?" drawled Whitley, glancing at the computer screen while Johanna navigated through Google to find a map of Manhattan.

"I think what we need to do is plot out Felicia's movements for the day."

"That's a great idea." Whitley lugged a chair out of the kitchen and put it down next to Johanna.

"So, her mom said that she and Mitch lived in Lenox Hill. That's here." She pointed to a spot on the screen that was just east of Central Park. "Her office is in Midtown, which is over here." She slid her finger almost straight west. "Both the dry cleaners *and* the nail place were within a few blocks of her office."

"Well, where was her body found?"

"Clear down here." Johanna slid her finger all the way

down to the southwestern quadrant of Manhattan, where the Hudson River separated Manhattan from New Jersey. "I mean, her mom's right. It would make no sense for her to be all the way over there on the day of her wedding rehearsal, *but* we know something that her mother didn't know and that's that she had a real estate showing at some point during the day."

"Do we know where that was?" asked Whitley.

Johanna shook her head. "I think that's the piece of this puzzle that's missing. If I were a betting girl, I'd place a bet that the property Felicia Marshall showed was somewhere in that neighborhood."

"Well, then, I guess that's what we need to find out!"

"Then what are we waiting for? Let's get to it!"

17

*J*ohanna stood in her apartment's small bathroom with her eyes closed, as still as she possibly could. One would think that was easy, but in fact, it was harder than it sounded. Somehow a person's balance shifted when standing for an extended period of time with their eyes closed. "I can't believe I'm letting you do this," she murmured as she struggled to stay erect.

"Quit talking. When you talk, you move," said Whitley as she carefully outlined Johanna's brown eyelids with a deep plum eyeliner.

"I can't help it," she said without moving her lips. "I'm getting dizzy standing here with my eyes closed."

Esmerelda pawed her forehead from the top of the vanity. "Oh, for heaven's sake, you're as awkward as a cow on crutches."

"Right, well, you're as subtle as a flying brick," Johanna snapped back.

"Doh!" said Whitley with a smile. "Good one, Han."

Johanna's eyes flashed open and she turned to stare into

the mirror. Her brown hair was freshly washed and bounced sprightly around her shoulders thanks to Whitley's expert styling. "Are you done yet? This makeup stuff takes *forever*."

Whitley frowned. "I literally just started on your makeup."

"Yeah, but the hair took forever. And now the makeup is going to take even longer. There's a reason why busy people like me don't wear makeup. It's because we have more important things to do."

Whitley grabbed hold of Johanna's shoulder to steady her again. "Quit complaining. This won't take that much longer. Es, go find Hanna a different shirt to wear."

Johanna looked down at the plain black shirt she was wearing. "What's wrong with the one I have on?"

"It's a long-sleeved t-shirt."

"Yeah?"

"I'm not going to let you go on a date wearing a long-sleeved t-shirt, Hanna," said Whitley, lifting one brow.

"Oh," she said, mulling it over as Esmerelda jumped to the floor. "Well, I have short-sleeved t-shirts. They're in my bottom drawer, Es. The good ones are on the right side, the lounging ones are on the left."

"You divided your t-shirts into good ones and lounging ones? Aren't all t-shirts lounging shirts?"

"No. The lounging ones have stains on them."

"And yet you keep them?!"

"Of course I keep them. I'm not going to throw out a perfectly good t-shirt just because it got a stain on it."

"Then when do you throw out a t-shirt?"

Johanna made a face. "Who throws out t-shirts?"

"Oh my God," sighed Whitley. "We need to take you shopping."

Esmerelda reappeared seconds later with a red sweater

between her teeth. She dropped it at Johanna's feet. "How about this?"

Johanna bent over and picked it up. "Mmm, you got this out of my closet?"

Esmerelda nodded.

"Yeah, this shirt is dry-clean only, which means it's dirty."

"But it was hanging in your closet," said Esmerelda.

"Yeah, everything that's hanging in my closet is dry-clean only. It's all dirty."

"You know there's a dry cleaners just down the street. I've seen it every time we go out," said Whitley.

"Yeah, well, who thinks of that? I've got books to write."

Esmerelda groaned and headed back towards Johanna's bedroom.

"Stick out your chin, close your eyes, and lift your brows," instructed Whitley as she pulled out an eyeshadow palette.

"Are you seriously putting eyeshadow on me? No. I'll look like a hooker."

"You're not going to look like a hooker, trust me. I'll blend it."

"How about the green blouse you wore to Christmas at your dad's?" hollered Esmerelda from the other room.

"No, I'm going to wear that this weekend to my uncle Jack's," Johanna hollered back.

"You can't wear that again!" breathed Whitley as if the thought disgusted her.

"Why not?"

"Because your sister and your family already *saw* you in it!"

Johanna's brows crinkled. "My uncle Jack and the rest of the family haven't."

"But your sister has. No, you'll have to wear something

else to the Christmas party. You can wear the blouse on your date." She turned her head to holler over Johanna's shoulder. "Bring the blouse, Es."

"I don't have anything else for Christmas. If I wear a t-shirt to Uncle Jack's, my sister will kill me," sighed Johanna.

"Then we'll go shopping," Whitley suggested. "I love shopping."

"We don't have time to shop, Whit. We have a murder to solve."

"Then you'll have to get the red sweater dry-cleaned in time." She blended the last of the eyeshadow. "Now let's do your lips. Maybe you should put the blouse on first so you don't get lipstick on it."

Johanna bent over, took the green blouse Esmerelda had dragged in and swapped shirts. When she stood back up, Whitley took hold of her chin and began to paint an almost-nude color onto her lips.

"That's the same color as my lips. What's the point?"

"To make Mitch think you look pretty."

Johanna was quiet for a moment. It had been years since a man had thought she looked pretty. She wasn't even sure that she *was* pretty anymore, but she didn't want to say that to the girls. "I don't think I can keep lying to Mitch," she said quietly.

Whitley stopped painting and met her eyes. "What do you mean?"

"I have to tell him about the dress and about our suspicions."

"You're going to tell him that she had a property showing the day she died?" asked Whitley.

"Yeah, what do you think?"

Esmerelda hopped back up onto the vanity. "Do you like him?"

Johanna grinned. It embarrassed her to have to answer that question. "I mean, sort of…"

Esmerelda nodded. "Thought so. Then I think lying is the best policy."

Whitley's green eyes widened as she turned to gawk at her sister. "Where did Mom and Dad go wrong with you?"

"No, I'm serious. If he finds out that you're seeing ghosts and talking to cats, he's going to think you belong in the loony bin."

"I think I'd rather have him think that than to keep withholding that information from him. If someone knew something about James's death and they didn't tell me, I'd be furious. I can't have Mitch furious with me."

"What happens when he doesn't believe you?" asked Whitley.

Johanna thought about it for a second. She had no idea how it would all play out, but whether Mitch thought she was a crazy woman or not, she had to give him all the facts of Felicia's case. "I don't know. I'll just have to figure that out as I go."

*B*undled up in her black wool coat and her trendy black newsboy cap, Johanna practically skipped down the Midtown streets at seven the next morning. The air, so cold that it stained her cheeks a scarlet red color and made her nose numb to the touch, puffed out in front of both her and Rocky in thick clouds and forced her to shove her mittened hands deeper into her pockets. She looked up into the sky and once again wondered where the snow was.

Knowing exactly where Bagels and Beans was located, Johanna turned a corner and then crossed the street at the next intersection. She'd visited the small coffee shop on more than one occasion, and the thought of the shop's bacon, egg, and cheese blueberry bagel made her almost as giddy as the thought of getting to see Mitch again. From a block away, Johanna could see the walnut-colored storefront and the black awning with festive green garlands draped beneath it.

"Almost there, buddy," she said, fighting back a squeal.

"Woof!" Rocky seemed almost as giddy as she felt.

As they passed the windows in front of the shop, she could see Mitch already inside, nursing a mug of steaming coffee. Her stomach flip-flopped.

"Oh man, Rock. I'm not sure I can do this. Where's one of Whit's motivational speeches when I need it?" she asked despite the fact that Whitley had stayed home at her own request. She hadn't wanted the constant monitoring; she'd thought it would only make her more nervous.

Rocky chuffed into the frosty air.

The line at the counter stretched all the way to the front door. A bald man in a tweed blazer opened the door for Johanna and Rocky. "Thank you," she said with a smile.

The minute they'd stepped inside the festively decorated shop, Mitch stood up and waved with a broad smile. *Gosh, he's handsome*, she thought as she made her way towards him.

Rocky saw him too, and as he dashed forward to greet his new friend, his path cut in front of Johanna. She stumbled over his hind legs and began to nosedive over the top of her beloved horse-dog. Jumping to her rescue, Mitch was quick to catch her and set her upright.

"Oof! Oh my goodness!" she said, thoroughly embarrassed, but thankful she hadn't doused him with hot coffee again. *Seriously, Rocky. Dude. You're making me look bad here. And I don't need any more help in that department.*

"Do I need to wear a football helmet when you two are

around?" Mitch asked, displaying a set of perfectly straight white teeth.

Johanna grabbed her hat from the floor and then raked her hair back into place. "I'm afraid you're getting to know the real me right away."

Mitch grinned from ear to ear. "It's possible that might just be what I like about you the most."

Johanna's eyes widened. "That I'm the biggest klutz you'll ever meet?"

He chuckled softly. "No, that you're just being you. If you can meet someone like that in this city, it's sort of like winning the lottery."

Johanna's cheeks felt like they were going to burst from the smile his statement put on her face.

Mitch gestured towards his table, where two mugs of coffee lay in wait. "I hope you don't mind, but the line was so long that I went ahead and ordered you a cup of coffee and a bagel."

While relieved that she didn't have to wait in the long line, she was also a tad bit disappointed. She'd been looking forward to her favorite treat the entire way there. "That's very sweet of you." She rubbed her hands together and peered at the little paper bag on the table. "What do we have?"

With a big grin, he opened the bag. "Well. I got two things and you can pick which you'd prefer, and I'll eat the other."

Johanna slumped back in her seat, "Well, I hate to make you eat something you don't like."

"Oh no. I'd be happy to eat either of these." He slowly pulled out a small wrapped bagel. Rocky put his chin on the table and his eyes swung upwards to stare at the bagel covetously. "Okay, this one is their new sandwich. It's a grilled cheese bagel with sliced apple, pear, cheddar cheese, caramelized onions, arugula, and a sunny-side-up egg."

Johanna's jaw dropped. "I'm surprised you remembered all that."

"Oh, trust me. My stomach has a good memory," he chuckled as he pulled out the other sandwich. "And this one is a little more conventional. It's a cheese bagel with bacon, egg, and cheese."

She brightened and reached across the table to snatch that one out of his hands. Rocky's eyes followed the bagel and a little whine emanated from his throat. "Oooh, I'll have that one. I usually order a blueberry bagel with bacon, egg, and cheese, but I've never had a cheese bagel before. It doesn't sound too bad."

He fake-gasped. "You've never had a cheese bagel before? Oh, Johanna, you're missing out! Especially theirs. Theirs are the best."

Hearing her name roll off his lips sounded so sweet that she couldn't help but smile. "Am I? Well, then, I cannot wait to try it."

He clapped his hands together. "Good. Because my stomach and mouth were in agreement. They wanted that grilled cheese bagel." He lifted the paper bag to remove it from the table and then realized there was something else weighting down the bottom of the bag. "Oh! I almost forgot!" He pulled out a little paper-wrapped item. "I got Rocky their blueberry bacon dog treats. I hope that's okay?"

Rocky heard his name and swiveled to look at Johanna as if to say, *Please, Mommy, can I have it?*

Johanna felt sudden tears spring to her eyes. She had to blink and then swallow hard to shove them back. "Of course," she whispered softly. *Where in the world has this man been all my life?!* "That was very sweet of you."

"I didn't want him to feel left out," he said, dismissing Johanna's praise. He opened the small package and then put it on the floor, where Rocky immediately devoured his treat.

Johanna felt herself at a loss. Here she was with this amazingly sweet and attractive man and she didn't know what to say. It occurred to her then that he was too far out of her league. As his eyes lifted off Rocky and swung towards her, Johanna shoved the bagel into her mouth so she wouldn't have to think of something brilliant to say.

"What do you think of that cheese bagel?" he asked.

With a mouthful of food, Johanna nodded. "Mmm-hmm!"

"Oh good, I'm glad you like it." He unwrapped his own sandwich but took the plastic silverware on the table to slice off a piece of it and put it in his mouth.

Johanna looked down at the sandwich in her hand. *Oh. So we're being fancy?*

They chewed for a few moments, and when he'd swallowed his first bite, he looked at her curiously. "So. You're a writer. Tell me about that."

Johanna fought to swallow the enormous bite she'd taken without choking. She held up a finger to ask him to wait as Rocky sat up and rested his chin on Mitch's lap to thank him for the snack. Mitch patted his head while Johanna gathered her thoughts.

"Well," she said, swallowing the last dry bite, "I write mysteries under the pseudonym Hanna Hughes."

"I wondered if that was you," he admitted, nodding his head. "I've heard of you."

Johanna felt her face flush red. Why it always seemed to embarrass her when someone had heard of her, she wasn't sure. "Oh, really?"

He nodded and smiled at her.

"I've had a few write-ups in the local papers," she admitted.

"So do you go by Hanna?"

She shook her head as she cut off a small piece of her sandwich. "Not really. I have one friend that calls me Hanna, but pretty much everyone else calls me JoJo."

"JoJo, huh? That's cute." His blue eyes twinkled when he smiled, and a new Christmas song fired up in the background. "You look more like a JoJo than a Johanna."

"I'm pretty sure that's why hardly anyone calls me Hanna. I only used Hanna as my pseudonym because I wanted a little bit of anonymity." She leaned forward then to admit something deeply personal. "I'm not much of a people person."

He leaned backwards in his seat with a fake look of shock on his face. "You? No! I'd have never guessed."

That made her smile. She giggled. "Is it that obvious?"

"Maybe a bit," he said, pinching one eye shut and holding his finger and thumb up parallel to each other about an inch apart. "It's alright. I've been described as a bit of a recluse myself," he admitted.

"I was better before James died. After that, I kind of holed myself up in my apartment, and days would go by and I'd realize I hadn't even felt fresh air on my face in a week. That was when I decided living like that wasn't healthy, so I got Rocky. I figured having to walk a dog every day would force me to get fresh air."

"And you had someone to talk to."

She nodded. "And I got Rocky out of the deal, and we've been best friends ever since."

"I think there's probably no better best friend to have."

"I agree." Johanna scratched Rocky's long body. "So did you find you wanted to hole up at your place too?"

He looked thoughtful for a moment and then began.

"After Felicia passed, I *wanted* to just disappear and like go to a remote island somewhere and live the rest of my life carving coconuts into bird feeders or something."

"Bird feeders?" asked Johanna with a chuckle.

His eyes crinkled in the corners. "I saw a documentary on that once. It looked peaceful."

They laughed comfortably together, and for the first time, Johanna felt her shoulders loosen up slightly.

"But then work called one day. It was an emergency, and I needed to go in. They got their initial condolences out of the way when I walked in, but then once that was over, it was like back to business as usual, and I realized that the world had continued to turn while I was gone. While I was burying my fiancée, the world hadn't even taken a pause. And I realized that I could keep up my existence, keep up my *job*, without having to be fully awake. I could keep going in this mind-numbed bubble that my conscious had settled into and I could just work. And time would pass. And so that's what I did."

Johanna felt her heart tug for him. She knew that mind-numbed bubble well. "Did going to work every day ever pull you out of that funk?"

"Oh, I suppose eventually I began to wake up more and more, but I don't know if I've ever really reawakened. You know?"

Johanna's head bobbed as she stared down at her sandwich. "I do." She didn't know if she'd ever really reawakened either. She swallowed and tried to summon any inner strength she had. "Mitch. There's something I need to tell you."

18

*H*e leaned back, crossed his legs, and looked at her curiously. "I'm all ears."

It was now or never for Johanna. She couldn't do this to herself. She couldn't start... whatever this was... with this wonderful man—the first man she'd met and *liked* since James—and then lose him down the road because he discovered the truth that she'd been keeping from him. She had to tell him *now*. But truths were *so hard*!

Johanna felt her palms go clammy and her mouth go dry. She took a sip of her black coffee. Then she looked up at him. He blinked back at her. His blue eyes were serene and easy. He tilted his head to the side, no doubt wondering what was up with the psychopath sitting in front of him.

"I got a wedding dress," she finally blurted and then struggled with what to say next, but Mitch cut in.

"A little presumptuous, but hardly the end of the world to justify the way you're sweating," he said with a light chuckle.

It occurred to her what he meant. She waved a hand in

front of her face and smiled. "Oh, no, I didn't mean for us—I mean, I…"

"It was a wedding dress for your wedding to James," he said knowingly. "I get it."

"No, I never got around to picking out my wedding dress for my wedding to James," she admitted. "I got this dress on the evening that Rocky and I bumped into you in the park."

He winked at her. "Okay, so we're back to presumptuous?" He held up two hands. "Kidding, kidding. Continue."

Johanna wrung out her wrists and avoided eye contact with him. She wasn't sure how much of the mystical stuff to include or conversely, to leave out. "Right. So… it was a wedding dress. I got it from a secondhand shop," she fibbed, deciding in that instance to leave out *all* of the magical stuff. She already had so much working against her, she didn't need to add mental patient to her dossier. "I don't know why I bought it. Something just seemed to call to me. It was so beautiful." She glanced up at him, wondering what he was thinking.

But he didn't look the least bit concerned at hearing that the woman he was having coffee with had bought a wedding dress the day she'd met him.

"So, anyway, I got the dress home and realized that it had never been worn, and I started to wonder who would have gotten rid of such a beautiful dress without ever having worn it? I noticed that it had a dry cleaning tag stapled to the manufacturer's label, so I thought maybe I'd just go see if the dry cleaners knew who it had belonged to."

"You seriously decided to go track down the owner of the dress?" he asked.

She shrugged. "Yeah. You know, I thought maybe it had

been mistakenly sent to the secondhand shop and, I don't know, I guess the mystery writer in me had her interest piqued."

"I see. So did you find anything out at the dry cleaners?"

"I actually did. I spoke to the woman who had altered the dress. She said she'd altered it years ago, and then the owner had never picked it up. It was the dry cleaners that had given it to the secondhand store."

"Someone took a wedding dress in to have it altered and never picked it up? That sounds like a giant waste of money."

Johanna smiled, her stomach doing flip-flops as she got closer to the painful punch line. "Right. Yeah. So I asked the seamstress if she knew who had owned the dress, and she gave me a name and a number and a little bit of information." Johanna swallowed hard. "I did some digging with that information, and I got some bad news about the woman who owned the dress."

He frowned. "Do I really want to hear it?"

"Probably not," whispered Johanna. But she had to tell him. She had to get everything out in the open and see whether or not he still wanted to talk to her, knowing the real reason she'd been to visit him at his office. "I found out that the woman died before she could pick up her wedding dress from the dry cleaners."

He nodded knowingly. "I was going to guess that by the look on your face. I bet that hit you pretty hard since James died before the two of you could get married."

Johanna swiped a hand across her forehead. "Yeah, it was very painful to hear," she agreed. "But there's more…"

"Oh man. More?"

She nodded. "I Googled the woman who passed away. I thought maybe it would be best to return the dress to her family or something. You know, to give them some closure.

Maybe it would even answer some questions," she added, preparing him for what was to come.

"Oh. Well, did you find her family?"

Johanna nodded. "I did, actually. I went to see her mother yesterday."

He winced. "Ooh, I bet that was hard."

"Excruciating, actually." Her voice was tiny then. She wasn't sure if she could continue.

He reached a hand across the table and covered her hand with his. "I'm so sorry. I can tell it opened a wound for you."

"I also went to see her fiancé," she whispered, without making eye contact. She wasn't sure that she could look at him while she was telling him.

His hand went stiff and he was silent. She wasn't sure if it was because he could guess what she was going to say next or if the idea of what she had done opened his own wounds.

She glanced up at him. His eyes were damp. "And you told him this whole story?"

Johanna shook her head, her eyes rimmed with red as tears poured down her face now. "I couldn't tell him," she admitted. "So I told a lie."

He refused to allow her to break eye contact with him. "What lie did you tell, Johanna?" he asked, and then she could see him damming his next breath in his lungs.

"I told him I was there checking on his muddied suit. I told him I'd found his business card on a path in Central Park. But I hadn't. The truth was, I didn't even know that man's name in Central Park. I'd seen him for years on the path, but I'd never known his name." She stopped talking and swallowed hard.

Mitch blinked, breaking their eye contact. He slid his

hand away from hers and sat back in his chair. "The dress was Felicia's?"

Johanna winced. "Yes."

Two fat tears slid down his cheeks and as he sniffled, he looked out the window next to their table. "You found Felicia's wedding dress. Wow, that's a lot," he admitted, his head bobbing in silence.

"I know," she agreed quietly. "I went there with the full intention of telling you. I'm sorry that I lied. It's just that when I got there and saw it was the poor man I'd nearly knocked unconscious in the park…"

"Yeah," he agreed. "No, I understand." He pulled a handkerchief from his jacket pocket and wiped his nose. "I tried finding the dress, you know. For her parents. I thought her mother might like to have it. The place she usually took our dry cleaning didn't have it. I tried a few other places in the neighborhood, but none of them had it either. I guess I didn't try hard enough."

She looked around the coffee shop uneasily. A few eyes were looking their way. Whispering. Making up stories about what was unfolding at their table. Johanna was sure someone thought she'd broken up with him. It was what she would have thought if she had witnessed the scene herself and didn't know better. No one would ever guess the truth about what was happening, though. Johanna never would have guessed she would be in this situation before she'd left for her walk last Thursday.

She cleared her throat and looked at him again. "There's more," she said uneasily.

He looked at her with his brows knitted together. "More?"

With her lips melded into her teeth, she nodded.

He sucked in a deep breath and then let it out slowly. "Okay. I'm ready to hear more."

"When I found out from the seamstress who the dress belonged to, she also told me something that I don't think you or Felicia's parents, or the police, knew."

He tipped his head sideways, listening keenly.

"She went to pick the dress up on the day of your wedding rehearsal."

He looked shocked. "She did! Well, then, why didn't she? Why was it still there?"

"Because as she was trying it on one last time, the zipper broke," explained Johanna. "And the seamstress told her it wouldn't take long to fix, but then Felicia got a text message from a client."

Mitch's head jerked back. "What?"

"Yeah. Apparently, it was a new client. He asked for her by name, and the commission on the sale would have been big enough to pay for your entire wedding *and* your honeymoon, so she decided to take the property showing."

Mitch's body language changed then. He sat up and his body grew more rigid. "She decided to take the showing on *the day of our wedding rehearsal*?"

"From what I've heard about Felicia, she was kind of a workaholic. Maybe that's not so crazy?"

His eyes scanned the table as he thought about it. "Maybe not so crazy," he finally agreed. "But she'd told me that morning that she had so many errands to run. She wanted to get luggage for the honeymoon and she had to get cash from the ATM. She had to get her nails and her hair done and pick up her dress. Her list was endless."

"I know," whispered Johanna. "But her plan also included showing that property, because she left and she never came back for the dress."

"But the police asked the company she worked for if she had any appointments scheduled for the day. They said she didn't."

"That's what they told me, too," Johanna agreed.

"You went to see her employer?!"

"Yeah, well, the seamstress didn't have a full name. Just a first initial, a last name, and a phone number. I called the number and the person with that number told us—I mean, *me*"—she swallowed hard—"that the person who had last had her number had been a realtor for Four Seasons Realty."

"Which was Felicia's employer," he filled in.

"Right. So, I went there and talked to some people she used to work with, and none of them mentioned she was showing a house or an apartment that day."

His mouth gaped open. "Is that why her body was found on the other end of Manhattan?"

"It's what I'm guessing," said Johanna sadly as she caught Mitch's defeated look. "Now, it's possible that I have an overactive imagination because I'm a mystery writer and because I twist situations to explain my murders all the time, but I feel like now I need to know if that showing she did before she died had anything to do with her death."

Mitch swiped his handkerchief across his eyes without unfolding it. "I always thought the mugging was a cover-up. It made absolutely no sense for her to have been in that park the day of our wedding rehearsal."

"I know it didn't. That's why I plan on going to talk to the people at her realty company again this afternoon. I feel like you and Mr. and Mrs. Marshall deserve to know who Felicia showed that house to the day that she died."

His face suddenly hardened. He wiped his nose and sat up straight. "Well, I'll tell you one thing. I am most certainly not going to let you go alone."

Johanna gave him a crooked grin. "I wasn't telling you all that to make you go with me. I can do that by myself. I told you because I didn't want to get to know you better and have everything we talked about be based on a lie. You needed to understand the real reason I came to your office yesterday morning."

"I appreciate that," he said quietly. "But I'm going with you. I've already spent the last six years wondering what really happened to Felicia. If there's a person out there who knows what happened to her and can give Dawn, Gene, and me the answers and the closure we need, then I'll go to the ends of the Earth to get that. Just like I know you'd do the same for James."

"I would," agreed Johanna in little more than a whisper. "When do you want to go?"

He stood up and pulled his coat off the back of his chair. "The realty company is only a few blocks from here. I don't have any meetings scheduled until this afternoon. I say we go now. That is, if you're up for it?"

"It's where I was headed when we were done with breakfast," she admitted.

He tugged his coat on and added a pair of black leather gloves. "You can finish that cheese bagel on the way. I'm not really hungry anymore, anyway. I'm sure Rocky won't mind finishing mine for me. Will you, fella?" Mitch shoved his bagel in Rocky's direction.

Rocky looked up at him with big grateful brown eyes and gave him a gruff sounding "Woof!" as if to say, *I got you, buddy.*

Mitch smiled and held a hand out for Johanna to go first. "Lead the way."

19

*J*ohanna cupped her mittened hands and peered inside Four Seasons Realty's darkened window. "I don't see anyone."

Mitch pulled back his sleeve and looked down at the white gold watch on his wrist. "It's not even eight yet. We're early."

Johanna turned and leaned her butt against the glass door while Rocky huddled against her side. Together they watched Mitch pace the sidewalk. "Well, their sign says they open at eight. You'd think someone would be here any minute."

"Wouldn't you think it's good business to open earlier than your posted times?" he said with a bit of annoyance coloring his voice.

Johanna blew out her breath and looked down at Rocky. This was all her fault. Mitch had finally packed away his feelings about Felicia's death and now she'd helped to unpack them. She felt horrible about it.

He stopped pacing then and stared at her. She felt his eyes burning a hole through her, forcing her to look up.

"What?" she asked quietly.

"Thank you," he said. His eyes were serious and his expression somber. He looked like a man who had just had his heart ripped wide open.

"Thank you?"

"For everything you've done, Johanna. You didn't have to take that dress to the dry cleaners to find out who it belonged to. You didn't have to go all the way out *to Brooklyn* just to talk to Felicia's parents. You didn't have to come and see me yesterday, and you most certainly didn't have to tell me the truth today. I know you're a self-proclaimed non-people person. I get that. I know how hard it is to put yourself out there after the kind of loss that we've endured, but you did, because you have a big heart. So for of all of that, *thank you*."

She felt her cheeks warming despite the biting cold. Her heart felt swollen and vulnerable in her chest. His blue eyes that burrowed holes in her forced her to look away.

"You're welcome," she whispered. "I just hope we get the answers you want."

"Me too," he agreed, throwing an arm over her shoulder in a side hug right in front of the realty company's front door.

Johanna sank into the scratchy warmth of Mitch's wool trench coat and let herself indulge in the familiar sandal-wood scent of his cologne as he squeezed her shoulder tightly. Aside from her father and her brother-in-law, Johanna couldn't remember the last time a man had hugged her. Even though it was only a side hug, she realized it felt good to be hugged.

Then she felt him lean his head on hers.

That was the moment it occurred to her that the hug wasn't an affectionate hug. It was only him mourning the loss of his fiancée and giving Johanna thanks for her role in helping to solve the mystery of Felicia's death. Her eyes flashed open and without moving her head, she swiveled them upward, though she couldn't see his face past the bill of her newsboy cap. She patted the arm he'd wrapped around her shoulder awkwardly. *There, there*, she thought, unsure of what to say to him.

The jingle of keys behind them and a man clearing his throat disrupted their moment. "Good morning," came a jolly man's voice.

Mitch's arm left her shoulder and the two of them swiveled around to see the realty company's managing broker, Tim Shaw, behind them. "I just need to unlock," he said, pointing at the door behind them. Then he narrowed his eyes and pointed at them both. "Oh, hey, I recognize you."

Johanna was just about to nod and say that, yes, she'd been in the other day, when he said to Mitch, "You were Felicia Marshall's fiancé."

Mitch extended a hand to him. "Yes, great memory. I'm Mitch Connelly."

Tim shook it slowly and then glanced over at Johanna. "And weren't you in the other day looking for Felicia?" He pointed at Mitch. "Are you two…"

"Together?" asked Mitch. "Oh no. No. We've only just met. It's a long story, but Johanna didn't know that Felicia had passed when she was in the other day."

"Ahh," said Tim, bobbing his head. "So, was there something I can help you with?"

"Actually, yes, we have a couple questions about Felicia. Do you have a minute?"

Tim glanced down at his watch. "I have a few minutes. I do have an appointment at eight thirty, though."

"Oh, absolutely, we'll keep it brief," Mitch promised.

"Well, then, come on in. It'll just take me a minute or

two to get the lights on and the heat and coffee going. But you can just have a seat in the lobby."

"Do you mind if he comes in?" asked Johanna, pointing at Rocky. "He'll be good."

Tim smiled at Rocky. "Oh, we don't generally allow pets in the office, but it's so cold out, I suppose we can make an exception for a friend of Felicia's."

"Rocky and I appreciate that very much."

"No problem," he hollered over his shoulder before scuttling off to get the office opened up.

Mitch led Johanna to a seat in the somewhat darkened lobby. The only light came from three long rectangular sunbeams pouring in from the windows facing the street. Seconds later, the secretary who had greeted Johanna on her first visit to the office approached. Her purse drooped from the crook of her elbow while she juggled a cup of coffee, a donut, and her keys. Mitch leapt up to open the door for the woman.

She glanced up sharply but softened when she saw who had flung the door open. "Oh, hello," she said, practically sang.

"Good morning," said Mitch. "Sorry if I scared you. Mr. Shaw is inside opening up. We were just waiting for him."

"Oh, no problem," she said, cracking her gum.

Another employee filed in seconds later. "Hey, Roz," said a tall, thin man in a dark suit. His brown hair was so thickly greased over to one side of his head that it shone in the sun as he passed by the window.

"Hey, Jimmy."

Jimmy gave Mitch and Johanna a polite nod before heading back to his office. The lights suddenly came on in the lobby, and Tim Shaw appeared again.

"Okay! Coffee's on, I can offer you a cup in a few minutes," he said, pointing at Mitch and Johanna.

"We're good," Mitch promised him. "We just had a cup."

"Alright, then, right this way," he said and pointed in the direction that Jimmy had just gone. "Good morning, Roz. Good morning, Janet," he said, nodding at the secretary and Janet Sandborn as she came in the front door.

As Johanna turned around, she thought she caught a brief glimpse of Janet's eyes narrowing as the female realtor realized who she was. But neither Johanna nor Janet said anything.

Inside Tim's office, Mitch and Johanna took a seat on the pair of chairs in front of his desk. Rocky sat down on the floor next to Johanna.

Tim dropped into his desk chair, which squeaked its complaints as it was forced to bear his weight. "So, before we get into whatever it is you two are here to discuss, Mr. Connelly, I know this is late, but I'm so sorry for your loss," said Tim. His hands were clasped together in front of him on his desk, his potbelly reaching the desk before his elbows could.

"Thank you," said Mitch quietly. "I appreciate that."

"No, really. Felicia was a wonderful gal. Everyone loved her. Our clients loved her. We were all devastated to lose her."

"Thank you."

Tim gave Mitch a tight smile. "Now, what can I help you with?" He glanced at both of them curiously.

Mitch cast a sideways glance at Johanna. She wondered if he wanted her to go first. She swallowed hard. *Time to woman up, JoJo.* "Right." She blew out a nervous breath. "Mr. Shaw…"

"Tim, please."

She gave him a nervous smile. "Tim. Something was

recently brought to my attention regarding Felicia Marshall's schedule on the day that she was killed."

He looked somewhat interested. "Okay?"

"I discovered that Felicia had a real estate showing scheduled for the day that she died."

Mitch leapt in next. "And I told Ms. Hughes that there was no way that was possible. Felicia told me she'd cleared her work schedule that day as she had so many errands to run to prepare for our wedding, and also your company never disclosed that information to the police or to the family."

Tim curled a finger around his top lip and cleared his throat as the pair stared at him. "Hmm. That's very interesting. I'll start by saying, unfortunately, that was six years ago. I can't remember *all* the things that happened around here six years ago, but I do remember Felicia taking an extended weekend off, plus the entire next week for your wedding and honeymoon. I don't remember her having a showing that day."

Johanna leaned forward. "It was a last-minute thing, from what I understand. She got a text message from a client asking to show her a very expensive property. He specifically requested her by name."

Tim shook his head and lifted his hands from his desk. "I mean, it's absolutely possible that happened. I'm just saying, she didn't report back to the office that she was showing any property."

"The police checked her personal phone records," said Mitch. "Do you know if they asked for her work phone records?"

Tim shook his head. "I honestly don't recall if they did."

"Her phone was stolen by the mugger," said Mitch. "But it would be really helpful to know if she actually got a text message from a client that day, and if so, to get that number. Is there any way to retrieve those records?"

"That was from six years ago, Mr. Connelly. I'm not sure how long our phone records go back. But I can most certainly have Roz do a little digging on that."

"I would appreciate that," said Mitch with a curt nod.

"Are you and Janet the only two who still work here who would have worked with Felicia back then?" asked Johanna.

Tim had to think about that for a second. He leaned back in his squeaky desk chair and propped up his chubby face with an equally chubby finger. "Jimmy got hired when Dean Klatworthy left. Dean was here when Felicia was here."

"I remember Felicia talking about Dean," said Mitch nodding. "Older gentleman?"

"Yeah. He left not long after Felicia was killed. I feel like it was just the four of us in the office around the time she was preparing to leave for her wedding. I remember because we literally didn't have enough agents to cover demand. It was a very busy time for us."

"Which might be why someone referred a client to her on her wedding rehearsal day," suggested Johanna.

Tim's brows lifted and he pointed at her. "Exactly!"

Mitch scratched his chin. "So, does Roz have time today to work on getting Felicia's cell phone records from that day?"

Tim nodded. "Absolutely. I'll get her on that immediately." Then his eyes narrowed. "So, can I ask what the sudden interest is in this?"

A deep V formed between Mitch's brows. "Felicia's family and I have never been convinced that we knew the whole story about what happened to her. The main question has always been, why was she over in the Meatpacking

District? All the errands she had to run were in the Midtown area, and the rehearsal and her parents' house were in Brooklyn. If we can find out if she really did show a house that day, it might tell us why she was even over there in the first place."

"And then we may have to consider whether this was truly a mugging or perhaps something else," said Johanna sadly.

Tim's eyes widened. "Oh, wow. You think it's possible that she wasn't mugged after all?"

Johanna shrugged. "Anything is possible, right?"

He nodded. "Most definitely. Well, let me get Roz started on this right now," he said, standing up.

Johanna lowered her chin. "Tim, is there any way we could speak to Janet Sandborn? She seemed to know Felicia as well as anyone else in the office. Maybe she knew about the showing."

Tim seemed to blanch. "They knew each other alright."

Mitch tipped his head sideways. "What aren't you saying, Mr. Shaw?"

Tim threw his hands up defensively. "I'm not saying anything. They knew each other. But you know how women can be sometimes."

Johanna shook her head. "No, I don't really."

Tim's face flushed then. "You know. Sometimes they don't get along with other women. I think it's a competitive thing. They knew each other, but let's just say they weren't the best of friends."

"I thought I sensed a little animosity from Janet when I spoke to her the other day," said Johanna, nodding her head.

Mitch rubbed his temples. "Felicia did mention there was a gal at her office who liked to make things difficult for her. I take it that was Janet?"

"It had to have been. Janet and Felicia were the only two women in the office at that time. Let's just say they had a healthy competition over scoring clients and listings."

"Can we talk to Janet again?" asked Johanna.

"Yes," said Tim, heading to the doorway. "Follow me."

He led them to Janet's office and knocked.

"Yes?"

He stuck his head in first. "Hey, Janet, do you have five minutes?"

"For what?"

"To speak with Felicia Marshall's former fiancé?"

"I spoke with that woman the other day," she said, clearly annoyed.

"They have some additional questions."

Johanna was sure she heard a groan, followed by an unenthusiastic, "Fine."

Tim nodded and pushed the door open, pretending like Mitch and Johanna hadn't just heard Janet's less-than-eager response. "Janet said she's got a few minutes. I'll just go see Roz about those phone records now."

20

*J*anet glanced up as Johanna, Mitch, and Rocky filed into her office. "You're back," she said, leaning back in her seat. She folded her arms across her chest and crossed her long legs.

"I am. Thank you for seeing me again." Johanna gestured towards Mitch. "Have you met Mitch Connelly? He was Felicia's fiancé."

Mitch held out a hand to Janet. "Hello, Ms. Sandborn."

She unfolded her arms and leaned forward, taking just the tip of his fingers in her hand. "Janet," she said, crossing her arms again.

"Janet," he agreed.

"No, I don't think we've ever formally met. You were in the office once, maybe twice."

Mitch gave her a tight smile. "Yes, I popped in a few times to take Felicia to lunch."

"So what's up now?" she asked, looking straight at Johanna.

"We have reason to believe that Felicia had a property showing on the day that she died."

Janet lifted a shoulder. "It's possible."

"But she wasn't scheduled to work that day," said Mitch. "She told me that."

"We get calls and texts all the time. Clients don't know it's your day off," she explained. "Clients don't call and say, 'Hey, are you busy today? Because I don't want to inconvenience you.' No. They don't do that. They want what they want when they want it, and what they want is for you to drop everything you've got going on and cater to them."

"Well, we're fairly confident that Felicia got a text that day and was asked to show a very expensive property. We heard that the commission on that property alone would have paid for her entire wedding and honeymoon. That's a pretty good chunk of change," said Johanna. She felt emboldened by Janet's flip attitude.

"Like I said, it's totally possible."

Mitch's eyes narrowed as he addressed her next. "Were you aware of any showings that Felicia had that day?"

Janet closed both eyes and shook her head. "I can't recall."

Johanna smiled at her and then stood up brazenly while Mitch and Rocky stared up at her. "Okay, that's fine. Tim's getting Felicia's phone records for the day from Roz. We'll find out exactly who texted her and ask them what they knew."

Janet's eyes snapped open and narrowed on Johanna. "Go ahead, be my guest."

"And I'm sure if the client is in any way connected to *you*, the police would like to know that, wouldn't they? Maybe we'll let them piece together if you were aware of any showings that Felicia had that day."

Janet groaned and sat forward in her chair. "Ugh, sit down."

Johanna sat trepidatiously, shocked that her scare tactic

had actually worked in a place outside of her novels, while Mitch gaped at her.

"She had a showing that day," she admitted.

Mitch turned his attention to Janet. "Well, why in the world didn't you tell the cops that? I know they asked!"

"Felicia and I didn't really get along that well." Janet shrugged. "I didn't want them to think I had anything to do with her murder."

"Why would they think that?" asked Mitch.

Janet lifted a blond brow. "Are you kidding? I watch all those crime shows. The cops are just looking for people to pin that kind of stuff on. Everyone else in the office loved Felicia. Dean and Tim both thought she hung the moon. All the clients loved her. She was taking business away from *me* —taking food out of *my* mouth. Can you see how that would look to a cop?"

"But she was *murdered*, Janet," whispered Mitch. "If you're claiming it *wasn't* you who did it, you could have at least given the cops some leads to go on. Maybe it was the client she showed the house to."

Janet sighed. "Or maybe she really was just mugged? They still haven't caught the guy who did it, did they? If I had come forward and said that she was showing a house that day, they would have discovered that the client was *my* client. And I would have had Felicia's blood on my hands just like that."

"*Your* client? Wait, what?" asked Mitch.

Janet rolled her eyes. "Yes. He was my client. And he asked for Felicia by name. At least, that's what she told me when she called me."

"She called you? That day?" demanded Mitch.

"Yes. She did. She called to *apologize*. If you can believe that. She called to say she *knew* that the property she was showing was to one of my clients, but that he'd requested her by name and she was taking the showing."

"So then what happened?" asked Johanna.

Janet's mouth twisted. "She never showed."

Mitch gasped. "She never showed?"

"That's what he said. Felicia never showed up for her appointment. After I found out that she'd been killed nearby in a mugging, we assumed she'd been on her way to the appointment when it happened."

"So the address of the property *was* near where she was killed?" asked Johanna. *I knew it!*

Janet nodded. "Yup. Just a few streets away."

"Do you have the address of the property she showed?" asked Mitch.

"It was on Bank Street," she said.

"Do you have the *exact* address?"

"Ugh," she groaned, uncrossing her legs. She turned to her computer. "I'll look."

"I can't believe this," Mitch whispered to Johanna. "You were right."

Before Johanna had a chance to respond, Janet pointed at her computer screen. "Oh, here it is. I'll write it down." She took out a sticky pad, jotted down the address, and handed it to Mitch.

"What about the client's name and number?" asked Mitch, handing the sticky note back to Janet.

"I wouldn't have his number anymore. That was six years ago."

"You can't look it up? Surely you keep records…"

"Of every client who ever looks at a house? No, we don't keep those kinds of records."

"You don't even remember his name?"

"He was some big producer or something. Lots of money. His name was Dutch."

"Dutch Erickson?" asked Mitch with his mouth open.

"Yeah, Dutch Erickson. You know him?"

"Not personally, but I mean, he's always in the news." Mitch narrowed his eyes. "You've never heard of Dutch Erickson?"

Janet lifted a brow. "Of course I've heard of Dutch Erickson. You think I live under a rock? I never said I didn't know his whole name."

Mitch leaned forward, his forearms on the desk. "Ms. Sandborn, did you have anything to do with my fiancée's death?"

She leaned forward too and shot him a cynical look. "Mr. Connelly, I might be a cutthroat real estate agent, but I'm most certainly not a cutthroat killer. I had nothing to do with Felicia's disappearance. See? This is exactly why I didn't go to the cops with what I knew. I *knew* I'd look guilty. But I didn't do it."

Mitch stood up and then helped Johanna to her feet. "Let's just hope you're telling the truth. For *your* sake."

"*N*ow what?" asked Johanna as the three of them poured back out onto the Manhattan street. Her mind was blown. She couldn't believe they'd just been delivered such a handful of information. Not only did they have the client's name and the address of the property Felicia was supposed to have shown that day, Tim and Roz had also come up with a list of phone numbers that had texted Felicia's work phone on the day that she'd died.

Mitch put an arm behind Johanna's back and ushered her and Rocky down the street. "Now we need to see Dutch Erickson."

"Like he's going to want to see us? He's a big music producer."

Mitch's jaw clenched. "He's going to want to see us. Otherwise, we'll be going to the cops with the new information we have."

"Do you think he had something to do with her death?"

"For his sake, he better not have," he growled. He pointed up ahead. "My office is just a few blocks up. Do you have a minute? We could stop in and call him."

Johanna looked down at Rocky, who was keeping up with their brisk walk between them. "If Rocky can come inside, then I've got a minute."

Mitch reached down and petted his head. "Of course Rocky can come in. So you're in?" He looked up at Johanna and gave her a warm smile.

Johanna nodded. "Yeah, I'm in."

"*Y*ou want something to warm you up?" asked Mitch while Johanna peeled off her wool coat and hat. "Coffee? Tea?"

"Coffee would be great," she said, looking up at the blonde woman in the pantsuit.

"I'll have coffee too, Darcy. And if we have any donuts, we'll take a couple of those too," said Mitch, giving her a smile.

Darcy nodded. "You got it." She pulled the door shut behind her.

"I'm starving. I let Rocky finish my breakfast," he explained as he shed his own coat and hung it on a coatrack beside his office door. From his spot on the floor, Rocky lifted his eyes when he heard his name.

"Yeah, I didn't finish mine either," admitted Johanna. "That cheese bagel was amazing, though, by the way."

Mitch gave her a toothy smile. "I told you!"

She let out a little giggle. "I know."

He stared at her softly then. "You sure have a nice smile."

"Thank you," said Johanna. She shifted on her feet and swung her arms, not sure what to do with them then. Compliments always made her feel uncomfortable. She pulled out a chair at the conference table and sat down. When Mitch wouldn't stop staring at her, she pointed at his desk. "Do you have a notebook? You know, in case we need to write down something he says?"

"Oh, great idea!" Mitch rummaged through his desk and pulled out a yellow steno pad and two sharpened pencils. He rushed back to the conference table, running a hand through his blond hair before setting the pad down on the table and dropping into the seat next to her. "What a morning we've had. Are mornings with a mystery writer always this exciting?"

Johanna couldn't help but laugh. "Always this exciting? Mornings with a mystery writer are almost *never* this exciting."

He leaned his chin on the heel of his hand. "I really don't believe you. Since I've met you, it's been one exciting event after the next."

She grinned as her memory replayed all of their encounters thus far. "Oh, I suppose it's been *interesting*."

"To say the least," he chuckled. "And I'm shocked at how much information we got today. Can you believe none of this was ever disclosed to the police? You might actually help me solve Felicia's murder."

"Yeah."

He shook his head at her with a soft smile. "Where have you been hiding yourself, Johanna Hughes?"

In my apartment, she thought, suppressing a giggle. "Buried in my work, just like you."

"Maybe we both need to start getting out more often," he said as Darcy came back in the office with two coffees and two donuts on a small tray.

She set the tray between them. "Can I get you anything else, Mitch?"

He shook his head. "Thank you, Darcy, no. But please hold all my calls. Ms. Hughes and I have an important call to place."

She nodded as she left. "Will do."

When Darcy had closed the door behind her again, he pulled his cell phone and the sticky note they'd written the number down on out of his pocket. "Are you ready?"

Johanna let out a nervous breath. She glanced over at Rocky, who had fallen asleep, and then she nodded. "Yes. I think so. You?"

"I've never been more ready to put this case to rest." He dialed the number, touched the speakerphone button, and laid the phone on the table. It rang and rang. He glanced up at her.

Felicia had been killed six years ago. They both knew it was more than likely that the number wasn't Dutch Erickson's number anymore. After all, six years ago, Dutch had been a newcomer to the music producer scene. Since then, he'd grown his business and had become a household name. There was no way he had the same phone number. But still. They let it ring.

"Hello?" said a man's voice finally.

"Dutch?" asked Mitch hopefully.

"Yeah. Who's this?"

Johanna wanted to scream. She had to press a hand against her mouth to keep from cheering.

Mitch glanced up at her, his eyes wide and hopeful. "My name is Mitch Connelly. I was wondering if I could ask you a few questions."

"How'd you get this number?" he asked gruffly.

Mitch swallowed hard and then continued. "My late fiancée got a text message from this number the day that she died."

"Is this some kind of joke?" he asked.

"No, it's not a joke. You might have been the last person to see my fiancée alive before she died."

There was a pause and then, "Who was your fiancée?"

"Felicia Marshall."

A longer pause. "Yeah. Just a second."

They could hear the sound of footsteps and then the sound of a door closing in the background.

"What did you say your name was again?"

"Mitch Connelly. Six years ago, Felicia Marshall was supposed to marry me. But before she could, she got a text message from you asking for her to show you a multimillion-dollar property."

"Six years ago. That's a long time. I think you got the wrong guy," said Dutch. His voice was deep, but unconvincing.

"I don't think so, Mr. Erickson. Someone at the realty company gave us your name, and this number was on Felicia's cell phone records from the day she died."

"Okay, so maybe I texted her to see a property that day. I don't really remember. Like I said, six years was a long time ago."

"Her death was all over the news," said Mitch. "Are you telling me you didn't see that and realize that was the real estate agent that you were working with?"

"I'm a busy guy. I don't sit around watching the *Today Show* every morning, ya know?"

"So, are you telling me that you never saw the house on Bank Street that you'd asked Felicia to show you?"

"I looked at a lot of houses back then. How am I supposed to remember if I saw that exact house?"

"Mr. Erickson, it sure would be a shame if news of this story leaked out to the press. I can't imagine a scandal of this nature being good for business," said Mitch, eying Johanna with one lifted brow.

There was a long pause on the other end of the phone and then a sigh. "She never showed me the house alright. I did text her to see it, but she never showed up."

"And we're supposed to just believe that? A few seconds ago, you claimed you didn't even know who she was," said Mitch.

"Yeah, well, I knew. I saw her name on the news. Popular Manhattan real estate agent murdered in Hudson River Park, ya know. I couldn't miss it. It was plastered all over the place. I figured that was why she didn't show up to her appointment with me."

"And you didn't think it was important to tell the cops you had an appointment set up with her?" asked Mitch, his teeth grinding together now.

"And tie my name to the murder? It woulda killed business. I couldn't do that. I was finally starting to take off. Why would I do that to myself?"

"To help solve a murder. To give her family some closure. I don't know, to be a decent human being."

"Look, I'm sorry I didn't come forward back then. I figured if someone pushed hard enough, they'd find me and then I'd clear my name. But they never did. Years went by and I just let it go."

Mitch cradled his forehead in the palm of his hand. "I'm

going to ask you one time and I want an honest answer. Did you have anything to do with Felicia's disappearance?"

Dutch's voice came through loud and clear. "Listen, man. I didn't touch a single hair on that girl's head. I swear."

"If you're lying to me—"

"I'm not lying to you."

"You'd better not be. Because if you are. I'll find you."

21

"Well, it's about time you got back," said Whitley with her face screwed up into a pout and her hands on her hips. "What took you so long?"

Johanna and Rocky went inside. Johanna stripped her winter attire off while Rocky trotted right inside to check his food bowl.

"Mitch and I ran some errands together."

"Oooh, so now it's *Mitch and I*," teased Esmerelda from a sunny spot on the floor.

"No, not like that. I told him the truth!"

"About us?" asked Whitley, her eyes shining.

"No, I decided to withhold the magic stuff. Not everyone's going to be as open-minded about it as I've been."

"Puh, I wouldn't exactly call you open-minded," said Esmerelda with a laugh.

"Well, I wouldn't exactly call you a cat, so I guess there's that," snapped Johanna.

"Touché." Esmerelda curled back up into a new ball and closed her eyes.

"So, what exactly *did* you tell him, then?" asked Whitley.

"I told him that I'd found the dress in a secondhand shop and that I followed the clues to him. I told him that was why I'd gone to see him the other day, but then when I realized who it was, I froze up and I couldn't. He completely understood."

"Oh, that's so awesome!"

"Yeah, it is. We went and saw the realtor again. We talked to Tim Shaw and Janet Sandborn and found out that Janet *knew* about Felicia's real estate showing that day. It was her client, but he asked for Felicia by name."

Whitley's eyes widened as she climbed onto the armchair next to Johanna and pulled her knees into her chest, wrapping her arms around them. She looked up excitedly. "Oh my God, do you think that *Janet* killed Felicia for stealing her client?"

Johanna shrugged. She couldn't help but consider that as a possibility. "I mean, she said she didn't, but who's gonna come right out and say, 'Yeah, I did it'?"

"Exactly! Oooh, this is *exciting*! We're finally getting somewhere!"

"Well, there's actually more to the story."

"More?"

"Rocky, can you tell Columbo and Sherlock Holmes in there to keep it down? I'm trying to sleep over here," snapped Esmerelda.

"Woof!" he barked before running over to her and giving her a big, sloppy lick right across the entire side of her body. It had happened so quickly that she hadn't even seen it coming.

Esmerelda's eyes widened and her head lifted. "Oh, you *didn't*!"

"Woof!"

"You're gonna pay for that, you slobbering piece of—"

"Can you not right now, Es? I'm trying to hear what

new information Hanna got today. Why don't you go lay down in her bedroom?"

"Not on my bed, though. You look disgusting," said Johanna with a half-smile.

"Oh, ha-ha, very funny," snapped Esmerelda, getting to her feet. With one side of her fur plastered against her body and her green eyes narrowed, she strode towards Rocky the way lions hunt their prey.

Rocky slowly backed away, lowering his head and whining.

"Essy," Johanna barked. "You leave him alone. He was just showing you how much he likes you. God knows *why* he likes you, but he does. You should feel honored, not angry."

Esmerelda stopped walking and spun around. "Oh. Yeah. I feel honored to have my fur smelling like bacon bits and looking like wet cotton."

Johanna shrugged. "What can I say? Rocky's just a touchy-feely kind of guy."

Whitley giggled. "And Esmerelda is more of the scratchy-bleedy type of girl. No wonder they don't get along."

Esmerelda stared her sister down and then strutted towards the bedroom. With her back paw, she slammed the door behind her and it hit the jamb with a thud.

"So tell me the rest," begged Whitley.

Johanna strode into the kitchen, refilled Rocky's food bowl, and then took a seat on the sofa in her living room.

"Okay. Where did I leave off?"

"Janet might have killed Felicia," said Whitley, her smile way too broad for a statement such as that.

"Right. Well, Janet gave us the address of the house that Felicia was supposed to show that day."

"She did? No way!"

"Yeah, *and* we also have the name of the person she was supposed to show it to and his number."

Whitley's jaw dropped.

"Yeah, so Mitch, Rocky, and I all walked back to Mitch's office and called the guy."

"The guy who had asked for the showing?"

"Yup."

"Did he answer?"

"Yup."

"This is amazing! *He* could be the murderer!"

"Yup. Of course he *swears* he didn't do it. But again, who's just going to come right out and be like, 'Yeah, I killed her'?"

"This is crazy. So now what do we do?"

Johanna sighed. She wasn't really sure what was next. Mitch had to get back to work because he had afternoon meetings, so she and Rocky had left, with Mitch making only a vague mention of getting together soon to discuss the case. And, of course, when he'd had to take a business call, she'd sort of snuck out because she'd felt silly standing around waiting for him to get off the phone, and it hadn't occurred to her to leave her number behind.

"I'm not sure, but you know what makes the most sense to me?"

"That we go check out the house that Felicia was supposed to show the day she was murdered?" asked Whitley, her hands clasped together.

Johanna grinned. "You read my mind!"

*T*hat's the house," said Johanna, pointing at the outside of a three-story brick townhouse on a narrow, tree-lined side-street in the West Village.

Whitley's jaw dropped. "That house is worth twenty-five million dollars?!"

Johanna smiled and waved her forward, pulling her hat on tighter over her hair. "Welcome to New York City."

"Wow."

"Yeah. Wow is right."

Whitley turned and looked back to where they had just come from. "So from here to the park where she was found was literally like just a few blocks away."

"Yup. I think it's pretty clear she was killed either right before the showing or right after it. We just need to figure that out next."

"And how are we going to do that?" asked Whitley.

Suddenly, something caught Johanna's eye. She looked at it curiously, tilting her head to the side. With her head cast upwards, she walked towards it.

"What are you looking at?" asked Whitley, following her.

Johanna pointed up to the top of the building. "Do you see that?"

Whitley's eyes swung upwards, but she wrinkled her nose. "I have no idea what I'm supposed to be seeing."

Johanna's finger poked the air harder. "There. Up there. That video camera. I think *that's* how we're going to figure out if Felicia ever did the showing!"

"But who would we ask to let us see those tapes?" asked Whitley.

A smile spread across Johanna's face. "Easy. I know a guy."

*T*he sun had barely risen the next morning when Johanna and Rocky burst through her apartment's front door.

Whitley shot off the couch. Empty Ben and Jerry's containers and an open half-eaten bag of Lays potato chips cluttered the side table. "What? Who's there?"

"Oh, sorry, it's just me and Rocky. We're back from our walk," said Johanna, putting her Styrofoam coffee cup and cheese bagel breakfast sandwich down next to her laptop.

"Your walk? You got up and got dressed and went out for a walk already? The sun's barely even up," said Whitley, grinding her fists into her eyes. Her brown hair was wild around her face, her mouth was smudged with last night's chocolate ice cream, and her sweatshirt was one from Johanna's lounge drawer.

"I know, but I wanted to get back early. I have a very important phone call to make this morning."

"Eee," squealed Whitley, pulling her legs up underneath herself. "You're going to try and get someone to help you get the surveillance camera footage, aren't you?"

Johanna pulled off her outerwear and went to the kitchen to fill up Rocky's bowl. "Yes. It's time to make a very important call." She padded, stocking footed, towards the computer. Sitting down in her desk chair, she took a sip of coffee and pulled out her phone.

Whitley pulled a blanket around her shoulders and took a seat next to Johanna. "You gonna do it right now?"

Pulling on her glasses, Johanna flipped through the contacts on her phone. "I want to catch him before he gets to work," she said as the phone began to ring.

"JoJo!" said the bouncy voice on the other end of the line. On speakerphone, the echoey sounds of wind whipping past the other end of the phone made the reception somewhat crackly.

"Hey, Kev," said Johanna with a broad smile. "You're not at work yet, are you?"

"Nope. On my way now. Did you change your mind about catching a ride with us to Uncle Jack's Christmas party?"

Johanna groaned and fell back against her seat back. "Ugh. Is that this weekend?"

He chuckled. "Yes, JoJo, Christmas is this weekend. Had you forgotten?"

"Well, it wasn't that I forgot per se. It was more that I lost track of my days. They come and go around here so fast, you know."

"Funny how that happens."

"Yeah, funny."

"Have you changed your mind about wanting to ride with us?" asked her brother-in-law with a hint of optimism coloring his voice.

"No. I haven't changed my mind. I'll get a cab or something. Don't worry about me."

"Why would you get a cab? That's just a waste of money, and I know how much you detest wasting money. You get that from your father."

Johanna tipped her head to the side as she stared at her phone. She did hate wasting money, but she hated people bugging her about her social life even *more*. She'd catch a cab or take the train. Or she wouldn't go. She was still debating her options. The latter option sounded better than the first, but of course she wouldn't tell Kevin that, because he'd only squeal to her sister.

"I just don't think there's enough room in the van for all of us. You know, with Dad and Maureen going, you, Mook, the kids, the presents, the food."

"Pretty sure we aren't bringing any food, but alright, whatever. Get yourself there on your own. If Mel asks, I tried to convince you. Oh, hey, I bet I know the real reason you want to drive yourself."

"Oh yeah?"

"Yeah, you and *Mitchell* want some quality *alone* time together. Is that it?"

"Me and Mitchell...how do you know about Mitchell?"

"You drinking too much eggnog this early in the morning, JoJo? You told us about Mitchell at Denny's the other night."

"I—" Johanna's jaw dropped. In the craziness that surrounded her sleuthing, it had *completely* slipped her mind that she'd told her family that she was dating Mitch. That was before she'd even *met* him. Well. That wasn't true. She'd *met* him, but she hadn't known it was Mitch. And how crazy. She'd actually named the guy Rocky had bowled over in the park correctly. How was *that* for fate or divine intervention? "Yeah. About that..."

Whitley knitted her brows together. Her eyes went from staring at the phone to Johanna.

"He's going with you to Uncle Jack's, JoJo. You can't change your mind now. Melissa and I were over at Denny's last night, and all he could talk about was how excited he was to meet your guy. We're all excited. He can't pull a no-show now. Denny would never let him live it down."

"And Mook would never let me live it down either, I suppose," sighed Johanna, more to herself than to Kevin.

"Exactly. So he's going, right?"

"Hey, listen, Kev. That wasn't why I called."

"Oh yeah? Why'd you call?"

"I need a favor."

"Oh, here it is. What?"

"What do you mean, *oh, here it is*?"

"Nothing. I'm just waiting for it."

"Waiting for what?"

"You need me to come snake your drain again, don't you? I told you to quit giving Rocky baths in your tub."

Her mouth hung open. "I have nowhere else to bathe him! You won't let me do it at your house."

"I'm pretty sure the city has places you can take your dog to give him a bath, JoJo. Either that or you need to put something in the drain to keep the hair from going down."

"Yeah, alright. I'll look for something to order online. But that wasn't why I called either. I need an IT favor."

"Oooh," he cooed. She could almost hear him rubbing his hands together on the other end of the phone. "Now you're speaking my language, sister. Spill."

"I need to get some surveillance video footage of a townhouse from six years ago."

"Six years ago!" he bellowed into the phone. "JoJo, most places only keep video of the last week. To some places thirty days is a long time."

"So it's not possible?" asked Johanna, disappointed.

"Well, I didn't say *that*. I do happen to be a miracle worker."

"No kidding. You made an honest woman of my sister," said Johanna with a chuckle.

"Oh man, I'm telling Mel you said that," he laughed back.

"Yeah. You better not if you want me to come to Christmas this weekend."

"Okay, okay, fine. Yeah, text me the address and the dates and times and what exactly I'm looking for, and I'll see what I can do."

"Really?"

"Yeah, really. No promises. What's it for?"

"Oh. It's a cold case I've been working on. I might use the facts of the case for a new mystery novel."

"Oooh. If I find what you're looking for, do I get credit in the book?"

"If you get me the goods, I'll totally give you credit in the book."

"My name in black and white, huh? Might be worth it."

"Then don't disappoint me, Kev. I really need this footage."

"Yeah, back at you. Don't disappoint your sister, Denny, and the kids. Lex and Henry are expecting Auntie JoJo and Rocky to make an appearance with their new uncle Mitch."

"Oh my God, Kev. If you call him that, I'm not bringing him!"

She could hear him chuckling on the other end of the phone. "Yeah, alright. We'll save that for another time. Don't let us down, JoJo. The family is counting on you to be our Christmas miracle this year."

Johanna laughed. "It's going to take a Christmas miracle for me to bring Mitch to the party. Listen, Kev. I gotta go. Don't take too long on that surveillance video, 'kay?"

"Yeah, text it over. I have some time this morning that I can give you."

"Thanks, Kev, you're the best big brother I ever had!"

"I'll take that as a compliment. Later, JoJo."

"Later, Kev."

22

*J*ohanna glanced up at the sky. "Not a single flake in sight, Rocky. No wonder I almost forgot Christmas was this weekend. How can it be Christmas without any snow?"

Rocky tugged Johanna forward along the path. *We don't have time to stare at the sky, JoJo. My squirrels are in the park. Let's go*, were his likely thoughts.

"Oh, fine," she agreed with a laugh. It had been a productive couple of days for Johanna, and she was in a good mood. For the first time in almost a week, she'd spent almost two full days behind her computer and put words on the screen. Putting words on the screen *always* made Johanna feel better and more in charge of her world. It was like it was the one place in her life that she wasn't a klutz, wasn't a social outcast, wasn't a thirty-five-year-old unmarried spinster. She was just a narrator who got to tell a story.

As the narrator, she got to tell whatever story she wanted. So what if the hero in her book had suddenly become a rugged-looking blond man in his late thirties? She'd changed his name from Benjamin to Miles, too. Miles sounded better—and was a better fit for the character anyway. She had nothing to prove to anyone. Did it matter that her heroine had gone from a blonde woman in her twenties to a thirty-two-year-old brunette? No, it didn't. Because her screen wasn't allowed to judge or make unnecessary hypotheses. It was only there to record her narration. Why the gritty mystery she'd been writing suddenly had romantic undertones and witty banter as the hero and heroine worked to solve the case together was of no importance to anyone else. It was simply the story in her head, and as the narrator, that was her prerogative alone. That was the way it went.

So when she and Rocky entered the park that evening, even though there was no snow on the ground or falling from the sky, the night felt that much more magical to Johanna. It was as if she'd gotten to live a couple vicarious romantic days with her hero, and it made her glow from within. So much so that she felt herself skipping down the path in the park without so much as a care that she'd never been very good at skipping and, if left to skip for very long, would most likely wind up tripping over her own feet and landing facedown on the path.

"Skipping!" said a voice from a bench on the side of the trail. "Isn't that a little dangerous with your proclivity for clumsiness?"

Johanna's feet ground to a halt as both she and Rocky saw Mitch sitting quietly on the bench cloaked beneath long shadows. She'd never seen Mitch this far into the park. Usually she and Rocky were nearing their way *out* of the park when they'd see him on his way home from work.

"Mitch!" she exclaimed.

Rocky let out several excited barks and bounced over to the man who had fed him blueberry bacon dog treats only a few days before.

"Hey, buddy." Mitch let Rocky jump up and give him a hug while he tousled his ears.

Johanna's heart felt like it might burst as she watched her beloved dog engaging so lovingly with Mitch Connelly.

Mitch looked up at Johanna. "Hey," he said with a crooked smile. "You left me in the lurch the other day!"

"Did I?"

He nodded. "Yes, you did. I had no way of contacting you. You didn't leave me your number *or* your address. I tried calling your agent, but she wasn't giving out either."

"You called my agent?"

"I had to! I had no way of contacting you. I still don't."

Johanna grinned and took a seat on the bench next to Mitch. "You were busy," she pointed out.

"Yes, but you've been at an advantage. You had my work number. You could have called and given me your number. How are we supposed to solve this case together if we can't get ahold of one another?"

Her eyes swung down towards the path as she nodded. "True, true. I was going to call when I got new information."

He leaned forward, forcing her to look at him. "Oh, really? You're expecting new information? See, I didn't even know that."

"I went and saw the house Felicia showed that day," she admitted.

"Without me?" His jaw hung open.

"You had to work!"

"I would have gone with you after work."

"It would have been dark by then," she said softly. "I'm glad I went when I did."

"Oh, really? Why is that?"

"Because I got an idea!"

He stood up and gestured towards the path. "You want

to walk together? You can tell me all about it on the way."
He extended his hand to her.

A slow smile spread across her face. Why the tiny action
made her slightly giddy inside, she wasn't sure. She took
his hand and allowed him to pull her to her feet. "Sure.
Come on, Rocky," she said, giving the leash a little tug.

"Woof!" he barked at the squirrel he'd been patiently
watching.

"He really likes his squirrels, doesn't he?"

"Rocky has a very big heart. He likes everything that
moves. We've been cat sitting the past week or so and he
really likes the cat. She doesn't exactly get along with him,
though."

"She's not into dogs, huh?"

"She's not into slobber," said Johanna with a chuckle. As
she laughed, she suddenly realized how easy it felt talking
to Mitch. It was like she was talking to an old friend now.

"So. What's the new idea you came up with today?"
asked Mitch, looking over at her. "It's fascinating to see the
mind of a mystery writer in action."

She giggled. "Well, I don't know about that. It's really
not that big of a deal because it might not even pan out."

"Oh? What is it?"

"I noticed that there were video cameras installed at the
front door, and it got me thinking that maybe there was
surveillance footage of that day."

Mitch stopped walking and looked at her with a slack-
jawed grin. "That's a wonderful idea! You're brilliant!"

To hide her blush, Johanna lifted the hand between them
and tucked a thick tuft of hair behind her ear. "You're
funny. I don't think that idea qualifies me for being called
brilliant."

"You're not very good at taking compliments, are you?"

"Not really," she agreed.

"So what award do you think it qualifies you for?"

She lifted her brows and looked at him. "I don't know. An observant award?"

"Ha-ha. Okay, you win the observant award, then. So, now that we know there are video cameras on the building, we contact the building owner to see if they would give us access to the records?"

Johanna made a face. "Well, not exactly. Because the people who live there now didn't live there then. Remember, Felicia was showing the property, so likely someone bought it since then. Which means we'd have to go back to the previous owners, but then it occurred to me that a house worth that much money surely goes through a big company for their surveillance, right?"

"Absolutely!"

"Yeah, my brother-in-law, Kevin, works for an IT company in Jersey. He was just telling me the other day that his company is getting slammed right now by people wanting tighter cybersecurity. Exploiting a computer system's vulnerabilities and then showing companies how to repair those weaknesses is kind of his jam right now."

"Your brother-in-law is going to break into the building's security system?"

"I didn't ask him to break into it, exactly, but I mean, if that's what he's gotta do..."

"Jo!" exclaimed Mitch.

"Jo? Since when are you calling me Jo?"

It was Mitch's turn to break eye contact then. "Oh, sorry. Is Jo not okay?"

Johanna lifted a shoulder.

"It's just that Johanna is a mouthful if I'm trying to tell you something fast. Like if I were to say, *Hey, Johanna, watch out for that car!* you'd already be smashed."

"Well, that's gruesome," she said with a giggle.

"I know, but it's true. Now, if I were to be like, *Watch out, Jo!* you'd get out of the way, right?"

She nodded somberly. "Oh, most definitely. You'd have saved my life!"

"See? Exactly what I'm saying. But you said your family calls you JoJo, and your friends call you Hanna."

"Friend. My *friend* calls me Hanna. She's the only one who calls me that."

"Right, well, I thought Jo wouldn't be stepping on anyone's toes."

She didn't know if she should tell him or not, but since she figured she was trying to stick to a lie-free diet, she opened her mouth. "James used to call me Jo sometimes. We grew up next to each other when we were kids, so he's always been like family, so he usually called me JoJo, but sometimes he shortened it to just Jo."

"Ahh," said Mitch, nodding. "Felicia used to call me Mitchell. I don't think she ever called me Mitch. Isn't that funny? Everyone else called me Mitch, but the woman I was going to marry liked to stretch my name out and make it *longer*."

Johanna giggled. "Mitchell's definitely more of a mouthful. *Hey, Mitchell, don't fall into that open manhole!*" she shouted, cupping her hands around her mouth. "It does *not* roll off the tongue."

His eyes widened as he turned to her and held a hand up by his waist. "I'd be up to here in Manhattan sludge if you said that to me!"

"Yeah, you would."

He gave her a little shoulder bump as they walked. "So can I call you Jo? Or is it too reminiscent of James calling you Jo?"

She grinned shyly. "You can call me Jo."

"So, you said your family calls you JoJo. Tell me about your family."

"Umm, well. My dad lives in Union City in the house that I grew up in."

"Ohh, so you're a Jersey girl, I should have known, I can hear it."

Johanna turned to look at him with reproach. "Hey! I've worked for many years to lose the accent. You should hear my sister! She's the stereotypical Jersey girl. Her name is Melissa, but we all call her Mook."

"Mook! Now *there's* a nickname."

"I invented it when I was one."

"Ahh," he said with a smile.

"Yeah. So there's Mook and her husband Kevin, the IT guy. They have two kids. Lexi and Henry. Umm, my mother passed away."

"Oh, I'm so sorry," he said, reaching out and giving Johanna's hand a squeeze.

She thought she could feel electric sparks through her mittens but tried to carry on normally. "It's okay, it was a while ago. Before James." She swallowed hard. "I went home last weekend. My dad wanted to have our family Christmas because next weekend is the *actual* Christmas at my uncle Jack's."

"You mean *this* weekend? Christmas is in like two days or something. You know that, right?"

Johanna grinned. Of course she knew that. Kevin had reminded her that very morning. "Duh. You'd have to be a real idiot not to know Christmas was this weekend."

He laughed.

"Anyway, I went home last weekend and we had our little family Christmas. Dad dropped a bit of a bombshell on me."

"What kind of bombshell?"

"He's got a girlfriend," sighed Johanna. She'd been trying not to think about it. Luckily, between her new book and the case she'd been working on, she hadn't had to.

"How long has your mom been gone?" asked Mitch.

Johanna looked down at her hands. He was missing the point. "When I was in college," she admitted quietly.

"I don't know how long ago college was for you, so I have no point of reference."

"Mom died almost thirteen years ago."

"We really do have a lot in common. My folks died when I was in college," said Mitch.

Johanna stopped walking and turned to face him. "Both of them?"

He nodded and pulled his lips back tightly against his teeth. "Yup."

"At the same time?"

"In an accident. They were on a vacation, in a rented car. They were having car problems and had just pulled over to the shoulder when a semi swerved off the road and hit them."

"Oh my God, Mitch! I'm so sorry." She reached out and squeezed his arm.

"Thanks," he said, giving her a smile. "That was almost seventeen years ago for me."

"Do you have any siblings?"

Mitch started walking again. "A brother. He's married. They live in Atlanta. No kids."

"Wow. We've both been through a lot of loss," she said quietly.

"How'd your mom die?"

"Cancer," said Johanna matter-of-factly. "By the time she found out, there wasn't a lot of time left, so it happened pretty fast."

"Oh man. I'm not sure which is worse. Having time to

say goodbye but watching them suffer or just having it over like that"—he snapped his fingers—"but not being able to say goodbye."

"Even though the end wasn't real great for her, I think Mom was thankful she got to say her goodbyes." They walked quietly for a few moments. Then Johanna looked over at him. "Do you go to your brother's in Atlanta for Christmas?"

He chuckled. "No, they really aren't the 'celebrate Christmas' type. He works for the airline out there and she's in HR for some big law firm. Christmas is his busy season."

"Yeah, I can imagine. So what do you do on Christmas?"

"Oh, it varies from year to year. I have an aunt and uncle who live in Staten Island. They usually invite me over. Some years I go, some years I don't. It just depends on what's going on at the office. I always treat it as just another day." He glanced over at her. "How about you? You said you're going to your uncle's?"

She lifted a shoulder. "I don't know. I'm thinking about skipping it," she admitted. Despite her new honesty policy, she had absolutely zero intention of telling Mitch about the whopper of a lie she'd told her family the last time she'd been home.

"Why?"

"My family is kind of funny."

"Aren't all families?" he asked, giving her a sly grin.

"Well, yeah, but mine are worse than most. They don't take no for an answer. They're pushy and embarrassing, and to be honest, they give me anxiety."

"So, you were telling me that your dad has a new girl-friend. Is that part of the problem?" asked Mitch.

"Oh. Some of it, I suppose. I know I sound like a spoiled little girl to be upset about my dad dating again, but this is his *first* relationship since my mom passed away."

"His first relationship in thirteen years?! I'd think you'd be happy for him by now. So he's not alone."

Johanna hung her head and gnawed on her bottom lip. Rocky glanced up at her, giving her a comforting look.

Mitch bumped her shoulder again. "Sorry. I wasn't trying to make you feel bad or anything."

"I know," she agreed. "Dad was ready to start dating again before James passed, and then when he died, Dad and I both kind of went into mourning again. Together. So it was almost like neither of us could date. You know?"

"Maybe," said Mitch with a little shrug.

"I guess it's hard to explain."

"Does your dad not want you to date?"

"Oh, no! Quite the opposite," Johanna admitted with a flourish. "They are all *pushing* me to date. They don't think it's healthy that I've been alone for so long."

"Yeah, my coworkers treat me like that too," he said with a knowing chuckle. "They don't understand that I've been perfectly content with my life the way it is. I haven't had any desire to learn how to date online or to start going to bars after work. It's just not my thing."

"Mine either!" Johanna agreed. "And my family got it in their heads that I should bring a date to Uncle Jack's for Christmas." She sighed. But she'd decided; there was no way she wanted to spend her Christmas listening to her entire family ask her why she was still single. She'd rather spend it cuddled up with Rocky and a big tub of popcorn. They could binge-watch *Dexter* on Netflix or something.

"I suppose you're vehemently opposed to taking a date to your Uncle Jack's for Christmas, huh?" said Mitch quietly.

She glanced at him from the corner of her eye. "Well, we

both just agreed we aren't much into online dating or going to bars. There just aren't a lot of dating options for introverts like us."

He shrugged. "Maybe you could find someone else who doesn't have any plans for Christmas, and they could go with you. You know just to take the pressure off. It wouldn't necessarily have to be a *date*, exactly. But just two single lonely people hanging out for Christmas... while meeting your entire family." His head nodded and a slow smile crept over his face as he said the words aloud. "Boy, that does kind of sound *datey*, doesn't it?"

Her eyes squinched as she smiled. "Yeah, it kinda does."

"So that's not something you'd be interested in?"

Johanna glanced at him again. Was he talking about *himself*? Surely he didn't want to spend his Christmas at her uncle Jack's house. But it did sound like he didn't have plans. Should she ask him? She swallowed hard.

What did she have to lose?

Her insides bubbled with anxiety.

Johanna cleared her throat.

"Mitch?"

"Yes...," he drawled with a toothy grin.

23

*J*ohanna's palms were clammy inside her mittens. She couldn't believe she was going to actually say it. *Mook would be so proud of me right now.* "Would you like to be my non-date for my uncle Jack's Christmas party this weekend?"

"Your non-date?"

"Well, you know, you said it didn't have to be a date...," she mumbled uncomfortably. Should she just have called it a date? Because he'd said...

"No, we can call it a non-date if you want." He grinned.

"Does that mean...?" Her voice trailed off as she looked up at him. "That you actually would want to go?"

"And get to spend my Christmas with the famous Hanna Hughes?" he asked. "Are you kidding? I'd be honored."

How did this man have the uncanny ability to make her blush constantly? "You're kidding!"

"Not kidding. Unless you really don't want me to go, in which case—"

"No! No! I want you to go," Johanna cut in before he

223

could finish. "I want you to go. I swear. Just be prepared. It might be a little uncomfortable. My family literally has no boundaries. No topic is off-limits in their minds. It's excruciatingly painful sometimes." She covered her face with her hands. What was she doing? He'd never want to hang out with her again after her family got done with him.

He grinned. "I'm a big boy, Jo. I think I can handle it." He reached out and took hold of her hand. "As long as you're there by my side?"

Johanna's body stiffened and her eyes froze in her head in the forward position. She didn't dare turn her head or look at him for fear that he'd let go of her hand. "Of course I'll be by your side," she promised. A nervous giggle bubbled out of her mouth. Why in the world was she giggling like a teen holding hands for the first time?

"Good," he said, seemingly oblivious to the sudden panic attack that was quickly growing from infancy to full-grown adult status inside her stomach.

And then, Johanna's phone rang. She pretended like she didn't hear it for a moment as it vibrated in her back pocket. Even though she felt awkward, she didn't want him to let go of her hand. She'd ignore it.

But Mitch heard it. He stopped walking and looked around.

And Rocky heard it. He stopped walking and barked.

Ugh.

"What's that noise?" asked Mitch.

"Oh!" sang Johanna, reaching into her back pocket and silently cursing technology. "I didn't even notice. I guess it's my phone. I'll just let it go to..." She looked down at the caller ID. *Kevin.* Suddenly the anxiety in the pit of her stomach dissipated. "It's Kevin, my brother-in-law."

"Answer it," said Mitch, pulling her towards the side of the path.

Johanna nodded and put it on speakerphone. "Hey, Kev."

"Hey, JoJo. You owe me one."

"I do?"

"Yeah, I spent most of my day working on your little case. I better get coauthor credit out of this or something."

"How about I just plug you and your IT company in the front of the book?"

"We can negotiate terms at Uncle Jack's."

"So what did you find out?"

"Well, the first thing I had to do was figure out what surveillance service was used six years ago."

"Oh, I never thought about that. Since it was likely sold during that time period, the surveillance company could have changed," said Johanna.

"Right," he agreed. "Okay, well, now the property is owned by Dutch Erickson. You've heard of him, I assume? He's a big music producer."

Johanna's jaw dropped and her eyes widened as she looked up at Mitch. His eyes were just as wide as hers. "*Dutch Erickson* owns the house on Bank Street?"

"Yeah, says here he bought it in 2011."

Johanna palmed her forehead. "I can't believe I didn't even think to look who bought it."

Mitch shook his head but remained silent. She could tell he was thinking the same thing.

"But the guy who owned it before that was Titus Matthews. Pretty unique name, so I Googled him and found out that he's an investment banker at a firm in Manhattan. I gave him a call and told him that I was moving into the area and asked him who he used for security when he lived at that address. People love giving recommendations."

"You're kidding! You just straight out asked him?"

"Yeah. And he straight out told me. He said he went through this small start-up company called Stealth Surveillance because the founder was a client of his."

"Sweet!" said Johanna, grinning from ear to ear. "Please tell me they kept records for six years?"

"Hey. I was getting to that."

Johanna spun a hand in the air. "Get there faster, Kev."

"You women, always demanding," he joked.

Mitch shot her a wink.

"Yes. They kept records all the way back to their first day of business."

"Yes," cheered Johanna. "Like I told you in the text I sent you, the house was for sale on that date. There probably wasn't a lot of action. Did you see anything?"

"Yeah. I most definitely saw action," said Kevin.

"You got the picture I sent, too? Of the realtor I was looking for?"

"Yup, I did."

"And did she show up?"

There was a pause, and then she heard Kevin's voice crackle through. "She most definitely *did* show up."

Chills shot down Johanna's arms and legs. Her head snapped up to look at Mitch. The blood drained from his face. As they stared at each other in stunned silence, Kevin's curious voice shot through on the other end. "JoJo? Is that good news? Did you want her to show up?"

Johanna winced. "I don't know if I can call it good news or not, Kev. Because either way, the woman in the picture I sent you was murdered not long after that footage was taken. But we had been told that she never showed up there. Having video surveillance showing that she was indeed there sheds new light on the case."

"Well, in that case, then I think you're definitely going to want to see the tape for yourself."

"Why's that?" asked Johanna, trying to prepare herself for whatever Kevin was about to tell her.

"Because that woman in the picture you sent me wasn't alone."

S ide by side, Johanna and Mitch trudged through the blustery cold parking lot to Kevin Donovan's Jersey City office.

After learning the night before that Johanna's brother-in-law had found images of Mitch's late fiancée on the surveillance video, he had wanted to drop everything that night and head straight for New Jersey. But Johanna had instead set up the appointment with Kevin for the next day at his office, and Mitch had volunteered to drive the two of them over there on his lunch break.

Mitch had tossed and turned that night, and he'd also gotten very little done at work that morning. He was too consumed by the snowstorm of thoughts that swirled inside his head. It was as if his brain were a snow globe that someone had shaken, and now bits and pieces of his mind were scattered everywhere. All he wanted was for everything to settle once and for all so he could move on with his life. He was starting to feel things he hadn't felt in years, but he couldn't relish the feelings because pieces of his past were now haunting him.

"I wish we'd asked him for a little more information while we had him on the phone last night," said Mitch, guiding Johanna towards the front door of the building with a leather-gloved hand on the small of her back.

"Me too," she sighed. "I didn't sleep very well last night. All I could think about was the possible scenarios that could have happened. Felicia could have met anyone there. It could have been Janet. It could have been Dutch or maybe another client."

"Or just some random off the street," said Mitch, feeling his intestines twisting. The image of someone hurting Felicia killed him inside. He had six years of anger towards her killer pent up inside him, and the minute he saw footage of someone laying a hand on her, he was scared of what he might do. He pulled the heavy door open. The bitter winter wind fought it, but the minute Mitch got it open, the wind tried to suck it off the hinge and he had to pull it shut.

"Boy, the weather is horrible today," he said, looking up into the sky.

"And still not a flake to be seen," sighed Johanna as they strode into the lobby.

"You want snow?"

"It'd be nice to have a white Christmas, wouldn't it?"

"If it could snow *on* Christmas and then melt the next day I'd be fine with it." He looked at the sign between the pair of elevators.

Johanna pointed at the words: *Cyber Solutions, Third Floor.* "Kevin's company."

He nodded and pushed the up button.

When the doors opened and they stepped inside, she crossed her arms over her chest. "We have to be prepared for the fact that maybe we won't see anything useful on the tapes."

He nodded. "I know. I thought about that last night too." As he stood with his back against the side of the elevator, his eyes finally had a moment to drink her in. In the car it would have been too obvious that he was gawking, even though all he'd wanted to do on the entire drive to New Jersey was to stare at Johanna.

She wore her wool jacket and her cute little newsboy cap

again today. Her shoulder-length brown hair poked out of her cap in all directions, thanks to the wind, but not only did the woman not seem to notice, she also didn't seem to care. Johanna Hughes wasn't like any other women he'd met before. She didn't appear consumed with looks, with clothes, with fancy jewelry. In fact, when he'd first met her, she'd been wearing the most hilarious pink dog hat with pink puffballs that draped down to her breasts and a hideous coat like he remembered girls wearing back in college. He'd yet to see her wear a single piece of jewelry or fuss with her appearance in any way. It was refreshing, to be honest. To meet a woman who valued her career, but who didn't put a heavy emphasis on *stuff*. Instead, the thing Johanna Hughes put a heavy emphasis on was her *dog*, and he found that endearing.

"Earth to Mitch," she said with a half-smile. "Come in, Mitch."

"Oh, sorry," he mumbled. "Did I disappear?"

"Yeah. Where'd you go?" she asked, tipping her head sideways and staring at him with her big, almond-shaped brown eyes.

He cleared his throat. "I was just thinking about what we're going to see on that tape," he lied. He was fairly confident that the other thing Johanna Hughes didn't put a heavy emphasis on was *dating*.

"Yeah," she said quietly.

The doors slid open and the two of them walked side by side towards the Cyber Solutions door. He wanted to reach down and take her by the hand again, as he'd done the night before in the park. But it had caused her to freeze up. That was when he'd realized just how skittish she really was about dating. Instead, he'd take it slow. A hand on the small of her back was all he'd chance for now.

He led her to the doors and opened them for her.

"Thanks," she whispered. "Kevin Donovan, please. He's expecting us," she said to the receptionist.

"JoJo?" asked the woman.

Johanna grinned and glanced back at Mitch. "Yeah."

"He just called up here to tell me you'd be here any minute. Go on back. You know where his office is, right?"

"Yeah, I know my way. Thanks."

Johanna led Mitch to her brother-in-law's corner office. She knocked.

"Come in!"

Slowly she pushed the door open. "Hey, Kev." She grinned.

The tall man behind the desk stood up and walked around his desk to give his sister-in-law a hug. "Hey, JoJo."

Mitch stepped inside the office and Kevin's eyes immediately swung up to check him out. He let go of Johanna and put a hand on his hip. "Who's this?"

Johanna's face went red, as it often did, making Mitch's heart melt. "Oh. Kevin, this is—"

"Let me guess. Is this Mitchell?"

Mitch lifted a brow as he glanced over at Johanna. She'd told her brother-in-law about him? "Yeah. Mitch Connelly." He held out a hand.

"Kevin Donovan. I'm Melissa's husband. It's nice to finally meet you."

Finally?

Johanna's face was beet red now. "Finally? Really, Kev? I mentioned this case to you *yesterday*."

"Well, yeah, but you mentioned—"

"So what did you find out?" asked Johanna, sprinting around the desk to look at his computer screen. "Is it pulled up?"

"Hey, don't touch anything," said Kevin anxiously, following her around the desk.

Johanna pulled her hands back and held them in the air. "I'm not touching."

"Why don't you two have a seat, and I'll put this on the big screen?" he said and pointed to a flat-screen TV hanging on one wall.

Mitch pulled out a chair, spun it towards the screen and gestured for Johanna to sit. When she'd sat, he pulled up a chair and sat next to her.

Kevin clicked on his keyboard. "Okay. There's not a ton to see, but I think it's definitely the woman in the picture."

As the TV on the wall fired up, Mitch and Johanna sat side by side. He sucked in a lungful of air and then reached out and covered Johanna's hand with his own. It was a split-second decision, but he needed the support. He felt her freeze momentarily, but it only took her a second or two to loosen up slightly.

Footage from the exterior surveillance video popped up. Cars passed by on the narrow street. A couple pushing a stroller with a toddler's legs poking out from beneath the visor went by. And then two teenagers with a basketball moseyed past. And then, a woman in a cream skirt, blazer, and heels came rushing up the street.

Mitch felt his heart stop. "*Felicia!*" he gasped.

24

"*I*t's definitely her?" asked Kevin, pausing the tape.

Mitch nodded, his jaw slacked. "One hundred percent. It's her." Mitch fought to keep his emotions under control. He knew Kevin thought Johanna was only doing research for a book and that he had no idea that Mitch had been *engaged* to the woman in the video.

Kevin nodded and pushed a button on his computer, and the video started playing again. Mitch couldn't take his eyes off the screen. The three of them watched as Felicia hustled up the front steps. She fiddled with the lockbox on the outside of the house, and seconds later she disappeared inside.

Mitch's heart had begun thumping wildly in his chest the minute he'd seen her. So much so that he almost felt out of breath. His fingers curled into two tight fists. "Do you have tapes of the inside of the house?"

"I found footage of the interior foyer, but not the rest of the house. I'll show it to you, but first, let's give it a minute and see what happens next."

Cars continued to whiz past, people strode up and down the block, and then a black car with darkened windows pulled up to the curb. A man stepped out of the back passenger side and approached the house. In two wide strides, he was to the top of the front steps.

"It's Dutch." Mitch's blood ran cold and he felt his jaw clench up tight.

"He lied to us," breathed Johanna. "He told us Felicia didn't show up for the showing."

Mitch's right hand unsnarled and he unconsciously ground his left fist into it. "That bastard!"

"Hold up, hold up," said Kevin, tamping the air with an open hand. "There's more."

Kevin pushed a button on the computer and the view changed from a street view to the entryway of the house. They watched Felicia greeting Dutch Erickson with a handshake. Then she extended a hand towards the rest of the house, inviting him in.

Mitch struggled to remain calm. He wanted to leap into the video and grind Dutch Erickson into the ground. Whether he'd been responsible for her death or not, he'd lied to them and he'd withheld valuable information from the police. Mitch leaned back in his seat and extended his legs while the tips of his fingers massaged his temples. He couldn't believe that everything about the mugging had likely been a lie. Had they known all these details years ago, the person who had committed Felicia's murder might have been behind bars by now!

Kevin hit the fast forward button. "They're in there for about ten minutes, and then they come back out to the entryway." He pointed at the screen as Dutch and Felicia returned to the entryway and shook hands, and then Dutch exited out the front door.

Mitch bolted upright. "He left!" As much as it sickened him to think it, he'd half-expected Dutch to kill her in the house and then take her body to the park. But they all watched as Felicia went back into the house, the lights in the foyer went out, and then Felicia reappeared in the entryway. She opened the door, went outside, and pulled it shut behind her.

Mitch stared at Kevin with his mouth hanging open. "That's it?!"

"Can we see the exterior shots now?" asked Johanna.

Kevin nodded. "Yeah, here we go." He flipped to the other camera. It began as Dutch exited the townhouse. He looked at his phone as he bounced down the stairs, opened the back door of the dark car and got inside. Seconds later, the car pulled away from the curb.

Mitch looked at Kevin. "Are you kidding? The guy just leaves?"

Kevin nodded. "Keep watching."

With their eyes glued to the screen, they watched as Felicia came down the same stairs only a minute or two later. She turned back in the direction she'd come from, and then she was gone.

"She's gone!" Mitch slid to the edge of his seat and swiveled to look at Kevin. His mouth agape. They'd driven all the way to New Jersey to see that she'd shown the house, but nothing had happened? Had she just been walking back to her car when she was mugged? Was that what had truly happened?

Kevin nodded. "I know it looks like a pretty cut-and-dried house showing, but I wasn't satisfied that that was all that happened. I Googled this woman and found out that the police said she was mugged in the Hudson River Park. It was never stated that she showed a house to Dutch Erickson only hours or minutes before her death. So, I was curious too. I rewatched the tape about ten times before I realized this…"

He rewound the footage and then played it again in slow motion. This time he pointed to the upper right corner of the screen. "Look. See that car?"

Johanna and Mitch nodded.

"I watched the tape from further back and found out that that car got there only a minute after Felicia arrived. It was there when Dutch's car pulled up." Slowly, the car inched forward. "There, see it? Once they're done with the showing and Felicia is down the block a little bit, it takes off in the direction that she went."

"You think the car was following her?" asked Johanna.

Kevin tipped his head sideways. "Well, it's a long shot, but I think it's very possible."

Mitch squinted at the screen. "How about a license plate? Were you able to get a license plate number off the car? Maybe if you blow it up?"

Kevin sighed. "No. The angle wasn't right to catch the plates, but when it goes by right here, you can see something on the door of the car." He rewound the video, played it again, then paused it. "Right there. See it?"

"It's like graphics or letters or something!" said Johanna. It was too grainy to make out what it said.

Mitch pointed at the door. "Felicia had that on the door of her car too."

"How do you know?" asked Kevin, jerking his head back in surprise.

Mitch suddenly realized what he'd done. He scrambled to fix it without revealing to Johanna's brother-in-law who he really was. "Well, Felicia was a realtor. Wouldn't you assume she had graphics on the side of her car too? I mean, that totally looks like a company logo or something."

Johanna caught his drift. Her eyes widened and she

nodded her head. "It does look like a realty logo. Especially the Four Seasons Realty logo."

Mitch shook his head. He couldn't believe it. For years he had fought to convince himself that the police were right and Felicia had been killed by a mugger. That meant he could put the issue behind him and move on with his life. And then, knowing that Felicia had gone to the showing, last night he'd convinced himself that Dutch Erickson had been her killer. Now, Dutch Erickson was long gone, and there was a Four Seasons Realty car following Felicia. He didn't know what to believe anymore.

"Can you zoom to see who's in the car?"

"I tried. The camera is at too high of an angle to see who was driving, plus it's so grainy at that distance."

Mitch let his head fall into his hands. His fingers combed through his hair. He struggled to know what to do next.

"You seem to be taking this very personally, Mitch. Did you know the girl?" asked Kevin, crooking a brow up curiously.

Johanna squeezed Mitch's hand. "He's just really invested in this story. You know… for me."

Kevin nodded. "Ah. I see. Well, Mitch. Now that I've got you here, you're planning to come spend Christmas with the family at Uncle Jack's, right?"

Mitch glanced up at Johanna. They'd only just discussed Mitch going to Christmas with her the night before. Was it odd that Johanna had already told her brother-in-law that she was bringing a date? "Umm, yeah. Jo and I talked about it last night. I volunteered to be her non-date date."

"Her non-date date?" asked Kevin, lifting a brow and glancing pointedly at Johanna.

She shifted in her seat uncomfortably. "I just don't want the family getting the wrong idea, you know?"

"But you said that—"

"Listen, Kev," interrupted Johanna. "Thanks so much for everything you did. You have no idea how helpful that video was."

Kevin nodded. "I only wish I knew if the rest of the buildings on that street had surveillance cameras. If I had all the footage, we might be able to piece together how far Felicia got or see if someone else snatched her up!"

"That would be helpful," agreed Johanna with a wide-eyed nod. She grabbed Mitch by the coat and tugged him gently. "Come on, we should probably get you back to work. I know you said you had an important meeting this afternoon."

Mitch stood up, dazed. His mind was still spinning after taking in so much new information. He held a hand out to Kevin. "Kevin, thank you so much for your help."

"Hey, no problem. It was really great to meet JoJo's guy. Finally," said Kevin, pumping Mitch's hand.

Johanna opened the office door and shoved Mitch out. "Goodbye, *Kevin*." She practically spat his name.

***

$\mathcal{A}$fter Mitch dropped Johanna off at her apartment, she raced up the stairs, taking them two at a time. Mitch had had to get back to work, but she had a brilliant idea, and she couldn't wait to get back up to her apartment.

She threw open the door to find her apartment destroyed. Shredded newspaper, pieces of unopened mail, and throw pillows littered the floor. The books that had been neatly stacked on her bookshelves had all been removed and were now strewn about in disarray. Two end tables were on their sides, and a lamp had been separated from its shade. In the kitchen, Rocky's entire box of dog food was dumped over with the lid popped off. Round dog food marbles created a walking hazard across the floor. Whitley was lying prone on the sofa sobbing, and Rocky had Esmerelda firmly ensconced in his mouth. Her fur was completely sopping wet and she had the most furious scowl on her face. Rocky glanced up at Johanna with big sad eyes.

"What in the...?"

Whitley's head sprang up when she heard Johanna's voice. "Oh, Hanna! Thank *God* you're home!"

Johanna ran into the room, and Whitley threw her skinny little arms around Johanna's shoulders. "Whit! What happened? Were we robbed?"

Whitley sniffed. "No, I just can't handle these two. They are at each other's throats *all day long*! He wants to lick on her. She wants to scratch on him. They fight like an old married couple and I can't take it anymore!" she sobbed, raking her face with her fingernails.

Johanna's jaw dropped. Was she serious? All of this had been caused by Rocky and Esmerelda's antics? "Well, you guys can just clean this whole house while I'm gone."

Whitley stopped crying and her head tipped back up. "You're going out?!" She clasped her hands together in prayer and looked up at Johanna with big sad eyes. "Oh, please take me with you! I can't stay here alone with these two. I can't!"

Johanna frowned. "You let a dog and a cat destroy my apartment, Whitley. I'm going to a lot of trouble to solve this mystery. A mystery that I didn't even ask for. You're staying here and cleaning this place up."

"B-but..."

Johanna shook her head. "No buts. Esmerelda can help."

"How am I supposed to help?" she howled. "Your

monster over here won't let me go. I've been trying for an hour to distract him, but he keeps coming back to me."

Johanna's hands sprang up into the air. "Then why didn't you just go lock yourself in my bedroom until I got home?"

"Rocky figured out how to open the door," sobbed Whitley. Her hair hadn't been touched all day. She wore the grossest sweat suit that Johanna owned, and she didn't have on a single bit of makeup. She was starting to look like Johanna looked after a week or two without leaving the apartment except to walk Rocky.

"Then you could have put Es in the hallway. She'd have found somewhere to hide until I got back."

"Have you been in your hallway? If this is the best apartment building you can afford, I think you need a new career," said Esmerelda, giving Rocky a dirty look as he sucked on her back end.

Johanna lifted a brow. "I think you could get out of that if you really wanted to. It's not like Rocky's really chewing on you or anything. He's just kind of *sucking* on your fur."

"Well, I mean, yeah, I could get away, but what's the point? He's just going to chase me again. I'm tired of running. I've been running all day."

Johanna pointed a finger at the grey cat. "You know what I think? I think you kind of enjoy the attention from Rocky. I think you *like* him playing with you. It gives you something entertaining to do."

Esmerelda turned around and swiped her claws at Rocky's nose, making him whine almost immediately. She stood up and sauntered over to Johanna. "I most certainly *do not* enjoy playing with this... this... cretin! He's disgusting. I wouldn't want him to spit on me if I were on *fire!*"

"Say what you want, but I think you're sweet on him," said Johanna with a crooked grin.

Esmerelda's green eyes widened. "Sweet on a *dog*?! You're crazier than he is!"

Johanna lifted a shoulder. "Whatever. So, do you two want to hear what I found out today?"

Whitley nodded excitedly and perched herself on the arm of the sofa. "Are you kidding? That's what I've been waiting for!"

"Well, here's the deal. I found out that Felicia *did* make it to the property showing on the day that she died, and she even showed it to Dutch Erickson."

"They both showed up? But didn't he say—"

"He lied," interrupted Johanna. "But, shockingly, he got in his car and drove away after."

"So it wasn't him?"

Johanna shrugged. "It doesn't look like it. *However*, there was a car that followed Felicia down the street after she left the house. No one knows for sure if the car was following her or just going in the same direction at the same time, but I'm going to run down there and do a little snooping around."

"Run down where?"

"Back down to Bank Street."

Whitley stood up excitedly and swiped a hand across her nose. "Oh, take me with you! I wanna go!"

Johanna grimaced. "Whit, I hate to tell you this, but you look pretty gross."

Whitley looked down at herself and then back up Johanna slowly. "So? No one can see me anyway."

"I know, but you'll feel better if you look better. Maybe you should just go take a shower or something," suggested Johanna.

Esmerelda leapt up onto the back of the sofa and then into Johanna's arms, where she put a paw up to feel Johanna's forehead. "Do you have a fever? What have you done with our old roommate?"

Johanna brushed Esmerelda's paw off her head and tossed the sticky cat down onto the floor. "What do you mean?"

"Literally a week ago when we showed up, you looked exactly like Whit does right now." She glanced over at her sister, who sniffled again. "Worse, actually. You hadn't washed your hair in weeks. You were wearing dirty clothes. No makeup. You were like a recluse and hadn't left your apartment in weeks. You were scared to talk to anyone. Now look at you. You're running around town, solving mysteries, following up on clues. Your hair is clean and styled. You're wearing actual *pants*. You have lipstick on and eyeliner. You sort of look like a real person."

Whitley's brows furrowed as she scowled at her sister. "Are you trying to say that *I* don't look like a real person?"

Esmerelda sighed. "You're a mess, Whit. I'm embarrassed to be in the same apartment as you."

"As if you can talk? You smell like garbage and your fur has little bits of dog food stuck in it."

Esmerelda lowered her ears and pointed a paw at the dog. "That's because of *him*! It's *his* fault I stink."

Johanna buttoned her coat back on and then pointed at her two roommates. "Here's the deal. This apartment better be spic and span by the time I get back from the West Village. If it's not, you can both find someone else in the building to bunk with tonight."

"Uh!" whined Whitley. "That's not fair! I didn't make the mess."

"You allowed *them* to make the mess. That makes you complicit."

"But I wanna go follow up on clues with you!" begged Whitley. She groaned. "Ugh, if I had my magic wand it would only take me a minute to clean this mess up. Can't you wait for me?"

"Nope. I can't. I'll be back soon. Have this place spotless!" Johanna shot them all warning looks before going back into the hallway and slamming the door shut behind her.

25

*J*ohanna flipped up the collar of her wool coat as she walked down the familiar tree-lined street. She'd been in this very neighborhood just a few short days ago, but today something was different. Today she couldn't stop a chill from zipping across her arms and legs and pebbling her skin. Johanna was sure it wasn't the December air making the tiny hairs on her body stand on end. Instead, it was the realization that Johanna was walking the very same path that Felicia Marshall had walked on the day she had been murdered.

Thanks to Kevin's help, Johanna felt closer than ever to the truth. Felicia had been alive when she'd left the house on Bank Street, and Dutch Erickson had driven away in his fancy black car. But surveillance video showed a strange car. Had it followed her? Or had that only been a coincidence? And if it *had* been following her, whose was it? The signage on the car almost looked like it could have been a Four Seasons Realty graphic, but that wasn't enough information to go on. Johanna and Mitch needed more.

With her newsboy cap pulled low over her eyes,

Johanna had to lean her head back on her neck to see the tops of each of the buildings on Bank Street. She was determined to find any other addresses that had surveillance cameras facing the street. Those that did, she photographed, jotting down their address and noting any signs that proclaimed their security system provider. It was her hope that perhaps she could get Kevin more places to check. Maybe they could put together a video timeline of Felicia's walk back to her car. Then they'd know what had really happened all those years ago.

Spying a camera installed beneath the soffits of a two-story walk-up, Johanna stopped, took a photo, and then put notes into her phone. "ADT," she murmured to herself as she typed. She shoved the phone back into her pocket and continued on her path towards Dutch Erickson's house. As she walked, she noticed a black car with completely tinted windows pull up to the curb just up the street. Curious, Johanna stopped walking and trained her eyes on the car. *It couldn't be?!*

The door swung open and a pair of black dress shoes emerged, followed by a pair of legs in black suit pants. Johanna's heart beat wildly in her chest. When the rest of the body emerged, she sucked in her breath. *It was Dutch Erickson!* Her jaw hung open.

Instinctively, Johanna hid herself behind a small tree, which did little to hide her body but made her feel somewhat invisible. She peered around the tree and watched as Dutch bounded up the stairs to his house, as he'd done in the surveillance video, and then disappeared inside. She glanced over at the car. Exhaust gas spilled from the muffler. It was still running. He wasn't going to be in there for long. She'd have to hurry.

Johanna skirted around the skinny tree and practically ran up the uneven sidewalk, careful not to stumble over the squares uprooted by tree growth and the expansion and contraction of water and ice over the years. She felt like the Pink Panther as she snuck along the street, hoping the driver of the black car wouldn't notice her as she tiptoed up the front steps to Dutch's house.

With her pulse beating a deafeningly steady rhythm in her ears, she sucked up her breath and knocked on the door before she could chicken out. Johanna held her breath until the door opened.

"Yes?" It was Dutch. He'd actually answered his *own* door. Did famous people actually answer their *own* doors? Johanna had assumed they had people for that—and people to hold their umbrellas in the rain, and people to run to the corner and get them a coffee and a bagel in the mornings.

So surprised that *he* had answered, Johanna blew out the breath she'd been holding. It emerged from her lips with an enormous *puh* sound.

Dutch blinked back at her, wiped a bit of spittle from his face, and then furrowed his brows.

"Oh, I'm sorry," gushed Johanna, now suddenly more embarrassed than afraid.

She felt her pockets for a tissue and found a wadded-up used one in her pocket. She reached it out to him in an offer of apology.

"No, thank you," he said stiffly. "Is there something I can help you with? I'm just home for a moment…"

"Oh, yes, Mr. Erickson, I do need a moment of your time. I just have a few questions."

At the sound of his name, he began to close the door. "I'm sorry, I'm afraid, I don't speak to reporters at my home. Call my office."

Johanna's mind blanked as her hand shot out to stop the door from closing.

Dutch let out an annoyed sigh. "Ma'am, I asked you politely to call my office for an interview. Please don't make me call the police."

"I'm not a reporter, and I'm not here for an interview, but you're welcome to call the police. And then you can explain to *them* why you neglected to report your meeting with Felicia Marshall on the day that she was killed, and maybe explain why her body was found only blocks away from your house." The second the words escaped her lips, Johanna's eyes widened. Where had *that* come from?!

Dutch stared at her with keen interest then. "Who are you?"

"I'm someone seeking justice for Felicia." Johanna had to stick her hands in her pockets so he wouldn't see them trembling with fear. Her stomach turned even as she spoke the strong words, making her want to vomit in the leafless bush next to his front step.

"Yes," he agreed, raising a single brow. "I gathered that." He poked his head out the door, scanned the sidewalk in both directions and then stepped back into his house, allowing her entry. "Come in. Hurry up before some paparazzi see you coming in here and assume I'm having an affair."

Johanna suddenly realized she'd been unprepared for this offer. Go *into* his house? Just because his black car had driven away from the curb the day that Felicia had died didn't mean that he was cleared of her murder in her eyes. He could have circled back and picked her up. There was no way to know what had *really* happened and now she was being invited into the lion's den! Oh! Why hadn't she brought Rocky with her after all?

"I—I ..." Her mouth gaped open as she stuttered.

He stared back at her with pursed lips. "Do you want to discuss Felicia Marshall, or don't you?"

Johanna nodded curtly and then took a step inside. She'd have to deal with the consequences of her actions later. She only prayed that there wouldn't be consequences. "Lots of people know I'm here," she told him.

He spun on his heel and motioned for her to follow him. "I'm not going to kill you. I didn't kill Felicia Marshall either," he added, leading her down a posh hallway of all-white decor, rugs, and furniture set against dark wood floors and trim. He brought her into the kitchen and pointed at the bar. "Have a seat. Would you like a water?"

She shook her head so rapidly she was sure her brain had been scrambled in the process. "N-no. Thank you." Would a killer offer her water? She wasn't sure.

He turned anyway and grabbed himself a bottle of water, cracked it open, and took a sip. He leaned back against his long granite counter and stared at her. "Okay. Who are you?"

"My name is Johanna Hughes."

"You were a friend of Felicia's?"

"I'm a friend of Mitch's," she said. "I never met Felicia."

"Who's Mitch?"

"He was her fiancé."

"Oh, right. The guy who called me the other day?"

Johanna nodded.

A smile covered Dutch's face then. "Ahh. I get it. You're dating him. He can't let go of her. So you're trying to solve her murder so he can fall in love with you." His eyes swung up towards the ceiling. Then he grabbed his cell phone. "That would make an amazing song, wouldn't it?"

Johanna's mouth hung open, "I—uh…"

"Gimme a sec. I gotta write this down before I lose it."

Johanna watched as he typed with his thumbs. "I-I'm not *dating* Mitch," she said nervously. She looked down at her hands. "Well, I mean, we've had breakfast together, b-but that wasn't a date. That was just, I don't know...breakfast, I guess."

Dutch furrowed his brows. "You had breakfast together?"

She nodded.

"He invited?"

She nodded again.

"He paid?"

A tiny smile crooked the side of her lips. She nodded a third time.

"Yeah. That was a date. Maybe you haven't slept together yet, but that doesn't mean you aren't dating the guy. Okay, so I think I got this figured out now. Continue."

Flustered, Johanna ground a mitten into her scalp and tried to think of what to say next. What did they need to know? "We found out Felicia showed you the house," she finally said. "You lied. You told Mitch she didn't show up for her appointment. And you certainly didn't tell him that you bought this house."

He screwed the cap back on his water bottle and set it on the counter. He rocked his head on his shoulders, cracking his neck. "Alright. You got me. I lied. But I *swear* I didn't kill that girl." He pointed at her. "See? This is *exactly* why I didn't go to the cops, and why I lied to your boyfriend—"

"He's *not* my boyfriend..." she cut in.

Dutch's mouth snapped shut and he glared at her. "Oh my God, are we in the seventh grade? Big deal if he's your boyfriend or he isn't your boyfriend. Do you want to know what happened between me and Felicia or don't you?"

Johanna sucked her lips in between her teeth and nodded.

"Alright. So, I texted her earlier that day and asked her to show me the house. She texted back and said alright. We set up a time. I showed up a few minutes late. She was already in the house. I had a meeting to get to, so we looked at the house rather fast, but I knew I liked it. I told her I was interested in putting in an offer. She said great, she'd get the paperwork all worked out. I had to go, so I left. That was it." He lifted a shoulder. "She stayed behind to lock up, and I drove away. The next time I'm seeing her face is on the news a couple days later."

Johanna had been studying his face as he talked. She felt sure that he was telling the truth. It helped that the information he provided seemed to match up to the video surveillance footage. "You didn't come back after you left the house?"

He held up his flattened palms on either side of his face. "No. I went straight back to the office. I had a meeting that day and didn't have time to hang around. She was going to send the contracts to my assistant."

Johanna leaned back in her seat. "But she probably never did that because she was killed before she could."

Dutch nodded. "Exactly."

"So how'd you buy the house, then?"

"Well, I actually knew another realtor in Felicia's office that I'd worked with before. She gave *me* a call a few days after Felicia's body had been found and asked how the showing had gone and if I was interested in putting in an offer or seeing any other properties."

"Janet Sandborn?" asked Johanna.

He nodded. "Yeah. Janet's mother and my mother go way back. I'd used Janet on another property deal a few years before that, so when I found this property online and I wanted to see it, I called her realty company again, but she was out of the office. They gave me Felicia's name and number."

"So you ended up buying the property through Janet?"

"Yeah. I mean, she followed up. What was I supposed to do? Not buy it because the realtor who showed it to me was mugged and killed?"

Johanna's brow lifted. "Did you see anyone outside the house when you left that day?"

"What do you mean?"

She debated showing her hand but then realized that it might be the only way she found out the truth. She'd have to give a little to get a little. "We actually found out that Felicia had indeed shown you the property because we were given access to the security video. We saw you and Felicia entering the house on the day she was killed."

He nodded and gave a half-smile. "Ahh. Clever."

"The footage showed a car following Felicia when she walked away. It almost looked like it was a business car, it had the graphics on the side. Like for a realty company."

"Oh-kay?" He furrowed his brows. "I don't get it."

"Did you see a realty car out front when you left the showing?"

"I guess I didn't really notice a car being outside when I left. I saw a realty car parked outside when I got there." He shrugged. "I only remember because that's how I knew she was there already."

Johanna leaned forward, resting her hands on the counter. "You saw a Four Seasons Realty car out front on the day Felicia was killed?!"

"Well, yeah. Was that not her car?" he asked.

"Video footage shows her walking in from the other direction. The car pulled in after she'd already gone inside, but we couldn't see who was driving it."

He shook his head. "I guess I didn't look inside the car. Or if I did, I don't remember seeing anyone." He looked at Johanna firmly. "Does that mean you believe that I'm innocent?"

Johanna shrugged, honestly, she didn't know. It didn't *look* like he had done it, but she couldn't be sure. It was beginning to look like Janet Sandborn had a lot to gain by killing Felicia Marshall. "Mr. Erickson, how much did you end up paying for this place, if you don't mind me asking?"

"I don't know. It was around twenty-five mil. I think Janet might have negotiated the seller down around twenty-three. I'd have to go back and look. I've got deals going in every direction, it's hard to remember those tiny details."

Tiny details! Oh, just two mil difference, she thought, choking back a sputter. "Do you know what Janet's commission was?"

"I have no idea, Ms. Hughes. I believe six percent is standard, split between the listing agent and the buyer's agent, but the seller might have negotiated that down. Plus, I'm sure Four Seasons Realty took a cut. Still, I imagine Ms. Sandborn made a tidy sum out of the deal."

Johanna nodded. That was exactly what she had been thinking. "Thank you, Mr. Erickson. I appreciate you speaking with me today." She hopped off her stool. "I'll see myself out."

"Hey," he shouted after she'd taken several steps towards the home's grand foyer. "He wouldn't have taken you to breakfast if he wasn't interested in dating you."

Johanna grinned. "Thanks, Dutch."

utch Erickson's parting words that Mitch wouldn't have asked Johanna to breakfast if he wasn't interested in dating her replayed on a loop through Johanna's mind the next morning as Whitley carefully painted makeup on her face in the bathroom.

"Hello? Hanna? Did you hear me?" Whitley asked, only inches from her face.

Johanna blinked and promptly caught a mascara wand in her eyeball. "OH!" Her eye immediately snapped shut. She backed up, holding her eye. Behind her, Rocky acted as a bathroom doorstop, causing her to fall backwards over the top of him. She landed with a thud on the floor outside the bathroom.

With one eye pinched shut, Johanna looked up at him. "Thanks, Rock," she whined.

"Woof!" Looking down at her with his big brown loving eyes, he gave her a lick on the cheek.

She gave him a good pat and then climbed to her feet to stare at her one-eyed reflection in the mirror. "Oh great,

Whit. Now I'm going to have to wear an eye-patch to Christmas at my uncle Jack's."

"Sorry," said Whitley, flipping one of her long brown braids over her shoulder. "I was talking to you, but you weren't saying anything."

"She was in la-la land thinking about her boyfriend," snapped Esmerelda from the floor. She had a red-and-green ribbon tied around her neck that jingled as she walked. She pawed at the musical collar and looked up at her sister. "Is this really necessary? I look stupid."

"No, you don't. You look like a festive holiday cat. They're gonna love you," Whitley assured her.

Johanna sighed as she forced her winky, watery eye open while staring at her reflection in the mirror. She blotted at it with a piece of toilet paper and shrugged. "Feel free to take the ribbon off. I told you. You don't have to go."

"But I can't stay here on Christmas Day. This has got to be the most boring place on Earth, and it's a *holiday*!"

Johanna glanced over at her. "Then you'll wear the ribbon. The ribbon tells my family you're a polite, well-behaved cat that wouldn't possibly topple over another Christmas tree."

Esmerelda pointed a paw at Rocky. "You're not making him wear a stupid bow."

"He's a boy," said Johanna, as if that answered everything.

"So. It was his fault the Christmas tree fell over last time, not mine."

"You climbed up it!"

"He chased me! He didn't have to chase me! I was only trying to get away from him!"

Johanna grimaced. The thought of there being a reenactment of the last family gathering worried her, but it was

Christmas, and she felt bad leaving Whitley and Esmerelda home alone. Rocky was going with her no matter what. They hadn't spent a Christmas apart since she'd gotten him, and she wasn't about to start now.

"Besides, Rocky's wearing an elf hat. I just won't put it on him until we're almost there."

"What time is Mitch picking us up, anyway?" asked Whitley, grabbing Johanna by the shoulders to turn her back around so she could finish applying her makeup.

"Any minute. And do me a favor, Whit. I know it'll be a boring ride to Jersey, but please don't talk in the car. I know Mitch can't hear or see you or anything, but I can, and sometimes I forget and respond. I don't want him to think I'm crazy."

Whitley sighed. "But it's so *boring* keeping quiet."

Johanna crossed her arms.

"Oh, fine," she finally pouted. "If Essy can keep quiet for the ride over, I'm sure I can too."

Esmerelda blinked up at Rocky as he stared down at her licking his chops. "All I'm saying is, *he* better keep his paws off me, or so help me, your boyfriend is going to hear exactly what's on my mind."

Johanna knew the only reason Rocky was being good was because she was keeping an eye on him. "Yeah, Rocky'll be good. I'll keep an eye on him today, I promise."

"There!" said Whitley, putting down the eyeshadow palette from Johanna's small makeup bag. "All done. You look great!"

Johanna stared at herself in her small bathroom mirror. She almost didn't recognize herself without the dark circles under her eyes or the faint wrinkle sketches around her mouth. Whitley had spent the morning applying makeup to Johanna's face, and yet, somehow, Johanna didn't look like she was wearing any makeup. She only looked better, younger, brighter, and fresher. It was like a new Johanna.

A slow smile covered her face as she patted the soft waves in her brown hair. She'd always seen wavy hairstyles on celebrities and wondered how they'd done it. But as far as Johanna was aware, her hair had only two options—Shirley Temple's curls or straight like Cher. There had never been any middle ground when she'd tried to fix her own hair.

"I'm shocked to say this, Whit, but I look really good."

Curled up in a ball on the carpeted toilet lid, Esmerelda agreed dryly, "You couldn't possibly be more shocked than I am."

Whitley frowned. "Es. It's Christmas. Can't you be nice for one day of the year?"

"Nope. I'm afraid you got all the nice genes in our mother's womb, dear sister."

Johanna spun sideways and assessed her outfit. Whitley had taken the liberty of putting together an outfit from the random pieces in Johanna's closet. She'd actually found a black suede skirt in the mess, along with black leggings and a pair of calf-high black boots. "And thank you for getting my dry cleaning done for me. My sister's gonna flip when she sees me in a skirt and tights."

Whitley grinned. "No problem. The place around the corner has a pickup service. I just left the stuff in the hall and they dropped it back off. Easy-peasy." She winced then. "Just don't be mad when you get your credit card statement. I gave them a hefty tip for pre-Christmas delivery."

Johanna smoothed her hand down the front of her red V-neck sweater. At one time, it had been her favorite sweater, until she'd accidentally spilled a bowl of ramen noodles on it during a particularly busy writing marathon. Thanks to the cleaners and Whitley, it was now fluffy again. "Shockingly, Whit, it was worth every penny."

Whitley giggled. "Well, thanks for letting me wear your green blouse. I realize no one can see me in it, but it feels good to get all dressed up again. It's been so long since I got to get dressed up for an event."

Esmerelda's head snapped up and she hissed at her sister. "Don't even say it."

Whitley's brows lowered and she frowned. "I wasn't gonna say it."

"Say what?" asked Johanna, her head ping-ponging back and forth between the sisters.

"Whitley Snow. If you dare…"

"It's just that…" Whitley eyeballed her sister carefully. "Oh, why can't I tell Hanna?"

"Because I don't want to be reminded about that night!"

Johanna was confused. "What night?"

Whitley looked down at her hands. "The night I got put in the globe and Essy got put in Sophie."

"Sophie? Who's Sophie?"

"Duh. The cat?" snapped Esmerelda.

"The cat? Wait. Your name isn't really Esmerelda?"

"Yes, my name is Esmerelda!"

"But you just said it's Sophie. I'm confused."

"*My* name is Esmerelda. The *cat's* name was Sophie. I got zapped into the cat."

"By who?"

"Did you not hear me say I didn't want to talk about this?!"

"Sorry, Es," whispered Whitley. "It's just that it doesn't even really feel like Christmas without Dad around. Don't you ever think about him? We never talk about him or what happened, and it makes me sad. It's hard to believe it's already been a year!"

"This happened last Christmas?" asked Johanna, trying to pick up the bits and pieces Whitley had shared.

"On the Winter Solstice, actually," admitted Whitley. "It's a long story."

"Of course I miss Dad too," said Essy, her voice softening. "I miss lots of things. I miss my room. I miss all the fun I used to have and all the boys I used to date. I miss taking real showers and eating real food."

"Where's your dad live?"

"Everland Cove," said Whitley as she wiped away a tear. "*If* he even still lives there. It's just him now."

"And you guys can't go back to him until the mysteries of all those dresses are solved?"

Whitley nodded her head sadly as her bottom lip quivered. "Yeah."

Johanna gave Whitley a hug then. "Don't worry. We're getting so close to solving the first mystery. After this, it'll all be a breeze!"

Whitley squeezed her. "Thanks, Hanna. And thanks for letting us spend Christmas with you and your family." Whitley shot a glance over at her sister, who was watching them with a faraway look on her face.

Esmerelda sighed. "Yeah, thanks for letting us spend Christmas with you and the mutt," she agreed gruffly.

Johanna knew they'd been through a lot. She walked over to her and gave her a little scratch behind the ears. "You're welcome."

Suddenly, Rocky was at the front door, barking like crazy.

Johanna froze. "It's gotta be Mitch." Her eyes flipped nervously towards Whitley. "How do I look?" she asked, feeling her heart suddenly pounding faster.

"You look amazing. Gorg!"

There was a knock at the door.

She blew out the breath she'd been holding. "Thanks," she whispered. She gave a little nod and then raced into the kitchen to grab Rocky's elf hat from its hiding spot. She walked to the door and opened it with a flourish. "Merry Christmas!" she said to the handsome man on the other side of the door.

He'd answered the door with a smile, but when he saw Johanna, his smile widened even more. "Merry Christmas, Jo!" he said, marveling at her. "Wow. You look ... radiant."

Johanna felt her cheeks heating up. "Thanks. You look great too."

Mesmerized, he crooked an arm out towards her. "Are you ready? I have a surprise for you."

"A surprise? For me?" she asked, looking him up and down and wondering where it was.

He nodded. "You're gonna love it!"

Johanna couldn't remember the last time she'd been surprised by anyone in a good way. The last time she'd been truly surprised was when she'd discovered her father had a girlfriend. That hadn't been a surprise that she relished.

"I can't wait," she said with a grin. She looked back at her apartment. "Oh. Rocky and Essy are coming with us," she said. She'd mentioned to Mitch when he'd volunteered to drive them to her uncle Jack's that Rocky was coming, but she hadn't mentioned Esmerelda's need for a ride as well. She hoped he didn't mind.

He crooked his head to the side. "Who's Essy?"

Johanna ran into her bathroom and hefted the furry grey cat into her arms. The little bell around her neck tinkled delicately. "Be good," she whispered under her breath into the cat's ear. Esmerelda hissed at her in reply but allowed her to carry her to Mitch.

"Here she is," she sang. "This is the cat that Rocky and I

are pet sitting right now. Her name is Esmerelda, but we call her Essy."

"We?" asked Mitch with a bit of a devilish smirk.

Johanna's eyes widened as she realized her faux-pas. "Rocky and I." She laughed. "Essy's a bit on the grumpy side, but I feel like her bow makes her look that much more festive for Christmas, you know?"

Mitch grinned. "I've never heard of anyone taking their cat to a Christmas party before."

Johanna nodded slowly. "Oh, I know it sounds a little odd, but I can't leave her here all alone on Christmas. Do you mind?"

Mitch threw up both hands. "No, of course not. I don't mind if your uncle Jack doesn't mind."

She giggled. She hadn't asked her uncle Jack. She swatted the air. "Oh, Uncle Jack won't mind. He's a great guy. You'll like him."

"I'm sure I will. You want me to carry the cat for you?" He held out his hands.

Johanna squatted down, scooped a festive gift bag from the floor and plopped it in his arms instead. "You better carry that instead. I'll carry Essy, she's not the friendliest cat."

"Sounds like a good idea."

"Can you handle Rocky's leash too?" She offered up the leash as Rocky panted at Mitch's feet, his tail swatting the floor exuberantly.

Mitch gave Rocky a loving rub. "Absolutely."

With the door hanging open, Whitley snuck out first, followed by Mitch, who led Rocky out into the hall. With Esmerelda slung over one shoulder, Johanna locked up her apartment, and then Mitch led the group down the stairs to the little lobby on the ground floor.

"Okay now," he said, stopping before she was off the

stairs. "Close your eyes!"

"Close my eyes? Why?" Johanna felt that the vision of her tumbling down the last step and shredding the knees of her tights was far too much of a possibility to consider closing her eyes and walking at the same time.

"Don't you want your surprise?"

Johanna frowned. "My surprise is *here*? *Now*?"

"Yeah, it's outside. Are you ready? Close your eyes!"

Though thoroughly uncomfortable with the idea, Johanna closed her eyes and held out her crooked arm. "You'll have to take my arm."

"Of course," he said with a chuckle. He took hold of her and led her and Esmerelda to the door. He threw it open and led her out to the street, where the blustery cold winter air bit at her cheeks.

"Alright. You can open them," he said excitedly.

Before she'd even opened her eyes, Johanna knew what her surprise was. She could feel it dropping on her nose and blowing delicately across her face. "It's snowing!" she gushed. "On Christmas!"

"It *is* snowing on Christmas. I ordered it just for you," he said with a twinkle in his blue eyes.

"Oh, did you? How sweet of you," she giggled. "Oh, it's so beautiful! It must have just started. I took Rocky out for a walk an hour ago and there wasn't a single flake in sight!"

"It did. It just started on the way over here. I knew you'd be excited."

"I am! Very excited."

Mitch opened the back door so Johanna could slip Esmerelda into the car. She ushered Rocky inside next and then stood in front of the door an extra moment longer, pretending to be enthralled with the snow when she was really allowing Whitley time to scoot in next to Rocky. As Mitch opened the front door for Johanna to get in, he didn't notice Whitley lifting Esmerelda over her lap to separate the two animals from each other and he also didn't notice his seat belt being fastened around Whitley's slim hips.

"Thank you," she whispered, slightly giddy from the romantic nature of it all. Snow on Christmas. A handsome man opening her door for her and playing her boyfriend for a Christmas party with her family. The talking cat and the invisible girl from the snow globe. Johanna suddenly realized she felt like she was in one of those Hallmark Christmas movies she loved so much.

Mitch hurried around the car and got inside next to her. "Oooh," he breathed, shaking off the cold. "It's really cold out. And the snow makes it feel like Christmas, that's for sure."

"I told you!" agreed Johanna with a smile. Her heart felt light and giddy.

Mitch shifted the car into gear, checked his mirrors, and pulled away from the curb. Johanna exalted in the feeling of being whisked away by her handsome driver. She truly felt like she was on a date. Even though they had agreed that it was a non-date, for the moment she was pretending that it was a real date. She looked out the window and watched the cars zip past as Mitch expertly dodged traffic and wound his way out of the city. The snow came down sideways across the blurry grey New York City skyline.

"You know where you're going, right?"

He turned and grinned at her. "I put the address in my GPS, no problem."

"So, you're ready for this?" she asked nervously. The idea of her nutty family interrogating the poor man made her stomach do flips.

"Ready? To meet your family? Why wouldn't I be?"

She leaned her head back against the charcoal-colored headrest and averted her eyes. "James is the only man I've ever brought home. And that was easy. He grew up next door, so everyone already knew him. This is going to be weird for them, and me. But especially for you."

"You think?"

Johanna nodded. "Trust me. My family is going to act like we've been dating forever," she warned, hoping like hell they'd not let on that she'd sort of made up their relationship before she'd officially met Mitch.

"Yeah, your brother-in-law Kevin seemed to let on to that yesterday."

"See? That's exactly what I'm talking about. So just ignore any crazy talk that comes out of their mouths. Please?"

"Ignore crazy talk, got it."

"Thank you," said Johanna.

"Why don't you tell me who I'm going to meet so I'm prepared?"

"Well, I don't know who all will be there, but you'll definitely see Kevin again. And my sister Mook."

Mitch crooked a brow. "Should I actually call her Mook?"

"Yes. You must." Johanna giggled. The thought of Mitch calling her sister Mook made her tremendously giddy inside for some odd reason. "And they have two kids, Lex Luthor and Henry the Eighth."

"Must I call them by their given names as well?"

Johanna laughed. Her hand shot out merrily, covering his, which rested on the automatic gear shifter in the center console. "Oh, you'd crack them up if you did! Or you can just call them Lexi and Henry." When her laughter had settled, she suddenly became blisteringly aware of the fact that her hand was now resting on his. She froze. How had that gotten there? Should she snatch it away? Would that be weird? Should she leave it there?

Did he like it? Did he hate it? Johanna didn't know what to do.

Mitch seemed to sense her ambivalence. Without him making a big production of it, his hand twisted around to take hold of hers. "I'll meet your dad, right?"

Her body heated up as she realized that he *wanted* to hold her hand. "Umm, yeah," she said stiffly.

"You might have already told me, but what's your father's name?"

"Dennis Hughes. Everyone calls him Denny," she said, relaxing slightly as she pictured her father's face.

"And what does he do?"

"He's a delivery driver for UPS."

"How long has he done that?"

"Almost thirty-five years," said Johanna. "He'll be retiring next year."

"Oh, wow, that's great. And you mentioned he has a girlfriend. Will she be there?"

"Yes, I believe so. Her name is Maureen. I don't know anything about her, other than he met her at work."

"And your uncle Jack, is that your dad's brother or your mom's?"

"My dad's." She'd all but forgotten about holding Mitch's hand by now. "Older brother. He's married to Aunt Lucy. She's the best. You're going to *love* her yams. They are amazing. I never loved yams until I had hers."

Mitch squeezed Johanna's hand. "Got it. Jack is Denny's brother, and Lucy makes amazing yams. Anyone else?"

"Uncle Jack and Aunt Lucy have three boys. Jack Jr. is the oldest. He's about six years older than me. Then Robert. Then Kenny. Bob and J.J. are married and each have a couple of kids. Kenny is still single. He's a Cadillac dealer in Atlantic City. Don't let him give you his sales pitch. He's good."

"See? This is good stuff. I need to know this stuff. We make a great team."

Johanna turned her head slightly and smiled at him. "Do we?"

"I think so. You don't?"

"No, I think so, too." *I'm just shocked that* you *think so too.*

27

*W*ith her free hand, Johanna adjusted the green-and-red elf hat on Rocky's head. "Oh, Rocky. You look so cute!"

"Woof!" he agreed, giving her a head bob and nipping at Esmerelda's tail.

Johanna swatted at his nose gently. "Nope. She's off-limits for the rest of the day, buddy."

Rocky hung his head and whined.

"He really likes her, huh?" asked Mitch as they stood on her uncle Jack's doorstep.

"Yes. They have a very interesting relationship." She glanced down at Esmerelda, who rolled her eyes at Johanna.

Suddenly the door burst open and Lucy Hughes's face broke out into a brilliant smile. "JoJo! Merry Christmas! I'm so happy that you made it!" A small woman with tightly curled almost-black hair reached her arms out to embrace Johanna.

"Merry Christmas, Aunt Lucy."

Aunt Lucy took a step back and surveyed the group

before her. A genuinely happy smile covered her wrinkled face. "And, my, just *look* at everyone you've brought with you!"

"This is my friend Mitch."

Mitch extended a hand. "It's nice to meet you, Mrs. Hughes, thank you for allowing me into your home on Christmas."

"It's so nice that you were able to make it after all. Denny said JoJo thought you had plans with your own family or something."

Johanna's teeth ground together. "Aunt Lucy, you remember Rocky, don't you? And this is Essy. Rocky and I are pet sitting, and I just couldn't leave her home alone on Christmas."

"Of course I remember Rocky! Welcome! And I'm so glad you didn't leave Essy at home on Christmas. That would be a shame." Aunt Lucy looked up and suddenly seemed to notice the weather. "Well, come in, come in. That wind is sure cold! And can you believe we're finally getting snow!"

The inviting aroma of a Christmas feast warmed the entryway inside the Hugheses' family home. Christmas lights strung over garlands twinkled across the doorways and bore little gold angels and red silk balls spaced every few inches. Flanking the staircase were poinsettia plants in green foil pots standing in front of carefully decorated miniature Christmas trees.

"You have a beautiful home, Mrs. Hughes," said Mitch, absorbing the atmosphere.

"Thank you. But, please, no formalities around here. It's just Lucy and Jack. Alright?"

Mitch nodded. "Understood."

Suddenly the sound of feet pounding the floor gave way to Lexi and Henry rushing towards Johanna. "Auntie JoJo!

Auntie JoJo!" they cheered in unison.

Rocky bounced around on his feet excitedly.

"Uh-oh, here comes the welcoming committee. Those two have been asking about you since they got here!" said Lucy, wiping her hands on her holiday apron.

Lexi and Henry threw their arms around Johanna first. "Lex Luthor and Henry the Eighth! Merry Christmas!"

"Merry Christmas, Auntie JoJo," said Lexi, quickly letting go of her aunt to give Rocky the attention he demanded. She kneeled down in front of him and hugged him around his neck. "Merry Christmas, Rocky." She giggled when he licked the side of her face.

"Merry Christmas, Auntie JoJo," said Henry, holding out his game console. "I already got to the sixth level on that game you gave me. Wanna see?"

"Of course I want to see, but first, do you two want to meet my friend?"

Henry glanced up at Mitch curiously. "Mom said you're going to be our new uncle."

Lexi stood up and kicked her brother in the shin.

"Ow! What'd you do that for? I'm gonna tell Mom," he groaned, grabbing his leg.

Lexi rolled her eyes. "You weren't supposed to say that *to him*."

Johanna wanted to crawl into a hole. "Right. So, guys. This is Mitch. Mitch, this is Lex Luthor, the most awesome niece in all the world, and this is Henry the Eighth, who as you might have noticed says completely random things whenever he feels like it."

Lexi giggled as she gave Mitch a shy little wave.

Mitch held out a hand to her. "It's nice to meet you, Lex Luthor. I love your name, it's very commanding. And dare I say it... slightly villainous." He touched his chin with a finger and pretended to be confused. "Though I'm not entirely sure why…"

She shook Mitch's hand weakly and smiled. "Lex Luthor's not my real name. Just Auntie JoJo calls me that. My real name is Lexi Ann Hughes-Donovan."

"Well, Ms. Lexi Ann, that's quite a lovely real name. It's a pleasure to meet you."

"And Mr. Henry the Eighth, is that not your real name either?"

He shook his head as he gnawed on his lip. After being kicked by his sister, he was scared to speak now.

"You can just call him Henry," said Lexi. "Come on, Henry, we have to go finish setting the table for Aunt Lucy." She looked up at Johanna. "Aunt JoJo, why did you bring that naughty cat again? She's not very friendly."

Johanna winced. "It was Rocky's fault too. But they've both promised to be on their best behavior today. See?" She showed her niece the cat's ribbon. "Essy's even wearing a ribbon with bells on so we all know where she's at at all times."

"Can Rocky come with us into the kitchen?" asked Henry.

"Of course he can," said Johanna. She squatted down to unfasten his leash from his collar. She straightened his little elf hat and looked him straight in the eye. "You better be good today. Understand?"

Rocky whined and looked away guiltily.

She patted his rump. "Okay, go on. Go play with Lex and Henry." Rocky happily trotted after the pair as Melissa and Denny appeared from the kitchen.

"JoJo! Finally, you're here!" Melissa said, throwing her arms around her sister.

"Merry Christmas, Mook!"

Denny waited his turn patiently and then hugged his daughter next. "Merry Christmas, JoJo."

"Merry Christmas, Dad," said Johanna with a smile. Then she turned and stepped aside. "Guys, this is my *friend* Mitch Connelly." She overemphasized the word *friend* so they would get the hint.

"Well, it's about time!" said Melissa, waving him in for a hug. "You realize she's been keeping you a secret for all these years?"

Johanna's face immediately went beet red and her stomach dropped.

"Oh, has she?" asked Mitch, turning to look at Johanna with a crooked smile and a twinkle in his eyes.

"Yeah. She didn't even tell us about you until last weekend. Imagine our surprise to find out that you've been dating on and off for the last five years."

Johanna palmed her forehead. Could her sister *be* any more humiliating? "I didn't say we'd been *dating* for the last five years. I said we'd *bumped into each other* on occasion."

Mitch elbowed her as he shook her father's hand. "Don't worry. You're not that out of the loop. I haven't told my family about Jo either."

Melissa looked disappointed. "So it's really not that serious, huh?"

Mitch shot her a Cheshire grin. "We're taking it slow, but that doesn't mean it couldn't *get* serious someday."

Both Melissa *and* Johanna turned to stare at Mitch. Johanna had to give the man props for his extemporaneous speaking abilities.

Melissa leaned her head on her father's shoulder. "Aww, our JoJo's got a nice guy," she cooed in her thick accent.

"So, Mitch. What do you do?" asked Denny, taking Mitch by the hand.

"I'm a structural engineer for an engineering company in the city."

"And how did you two meet again?" he asked.

Johanna's palms went clammy as she caught Mitch glancing over at her. "Are you two seriously going to start the inquisition again the minute we walk in the door? How about you at least let us take off our coats and put down the cat and the presents."

"Yeah, about that. Why'd you bring the cat again?" asked Melissa, lifting a lip. "She didn't do enough damage last weekend?"

"Because she needed a place to go for Christmas, Mook, alright?" Johanna's nerves were already almost shot, and she'd literally been there for all of five minutes.

"She couldn't have stayed in your apartment?"

Mitch shook his head. "Jo has too big of a heart. She didn't want to leave her home alone on Christmas."

Melissa nodded. "I see."

Johanna set Essy down on the rug. "Go play, Essy, but *be good*," she suggested sweetly. Standing up, she looked around. "Where's Uncle Jack and the rest of the family?"

"Jack and the boys are in the garage, having their annual Christmas cigar. All the ladies are in the kitchen, and the rest of the kids are upstairs," said Melissa.

Johanna looked at her father then. "Did Maureen come?"

Denny rubbed a hand across the back of his neck. "Mo's in the kitchen with the girls," he said. "You want to talk about that some more?"

No way in H-E-double-hockey-sticks do I want to talk about that today, thought Johanna. She gave him a tight smile and touched his arm lightly. "Another time, Dad. Alright?"

He patted her hand. "Okay, pumpkin. Whatever you

say. So, Mitch, do you smoke cigars? I was just heading out to the garage."

"I really don't, but I'd be happy to meet the rest of the family," Mitch suggested, giving Johanna a wink.

"Alright, then. Leave your coat on. It's a mite bit cold out there."

Johanna grinned at Mitch as he pulled back on the coat he'd just been shrugging off. He wrapped an arm around her waist and hugged her to him sideways. Johanna leaned her head towards him, and to her surprise, he planted a chaste kiss on the side of her forehead.

"I'll be right back, sugar."

Johanna's eyes widened in shock. She stared after Mitch as he followed her father to the garage. He wouldn't even turn around so she could shoot him a *what the heck was that?* look.

Whitley giggled behind her, causing Johanna to shoot a glance over her shoulder. "You should see your face!" she whisper-hissed.

Melissa and Lucy both stared at her. Lucy had her hands clasped her to her chest, and the sappiest smile Johanna had ever seen was plastered on her time-worn face.

"He's cute!" said Melissa when she was sure Mitch was out of earshot. "You've been hiding that man for all these years? And to think! I felt sorry for you because you didn't have a man."

"I don't have a man, Mook," Johanna sighed. Would she seriously have to explain herself all night? Maybe it had been a bad idea to come after all.

Melissa winked at her big sister. "He sure looks like a man."

Lucy nodded excitedly. "Your sister's right. He's a very attractive man. He looks a little rugged. I find that incredibly sexy!"

"Aunt Lucy!" breathed Johanna. She'd never heard her aunt use the word *sexy* before, and something about hearing it for the first time at Christmas made Johanna feel dirty.

"Oh Gawd," drawled Melissa. "Lighten up, JoJo. Sexy's not a bad word, you know."

Johanna's eyes flitted down. "I know."

"Alright, then, so why have you kept him a secret all this time? Why wouldn't you just tell us you had a boyfriend?"

Johanna put a hand on either of her sister's shoulders and stared her in the face. "I'm going to tell you one more time, Mook, and then you're going to drop it or I'm leaving. *Mitch isn't my boyfriend. He's a friend.*"

"But he said it could be more."

Johanna put a finger to her sister's lips. "Bup-bup-bup," she chided, taking a page out of Esmerelda's playbook. "I'll leave."

Melissa's shoulders crumpled slightly. "Oh, fine. You're no fun. What are we supposed to talk about now?"

"I don't know. The weather. Did you see all that snow coming down out there?"

***

A cloud of cigar smoke wafted into the foyer as Denny ushered Mitch into the garage. Mitch could hardly make out any faces through the thick, swirling smoke. He held a hand over his mouth and coughed, wishing he wasn't wearing his good coat.

Denny nodded. "Yeah, it's a little smoky in here. Jack, I'm gonna open up the overhead."

"The wind picked up out there. It's blowin' the smoke back into the house," said a gravelly voice through the smog. Mitch could only assume it had come from Denny's brother, Jack.

"Well, then, crack a window or something. I can't even see where I'm going," said Denny.

"Who ya got over there, Uncle Denny?" said another voice.

"Oh, uh. Yeah, fellas. I wanted to introduce someone to ya, but we can't even see your faces." He pushed a button on the wall and the overhead garage door slowly went up. The smoke in the garage circled and snow blew in. Complaints filled in the garage.

"Ay! Uncle Den, don't open it. We're already freezin' our asses off out here," said one voice.

"Yeah, I didn't even wear my coat out here. Carol didn't want my church coat stinkin' like cigars," said another.

Denny nodded his head and patted the air. "Yeah, yeah, yeah. If you're so cold, go inside and stand next to the oven with the rest of the girls."

Good-natured moans filled the room.

When the thickest puffs of smoke abandoned the garage, Denny turned slightly and gestured towards Mitch. "Alright, alright. Settle down. This here's Mitch. He's JoJo's fella."

A couple voices shouted. "Hey, Mitch."

Mitch was pretty sure he heard a "How ya doin', Mitchie?" and a "Welcome to the family, fella."

Mitch smiled back at the group of men, feeling only slightly uncomfortable. They seemed like a friendly bunch. "Hello, thanks for the invitation. I appreciate it."

"JoJo told Denny you had your own family get-together today," said the deepest voice, the one Mitch was sure was Uncle Jack's.

Mitch wasn't quite sure what Johanna had told her family, but he knew better than to mess up whatever ruse she'd told them. He certainly understood what it felt like to be pressured into finding a wife.

Mitch shrugged. "I was thinking about going to see my brother in Atlanta, but it didn't work out."

"Where ya from, Mitchie?" said a tall guy with beefy arms and thinning hair, holding a can of beer in a blue Bud Light coozie.

Mitch pointed at him. "What's your name?"

"Oh, yeah. I'm J.J., Jack's oldest."

"Oh, right. Jack Jr. It's nice to meet you. I lived in Brooklyn when I was a kid. I live in Manhattan now."

"Oh, yeah? Did your folks move, or they still livin' there?"

Mitch drew up his cheeks. "Actually, they were killed in an accident when I was in college." He said it knowing full well that it would be a mood squasher, but at least they had gotten it out of the way right off the bat, and maybe then they wouldn't ask him about his family anymore.

He was right. The room went silent for a second. Until J.J. pointed a finger at him. "Oh, hey man, I'm sorry."

Mitch waved his hand. "Oh, it's alright. It was a long time ago." When no one else said anything, Mitch pointed at the next guy, who sat on the seat of a Harley, also holding a beer and cigar. "So, you're Kenny or Robert?"

The shorter guy pointed a finger at himself. "I'm Bobby, that's Kenny." He pointed at a slim guy in a slick suit. He looked like a car dealer. Mitch made a mental note to avoid discussing cars with that one.

"Nice to meet you both." He looked over at the oldest of the group, who sat comfortably in a tweed Barcalounger in the corner of the garage. "You must be Uncle Jack?"

The man lifted his chin and Mitch made the short trek across the garage to shake his hand. "I appreciate the invitation."

"Nice to meet you, Mitch. Glad to hear JoJo's got a new fella. It's been too long."

Mitch grinned and held a hand out to the next guy, who was sitting on a barstool next to a workbench. "Hey, how you doin', Kevin?"

Kevin pumped his hand. "Good to see you again, Mitch."

"Oh, you two know each other?" Denny's brows lifted in surprise.

"We met the other day. Kevin helped us out on a little project that Jo's working on for one of her books."

"She tell you about all her stories?" asked Denny. "She's kind of a big deal, ya know. They did a thing in the paper about her. Put a picture of her in there and everything. All my friends saw it. They called her one of the city's hidden treasures."

A smile curved Mitch's lips. "One of the city's hidden treasures, really? And what did Jo think of that?" He chuckled to himself as he could only imagine how the self-proclaimed introvert felt about seeing her name and picture in the paper.

Denny grinned. "She took it about as well as you can imagine. She wasn't thrilled, but she did say it made for some good sales for quite a while after that."

"I bet."

"Hey, uh, Mitch, you wanna beer?" asked Uncle Jack, pointing at Mitch. "Kenny, get Mitch a beer."

"So what's the story with you and JoJo?" asked Bobby from the motorcycle.

Kenny handed Mitch a beer. He immediately cracked it open and took a hard swallow. "Story?"

"Yeah, you know. Give us the lowdown on how ya met and stuff."

Mitch grinned. "We bumped into each other in the

park." She was pretty sure that's how he'd heard Johanna describe it to her sister in the entryway.

"Well, that's what *she* says. You pick her up?" said Bobby skeptically.

"Not exactly. It was actually Rocky that brought us together."

"Oh, yeah? How so?"

"Literally. He ran over me. I think he was after a squirrel or something. Jo offered to pay for my dry cleaning. We've pretty much been friends ever since."

"So you two really aren't dating?" asked Denny, with a bit of a glum look on his face.

Mitch wished he had an answer to that. There was something special about Johanna Hughes. She made him feel things that he hadn't felt since Felicia died, and he most definitely had a very strong urge to kiss her. But Jo was like a spooked horse, ready to bolt at the tiniest thing. He wasn't sure if *she* was ready to be dating.

"Let's just say we're getting to know each other. I don't know if Jo's ready to date anyone, to be honest."

Denny sighed. "I was afraid of that," he said quietly. "Did she tell you about James?"

Mitch nodded. "And her mom. I know she's scared." The air in the room had taken another somber turn. He felt bad for weighing down the festivities. Mitch took another sip of his beer. "Hey, how about those Giants?"

28

"*M*itch sure seems like a nice man," said Maureen Hamilton to Johanna as she moved the mashed potatoes from the pot on the stove to a serving bowl.

Johanna nodded as she finished arranging deviled eggs around the outer edges of Aunt Lucy's vintage green glass relish tray. "He is."

Whitley was hunched over, leaning on her elbows on the counter, trying like mad to keep from chatting with the women.

Maureen glanced at Johanna out of the corner of her eyes. "He seems to fit in well with the boys."

"Yup."

"Hanna," chastised Whitley. "She's trying to have a conversation with you! You have to at least *try* to get to know the poor woman."

The women had all spent the better part of the day slaving away in the kitchen, and the food was almost ready to be served. Ginny and Carol, Bobby and J.J.'s wives, had gone to round up the kids for dinner, and Melissa and Aunt

Lucy were in the dining room, putting the final touches on the dinner tables. Of course the men were nowhere to be seen, which left Johanna, Maureen, and Whitley to themselves in the kitchen.

"And you met him in the park?"

"Mm-hmm."

"You're going to hurt her feelings," said Whitley with a glum expression.

Maureen put her spatula in the sink and turned to face Johanna squarely. "I'm really sorry you didn't know your dad and I were dating, JoJo. I'm sure it hurt your feelings to be the last to know, and to find out at a family holiday at that."

"I'm okay." Johanna pressed her lips together. She felt awkward being left alone to chat with the random woman her father was dating and obviously had feelings for, but she didn't know how to make the awkward feeling go away.

"It's easy to *say* you're okay," said Maureen, turning her attention to finding a gravy boat in the cupboard. "But I want you to really be okay. I think your dad is a pretty great guy, JoJo."

"He is."

Without moving her head, Maureen's lashes flickered up and towards Johanna. "I want to get to know you better. Someday I hope to maybe be part of your family."

"Part of my..." Johanna bit her lip. Surely, she wasn't talking about marrying her father! Marriage! Already? Johanna had barely gotten accustomed to the idea of her dad *dating*! Now they were talking *marriage?!* Her eyes flickered up to meet Whitley's.

Whitley smoothed her hands over the kitchen counter. "Relax, Hanna. She said *someday*. Not tomorrow."

Maureen smiled lightly. "I know, I know. We haven't

even been together for a year." She shook her head as she lifted the pan of gravy. "But I think when you know, you know. You know?"

Johanna remained silent. *No.* She didn't know.

Maureen waited for a response, but when she didn't get one, she continued on with a smile. "Well, at least I think *I* know. Denny seems sure, but I worry that he hasn't dated anyone else between your mother and me. What if he only *thinks* he's sure because he hasn't experienced anyone else? What if I'm like the rebound girl?"

"Han, tell her she's crazy!" cried Whitley.

"Mom's been gone for almost fifteen years. I highly doubt you're the rebound girl," said Johanna.

"Would you have liked to see him date around before settling down with someone?" she asked. "You can be honest."

Johanna thought about it for a minute while Whitley stared at her expectantly. Would she have liked to see her father dating a stream of women just to find another Maureen? The answer was a resounding no.

"Dad's not that kind of guy," she said.

"That's what your sister said. She said Denny's a one-woman kind of man. He always has been."

"So you should feel good about that," said Johanna lightly. She straightened the pickles one more time so they all fit perfectly on the tray. She could feel the sting of tears threatening. "He picked you to be that one woman."

Maureen grinned to herself. "Yeah. I do feel good about that," she admitted, almost as a realization to herself.

"He said you two work together?" asked Johanna, realizing she knew very little about Maureen.

"Yeah. I'm the local delivery sorter at his UPS center. I've been loading Denny's truck in the mornings for the last five years. One day about a year and a half ago, your father came in early so he could arrange his truck so he knew where everything was. Lexi and Henry had a school concert that night, and he wanted to make sure he got off on time. He and I had our first *real* conversation that day. The next day, he came in early to arrange his truck just because he wanted to talk to me again. He's come in early every day since."

"Awwww," cooed Whitley, wiping a tear from her eyes.

Johanna stopped arranging the black olives and looked up at Maureen. The woman was lost in thought and had a silly grin on her face. That was the first time Johanna had seen Maureen for who she was: a woman in love with her father.

She was about to say something; what, she wasn't sure. But she was interrupted by the onslaught of men suddenly flooding the kitchen.

"Is dinner ready yet?" asked Denny, giving Maureen a little squeeze around the waist.

"We're starved!" said J.J.

"Nothing like a little football to work up an appetite," said Kevin, holding a ball under his arm.

Mitch rounded the corner of the counter and put an arm around Johanna's waist. His coat was chilly and his hands cold to the touch. "Miss me?" he asked with a little grin.

Johanna glanced over at her father and Maureen, who were both staring at her. She cleared her throat and gave Mitch a forced grin. "Yeah. Of course. Did my cousins drag you outside in the snow?"

Mitch popped a pickle in his mouth and gave her a little lopsided grin. "Something like that."

Bobby pointed at him. "Don't let him fool ya, JoJo. He's got skills. He tried to pretend to be all *nah, I'm not very good*, but four interceptions an' two touchdowns later, we realized he was bamboozling us."

Johanna grinned up at Mitch. "Ah, I didn't know he was a bamboozler."

"A big one. You gotta watch out for that guy," said J.J. playfully.

Suddenly the rest of the women and the kids were in the kitchen too, and all hell broke loose. Rocky barked from the other side of the room. Noises and people surrounded Mitch and Johanna, smashing their bodies together.

With their faces only inches apart, Mitch looked down at Johanna. "Yeah, you gotta watch out for this guy."

"Do I?" She swallowed hard, shocked by her sudden desire for him to kiss her.

"Yup." He crunched on his pickle while smiling from ear to ear, exaggerating the little creases by his eyes.

Johanna's whole body tingled with excitement to be so close to Mitch that she could feel the warmth of his pickle breath on her forehead.

"Your nose is red. You look like Rudolph." She reached up and touched it with the tip of her finger. "Brr, it's cold. I should warm it up." She smiled as she rubbed his nose into the indentation of her palm.

He reached up and grabbed her hand and pressed it to his lips. "My lips are cold too. I feel like you should help me warm those up too."

Johanna was speechless then. The way he smiled at her when he said it... she felt like it had been an invitation for her to kiss him.

"Hey, JoJo, you guys ever find anything else out about that girl?" asked. Kevin from behind them.

"What girl?" asked Denny curiously.

Johanna's whole body tensed up then. *Dammit, Kevin,* she wanted to holler at him. Her whole family didn't need to know about her investigation, and they certainly didn't need to know about Mitch and Felicia. "No girl," she grumped, staring over her shoulder at her brother-in-law.

Denny looked at Kevin. "What're ya talkin' 'bout?"

Kevin glanced at Johanna and then at Mitch. He could tell he'd screwed up. "Ah, nothing. Just a character in one of JoJo's books."

"Why do *you* know about a character in one of JoJo's books?" asked Melissa, pulling a stack of plates from a cupboard behind Kevin's head.

"She asked me some IT questions. I-I was just helping her out," he stuttered.

Johanna pointed to the other room. "Kevin, can I see you for a minute?"

He swallowed and then said gloomily, "Yeah, sure."

She led him to the little mudroom off the back of the kitchen that led to the backyard. Mitch followed.

When they were safely out of earshot of the rest of the family, Johanna threw her arms down on either side of her. "Kevin! Why would you say that in front of the whole family?"

Kevin crossed his arms and sighed. "Sorry, JoJo. I wasn't thinking. I was just curious. You find anything else out?"

Johanna scowled at him. She was still annoyed that he'd mentioned the case she was working on in front of her family, but she needed to ask him to look up some more addresses for her. "Yeah. Some stuff."

Mitch looked at her curiously. "You found out more stuff?"

Johanna dug in the pocket of her suede skirt and pulled out a folded-up piece of paper. She handed it to Kevin. "I went back to the street and walked the path that Felicia would have walked. I wrote down the address of every house that had a video camera aimed at the street. There were five on just the first two blocks alone, that I could see anyway. A couple of them had signs that said what company their cameras were through, but not all of them."

Mitch turned Johanna's shoulders so she'd look at him then. His expression changed from easy-going to suddenly uptight. "Wait, you went back to Bank Street? You didn't tell me."

Kevin looked at the list that Johanna handed him. "JoJo, I can't keep hacking into security camera systems for this. I mean one time, you know, I made it look like I was helping those people out by exposing their firewall weaknesses, but I mean, three of these are through ADT. There's no way I'm hacking into ADT's system."

Johanna's face crumpled. She'd been banking on Kevin getting her access to those tapes. "But you said if only we had the rest of the tapes..."

Mitch lifted Johanna's chin so that her eyes had to meet his. "Jo, why didn't you tell me you went back to Bank Street? I would have gone with you."

"It's not a big deal. I went after you dropped me off at home. You had to get back to work, and I didn't want to bug you."

Kevin grimaced. "Listen, JoJo, I'll do my best with this list, alright?"

"Thanks, Kev. Whatever you can do, I'll appreciate."

Kevin nodded and made a hasty exit, leaving Mitch and Johanna staring at each other.

"So you found more cameras? Is that it?" asked Mitch.

Johanna looked up at him wide-eyed. "Well, actually there's more," she admitted. She had planned on telling him while they were driving to Aunt Lucy and Uncle Jack's, but they'd been having such a comfortable visit, she hadn't wanted to bring it up. "While I was there, I saw Dutch Erickson pulling up to the curb, so I knocked on his door."

Mitch's face went ashen. "You knocked on Dutch's

door? Jo, what were you thinking? He might've been the one that killed Felicia!"

Johanna shook her head. "I really don't think so, Mitch. I mean, we saw him drive away in the surveillance video."

"He could have circled back!" Mitch ran both hands through his blond hair in frustration. "I can't believe you went to see Dutch alone! What if something had happened to you?!"

Johanna shrugged. "I don't know. I would have figured it out. But nothing happened. Dutch did admit to using Janet Sandborn as his realtor to purchase the house. So obviously she made a tidy little profit off Felicia's death. Plus, Dutch was pretty sure there was a Four Seasons Realty car parked in front of the house when he got there that day."

Mitch stared down at her, and Johanna wished she could read his mind. His stone-cold expression made her wonder if he was mad at her for going to see Dutch without him.

She swallowed hard. "I wasn't *planning* to see Dutch, Mitch. He just showed up while I was scouting for more security cameras."

"We could have made an appointment together to go see him."

"Yeah, but he might not have taken the appointment. I think it was fate that I saw him pull up when I did. My body just kind of went on autopilot after that. I don't know what came over me."

"I don't know what came over you either. You could have been killed for snooping around," said Mitch with his brows knitted together.

"I really don't think Dutch was the one who killed Felicia," she said lightly.

Mitch nodded, but she could tell he wasn't as sure.

"JoJo, Mitch," hollered Melissa from the kitchen. "Time to eat."

"Be there in a second, Mook!"

Mitch took hold of both of Johanna's hands then. "Jo. Promise me you won't go do any more sleuthing without me. Okay?"

"But I—"

"Please?" he asked. He looked down at their joined hands. "I would be devastated if something happened to you."

Johanna swallowed hard. At first, she'd thought he was just mad at her for finding something out without him, but now, she thought she saw something else in his face. He was worried about her. She couldn't remember the last time someone besides her family had worried about her.

"Okay," she finally agreed. "I won't put myself into any dangerous situations without you anymore."

Before she could say another word, Mitch was leaning forward. His arms wrapped around her, embracing her in the kind of hug you give someone when you're thankful they're still alive and well. Then his face nuzzled her ear and he whispered, "Thank you, Jo."

29

*A*unt Lucy wrung her hands in the doorway only a few hours later. "I can't believe you have to rush off like this." Mitch and Johanna, along with the rest of their crew, were headed out the door. "We were just about to get holiday charades going."

"Sorry, Aunt Lucy. You know I love game night, but this snow is crazy! For months we haven't gotten a single flake, and now it's practically blizzarding! We'll be lucky to make it home now."

Johanna gave her aunt a kiss on the cheek before lumbering down the front steps with Esmerelda slung over one shoulder and Rocky's leash wrapped around her wrist. She waved backwards at the multitude of faces crammed in her aunt's doorway. "Bye, everyone!"

From the top step, Mitch watched Johanna and Rocky trudge through the snow. He watched as heavy wet flakes piled up on the hood of his car. His wipers chased each other across the windshield, keeping it cleared, but even the warmed-up engine couldn't compete with the heavy snow-fall they were getting. In the ten minutes since he'd started the car and cleared off the first six inches, another inch had accumulated. He hoped they hadn't waited too long to leave. The roads were going to be snow-packed, and likely filled with bad half-drunk drivers on their way home from Christmas in Jersey. And, if he had to guess, the snowplows probably hadn't even been out yet.

"Drive careful," said Denny, wagging a finger at Mitch. "Watch that speed and keep a safe following distance. You're carrying precious cargo."

Mitch nodded. *How right he is!* "Of course."

Melissa hollered out the door at her sister. "And JoJo, make sure to call me when you get home!"

Johanna was already to the car and had Mitch's back driver's side door open to let Rocky and Esmerelda into the backseat. She waved a hand over her shoulder at her sister. "I will!"

"Thanks for everything, Lucy. Dinner was amazing. It was great meeting you all," said Mitch as he walked down the shoveled walk.

Seven hands waved back at him.

"Don't be a stranger!" said Melissa, shooting him a wink.

Mitch grinned back. He was pretty sure that wasn't going to be up to him. By the time he got to the car, JoJo already had Rocky and Esmerelda inside and was trudging around the back of the car to the passenger's side. "I cleared a path around the front, Jo," hollered Mitch, watching her boots get covered in snow.

But she kept walking, so he went around the front of the car and beat her to her door. "I cleared a path around the front," he said again.

She peered up at him from beneath the bill of her cute black hat. Her teeth chattered. "Oh. You should have told me," she said, squinting against the falling snow. "I got snow in my boots."

"I did tell you, I yelled at you."

Her big brown eyes blinked back at him. "I didn't hear you."

He grinned. "Well, obviously."

He stared at her then. The streetlights illuminated the inky night sky, and snowflakes fell around her head in an almost magical way. It was such a perfect moment. She looked so angelic, with her nose scrunched up and her head tilted slightly to the side. In that moment, he wanted to ignore the fact that she spooked easily and ignore the fact that her entire family was standing on the doorstep watching them like hungry hawks. He wanted to wrap his arms around her and plant a kiss on those perfectly formed lips of hers.

He'd gone six years without wanting to kiss anyone but Felicia. Six years of not having a single lustful thought towards any other woman in his life, and now the most perfect creature he'd ever met was staring back at him, completely oblivious to how adorable she was, and he felt like there was something standing in the way of him making a move. Was it just her family staring at them? Was he scared of her reaction? Mitch didn't know.

"It's cold out here," said Johanna, eyeing the door he was blocking.

Mitch was pulled from his trance. "Oh! Right, sorry." He stepped back and opened the door for her, shutting it once she was safely ensconced in the car. Then he rushed around to the other side. As he did, the whole family waved at him from the door once again. He waved back, for a moment thankful he hadn't laid one on Jo while they were all staring. That would have been awkward.

Back inside the car, she waved at them too. "I wish we

didn't have to leave so early," said Johanna sadly. "For the first time in forever, I was actually having fun with my family. They really seemed to like you."

Mitch put his seat belt on and then put the car in reverse. "I really liked them too." He glanced over at Johanna. "You have your seat belt on? This could be a white-knuckle drive home."

"It's on." She glanced over her shoulder into the backseat. "I wish the seat belts worked for Rocky and Es."

"They're going to be fine," he assured her, patting her hand. "I'll drive slow. Don't worry."

They drove in a comfortable silence for several blocks. Lost in his own thoughts, Mitch took a few blocks to realize just how quiet it had gotten in the car. He glanced over at Johanna, who stared out the window, marveling at the snow.

"Jo? You alright?"

She nodded. "Yeah. I just can't believe my Christmas wish came true."

He chuckled. "Looks like you're getting more than you bargained for."

"Looks like it. I didn't think we'd get quite this much, though. You think we're going to make it home? They haven't even started plowing yet."

Mitch's car pushed ahead unfazed. "Silver Dragon's a beast. She'll make it."

"Silver Dragon?" Johanna laughed. "You named your car?"

"I did. Don't laugh. You brought your cat to Christmas."

"This is true."

They both stared ahead as the snow mixed with Mitch's headlights, forming a hypnotizing tunnel.

"Warp speed ahead," whispered Johanna under her breath.

Mitch leaned sideways. "Did you just say warp speed ahead?"

Johanna looked up at him in surprise. "Oh. Yeah," she smiled. "Don't you think it looks like we're going into hyperspeed when you drive fast in the snow or look up into the rain?"

"Yeah, I guess it does."

"James and I used to have this thing when we were kids. We'd lie on the grass when it was raining, and he'd hold my hand and he'd say, 'All systems are a go. Warp speed ahead!'"

"Is that from *Star Trek*?"

Johanna nodded. "James was a Trekkie."

"You guys grew up together, right?"

She nodded. "Yup. His house was literally just the next house over from mine. I feel like that's actually why James and I ended up together. He saw past my obvious flaws because he knew me so well for so many years."

Mitch quirked up an eyebrow. "What obvious flaws are those?"

"Are you kidding?" deadpanned Johanna. She held out her hand and started ticking off her fingers. "My clumsiness. My aversion to people. My social awkwardness."

"I'd hardly call a single one of those a flaw," said Mitch with a laugh.

"I haven't even told you all about my love for old crime TV shows."

"Which ones?"

"Oh, any of them, really. *Matlock*. *Columbo*. I *love* Jessica Fletcher, of course."

"Well, who doesn't love those old shows? You consider that a flaw?"

She shrugged. "I also watch a lot of those Hallmark Channel Christmas movies."

He smiled reminiscently. "Felicia liked those too. She wasn't a big television watcher, because she was so busy, but she did like the Hallmark Channel from time to time."

"Well, I'm kind of a Hallmark snob. I don't usually watch it like *anytime*, just for Christmas." She picked at a piece of cat hair stuck to her skirt. "So, how did you meet Felicia?"

Mitch leaned his head back against the seat rest and stared into the mesmerizing flurry coming at them. "Well, I was at a place in my life where I was tired of renting and ready to buy. I passed the Four Seasons Realty office at least twice a day on my way to and from work. Usually they were closed by the time I'd walk past in the evenings, but one day in March there was a light on in the front office, so I took that as my sign to stop and see if there was a realtor in. I walked in and there was this redhead behind the desk." He chuckled. "I thought she was the secretary. She was eating Chinese takeout and watching something on her phone, and it was making her giggle. I just remember thinking what a great laugh she had."

Johanna smiled at him from the other side of the car. "Awww."

"Yeah, she was pretty adorable. Anyway, I asked her if there were any realtors around that late, and she told me that she *was* a realtor and we started talking about what I was looking for. She told me that she had this great new place that was one of her new listings and she thought it was just what I was looking for. She took me to see it the next day. I wasn't quite sure about it, but she said it was in an up-and-coming neighborhood and the property values were going to appreciate very quickly, and at the very least I'd make a bundle on it if I kept it for a few years. She seemed to really know what she was talking about, so I went for it. I invited her over for a glass of champagne to celebrate the day that we closed on it, and I guess the rest is history!"

"You know I went to see Felicia's parents. I met her mom, anyway."

"Yeah, Dawn's great."

"She said that you and Felicia had only been dating for a few months before you got engaged."

He nodded. "I don't know what to say. When you know, you know, and I knew. She was something special, and everyone around her knew it."

Johanna's eyes darkened. "Obviously not everyone thought she was so great. Someone killed her."

"Yeah," whispered Mitch. "I know."

They drove in silence for a while, the idea of Felicia's fate sobering the energy in the car. Finally, Johanna spoke up. "The snow's really getting worse. Maybe we should have stayed at Aunt Lucy's."

Mitch's vision narrowed as he squinted into the snow. He suddenly became aware of his tensed shoulders and the tight grip he had on the steering wheel. "It is pretty bad. In hindsight, staying there might not have been a bad idea. At least by morning the snowplows would have been out."

Johanna pulled her feet out of her boots and curled her legs up underneath herself, tucking her coat in around her tights.

"Cold?"

"A little."

Mitch adjusted the car's thermostat.

"Thanks," she said, grinning at him sleepily. "And if I forget to tell you later, thank you for going with me to see my family."

"Hey, it was my pleasure. Thanks for giving me somewhere to be on Christmas."

Johanna leaned her head back against the headrest and

yawned. "And thanks for playing along. I know you were playing it up for my benefit."

"I wasn't playing anything up," he said, patting her hand. "Everything I said while I was there was the truth."

She grinned. "My family really seemed to like you. They probably like you better than me now."

"Oh, I highly doubt that. Your niece and nephew are all over you, and your dad couldn't stop singing your praises."

Johanna gave him a sleepy smile. "Yeah, Dad's very proud of my accomplishments."

Mitch looked over at her as she cuddled into his upholstered bucket seat. He wished he was sitting next to her on a sofa, not behind the steering wheel. He'd get to cuddle up with her then. "Getting tired? You're welcome to fall asleep."

"No, I'd like to help you stay awake," she said through the middle of a yawn.

"Okay," he agreed. "But I think it sounds more like I'll be the one helping *you* stay awake. I'm wired. I drank two cups of coffee before we left. I never have coffee this late at night. I'll make it home just fine."

"Mmm," agreed Johanna with a slow nod, her eyes little more than slits now.

"I promise, I'll wake you when we get there." Before the words were even out, Mitch could see the muscles in her neck give out as her head bobbed towards her shoulder. "Sweet dreams, Jo."

30

*J*ohanna awoke to a cold burst of air spiraling in around her. She unfolded her legs quickly, sat up, and realized her neck hurt and there was a little puddle of drool on her cheek. Where in the world was she? As her vision focused, she realized she was sitting in Mitch's car and the backdoor was open. She wiped the slobber from her face with the back of her hand.

"Brrr," she said, pulling her coat tighter around herself and slipping her feet back into her boots, where melted snow lay in wait for her stocking feet. She ducked her head and peered out the window. They were back in the city, but she didn't recognize the neighborhood. She looked over her shoulder to realize that Mitch was extracting Rocky and Esmerelda from the car. Whitley was already standing knee-deep in snow on the curb, with her arms wrapped around herself, shivering.

Mitch slammed the door shut and then opened Johanna's door. "Come on," he hollered over the wind, holding out one gloved hand.

Johanna looked up at him curiously. "Where are we?"

"Lenox Hill."

"Lenox Hill! What in the world are we doing in Lenox Hill? I live in Kip's Bay." She stared out the window, reluctant to get out of the warm car and into the freezing cold and snow.

He pointed over Esmerelda's furry grey head to the building behind him. "This is my apartment building. It was closer. We barely made it here, Jo. You and the kids are going to have to stay with me tonight. I'll take you home in the morning."

Johanna's mind raced. *Stay with Mitch? As in overnight? Is he crazy?* Johanna shook her head. "I—I can't *stay* with you…"

He grinned down at her, but still waved her forward. "I'm not talking about *sleeping* together or anything. I'll take the sofa. Come on, it's *freezing* out here. I just about got stuck six times. Cars are stuck in drifts all over the city. If we don't stay here, we'll be lucky to make it to your place and then I really don't think there's any way I'll make it back home. Which means I'll either have to stay with you at your place, or freeze to death in my car. I mean, your choice, but obviously I'd rather you not pick freezing to death in my car."

Johanna looked out the front window at the pile of snow and the flurry that seemed relentless in its pursuit of blanketing New York City for Christmas. "You don't want Rocky and Es at your place, though…"

"If it means we get to go inside where it's warm, then *yes*, I do want Rocky and Es in my place." He prodded her along with his hand. "Please, Jo? I'll be a gentleman, I swear."

Grudgingly, Johanna took hold of his hand and let him pull her out of the car. When she wobbled on her feet in the snow, he steadied her. Then, only inches away from her face, he stared down at her. "See? I'm only here to help. Come on, the kids are cold."

She couldn't help but smile at Mitch calling Rocky, Es, and by default, Whit *the kids*. She guessed Esmerelda wasn't getting as big of a kick out of it, but when she actually looked, she realized that the ball of fur was so tightly wound around Mitch's neck that she couldn't find where her head began and tail ended.

Mitch led the group of them to the front of his building, where a black-and-gold awning lit with white Christmas lights provided a smidge of protection against the elements.

"This is where you live?" asked Johanna as they hopped through the snow.

"Yeah, why?"

She shrugged as she stared at the two fully decorated Christmas trees in oversized pots flanking each side of the doorway. She wasn't sure where she'd expected Mitch to live, but she was shocked when she saw just how nice his apartment building was. "Fancy."

He grinned. "I told you, Felicia picked this place out for me. I just wanted something close to work, with an extra room for an office, and a nice view."

"She must have thought you wanted the luxury suite, huh?"

"I guess," he said with a smile before leading them to the elevator. As the elevator smoothly took off for the fifth floor, he leaned back against the wall and gave Johanna a little grin. "Have a nice nap?"

She grinned sheepishly. "I didn't realize I'd fallen asleep. I'm sorry. I wanted to help you stay awake."

"It's okay. It was probably better that you slept. It was a harrowing experience. I'm extremely thankful we made it as far as we did. There were a few times when I thought we were going to be stranded on the side of the road."

"Oh, wow. It is probably better that I missed it."

His blue eyes burned a hole into her as he stared. "You know, I would have never guessed you to be a snorer."

Her eyes widened and a hand flew to her mouth. "Did I…"

"Yup. A little."

"Just a little?"

"You sounded a little bit like a symphony of tree frogs, if you want honesty. But it was cute."

"Cute?" said Johanna, nearly choking on her own saliva. How embarrassing! "I'm sorry, me snoring is not cute. I swear I don't snore all the time. Something about car rides and the position of my head makes me snore."

He reached out and squeezed her arm. "It's alright, Jo."

"Here, you want me to take Es?" she asked, suddenly realizing that the cat was still wrapped around Mitch's neck.

He touched her fur absentmindedly. "Oh, she's keeping my neck warm, actually. She's better than a scarf. I think she might like me."

"Doubtful," said Johanna, rolling her eyes.

"Thanks!"

"Oh!" She covered her mouth. "I didn't mean it like *that*. I just meant that she doesn't like *anyone*. Not even me. She's pretty snarky. I've nearly kicked her out of my apartment at least a dozen times."

"A snarky cat, huh?"

The elevator door dinged and the group piled out. Mitch led them down the hall, past doors covered in Christmas wreaths and other holiday placards.

"Wow! Why doesn't your apartment building look like this, Hanna?" marveled Whitley, still trying to chase the chill away by rubbing her arms.

Mitch stopped in front of a completely plain door devoid of any holiday cheer.

Johanna looked around curiously and then pointed at the door in front of them. "Wait. Is this your apartment?"

He looked both ways down the hallway and then held up his key. "It's the only one they gave me a key for."

She giggled. "You're literally the only door without any Christmas decorations."

"Everyone else on my floor either is married, has a live-in girlfriend, or has children. I'm the only single guy. Single childless guys don't decorate for Christmas."

"Why not?"

He shrugged, pushed the door open, and flipped on the light. Rocky ran inside. "I don't know. Maybe *some* single guys decorate for Christmas, but not me. I have a job. I don't have time for holiday cheer. Bah humbug." He grinned at her wickedly.

"You're not funny." Johanna glanced inside at his beautiful, albeit bare apartment. "If I'm staying here for the night, the first thing I'm doing is putting on the Hallmark Christmas channel to add a little bit of holiday excitement to the place."

He unwound Esmerelda from his neck and put her down on the floor. "That might be the only festive merriment this apartment will have seen for the last six years."

Johanna pulled her hat off and ran a hand through her damp hair to smooth it. "Then it's probably a Christmas miracle that we showed up when we did."

"You have no idea," he said softly, unable to peel his eyes off her for a moment. After a particularly long stare down, he pointed at a small built-in fireplace in the wall below the television screen. "I could start a fire?"

"Oh my gosh, please do!" cried Whitley, still rubbing her arms. "I'm freezing!"

Johanna nodded. She'd always wanted a fireplace in her apartment. "That would be great."

"I have wine too, if you want some with the movie. It's in the kitchen. You could pour us a couple glasses?" He pointed towards his gourmet kitchen, complete with over-sized stainless steel appliances, black granite waterfall counters, and sleek white cabinets. Not a single item appeared out of place or like it had ever even been used.

Johanna ran her finger along the island counter. "This is a very nice kitchen. Do you cook?"

"I *can* cook," he said, turning on the fireplace, "but, alas, I don't."

Johanna pulled two wineglasses from the hanging rack below a cabinet. "Why not?" She was pretty sure she'd cook all the time in a kitchen like his.

"Work, mostly. I get home late. I usually just pick something up on the way. Plus, it's just me. Why would I want to cook just for me?"

Johanna knew the feeling well. It was just her and Rocky, and he was satisfied with dog food and whatever leftovers she brought him. She glanced over at the girls. Whitley stood in front of the fire with her palms facing it and Esmerelda had curled up in a ball on the furry rug in front of the fireplace.

Johanna nodded her head towards them. "The girls seem to like the fire."

"The girls?" He glanced back at her.

She winced. *Crap.* "I meant, Essy seems to like the fire. Where's Rocky? Rocky!" she called, trying to draw attention away from her faux-pas.

"Woof!" he barked from another room.

Following the sound of his bark, she found him curled up on Mitch's bed. "What are you doing, buddy?" Johanna patted his rump. "That's Mitch's bed. You get down from there."

Mitch was right behind her. "He's fine. He's not hurting anything. I'm going to let you and him have the bed tonight anyway, so he might as well get in bed." Mitch's deep, sexy voice spilled over her shoulder, his proximity to her drowning out the silence in the room. Her heart began pounding wildly. She was in a bedroom with a man she was incredibly attracted to, and every fiber of her body was suddenly *very* aware of it.

She spun around so that they were face-to-face. "B-but I can't, *we* can't, kick you…"

He put a finger on her lips. "Shhh. No arguing. My place. My rules. You get the bed and I get to sleep on my incredibly comfortable sofa." He strode over to his closet. "You want something a little more comfortable to wear to watch the movie? I've got some sweatpants that might fit you if tie the drawstring tight."

Johanna's heart was still having problems settling down, but she nodded and tried to force herself to look at ease. "Umm, sweatpants? Yeah, sure."

"Ask him if he has some I can wear!" shouted Whitley from the living room.

"Do—" Johanna's mouth clamped shut. She'd almost just lost her wits and asked him if he had clothes for her invisible friend. She palmed her forehead.

"Do? What? What is it?"

Johanna cleared her throat. "Do…you…have any popcorn?" She rubbed her stomach. "I'm hungry."

"Of course I have popcorn! That's one thing I do know how to make."

She smiled, relieved she'd been able to cover and he hadn't noticed yet again what an imbecile she was. "Good."

He pointed at the sweatpants, t-shirt, and socks he'd

thrown on the bed. "Bathroom's in there. I'll change out here."

From the bathroom minutes later, Johanna could hear clanging in the kitchen and then the humming of a popcorn maker. She did the best she could with her wet hair and her faded makeup and then slid out across his hardwood floors in the socks he'd lent her. She was suddenly very excited for popcorn, a glass of wine, and a Christmas movie all on Mitch's couch. It was *almost* like she had a boyfriend for Christmas.

She slid into the kitchen. "This is actually kind of fun," she said, merriment giddy in her heart. "Like a sleepover."

He put a bit of butter in a little plastic bowl and stuck it in the microwave. "It's *exactly* like a sleepover," he chuckled. He pointed at the television. "I turned it on, but I don't know what channel you want."

Johanna darted into the living room and scooped up the remote, flipping it to the movie she wanted. "Yay, it only started a few minutes ago. We didn't miss much," she said, looking at the time and then pausing the movie.

"Perfect. Popcorn's almost done."

The minute the smell of butter was in the air, Rocky was in the kitchen, barking. He wanted a treat too.

Mitch frowned. "Sorry, bud. I don't have any dog food around here."

"He'll eat anything," said Johanna. "He likes popcorn."

"Rocky eats popcorn?"

Johanna nodded. "He prefers it with extra butter, but the vet says plain is better for him." She held a hand aside of her face and added in a whisper, "But it's Christmas, so what I don't see won't hurt him."

Whitley, who had still been warming herself by the fire, strutted over to them with a pout on her face. "Hanna, I'm just going to go to bed. I'm cold and tired. It's Christmas and I miss my dad. I just want today to be over."

Johanna looked at Esmerelda, who was curled up in a ball snoozing in front of the fire. "Maybe I'll just put Essy in your room too, if that's okay?"

"You're going to put the cat to bed?" Mitch asked, lifting one brow while filling a small bowl of popcorn for Rocky. He put it on the floor.

"Yeah, you know. I don't want her to be too cranky in the morning." Johanna scooped Esmerelda up off the floor. "Bedtime, Essy," she cooed in her ear.

"Oh, you're kidding me. I don't even get to watch the movie?" Es hissed back under her breath as Johanna carried her towards the bedroom. Johanna smiled at Mitch, hoping she wouldn't have to spend the rest of the evening explaining why her cat was talking. Luckily, he hadn't seemed to have heard anything.

When they got to the bedroom, Johanna shut the door behind her. "Sorry, Es. You fell asleep. Whit's going to bed. Maybe you girls can let me have a little alone time with Mitch?" She handed Essy to her sister.

Esmerelda yawned. "Oh, fine. Call it my Christmas gift to you."

Johanna nodded excitedly. "Deal!" She ran back out into the kitchen to discover that Rocky had already scarfed up all of his popcorn.

"Bedtime, Rocky," she sang.

"Woof!"

Mitch patted his head. "Night, buddy. See you in the morning."

She led Rocky to the bedroom and handed Whitley his leash. "Can you please keep him in here with you too?" she begged.

"I suppose," Whitley sighed glumly. "One of us might as well have a good Christmas night."

"I'll make it up to you tomorrow, I promise."

"Really?" Her green eyes brightened.

Johanna nodded. "We'll have our own Christmas at the apartment or something. We'll play games and put on Christmas music and have cocoa and popcorn."

"Deal!" cried Whitley. "Come on, guys, bedtime." She put Esmerelda on the bed, and when she patted the spot next to her, Rocky hopped up next to her.

"He's sleeping on the other side of the bed," said Essy, pointing at the foot of the bed.

"He knows," promised Johanna from experience. She threw her arms around Whitley. "Thanks, Whit. I owe you. Good night, everyone!"

"G'night, Hanna," said Whitley as she crawled into bed too.

"Woof!"

a bright orangey-red fire danced in the fireplace only minutes later. Mitch and Johanna sat on opposite ends of Mitch's three-person sofa with a bowl of popcorn separating them. With both of their stocking feet up on the coffee table, they stared mindlessly at the people in the Christmas lodge on the screen. Every once in a while, Mitch's hand would accidentally graze Johanna's hand and he'd feel Jo tense up, or she'd glance over at him and smile awkwardly. It was cute, the way she seemed nervous around him, that much Mitch would admit. But the sexual tension between them was stifling, and the silence—deafening. So deafening that he couldn't even hear what was going on in the movie. It felt like they were on a first date, even though they'd agreed that this was to be a non-date date.

Jo's stifled laughter made it appear that she felt the same way. Even without looking at her, Mitch could tell that she was up in her head and not relaxing at all.

Finally, he couldn't take the awkward silence any longer. He decided he had to do something bold. He bolted upright, sliding his feet to the floor. He picked up the popcorn bowl and put it on the coffee table.

She looked over at him curiously and opened her mouth to say something.

But before she could ask him what he was doing, he reached across the sofa and grabbed hold of her, and in one easy tug, he'd slid the two of them together in the middle of the couch. He wrapped his arm around her body and leaned over her so that their faces were only inches apart. He inhaled, drinking in her intoxicating aroma of peppermint and wine.

For a split second, he saw a streak of panic flash across her eyes. He had known he would. But, he was pleased when the panic quickly gave way to a sweet tenderness and silent longing that tugged at his heart. In that moment, he could see that she wanted to kiss him just as much as he wanted to kiss her.

It was that tiny bit of encouragement that gave him the nerve to lift her onto his lap. Entranced by her big brown eyes, he slid his hand up into her hair. Staring into each other's eyes, he silently gave her the briefest of moments to push him away, to slap him, to decide this wasn't what she wanted. But when her lips curled into an almost imperceptible smile, he pulled her head down to meet his and their lips touched for the very first time.

At first, he felt her body freeze. Her lips were tight, her body rigid and full of panic. But instead of forcing the kiss harder, he let his lips soften and he hugged her to him. He wanted to convey something to her. She *meant* something to him. This wasn't just a kiss he was giving her. It was his heart.

Slowly, Johanna began to respond. Her lips softened too, and her body melded into his embrace. She wrapped her arms around him, curling her fingers into his hair.

Mitch wanted that kiss to go on forever. He wanted to lift her up and whisk her away to his bedroom. But he knew better. The minute his body began to respond, he pulled his head back.

She stared down at him, her big brown eyes shining in the dim light. "What was that about?" she asked breathlessly.

He grinned. He could stare at her like this all night. "I wanted to get it out of the way. It was hanging in the air between us like a curtain. We couldn't see past it. All I want is to enjoy my time with you, and I didn't want there to be this awkward tension between us."

Johanna touched her lips gently. "Oh," she said. "So you *wanted* to kiss me?"

His head lolled back on his shoulders as he smiled.

He lifted it back up again and looked her in the eyes. "Are you kidding, Jo? You couldn't tell by that kiss that I *wanted* to kiss you?"

"Well, I mean, I…"

"Did you *want* to kiss me?"

Johanna's face froze. She swallowed hard. She was speechless.

Mitch tipped his head sideways. "I know you're scared. I'm scared too."

Her eyelashes fluttered and she broke eye contact. "You are?"

He lifted her chin so that she would look at him again. "I am. I haven't had feelings for anyone since Felicia. I'm not sure I know how to do this anymore."

That made Johanna grin. "Really?"

He nodded.

"I'm not sure how to do it either," she whispered.

"Then we'll learn together. No rush, okay?"

She nodded as a smile like warm honey poured across her face. "Okay."

Mitch pulled her head down one more time. This time, he laid a kiss gently on her forehead. "Well, now that the first kiss is out of the way..." He pulled her off his lap and tucked her in beside him under his arm. He leaned forward and put the popcorn bowl on their lap and put his feet back up on the coffee table. He looked at her happily. "We can watch this Christmas movie."

*J*ohanna awoke the next morning to a hissing sound. Her eyes blinked open, and the first thing that caught her eye was the fireplace, which still burned brightly. She realized that she had fallen asleep on Mitch's sofa. She rolled to her side and peered around the edge of the sofa to see Mitch crammed up on the love seat, still sound asleep. *Aww, he let me sleep on the big couch*, she thought.

She heard the hissing sound again. "Psst!"

Johanna's brow crinkled. Slowly, she raised her torso to peer over the back of the sofa towards the sound. She saw Whitley in the doorway of Mitch's bedroom, waving wildly at her.

"Hanna!" she whisper-hissed. "Come here! Hurry!"

Johanna glanced back again at Mitch, who was oblivious to Whitley's presence. She let the blanket Mitch had covered her with the night before fall into a heap on the sofa as she stood up and rushed to the bedroom.

"What?!" she whispered.

Whitley tugged Johanna into the bedroom. "Get in here!" She shut the door behind her.

Rocky sat on the floor, looking up at Johanna with a big sloppy grin. "Woof!"

Johanna patted his head as she ground the sleep from her eyes. "Mornin', buddy."

Esmerelda was sitting on the edge of the bed. "Well, look at what the cat dragged in."

"You realize *you're* the cat, right?" asked Johanna with a grin.

"Yeah, I might be the cat, but you're the one who spent the night in the living room with your boyfriend."

Johanna's face flushed. "Nothing really—*happened*."

"Oh, sure. Yeah, I believe that," quipped Esmerelda.

"Seriously!"

The long whiskers over Esmerelda's eyes flinched. "He didn't kiss you?"

"Well, I mean… a lady doesn't kiss and tell," said Johanna as the memory of the kiss the night before came flooding back to her. It had been so perfect, she almost couldn't take it.

"Uh-huh. Say no more. We know what happened, don't we, Whit?"

Whitley nodded slowly, but her face was definitely *not* excited for her. "Yeah, I guess so."

"Whit? What's the matter? You look like you saw a ghost!"

Whitley sighed. "I feel like I have," she admitted.

Johanna shook her head. "Like you have? What do you mean?"

"Es and Rocky found something this morning, Hanna."

"You're not making any sense. What do you mean they *found* something?" She looked at Esmerelda.

"They were playing around this morning. I was trying to keep them quiet so you and Mitch could get some sleep, but Es smelled something in Mitch's closet."

Johanna felt a wave of panic grip her body. "What did she smell?"

Whitley nudged Essy. "Tell her."

"I smelled perfume in Mitch's closet," she said with a sigh. "I thought maybe he was keeping another woman from you or something, so I had to check it out."

Johanna's head bobbed. She just wanted Esmerelda and Whitley to get to the point. "And?"

Whitley handed a small book over to Johanna. "One of the baseboards wasn't nailed very tight. Once Essy's nose told her where the smell was coming from, Rocky took over. He pulled off the board and we discovered there was a hole in the wall behind it. We found this in there."

"What is it?" asked Johanna as she looked down at the small leather-bound book.

"We're pretty sure it was Felicia's journal."

"Her journal!"

Whitley nodded. "I glanced through it. I didn't have time to really look. She was scared of someone, Hanna. It was a man."

"A man? Like who?"

Whitley shrugged. "As soon as I realized it was Felicia's, I knew I had to wake you up."

Johanna's mouth went dry as she stared at the book in her hands. *Please tell me it wasn't Mitch.* "Who was it? Who was she scared of, Whit?"

Whitley pointed at the book. "I told you. I-I didn't read it all. I wanted to read with you."

Johanna touched the top of the book. Her fingers trembled as she slowly peeled the leather cover back and stared down at the sprawling feminine handwriting. She flipped through the pages and saw dates heading each page. She swallowed hard as she flipped to an earmarked page and one passage jumped out at her. *"I don't know what to do anymore. I'm scared."*

Jo's blood ran cold. Suddenly, she heard the door behind her creak. She snapped the book shut and shoved it under her shirt and into the waistband of her sweatpants.

"Good morning," said Mitch, sticking his head into the doorway.

Johanna felt her body freeze. *What if it was Mitch that Felicia was scared of?* "Good morning," she said stiffly.

"You hungry?"

Johanna shook her head. "Mmm, nope."

She glanced over her shoulder to see him rubbing a hand across his stomach. "I am. I'm starved. I could run out and get us a couple of bagels, and then I could call the office and tell them I won't be in today. There aren't going to be that many people there anyway. The Monday after Christmas is always pretty dead." He spun her around to face him. "We could watch Hallmark movies together all day if you want?"

Johanna didn't know what to say. She now wondered if all her instincts about Mitch had been wrong, if maybe she hadn't looked closely enough at him as a possible killer. Had she been blind all this time because of her attraction to him? Her heart did flip-flops in her chest as her hands began to tremble. "I-I need to take Rocky for a walk," she mumbled awkwardly.

"Oh, well, there's almost a foot of snow out there, Jo."

Johanna looked at Rocky who didn't look the least bit anxious for his walk. "I know, but you know, nature calls. When he's gotta go, he's gotta go. I wouldn't want him to *go* in your nice apartment."

Mitch grinned. "Say no more. Let me get my coat. I'll go with you."

Johanna shook her head as she rushed towards the front

door of his apartment. "No, it's alright. I better go by myself. He—he's kind of shy. You know, *going* in front of strangers."

Mitch looked at Rocky curiously. "I've never heard of a dog having bathroom anxiety in front of strangers."

Johanna nodded, wide-eyed. She'd totally just made that up. "Yeah, it's a real thing. They've done studies on it."

"Uh-huh. Well, are you coming back after your walk?" he asked as she tugged on her coat and boots.

Johanna glanced over at Whitley, who gave her a sideways look.

"Tell him no," hissed Whitley as Esmerelda strolled into the kitchen behind Rocky.

Johanna pursed her lips. "Umm, I don't think so."

"Really? Why not? I was hoping maybe we could spend the day together."

"Tell him you have to go home to take your medicine!" said Essy from the floor.

Without thinking, Johanna parroted Essy's suggestion. "I have to go home to take my medicine."

"Your medicine? You're taking medicine? Is everything okay?"

Her face flushed. She wanted to palm her forehead, but she was too busy tugging on her last boot. "Oh, no. Not *my* medicine. The *cat's* medicine. You know, I'm watching her for a friend and she's supposed to take this de-worming stuff every day. Otherwise her worms might come back."

Mitch made a face. "Oh. I see."

Johanna nodded. "Yeah. It's really, you know. Gross. So, I better go. And take the kids."

Mitch grabbed Johanna's hand as she went to reach for the door. "Well, when am I going to get to see you again? I had a really great time last night."

Johanna swallowed hard. *I had a really great time last*

night too. "Oh, umm. You know, I have this book I'm trying to finish, and I'm really behind. So, umm. I'm not really sure."

"Well, are we going to try and figure out the truth about what really happened to Felicia? Do you still have time to work with me on that?"

Johanna stared at her hands then. She didn't know what to say. Felicia's leather journal dug into the soft flesh of her stomach, begging her to read the contents. "Can we talk later about that? I really don't want Rocky to have an accident in your apartment. I'll feel terrible."

He let go of her hand then. Johanna couldn't help but feel bad about the way she was leaving. "Okay. Is everything alright, Jo?"

Johanna nodded and silently prayed that it was. "Yeah. I just really need to get home."

"Hey, Jo, listen, I'm sorry if I moved too fast for you last night." His face looked concerned.

She gave him a tight smile. "No, it's not that. I just need to get home."

Mitch leaned forward and held his arms open. "Can I at least give you a hug goodbye?"

Johanna felt tears burning behind her eyes as she nodded. He wrapped his muscular arms around her. She closed her eyes and put her head on his shoulder, silently praying that it hadn't been Mitch that Felicia was scared of. It just couldn't be.

She pushed herself out of his arms before he could see the tears falling. "Goodbye, Mitch."

"Bye, Jo."

ohanna's teeth chattered as she, Whitley, Rocky, and Esmerelda trudged through the snow while heading south on Lexington Avenue towards her apartment.

"Remind me again why we didn't just let Mitch drive us home?" asked Whitley's tiny voice.

Johanna glanced over at her. "I don't know, Whit. I panicked. What if he's the one Felicia was scared of?"

Esmerelda teetered around Johanna's shoulders, searching for a comfortable way to lie on their walk home. "I thought you said Mitch was working the day she was killed," she said before finally getting comfortable.

Johanna's mind had already gone back to Felicia's mother telling her that he'd had a pretty good alibi the day that Felicia was killed. "He was. But it never occurred to me that he might have had someone else do the dirty work for him. You know, to make it look like it wasn't him."

Whitley hugged her arms around herself. "You really think Mitch was capable of killing her?"

Johanna winced. Of course she really didn't think Mitch

was capable of murdering Felicia! He seemed to love her too much. But in her mystery novels, it was always the person they'd least suspected that had done the dirty deeds. And in this investigation, *Mitch* was the person she least suspected. Had she let her feelings for him cloud her judgment? "My instincts tell me it wasn't Mitch, but that doesn't mean my instincts are always right."

"My instincts tell me he didn't do it either," agreed Whitley, patting Rocky's side as he trotted between her and Johanna. "And I certainly don't think it would have been a big deal if he'd driven us home. It's freezing out here!"

"I'm sorry! I told you! When he came in the bedroom, I panicked!"

"We noticed," said Esmerelda. "He's literally got to be wondering what in the hell just happened."

Johanna's mittened hands went to her mouth as she sucked in her breath. "You think?"

Whitley nodded. "Yeah. It was a little bit of a rush to get out of there. He probably thinks you don't like him anymore."

"Well, what if we get home and read Felicia's journals and find out Felicia had been scared of Mitch?"

"What if we get home and find out that it *wasn't* Mitch that she was scared of?" said Whitley. "Then you just totally bumbled this whole thing up for nothing."

Johanna rolled her eyes. "It wouldn't be the first time, trust me." She adjusted the journal in her waistband. "Alright. If we get home and find out that it wasn't Mitch, then I'll text him and apologize."

"You can't text him, Hanna. You've got to call him!" countered Whitley.

"Fine. I'll call him. Happy?"

Whitley snuggled up next to Johanna. "Yes!"

$\mathcal{T}$he minute they got inside, Whitley rushed to pull one of Johanna's blankets around her shoulders. Johanna shed her coat, hat and boots, and strode into the kitchen to put on some hot coffee, while Esmerelda and Rocky and their frozen fur, headed straight for the furnace to defrost.

"That was the longest walk of my life!" said Whitley through chattering teeth.

"Mine too," agreed Johanna. She raced into the living room to curl up on the sofa with a blanket and Felicia's journal. It hadn't been the longest walk of her life because of the cold, but instead because she'd worried the entire thirty-five-minute walk that she'd get home to discover that Mitch wasn't who he seemed to be after all.

Whitley crawled onto the sofa and snuggled up next to her. "My heart's pounding like crazy right now."

"Ditto," said Johanna as she cracked open the journal and began to flip through the pages, scanning for Mitch's name. "Where do we start?"

"I don't know. When did Mitch and Felicia meet?"

Johanna thought about it for a second. "I'm pretty sure he said that they met in March." She flipped through the book and began scanning pages from March 2011 forward, looking for Mitch's name. Finally, she found an entry. "Aha! I found something."

Whitley squealed. "Eee!"

"Read it out loud," hollered Esmerelda from in front of the furnace.

Johanna nodded and began to read. *"April 11, 2011. A few weeks ago, a man came into my office looking to buy an apartment. His name was Mitchell Connelly. Nice guy. We closed on the property today. He brought a bottle of champagne and invited*

321

me to celebrate with him at his new apartment. Something about this guy is different. He makes me giddy."

"Aww," cooed Whitley, looking up at Johanna. "That's kind of how you feel about him, isn't it?"

Johanna suddenly found herself feeling guilty. Maybe she shouldn't be reading this without Mitch. But she couldn't help thinking, *but what if...*

She ignored Whitley and flipped the page. "*April 12, 2011. After work I stopped for a slice at that new pizza place that just opened up on the corner across from the bodega by my building. Oh my God, I have no idea how that place passed its health inspection. Memo to myself. Don't go back there ever again.*"

"Skip the food talk and get to the good stuff!" said Esmerelda.

Whitley nodded. "Yeah, we just want to hear the juicy details."

Johanna scanned the pages, looking for more stuff of interest. She had to know the truth.

"Okay, here we go... *April 27, 2011. Ugh. Some days I hate my job. One of my coworkers won't leave me alone. I'm pretty sure it could be considered sexual harassment at this point. Told the boss, he said we'd keep an eye on it. Let's hope he quits.*"

Whitley lifted an eyebrow. "Maybe it wasn't Mitch she's scared of after all!"

Johanna's heart began beating faster in her chest. She flipped forward further.

"*June 16, 2011. It happened again. I was working late, and same coworker cornered me in the storage room and asked me out yet again. I told him I had a boyfriend, but he didn't really seem to care. He wouldn't let me out. I just about dropped a knee on him. I really wish I would have. I haven't said anything to the boss yet. Maybe I'll tell him tomorrow.*"

"Aww, that poor girl!"

Johanna nodded and flipped the page, curious if Felicia

had indeed told her boss what was going on the next day. *"June 23, 2011. Mitchell stopped into the office to take me out for lunch today. I introduced him to everyone at work. I really really really like this guy. I sort of wonder where he's been all my life."* She glanced up at Whitley and stuck out her bottom lip. "Aww, she didn't tell her boss."

"She didn't write about it anyway."

"Yeah," agreed Johanna, flipping through more pages. One page was highlighted with a big doodled heart. *"July 4, 2011. OMG! Mitchell proposed! I am an engaged woman! We went to the fireworks together and he popped the question right there beneath the light show! It's only been three months since we met. Is that crazy? Yes! It's crazy! I know, he hasn't even met my parents yet! But he's the one. I can tell. He's perfect! Setting a date soon. We don't want to wait!"*

A soft grin covered Johanna's face. She could feel Felicia's excitement in her words and in the way the ink pressed harder into the paper. She had been so happy. Johanna's heart hurt for both of them.

"Keep reading!" pushed Esmerelda from the floor.

Johanna glanced over at her and smiled. "I thought maybe you fell asleep."

"Of course I'm not sleeping! I want to help solve this case too!"

Johanna looked down at the journal and flipped through another page. *"July 6, 2011. Welp. Mitchell and I set a date! We're getting married on August 13th. Can you believe that? I know, I know. It's less than a month away, but the church was available that day. Mom thinks we're crazy. She hasn't really come out and said it, but I know that's what she's thinking! I can't wait to be Mrs. Mitchell Connelly!!"*

Johanna turned the page and kept reading aloud.

"July 8, 2011. Ugh! I am so mad I could just about burst! Stupid problem child at work groped me again today! I told him I

was getting married and my fiancé wouldn't like him putting his hands on me, but he just laughed. I really want to tell Mitchell what's going on, but I know what will happen. He'll either want me to quit and find a different job, or he'll go down there and pound this guy. I can't quit now. I'm up for a big promotion and I have a real shot at getting it. And I don't want Mitchell to do anything to him, because I don't want him getting in trouble, especially right before the wedding. I'll just have to stick it out. If this keeps happening after I'm married and the boss won't handle it, I'll have to take matters into my own hands."

"Wow," said Essy. "That really sucks. I would have punched him."

Whitley nodded. "Me too!"

"At least it doesn't sound like it was Mitch," said Johanna with a smile. "That's such a relief."

"A *huge* relief," agreed Whit.

"July 15, 2011. Things at work are getting worse. Yesterday when I was going out to my car, he raced to catch up to me. He told me he and the rest of the office were going to Syd's for a drink and he wanted to know if I wanted to go too. I told him no, and he asked if I thought I was too good for them now that I was getting married. I said of course not, I just had a lot of wedding plans to take care of, and he immediately got upset about me marrying a total stranger. I kind of laughed at him, like he couldn't possibly be serious! When I laughed, he shoved me up against my car. Made me hit my head and everything! If Mitchell knew, I think the guy would be a flattened pancake right about now. I'm so mad that I'm tempted to tell him."

"Tell him!" shouted Whitley, crossing her fingers.

"No doubt!" agreed Essy.

"July 23, 2011. I had my first dress fitting today!! Mitchell's going to love my dress! I can't wait to be Mrs. Mitchell Connelly! Just a few more days!"

Johanna flipped the page.

"July 26, 2011. I am freaking out right now! Stupid a-hole at work told me if I married Mitchell he'd make me regret it. And this time he told me if I said a word about it to him or the boss he'd shut me up permanently. **I don't know what to do anymore. I'm scared."**

Johanna flipped the page again and frowned. "That's it, guys. That was the last entry."

"That was it?" Whit's brows lifted.

"She probably got busy with wedding stuff and work," said Johanna. Her heart hurt for Felicia. That bastard of a coworker! Johanna knew exactly who had killed her now, and she wasn't going to let him get away with it!

"I know where we're going now, girls. Get warmed up, and then we're off to trap a murderer!"

33

*J*ohanna glanced down at her phone as they approached the apartment building on the Lower East Side but was disappointed to see that there was still no response from Mitch.

After speaking to Roz, the secretary at the Four Seasons Realty office, and getting the address, Johanna had thrown Esmerelda into an oversized canvas tote and slung her over her shoulder, and the group of them had headed out. On the way, she'd called Mitch, but he hadn't answered, so she'd left him a somewhat cryptic voicemail asking him to meet her right away, and then she'd texted him the address where she wanted him to meet her.

Now, as they stood in front of the building, Johanna didn't know what to do. She hadn't gotten a response from Mitch, and she couldn't help but wonder if her odd behavior that morning had made him change his mind about her. She wrung her mittened hands and stared up at the tall apartment building, wondering if she should go in without him.

"Did he text back?" asked Whitley, staring over her shoulder.

"Nope." Johanna looked at her phone again and sighed. "He's probably mad because I rushed off this morning. He probably decided I'm too weird to bother with."

Esmerelda poked her head out of the bag. "It's what I'd think."

"Oh, Es. Hardly," said Whitley, swatting at Johanna's arm. "He really likes you, Hanna. There's no way he's thinking that. He probably just got busy and didn't see his phone. Maybe you should call him again."

Johanna nodded and dialed Mitch's number. It rang and rang and then went to voicemail once again. Her heart dropped.

"Hey, Mitch. Once again, I'm really sorry about this morning. I hope you're not angry with me. Listen, I think I know who killed Felicia. I'm here, at the address I texted you. I really hope you're on your way, though. If I don't hear back from you soon, I'm going to go in. Don't worry, I'll be careful. I have a plan!" She hung up the phone and gave Whitley a tight smile.

"What's your plan?" asked Whitley, lifting a brow.

Johanna reached in her bag and pulled out a little recording device that she often used when interviewing people for research for her books. "I'm going to record our conversation. You know, so I have something to give to the cops."

"That's your plan?" asked Esmerelda with a little laugh. "What's your plan if he pulls out a gun and decides to shoot us?"

Johanna bit on her lip. "That's why I brought Rocky. He won't let anyone hurt me."

"You really think Rocky could save you from a bullet?"

Johanna patted the top of his head. "Are you kidding? Rocky's ferocious when he wants to be. Aren't you, bud?"

Rocky seemed to give a sloppy grin as she patted his head.

"Oh yeah, he looks like a raging beast."

"I think we'll be fine," said Johanna. "I'll tell him that lots of people know I'm there. He's not going to kill me if he knows that. Are we ready? I don't think Mitch is coming."

Whitley nibbled on her fingernails. "I'm nervous."

"Oh, come on, girls!" said Johanna breathlessly. "You two came into my life and forced me to help you solve this mystery! We've almost got it solved and now you're going to wimp out?"

Whitley looked up at the tall building and then at Rocky. "Alright. If you really think Rocky will protect you, I'm ready."

"He will, don't worry. Let's go?"

Whitley gave her a little nod.

Together the group of them made their way to the fifth floor. Johanna knocked on the door to apartment 516 and then quickly turned her voice recorder on. Then she waited, holding her breath. Every fiber of her body trembled. She wanted to throw up, she was so nervous. She had no idea what she was going to say or what he would say. She held Rocky's leash close by her side and patted him, praying that he'd take care of her.

The door swung open and a lanky grey-haired man stood in front of her.

"Dean Klatworthy?"

"Yes?" said the man, adjusting his glasses.

"Dean, my name is Johanna Hughes. I am a writer, and I'm writing a book about the death of Felicia Marshall. I was told she was a coworker of yours at one time, and I was hoping maybe you'd allow me to ask you a few questions."

The man looked surprised to hear Felicia's name.

"Who is it, sweetheart?" asked a woman's voice from inside the apartment.

He glanced back into the apartment. "It's a writer. She's writing a book about Felicia Marshall."

Suddenly a woman stood in the doorway next to Dean. "Hello, I'm Elise Klatworthy." She held a hand out to Johanna, but as she saw the stranger's face, her smile faded in shock. She sucked in a breath. "You're Hanna Hughes!"

Whitley squeezed Johanna's hand. "It's like you're famous, Hanna!"

Johanna grinned and nodded. "Yes."

Her eyes widened. "Dean! This is Hanna Hughes!"

Dean adjusted his glasses and narrowed his eyes at Johanna. "You've heard of her?"

"Yes! She's the author of the *Clue Mystery* series." She looked at Johanna then. "I've got the whole series! Come in, come in!" She waved Johanna in, pulling Dean aside to give her room to walk.

"Do you mind if Rocky comes in?" asked Johanna, feeling a lot more at ease to see that his wife was present. "His feet dried on the carpet on the way up here."

"Oh, don't worry about it for a second. We've got hardwood floors," she said, leading them over to her comfortable living room. "So you're writing a book about Felicia Marshall?"

Johanna glanced up at Dean furtively, wanting to take in his expressions carefully so she could analyze them in her mind later. He seemed pensive and a tad uncomfortable. "Yes. Do the two of you remember her?"

Elise nodded emphatically. "Of course we remember Felicia! What happened to her was horrible, just horrible!"

Whitley frowned at Elise. "It's going to be even more horrible for her when she finds out that her husband was the one who killed her!"

Johanna swallowed and gave Elise a tight smile, trying to ignore Whitley. "Yes, it was very, very sad. They say she was mugged in the park, but I have reason to believe that that might not be the whole story."

Dean very clearly rubbed a hand across his brow, but he remained silent.

"I knew there had to be more to the story!" said Elise. "What do you think happened?"

Johanna knew she had to tread carefully. She couldn't just admit her suspicions to the Klatworthys. She had to lay some careful groundwork and get him to incriminate himself on tape. "Well, I'll get to that. First, Dean, do you mind if I ask you a few questions about Felicia?"

Elise's eyes flickered over to her husband expectantly.

Dean blinked and took a long moment to consider the request. "Well. That was a long time ago. I don't remember a whole lot."

"But you remember Felicia, don't you?"

Elise swatted at her husband. "Of course he remembers Felicia," she said to Johanna. She turned to her husband. "What are you talking about, Dean? You remember it all like it was yesterday! You mention Felicia quite often."

That raised Johanna's eyebrows. "Oh, is that so? Why's that?"

"Well, she was such a sweet girl. She worked so hard, and for her to be killed like that, on the day before her wedding, nonetheless, was just heartbreaking. For both of us!"

I bet it was, thought Johanna, staring at Dean's face. It seemed to get redder by the second. "Dean, how did you feel about Felicia?"

Dean swallowed hard. "Oh, well, Felicia was a great woman. She was a very hard worker. She had the highest conversion rate in the office. Our clients loved her. She was personable and attentive. She followed through on everything she promised to do. She was really just great."

It turned Johanna's stomach listening to Dean sing her praises, knowing how he'd been harassing her for months before her death and knowing what he'd done to her.

"What a creep," snapped Whitley, who was perched next to Johanna on the arm of a chair. "And to think his poor sweet wife didn't know anything about how he was harassing her!"

"Dean, can you think of anyone who *didn't* like Felicia?"

Dean's eyes flitted around the room, unable to focus squarely on Johanna's eyes. "Oh, umm. I think Janet Sandborn wasn't a big fan," he said quietly. "There was some competition there."

"I heard about that competition," said Johanna. "Do you think it's possible that Janet had anything to do with Felicia's death?"

Dean's eyes widened, as did his wife's.

"You think *Janet Sandborn* had something to do with Felicia's death?!" breathed Elise.

Johanna waved a hand. "Oh, no. I didn't say that at all. I was just asking if Dean *thought* she could have."

Dean looked uncomfortable. "It would really shock me if she did. Janet's a tough cookie, but she has a couple of kids and a big mortgage. I truly don't think she would risk prison just to kill her competitor. As far as I'm aware, that was their only beef. I mean, I think they got along otherwise."

"Who else was in the office when Felicia worked there?"

"Umm, at that time? I think it was just Felicia, Janet Sandborn, Tim Shaw, and myself. We were shorthanded for a while there. We didn't even have a secretary. She'd walked out a few weeks before Felicia was killed."

"Why'd she walk out?" asked Johanna. She'd never heard that before.

Dean sighed and tilted his head to the side. "I don't know. She may have mentioned something about having a conflict with a coworker."

Johanna narrowed her eyes at Dean. She wondered if he'd been making sexual advances towards the secretary too and scared her off! "Oh, really? That's interesting. What was the secretary's name?"

He cleared his throat. "Umm, you know, I don't remember for sure. It's been so long."

"Amy. Her name was Amy," said his wife, giving him the stink-eye.

"Who did Amy not get along with in the office? Janet?"

Dean shook his head like that sounded crazy. "Janet? Oh, no. Janet pretty much got along with everyone, except Felicia."

"Did Felicia not get along with Amy?"

"No, Felicia and Amy got along just fine."

Johanna felt like she had his feet to the fire now. She could almost see little beads of sweat forming on his forehead. Johanna tipped her head sideways. "If Amy didn't quit because of Felicia or Janet, it had to be because of either you or Tim Shaw, but you said she was having problems with a coworker, and Tim's the boss. So does that mean she left because of you?"

"Oh, go Hanna!" said Whitley as she stared at Dean's face.

Elise sucked in her breath. She leaned forward almost immediately, before Dean could even say anything. "Oh no! You've got it all wrong! *Dean* was Amy's boss. *Tim* was her coworker!"

Johanna made a face. "No, Tim's the boss."

Dean nodded. "Well, he's the boss *now*. I was the boss when Felicia worked there."

Whitley gasped. "Hanna!"

The flesh on her arms and legs suddenly pebbled as a tingle shot through her body. She had the wrong guy! *It was Tim!* Johanna gave an almost unnoticeable nod for Whitley, but she had to roll with it until she got to the truth. "*You* were the boss back then?"

Dean moved his head from side to side, cracking his neck. "Yeah. I had some health issues and retired not long after Felicia was killed. That October, Tim took over my position and they hired a guy named Jimmy to take Tim's place."

Johanna's mind flashed back in time. She remembered seeing the picture of Tim in the office when he'd gotten the promotion. She couldn't believe she'd missed the sign! "Was Felicia up for the same job?" asked Johanna.

Dean nodded. "Yeah, Tim and Felicia were both after the managing broker position, which was my old job."

Elise looked at her husband with surprise then. "Dean, are you saying that Amy left because of Tim?"

Dean frowned slightly. "I don't know. She might have mentioned something about him creating a hostile work environment."

Elise swiveled so she could look at her husband more closely. "You never told me that."

He shrugged. "She quit before I had a chance to look into it."

Johanna's stomach turned. "Dean, were there ever any issues between Felicia and Tim?"

Dean looked at his wife nervously. "I mean, she was an attractive woman."

Elise frowned at her husband. Johanna could tell that

had gotten her dander up. "What's that supposed to mean?"

"You know. I mean, I think maybe Tim was *interested* in her."

"Romantically?" gasped Elise.

He nodded. "Yeah, she mentioned he'd asked her out a few times and didn't seem particularly keen in taking no for an answer."

"But she was engaged!"

"Yeah, but she was only with that guy for a few months. She'd worked with Tim for a lot longer than that."

"So Felicia *told* you that Tim wasn't taking no for an answer?" asked Johanna, suddenly feeling the need to get out of there.

Dean seemed to shrink in his seat. "She mentioned it."

Elise looked at her husband. "Dean Klatworthy! Did Felicia Marshall *complain* to you about Tim Shaw?"

"I mean, she *mentioned* he'd come on to her…"

"And did you have a talk with Tim about it?"

"I offered to have a talk with Tim about it, but she told me to wait. She didn't want to appear weak or make things any more uncomfortable between them," said Dean. "She said she'd come to me if anything else happened."

"Dean! You were her boss! You should have spoken to Tim about it anyway. If both Felicia and Amy were having problems with him, that's a hostile work environment for sure!"

Johanna glanced furtively towards the door.

"Yeah, we need to go. We got the wrong guy," said Whitley, standing up and heading for the door. Rocky glanced over at her and barked.

Johanna patted his head. "Oh, gosh. It looks like Rocky needs to go outside." She smiled nervously. "Nature calls.

Listen, I think I got everything I needed for my book." She stood up.

Dean looked up at her curiously. "That was it?"

"Mm-hmm." Johanna nodded. While she wanted to rip Dean apart for not doing anything about Felicia's problems, that wasn't her job. Her job was to put a murderer behind bars, and that was what she needed to do. "Thank you both. I'll just see myself out."

Despite her offer to walk herself out, Elise followed her to the door. "I feel horrible that my husband didn't help Felicia if she was having problems with Tim. I didn't even realize it was happening. I certainly would have made him help her if I had known."

"I know. Thank you for your time, Elise." Johanna shook her hand. "I really appreciate your help."

"Anytime." She was just about to shut the door when she stopped and peered out at Johanna in the hallway. "Oh, say, when will Felicia's story be out in paperback? I'd love to read it."

Johanna smiled. "I haven't decided yet if I'm going to be able to write it. This case has hit really close to home. I'll send you a copy if it gets written. Thanks for your help. Merry Christmas."

"Merry Christmas, Ms. Hughes."

As Johanna and her crew headed back down the hallway, she pulled out her phone and began texting again.

"Who are you texting?" asked Whitley, looking over her shoulder.

"Mitch. I'm telling him there's been a change of plans. He needs to meet us over at the Four Seasons Realty office immediately. And this time, I hope he shows up."

34

*J*ohanna pushed open the glass doors at the Four Seasons Realty office. "Hello, Roz, is Mr. Shaw in?"

The secretary, glanced up from her computer and smiled at Johanna. "Oh, hello, Ms. Hughes. Yes, Mr. Shaw is in. Do you have an appointment?"

Johanna shook her head. "No, I don't, actually. Would it still be possible to see him?"

"Umm, let me just check his calendar." Roz clicked through a few screens on her computer.

"While you're checking his calendar, would you mind if my cat and dog come inside? I know your sign says no pets, but it's really cold out there." Johanna pointed through the glass to Rocky and Esmerelda who stood next to Whitley on the sidewalk.

Roz winced. "Oooh, I'm so sorry, Ms. Hughes. I'm not supposed to allow pets in."

Johanna swished her lips off to the side. She'd assumed they would be allowed in since Tim had allowed Rocky in a few days ago. "They're really well behaved. Tim let Rocky in, just the other day in fact."

Roz nodded conspiringly. "Yeah, Janet had a fit about that. She's got allergies and said that the dog made her sneeze for the rest of the day. Mr. Shaw said we needed to enforce the policy after that. I'm really sorry."

Johanna sighed and debated her options. Was it a good idea to go in without Rocky *or* Mitch present? She knew deep down in her heart that it wasn't, but where was Mitch?

Roz pointed at her computer screen. "It looks like Tim's free. I'll just give him a buzz real quick and let him know you're here. Hang on." Roz picked up the receiver and called Tim's office before Johanna could change her mind. "Mr. Shaw, Johanna Hughes is here to see you again." She paused for a moment. "No. Mm-hmm, she's alone. Okay, thank you." She hung up the phone and looked at Johanna brightly. "He said you can go back."

Johanna's heart had already begun beating wildly in her chest. She looked out at Rocky and wondered if she could actually confront Tim without him. She gnawed on her bottom lip. Tim wouldn't dare do anything to her at the office, would he? After all, then everyone would know what he'd done. They were in a public building. She was safe. She could do this. She gave Roz a tight grin.

"Thank you. Let me just make sure my pets are okay out there," said Johanna as she headed for the door.

"Sure thing," agreed Roz with a smile.

Johanna went outside to update everyone. "The secretary said no pets this time, but Tim is here, and I can see him."

Whitley's hands cradled either side of her face. "But Hanna! You can't go in to see that creep alone! What if he figures out what you know?!"

Johanna had the same worry, but she was trying to think logically, and her logic told her that he wasn't going to hurt her in such a public location. "He's not going to hurt me in there, Whit. I just wish Mitch were here. I wonder where he is!"

Whitley shook her head. "I don't know, but you could easily wait for him."

Johanna groaned. "It's freezing out here, Whit. We can't wait. He might never come. Listen, I'm going to take the recorder in there and get Tim to incriminate himself. Then we'll take the tape to the police and get him arrested. Alright? You need to stay out here and watch Rocky and Es. I'll let Roz know that I'm waiting for Mitch so when he gets here, she'll send him back. Okay?"

Whitley nodded, but her eyes told of her hesitation. "Okay," she said slowly. "Be really careful, Hanna. I don't want anything bad to happen to you."

"Nothing bad is going to happen to me, Whit. Tim's not dumb. Even if he thinks I suspect him, he's not going to do anything to me in his office."

Johanna hung the tote bag around Rocky's neck. Esmerelda poked her head out of it and looked up at her. "Maybe this isn't such a good idea, JoJo."

Johanna gave her a funny look. "Since when do *you* call me JoJo?"

"I don't know," sighed Esmerelda. "Just be safe, alright? We can't have anything happening to you."

Johanna smiled at her. "I will, thanks for caring. Even though I know the only reason you don't want anything to happen to me is because I'm solving the mystery for you."

Esmerelda rolled her eyes. "You've been telling me to be nice since I met you. Now I'm finally trying to be nice and you don't buy it. Jeez, I can't win!"

Johanna scratched the back of her ear. "You're right. I'm

sorry. Thanks for caring." She gave Rocky a hug next. "Take care of these two, alright, buddy?"

He gave her a big lick on the side of her face, making her giggle despite the trepidation she felt in the pit of her stomach.

Johanna stood up, wiping the slobber from her face, and smiled at Whitley. "Welp, here I go. Wish me luck."

Whitley sighed and threw both of her arms around Johanna's shoulders. "Be careful, Hanna. I mean it."

Johanna glanced around the street. Sure that no one was paying any attention to her, she hugged Whitley back. "I will." She pulled open the glass door again.

"Good luck, Hanna!"

*M*itch's feet pounded the treadmill in a perfect cadence with the music blaring in his ears. It felt good to get a workout in. It had been a while since he'd made the time for one. But today, he'd called in to the office and taken a personal day. Darcy, his office assistant, had been shocked to hear it as Mitch rarely took days off work, but today he needed to clear his head.

Since the run had begun, Mitch had done little else but think about Jo. He smiled as he replayed their trip to her family's house in New Jersey and how she'd fallen asleep on the ride home. And then he replayed what had happened when they got to his apartment. He'd dared to kiss her. At the time, he'd thought she was okay with it. He knew she spooked easily, but last night it seemed like she'd finally gotten over her fears. After the kiss, she'd been relaxed and at ease with him. They'd watched movies and laughed and talked together until the early-morning hours, and then they'd fallen asleep. The day they'd shared had been everything to him, and then in the snap of a finger, it was morning. And it was as if the magic from the day before had worn off. She'd bolted so fast and furiously from his apartment that he almost hadn't seen what'd hit him!

Since she'd gone, Mitch had picked up his phone at least two or three dozen times. He'd typed out a few messages to her, edited them, and then promptly deleted them. She'd said she'd call when she was ready. He had to give her a minute.

It was just that the thought of having feelings for someone again and then promptly losing them? It killed him. He hated the idea of it, literally couldn't bear the thought. He'd sat around in his apartment and nearly driven himself mad long enough. He *had* to get away. He *had* to stop checking his phone like a crazy person and clear his head. He grabbed his iPod, put on his favorite playlist, and took off for the gym in the basement of his apartment building.

By the time his mind was clear, he'd been gone for several hours. And while he hadn't come up with any new answers, he hoped like mad that when he got back to his apartment, he'd have a call or a text message from Jo waiting for him.

Mitch caught the elevator before the doors slid shut. Inside, he pulled out his earbuds and bent over, breathing heavily, fighting to catch his breath. By the time the elevator doors reopened, he was breathing a little more normally, but his heart was still racing. He let himself into his non-decorated apartment and wished he'd put some effort into the holiday. Of course, he'd had no way of knowing that he'd end up getting snowed in with Jo.

Inside his apartment, Mitch dropped his iPod and

earbuds down on an end table and went straight to the kitchen to grab a bottle of water. He pulled one from the fridge and cracked it open, guzzling half of the bottle in one big slug. Feeling a bit better, he reached for his phone, next to the empty popcorn bowl from the night before. He pushed the home button and was *shocked* to see his front screen littered with missed notifications. They were all from Jo!

His heart began pounding faster again. He had two missed voicemails and two text messages. He looked at the text messages first. The first one was just an address on the map. Somewhere on the Lower East Side. He read the second text message aloud. *"Hey, Mitch, change of plans. Meet me at Four Seasons Realty in forty-five minutes. I've got huge news about Felicia."* His eyebrows pinched together. "Change of plans? What plans?" He dialed his voicemail and Jo's voice poured from his speakerphone.

"Hey, Mitch. Once again, I'm really sorry about this morning. I hope you're not angry with me. Listen, I think I know who killed Felicia. I'm here, at the address I texted you. I really hope you're on your way. If I don't hear back from you in the next couple of minutes, I'm going to go in. Don't worry, I'll be careful. I have a plan!"

And then the first message played. "Hey, Mitch, sorry for rushing out of your place this morning. But, hey, big news. There's been a major break in Felicia's case. Drop whatever you're doing. I need you to meet me somewhere in a half hour. I'll text you the address. See you soon!"

Mitch stared at his phone, mentally piecing together all the information he'd just been given. What was the break in the case? How had Jo suddenly figured out Felicia's killer? What was going on? He didn't understand, and he didn't have time to think about it. Whatever her plan was, she'd already put it into motion, and she'd gotten started without him!

He grabbed his car keys and his wallet from the counter. One thing was for certain, even though the realty company wasn't very far from his apartment, there wasn't going to be time to walk there. He was driving.

35

*J*ohanna smiled despite the bubbling in her stomach as she took a seat in front of Tim Shaw.

"So, Ms. Hughes, you're back. What can I do for you today?"

Johanna cleared her throat and fingered the tape recorder she held in her pocket. It was running, but she worried it would be muffled in her pocket, so she snuck it out and held it under his desk. "I had a few more questions about Felicia Marshall's case."

"Boy, you're really interested in her story, aren't you?" he said, his face red.

Johanna felt like she was navigating a field of land mines. She had to say the right things, something that wasn't particularly her forte. "Yeah. Well, I don't know if I mentioned it to you before, but I'm a mystery writer."

His eyebrows shot up animatedly. "Oh, no, I don't think you mentioned that before."

She gave him a tight smile. "Yes. To be honest, that's actually how I got mixed up in the whole Marshall case in the first place. I was doing a little research on something else kind of unrelated, and it led me here when you told me that Felicia Marshall had been killed in a mugging."

He nodded, pretending to be intrigued. "Oh, I see. Uh-huh. Interesting."

"Right. So, long story short, Mr. Shaw, I came back because I was recently given information from a source that Felicia Marshall was having conflicts with some of her coworkers while she was here at Four Seasons Realty."

"Conflicts, huh? I suppose you're referring to the conflicts between Janet and Felicia?" he prodded.

Johanna tipped her head to the side. "You did mention the last time we'd spoken that Janet and Felicia didn't really get along very well."

"Yes, and you know, I got to thinking about that," said Tim carefully. "And I did a little digging, and I found out that the man Felicia had shown the house to the day that she was killed ended up buying that very property from Janet! Isn't that sort of an interesting fact?"

Johanna narrowed her eyes as she stared at Tim. He was trying to cast suspicion on Janet, the creep! She wanted to leap across the desk and maul the man sitting in front of her for trying to put the blame on Janet, but she fought hard to keep it together. "Mm-hmm," she said. "There are definitely some very interesting facts surrounding this case." She glanced up at the door and wished that Mitch had been there. "You know, Mr. Shaw, there's one thing that I don't know if I quite understand about how things work in the realty world. Maybe you can help me out with that?"

"What's that?"

"Well, the last time I was here with Mitch, Janet told us that Felicia had stolen her client. Janet admitted that she was upset about that fact, even though Felicia had actually *called her* to apologize for stealing her client, so to speak.

But, would it really be considered *stealing a client* if the client asked for Felicia by name?"

Tim leaned back in his seat. "No, if a client asks for a realtor by name, that's completely aboveboard."

"Right, so obviously it wasn't Janet who gave Dutch Felicia's name and number the day of her wedding rehearsal. I mean, why would she have done that?"

He nodded. "Yeah, that's very true. I'm not sure how exactly Dutch wound up with Felicia's name and number."

"You know, I was curious about that for a while. You know, I actually spoke to Dutch the other day."

"You spoke to him?"

"Yeah, and he explained to me how he'd gotten connected with Felicia in the first place."

Tim cleared his throat uncomfortably. "He knew who had given him Felicia's name and number?"

Johanna waved a hand in the air dismissively. "Well, he didn't mention the person by *name*. He just said he called the office and was given her name and number that day."

Tim nodded. "I see. Well, I'm sure the secretary gave him her name."

"But that's the funny thing. The other day, you mentioned that it was just you, Felicia, Janet, and Dean working at that time."

Tim shook his head. "Oh, yeah. I guess we might not have had a secretary at that time. It's hard to remember, you know? Six years ago and all."

Johanna nodded and continued, "Well, if it wasn't Felicia or Janet who took Dutch's phone call, and there wasn't anyone else in the office, then it had to have been either you or Dean. Would you say that sounds accurate?"

Tim shifted in his seat, leaning on his right arm and hip. "Well, I guess it would have to have been either Dean or me. I certainly don't remember taking the phone call, so I'm going to have to assume it was Dean."

"Mr. Shaw, if you don't mind me asking, how did you and Felicia Marshall get along?" asked Johanna. Her hand shook as she held the recorder under the desk.

"We got along fine. I think I mentioned before, everyone really *loved* Felicia. You know, she was a nice woman and a good agent."

"How did she get along with Dean?"

Tim frowned and gave a little shrug. "I don't really know. I mean, he was her boss. I think they got along just fine. Why?"

"Well, like I said, I was given information from a source that told me that Felicia Marshall was having conflicts with some of her coworkers. I don't think they were specifically referring to Janet, so I was wondering how Dean got along with her."

Johanna could see Tim's mind spinning then. He rocked back and forth on his squeaky office chair. "Well. I mean, I certainly don't know what goes on behind closed doors, but I think that you could say that Felicia could be considered a promiscuous woman."

Johanna's eyes widened intentionally. "Felicia? Promiscuous? I was under the impression she was a very focused and dedicated woman and that she really didn't have *time* for relationships and the like."

Tim looked put off by that statement. His cheeks turned even more crimson than they already were. "Well, Ms. Hughes, I'm sure I don't have to tell you that your friend Mitch was a client of hers at one time. That doesn't sound like the behavior of a professional woman, does it?"

"Mr. Shaw! Are you referring to Felicia's fiancé?"

"I am."

"I think you might be exaggerating that statement a tad, don't you? I mean, they met and kind of fell for each other."

Tim gave a one-shouldered shrug. "If that's how you see it. They'd only been together a few months before she coerced a proposal out of him. I find that a little disturbing."

Johanna wanted to laugh in Tim's face. "Disturbing! I hardly find that disturbing. I think they found their person, nothing wrong with that."

He cleared his throat again.

Johanna could tell she'd gotten him fired up. She felt like he was on the cusp of admitting something. She glanced back at the door again and wished that Mitch was there!

"Yes, well, what's your point, Ms. Hughes?"

"I just wondered if perhaps *you* had any kind of issues with Felicia Marshall."

"Issues?"

"You know, hard feelings, disagreements, confrontations."

"No. We got along just fine," he said curtly.

"No issues?"

He shook his head resolutely. "Nope. None."

Johanna lowered her brows. It was time to take another approach with Mr. Tim Shaw. "Mr. Shaw, was Felicia Marshall up for the managing broker position before she was killed?"

That caught him off guard. He put a fist to his mouth and cleared his throat once again. "Yes, I believe we were both up for the same promotion at that time."

"And you said it yourself, she was really liked by the entire office, huh?"

"Yes, she was."

"And she had really great results with the clients?"

He nodded.

"I bet she had a really good shot of getting that promotion had she still been alive."

Tim frowned. "Yes, she had a very good shot at it," he was forced to agree.

"Mr. Shaw, I find it kind of odd that there wasn't a secretary working here back then. Your realtors had to answer your own phones."

"Well, we had a secretary. I think we were just between employees at that time," he said.

"But you'd *had* a secretary before?"

"Of course. We'd been through numerous secretaries."

"They didn't like to stick around, huh?" asked Johanna.

He shrugged. "I don't know. I guess not. What's your point?"

"Well, I was just kind of wondering *why* the secretary left around the same time that Felicia was killed. It occurred to me that *maybe* she was having the same problems with a coworker that Felicia was having."

"I really wouldn't know, Ms. Hughes. Now, you know, I have a lot of work to do, so if you could get to your point… or I'll have to ask you to leave."

Johanna held her ground. She knew she was close. "Mr. Shaw. Did the secretary leave because perhaps she was being sexually harassed in the workplace?"

"Sexually harassed?" He frowned and leaned forward in his seat so his big belly touched the desk. "I don't know what kind of work environment you think we run here, but I can assure you—"

"Mr. Shaw, I don't need your assurances. I think I have a pretty good idea of the kind of work environment you run around here. I bet if I went out and visited with Roz, she might give me a pretty good idea just what kind of boss you are to work for."

His face went pale then. "Ms. Hughes, I'm afraid I'm going to have to ask you to leave."

Johanna gripped her handheld recorder tightly. "Mr. Shaw, isn't it true that *you* were the one creating the hostile work environment that both Amy and Felicia Marshall complained to Dean Klatworthy about?"

He stood up then and pointed at the door. "Ms. Hughes, I don't appreciate what you're insinuating."

Johanna wanted to stand up too, to challenge him, but she couldn't. Her recorder was still in her hand. So she stayed seated.

"Mr. Shaw, I'm not *insinuating* anything. Felicia Marshall shut down your advances, and you didn't like it. So eventually your harassment turned into threats and she became scared of you. Yet, despite your threats, you were infatuated with her, and you were jealous about the fact that she'd met someone so easily and agreed to marry him without even hardly knowing him. It drove you mad, didn't it?"

"That's not even remotely—"

"*And* you didn't like the fact that she was probably going to get the managing broker position over you. So then, she'd be your boss, wouldn't she? I bet she wouldn't keep someone around the office who was threatening her, would she?"

He was speechless.

She could see it in his face. She had him now. "So you decided you'd had enough of Felicia Marshall, didn't you?"

"I've had about enough of you. That's who I've had enough of."

"So when Dutch Erickson called the office on the day of her wedding rehearsal, you assigned Felicia to him because *then* you'd know exactly where she was. You waited for her outside that three-story townhouse. And when her showing was over, you followed her, didn't you, Mr. Shaw?"

His mouth opened, but no words came out. Only a hissing sound escaped his throat.

"And then you killed her, took her jewelry, her purse, and her keys and dumped her body in the park to make it look like a mugging. Didn't you?" Johanna's heart was pounding a mile a minute and her limbs pulsed from the pumping adrenaline.

His brows lowered then as he scoffed at her. "Like anyone in the world would believe a cockamamie story like that?"

"Oh, trust me. I have proof. They'll believe it alright." Johanna glanced over her shoulder at the door, wishing like mad Mitch were there to see the police roll in and arrest Mr. Tim Shaw. All she had to do was go tell Roz to call 911 and it would be over.

But when she turned to face Tim again, this time, there was a gun pointed at her face. "Oh, I'm sorry, Ms. Hughes, but I don't think you're going to be around long enough to show anyone that proof." He flicked the end of the gun towards the ceiling, motioning for her to stand. "Get up."

$\mathcal{P}$ulling up to the realty office, Mitch felt unease settle into the depths of his belly. The first thing he caught sight of was Rocky sitting unattended outside the front door with Esmerelda suspended inside a canvas tote hanging around his neck.

He navigated his car towards the curb. "Where's Jo?" he murmured, his heart thumping in his chest. He pulled the car to a stop, double-parking but unfazed by the likelihood of getting ticketed. He didn't have time to hunt down parking. Jo could be in danger.

He threw open the door and rushed around the car to Rocky's side. "Rocky! Where's Jo?"

"Woof!" said Rocky excitedly, happy to see Mitch and unaware of his concern for Jo.

Mitch patted his head. "She went inside without me, didn't she?" He squatted down to unfasten Rocky's leash from the pole he was tethered to. Esmerelda poked her head back out of the bag she hung in, and Mitch gave her a little scratch behind the ears. "Jo's got you cat sitting, huh, Rock?"

Rocky put a big heavy paw on one of Mitch's shoulders. He shook it and then stood up. "No time to play today, buddy. We gotta find Jo. Let's go." He led Rocky in by the leash, allowing Esmerelda to continue hanging around his neck. Inside, the secretary was busy typing on the computer.

"Hello, may I help you?" she said without taking her eyes off of the computer screen.

"I'm Mitch Connelly. I was supposed to meet Johanna Hughes here a little while ago, but I'm running late."

Roz nodded. "She's in with Mr. Shaw right now. I'll just give him a quick call to let him know you're here before I send you back." She picked up the phone and pressed a button. While it rang, Roz pointed at Rocky. "I'm sorry, but you'll have to leave him outside. Pets aren't allowed. It's an old rule, but Mr. Shaw said I have to enforce it now."

Mitch looked at Rocky. "Ah, so that's why Jo left you outside." He felt his body relax only slightly.

Roz's brows furrowed. "Mr. Shaw's not answering his phone. They should be in there."

"How long ago did Ms. Hughes get here?"

"Maybe about fifteen minutes ago?"

"Did they leave together?"

"No. I didn't see them go," said Roz. "I haven't left my desk since she got here. I'll try ringing him again."

Mitch shook his head. Something didn't feel right. "I'm sorry, Roz, I don't have time to wait." He barged past the woman with Rocky close by his heels and went straight for Tim Shaw's office.

He could hear Roz behind them. "Wait, Mr. Connelly. Your dog can't go back there!"

He threw open Tim's door, unsure at what he was going to find, but was surprised to find the room empty.

Roz was right behind him. "Mr. Connelly, your dog

can't..." She stopped talking when she entered the room and discovered that it was empty.

"Where are they?" asked Mitch, pointing at the empty room.

Roz's brows furrowed and a look of confusion covered her face. "I have no idea. They were just in here."

Rocky sat on the floor in Tim's office while Mitch ran back out into the hallway. "Do you have a conference room or something?"

Roz nodded and went to a door at the end of the hallway and poked her head in. "The lights are off. It's empty."

"Check all the rest of the offices," commanded Mitch authoritatively, suddenly extremely worried about what had happened to Johanna.

Roz narrowed her eyes. "Is there something wrong, Mr. Connelly?"

Mitch shook his head. He didn't have time for questions. He had to find Jo. When she didn't immediately do what he'd requested, he took it upon himself to walk up and down the hallway, opening doors and poking his head into offices. Most of the rooms were empty, except one. Jimmy, the slick realtor he'd seen the other day, was in one of them with a client. "Excuse me," Mitch interrupted. "Have you seen Mr. Shaw or a woman with brown hair?"

Jimmy looked confused but shook his head. "Not in the last few minutes. I saw Tim this morning."

Mitch slammed the door. Roz followed him back into Tim's office. Rocky was howling then.

"You're sure you didn't see them leave?"

Roz shook her head. "I swear. I didn't see anything. Mr. Connelly, what's going on?"

"I don't know what's going on. I just have a really bad feeling."

Rocky circled Mitch and then stopped underneath his hand. "Woof woof!"

Roz looked down at Rocky. "Mr. Connelly, I'm going to have to ask you to take your dog outside."

"I just need to find Jo, and then I'll take the dog outside."

Rocky barked again. This time Mitch looked down at him curiously. "What, Rocky? Do you know where Jo is?"

Rocky put his head down and walked over to the desk, sniffing at something dark on the floor hidden beneath a chair.

Mitch squatted down and looked at it curiously. "It's a mini recorder." He looked up at Rocky. "Rocky, is that Jo's?" He hit rewind and listened to the last thirty seconds of the recording.

"Mr. Shaw, I don't need your assurances."

"It's Jo voice!" said Mitch, looking up at Roz.

"I think I have a pretty good idea of the kind of work environment you run around here. I bet if I went out and visited with Roz, she might give me a pretty good idea of what kind of boss you are to work for."

"Ms. Hughes, I'm afraid I'm going to have to ask you to leave."

"Mr. Shaw, isn't it true that you were the one creating the hostile work environment that both Amy and Felicia Marshall complained to Dean Klatworthy about?"

"Ms. Hughes, I don't appreciate what you're insinuating."

"Mr. Shaw, I'm not insinuating anything. Felicia Marshall shut down your advances, and you didn't like it. Eventually your harassment turned into threats and she became scared of you. Yet, despite your threats, you were still infatuated with her, and you were jealous about the fact that she'd met someone so easily and agreed to marry him without even hardly knowing him. It drove you mad, didn't it?"

"That's not even remotely—"

With his pulse racing wildly now, Mitch fast-forwarded the tape a few seconds.

"And then you killed her, took her jewelry, her purse, and her keys and put her body at the park to make it look like a mugging. Didn't you?"

"Like anyone in the world would believe a cockamamie story like that?"

"Oh, trust me. I have proof. They'll believe it alright."

"Oh, I'm sorry, Ms. Hughes, but I don't think you're going to be around long enough to show anyone that proof. Get up."

And then the tape ended. Just like that, Johanna's voice was gone. Mitch stared at the recorder in stunned silence. He glanced up at Roz, whose mouth hung open. "Roz. Do you know what Johanna was talking about? What kind of hostile work environment?"

Roz blinked several times as the words she'd just heard sunk in. "I—I don't..."

"You have to tell me. Johanna's life might be at stake right now."

"I mean, Mr. Shaw..." Her voice trailed off and she refused to make eye contact with Mitch.

Mitch stood up. "You can tell me, Roz."

"He can be kind of scary," she admitted weakly. "I'm not supposed to tell anyone." She swallowed hard. "He said he'd hurt my kids."

"Dammit!" snarled Mitch. "Is there another way out of this building?"

Roz pointed with a trembling finger towards the hallway. "Back door."

Mitch raced back out of the building and down the hallway, where he found an exit sign. He threw open the door and realized it was an alley exit. Jo was nowhere to be seen.

He raced back inside. "I need Tim Shaw's home address. Immediately."

"B-but I could get in trouble..."

"Roz. A woman's life is at stake. You need to give me his address, and then I need you to call 911."

Mitch led Rocky and Esmerelda to the front office when Roz clicked through her computer screens and found Tim's personal address. She wrote it down on a sticky note and handed it to Mitch.

"Now, call 911 and send them to that address. Tell them Tim Shaw is the person who killed Felicia Marshall back in 2011 and he's at that address. It wasn't a mugging after all. And he's kidnapped Johanna Hughes!"

---

*W*ild tears streamed down Johanna's face as she struggled to free herself from the duct tape that bound her wrists behind her. Now that there was no doubt in Johanna's mind that Tim Shaw had been the person who'd killed Felicia Marshall, she realized that she was about to be his next victim.

Johanna closed her eyes and struggled to relax her body for a moment. She needed to clear the panic that clouded her mind and focus if she was going to get out of the situation she was in.

She had to assess her environment. She looked around the room. From her wooden chair in the middle of a kitchen, she could see one small window over the sink, and she could almost see the back door from where she sat. She had to get to that door.

Johanna had no idea what part of the city she was in. When Tim Shaw had taken her, he'd led her out of the realty office's back door and forced her down the alley to the parking garage where his car was parked. He'd dealt her a blow to the head with the gun, and the next thing Johanna knew, he was unloading her out of his trunk in an alley and forcing her up a short flight of stairs. Within minutes of their arrival, Tim had Johanna bound to a wooden chair, securing her wrists behind her and her ankles to the chair. He'd stuffed a rag in her mouth and then wrapped tape around her head to keep her from screaming. Then he'd disappeared into the house, mumbling something under his breath.

Now she could hear him upstairs, walking around. She heard a door slam and then his heavy footsteps again. He could be back any minute. Johanna had to work fast!

She set about working on the tape binding her wrists. She had to tear it or cut it. There had to be a way to get her hands free. As she worked, breathing from her nose, she kept a close eye on the sliver of light she could see streaming in through the back door. She had to get to it.

With the pads of her feet, she gave herself a little push and tipped her chair backwards slightly, rocking on the two back chair legs, trying to get a better look at the alleyway. Was anyone out there? Something moving outside caused a brief change in the light. Johanna's heart thumped wildly in her chest. She had to get back there. People were out there. They could help her!

Giving herself another little push with her feet, she rocked back on her chair again. This time, she gave herself too much of a push and she tipped backwards, making a loud boom as she and the chair smacked down onto the hardwood floor. Both panic and pain rippled through her body. Had he heard that? Would he be back now?

She tried to slow her breathing and her choked sobs so she could listen for his footsteps on the ceiling above, but she couldn't hear anything. Petrified, she fought with all of her strength to roll onto her side with the chair still attached, and she began to wiggle her body, inching towards the door.

Then she heard him again. The footsteps rushing down the stairs. Panic filled her once again, and with her eyes trained on the door, she fought with everything she had to get to it. But the footsteps were getting closer and closer. Before she knew it, he had her by the hair. He dragged her back the few inches she'd moved and set her upright.

"Going somewhere?" he sneered, his chubby face beet red and sweating.

Johanna's muffled screams came out as a high-pitched nasal sound.

He grinned at her wickedly. "That's what I thought." He slapped her across the face. "I thought I told you to be a good girl?"

Where his hand struck her cheekbone, Johann's face felt like it might explode. She felt her world spinning then. *Oh, my God. This is it! This is where my life ends. Just as it finally felt like it was beginning again. Now it's over.*

"If only you'd been good, I might have considered keeping you alive for a little while. Then you and I could have had a little bit of fun together before I had to kill you." He pulled his gun out of the back of his pants and aimed it at her. "But you had to go and be naughty. Just like Felicia Marshall was naughty."

Johanna huffed into her muzzle, her eyes frantic, her heart throbbing out of control.

"Yeah, see, no one can hear you," he jeered. "No sense in wasting your energy trying to scream." He hit her across the head with the back of the gun.

Johanna's mind dizzied, and just before she passed out, she thought she heard the sound of Rocky's bark. *Rocky.*

37

"*T*he destination is on your left," said the robotic woman's voice on Mitch's phone.

Pulling up to the curb in front of the two-story brick house, Mitch glanced out the window. His pulse pounded wildly in his ears. He didn't even have the car in park yet when he threw open the door and Rocky burst out over his lap. He slid the gear shifter into park and jumped out to follow the dog to the front door.

Rocky barked anxiously as they approached the quiet-looking house on the unassuming street. It was as if Rocky *knew* Johanna's life was in danger. Mitch tried the handle, but it was locked. He peered inside but couldn't see anything. He took a few steps back to look up at the house and realized they were next to an alley. "Let's try the back. Come on, buddy."

With Rocky hot on his heels, Mitch ran around to the back door to discover that it was unlocked. Mitch sucked up his breath and pulled the door open. Rocky barged in first, barking wildly. Mitch hollered into the house. "Johanna!"

A split second later, the sound of a gun firing rang out as a bullet blazed passed him. Missing his shoulder by a narrow inch, it buried itself into the wall next to him. As he pulled back behind a dividing wall, Rocky lunged forward into the house, barking.

Another gunshot went off.

Mitch's adrenaline raced as he envisioned Johanna dead in the house. But he couldn't think about that right now. He had to focus on finding her.

Tim screamed as Rocky tore into him.

He heard a loud clack and prayed it was the sound of Tim's gun hitting the floor.

Keeping low, Mitch duck-walked around the dividing wall to find a splattering of blood drizzled across the kitchen floor. "Oh God, Rocky!" he breathed. His eyes swept across the trail of blood to witness Rocky on top of Tim Shaw. He had him by the jugular.

And then he saw her.

Gagged and bound to a wooden chair, Johanna wasn't moving.

In that moment, his heart stopped beating. He wanted to die, seeing her like that. "Jo!"

As much as he wanted to go to her, he had to help Rocky secure Tim, or they'd all be dead. The gun, which had clattered to the floor when Rocky lunged and toppled the man over, was next to the kitchen table. Mitch clambered over to it and picked it up, holding it on Tim. "Don't move," he shouted at him.

Tim flinched, causing Rocky to clamp down harder on his throat, a low, menacing growl emanated from the dog's throat.

Tim's eyes were wide, terrified of the grip Rocky had on his neck.

"Good boy, Rocky." Mitch noticed blood draining from

Rocky's hindquarter. "Oh jeez, Rocky. You've been hit! We gotta get you help!"

Suddenly, sirens sounded. Still holding the gun on Tim, Mitch rushed to Johanna's side. "Jo!" he said, cupping her face with his free hand. She didn't respond. Scared that Tim had already killed her, he checked her for a pulse.

Feeling the little throb in her veins against his finger was everything. "Oh, thank God! You're alive, Jo!"

He checked her body for any signs of gunshot wounds, but didn't see anything. "Jo!" he said again, patting her face gently.

He heard the police banging at the front door. "Police! Open up!"

"Around the back!" he hollered. He looked down at Johanna, praying for her to wake up. Suddenly, he heard a thump and then Rocky's whine. And in the blink of an eye, Tim was on top of Mitch, lunging for the gun.

Mitch fell to the ground with the gun still in hand. Tim surged forward over the top of him and dealt him a blow to the head. Then Rocky was on Tim's back and there were officers at the back door.

"Police!"

"Help!" hollered Mitch, as he and Rocky fought Tim.

And then the police were inside with guns drawn. "Police! Freeze!" Officers swarmed the kitchen, dragging Tim off Mitch and fighting to hold Rocky at bay.

Mitch's mind swirled with fear as he panted on the ground. "You've gotta help her." He pointed at Johanna's limp body. "She needs an ambulance. He tried to kill her! That man killed Felicia Marshall."

The next thing Mitch knew, someone had helped him to his feet. While officers worked to free Johanna from her restraints, others cuffed Tim Shaw and began heaving him out of the house.

His world was spinning. Had all of that really just happened? "Rocky was shot. He needs an ambulance."

"We'll take care of your dog, sir. Don't worry."

Mitch rushed to Johanna's side. "Jo! Wake up!" His heart throbbed wildly. What would he do if he lost her? He'd only just *found* her. Felicia had somehow led him to her. He knew it. It was a mystical connection that he just couldn't explain, like the fabled Christmas miracles they both loved so much. "Jo! Please talk to me!"

And then, her eyes fluttered open. It took her a moment to regain her bearings, and when she did, she smiled. "Mitch, thank God!" she whispered weakly.

Tears streamed down his face as he threw his arms around her. "No, it's me who's thanking God," he cried.

$\mathcal{R}$ocky limped over to Johanna's side of the bed and laid his head in her lap.

"Aww, how ya feelin', Rocky?" she asked him, scratching him behind his ears.

He merely whimpered as his eyes moved animatedly, garnering more scratches from his master.

Snuggled up next to Johanna, Whitley reached a hand across her lap and patted his head too. "Poor Rocky. It's got to be pretty painful getting shot."

"He's tough. Pain doesn't faze him," said Esmerelda, perched on the side of the bed between Johanna and Rocky. She reached out and gave her supposed nemesis a gentle pat. "Right, Rocky?"

Rocky let out a little noise from his throat.

"Aww, Essy, you love Rocky!" said her sister with a big smile.

Esmerelda pulled her hand back and scowled. "No, I don't. I just think it was pretty cool how he saved JoJo's life. I guess he's not so worthless after all."

"You love him!"

Esmerelda's energy to rebuff her sister waned. "Eh, he's alright."

Johanna grinned at the two. Somehow both of them had managed to grow on her over the past two weeks. "I can't believe we actually solved the mystery of the wedding dress."

Whitley laid her head on Johanna's shoulder. "You mean *you* solved the mystery. Essy and I only helped. It would have been impossible for us to do it without you, Hanna," she sighed.

Esmerelda licked a paw and smoothed out her fur. "I suppose JoJo played a significant role in solving the mystery."

"Es!"

"Kidding, kidding," sighed Essy. "She rocked it out."

Johanna grinned at her. "Thanks, Es. But we did it together. Everyone pitched in. Mitch would have never found me if you hadn't pointed the recorder out to Rocky."

Essy grinned. "This is true. I helped save your life! You're welcome. All I require is your eternal gratefulness."

Johanna laughed. "You all pitched in and saved me, and for that I'll be eternally grateful to the two of you, and to Mitch, and to Rocky," said Johanna, giving her trusty companion a hug. She winced as she moved, lightly fingering her forehead.

"Head still hurt?"

"Yeah, kind of throbs. Mitch said he'd bring in some more ibuprofen when he's done making lunch."

"That's pretty cool that he took the week off to nurse you and Rocky back to health," said Whitley, her green eyes shining brightly.

A soft smile spread across Johanna's face. "Yeah," she whispered. It was *incredibly* sweet. She swallowed hard to fight the tears threatening to fall and then whispered, "I owe you both a lot."

"Oh, Hanna! Don't cry! You'll make *me* cry!"

"If it wasn't for the two of you, and your magic snow globe, and that dress... I never would have met Mitch. I feel like I got a new start to my life."

"Well, if it wasn't for you, we never would have solved the mystery of that dress, so... I guess we're even."

Esmerelda sighed. "One dress down, a *ton* to go."

Johanna peered into the snow globe on her nightstand. She could see the tiny little dresses hanging inside the wooden wardrobe. "You guys have to solve the mystery of *all* of those dresses, huh?"

"Yup," said Whitley.

"It's gonna take you a while."

"We know."

"So what are you going to do now? How does it all work?" asked Johanna.

Whitley shrugged. "I don't know. I was wondering the same thing." She flicked her magic wand and it let out a little sputter. "I still haven't gotten my magic back yet."

"Maybe I have to shake the globe again," suggested Johanna, lifting the globe off the nightstand.

Whitley held out a hand to stop her from shaking it. "Wait!"

"What?"

"What if it works? What if I get zapped back into the globe and Essy goes back to not being able to talk?" Johanna could see the fear in Whitley's eyes.

Johanna put her arm around her friend's shoulder. "I don't know, Whit. I don't have the answers, but I assume it'll be time for you to solve a new mystery."

Esmerelda leapt over Johanna to sit on her sister's lap.

"Don't worry, Whit. I'll keep an eye on you. We'll stick together. Just like we did the last time."

"Promise?"

Essy tipped her head and held a furry paw up to her sister. "Yup. Cat swear."

Whitley giggled as she shook her sister's hand. "Cat swear."

"So, should I shake it?" asked Johanna, holding up the globe.

"What will you do with it when I've gone back in there?"

"I don't know. I guess I should take it back to the antique shop," said Johanna.

Esmerelda sighed. "Can't you find a new antique shop? That old guy wasn't very friendly to me."

Johanna smiled as a tear rolled down her cheek. "I'll pick a really great shop, okay? And I'll hang a sign around your neck that says *does not like dry cat food*."

"Yeah, okay," said Essy with a grin. She sucked in a deep breath. "I guess I'm ready."

Whitley nodded, squeezing her sister tightly. "I'm ready too."

Johanna sighed as she wiped away her tear. "Wow, I never thought I'd actually say this, but I think I'm going to miss you both." She put an arm around Whitley's shoulder and hugged her.

Esmerelda leapt over Johanna's lap to hug Rocky. "I guess I'll miss this big old oaf too."

Rocky gave Essy a big lick across the face. "Woof!"

"Eww, Rocky!"

Whitley and Johanna laughed.

Johanna took a deep breath. "Alright, here goes nothing!"

Whitley squeezed her eyes shut as Johanna shook the

snow globe, working the flakes up inside into a flurry. She shook it again, and again, mesmerized by the way the flakes fell, and suddenly, it was snowing in her bedroom.

"It's snowing!" cried Whitley. "It's working!"

Esmerelda hopped up onto her sister's lap again.

Suddenly, a brilliant stream of light lit up the globe, drawing Johanna and Rocky's eyes to it. A loud cracking sound filled the room. Johanna pinched her eyes shut, suddenly remembering how loud that sound had been.

When it was over, she opened her eyes. The snow had stopped and Whitley was gone!

Suddenly, Mitch tore into her bedroom. "Jo! Are you alright? What was that noise?!" he cried in a panic. He looked around the room and saw snow on the bed. "Is that *snow*?!"

Johanna's heart thumped in her ears. She felt a cold breeze circling her. She glanced over at the window to see that it had blown open. She pointed a finger at it. "Oh, I opened a window. The noise and the snow came from out there."

Mitch put his hand to his chest. "You scared me! I thought something had happened to you!"

Johanna grinned. "Nope. I'm fine."

Mitch sat down on the side of her bed and took her hand in his. "Good, because I'm never letting anything happen to you again!"

Johanna squeezed his hand tightly. "And I'm never going to interview a murderer without you again."

Mitch smiled. "Well, I appreciate that."

"I thought you might." She touched her head. "I have a splitting headache."

He nodded. "Your soup is almost ready and then it'll be time for your ibuprofen. How's our superhero doing?" he asked, patting Rocky's head.

"Woof!"

"He's sad because he can't jump into bed with me," said Johanna. "I think his backside hurts too much."

Mitch laughed. "No problem. That's what you've got me here for!" He lifted Rocky up onto the bed and scooted him next to Johanna.

Rocky licked Mitch's face thankfully.

"He really likes you, you know."

"I really like him," said Mitch. Then he looked at her with his heart shining in his eyes. "I really like you too."

Johanna's heart felt so full that it might burst. "I really like you too."

Mitch gave her a kiss on the forehead and stood up. "I'm going to go get that soup and your medicine now."

"Thanks, Mitch."

"My pleasure."

When Mitch left, Johanna stared anxiously into the cat's eyes. "Essy!" she hissed. "Can you still talk?"

The cat blinked her eyes back at Whitley and opened her mouth to speak. "Meow."

Rocky barked.

Johanna leaned forward and reached for the snow globe, which had fallen into the soft mounds of blanket on her bed. She peered inside the snow globe to see Whitley, seated behind her sewing machine. Johanna gave the globe a little shake, whipping up the flakes inside. Whitley looked up at her and gave her a little smile and a wave.

Esmerelda stared down at her sister in the globe. "Meow," she said sadly.

"I know, Es. I know. But soon, you'll get all the mysteries solved and both of you will be able to go back to where you came from."

"Meow."

39

One Year Later

"Oh, JoJo! You look beautiful!" gasped Dawn Marshall, dotting at her eyes with a tissue.

Johanna stared at her reflection in the mirror. "You think so?"

The woman nodded, nearly unable to speak. "I do."

Johanna threw her arms around Felicia Marshall's mother. "Thank you, Dawn. And thank you for letting me wear Felicia's dress. You have no idea how much it means to me."

Dawn squeezed her hand tightly. "Felicia would have wanted you to wear it. That's why you found the dress, you know. You were meant to find it. Not only did you find out what really happened to my daughter, but you gave Mitchell his life back."

Johanna grinned. "No, he and Felicia gave me *my* life back."

Suddenly a door burst open. "JoJo! They're ready to start!"

"I'll be right there, Mook. You and Maureen can go ahead and start."

Melissa nodded from the doorway in her red bridesmaid dress. "Oh, JoJo, you look beautiful!"

Johanna smiled. "I know! You've told me at least thirty times today!"

Melissa wiped away a tear. "I know, but I never thought this day would come. I'm so happy for you!"

Johanna swallowed hard. "I'm happy too."

They heard the music firing up outside the doors.

"Mook! They're ready for you!" said a voice.

"Okay, okay! I'm coming, I'm coming," said Melissa, rushing out the door.

Dawn touched Johanna's arm. "I'm going to go take my seat now. Good luck, Johanna!"

"Thanks for everything, Dawn."

Dawn wiped the tears that spilled freely down her cheeks. "It's my pleasure. I didn't get to see my own daughter walk down the aisle, but I'm so thankful that I get to be a part of your big day. It's sort of like I got a piece of my daughter back."

Johanna hugged her honorary mother one more time. "It's sort of like I got a bit of my mother back, too." She swatted at the woman softly, fighting tears. "Now go! Before you make me mess up my makeup! Mook would kill me if I did!" She giggled.

When Dawn had gone, Johanna looked at herself in the mirror one last time. She adjusted the little capped lace sleeves on her dress and patted her hair and then the door burst open.

"Alright, JoJo, it's time!" said Denny, extending a crooked elbow to his daughter.

"I'm ready." Johanna turned around to face her father.

His face brightened as he saw her in her wedding dress. "Oh, Johanna! You look so beautiful. I wish your mother could be here to see your wedding."

"I have three mothers here to see it today," she whispered. "Mom's watching me from heaven, my honorary mother, Dawn is watching me from the audience, and my beautiful stepmother is watching beside me as my bridesmaid. I couldn't be any more lucky, Dad."

He nodded as tears filled his eyes. "I know, pumpkin. I'm so proud of you, you know that?"

Johanna's head bobbed. "I do know that, Dad."

And then the music changed and the wedding march began. The doors to the church split apart. Johanna took her father's arm and he led her to the beginning of the aisle.

Standing at the front of the church was Mitch, more handsome than ever in his tuxedo, with Rocky by his side. When he saw her, a smile covered his face from ear to ear.

"Are you ready, JoJo?" whispered Denny.

Johanna nodded. "Yeah, Dad. I'm ready. I've been ready my whole life. It's time to marry my best friend."

ALSO BY M.Z. ANDREWS

Curious about how Whitley and Esmerelda Snow managed to get themselves into the predicament they're in? Then you might be interested in reading the prequel to Snow Cold Case. The prequel is available in digital form only on my website www.mzandrews.com.

The Mystic Snow Globe Mystery Series

Prequel: Deal or Snow Deal

Book 1: Snow Cold Case

Book 2: Snow Way Out

Other Series by M.Z. Andrews

The Witch Squad Cozy Mystery Series

The Coffee Coven's Cozy Capers Series

The Witch Island Series

ABOUT THE AUTHOR

I am a lifelong writer of words. I have a wonderful husband, whom I adore, and we have four daughters and two sons. Three of our children are grown and three still live at home. Our family resides in the midwest United States.

Aside from writing, I'm especially fond of gardening and canning salsa and other things from our homegrown produce. I adore Pinterest, and our family loves fall and KC Chiefs football games.

If you enjoyed the book, the best compliment is to leave a review - even if it's as simple as a few words - I tremendously value your feedback!

Also, please consider joining my newsletter. I don't send one out often - only when there's a new book coming out or a sale of some type that I think you might enjoy.

All the best,
M.Z.

For more information:
www.mzandrews.com
mzandrews@mzandrews.com

Made in the USA
Lexington, KY
21 November 2018